Welcome to the Temple of Valor

About a fourteen-hour journey east of the village of Homestead, the Temple of Valor sits atop a strange geological anomaly called the Oracle Mount. This geological anomaly can best be described as the remnants of an ancient crater, possibly a meteoric impact, from thousands of years in the past. The Oracle Mount consists of a rising round hill in the center of the crater's ridge. The whole site, as seen from above, resembles a circle inside a circle, about four miles in diameter. In between the crater's high ridge and the Oracle Mount in its center, a valley of lush grassland divides the two areas. Rising gently from the valley, the Oracle Mount levels off to a flat top. There an ancient temple, rumored to have been constructed by the ancient acolytes of the Goddess Ehlona, is where we find the Temple of Valor.

ASTAR'S BLADE

TEMPLE OF VALOR

AN EPIC FANTASY

JOE LYON

Thank you to a wonderful team of contributors:

Developmental Editing by PJ Hoover
Copy Edited by Anne-Marie Rutella
Proofreading by Deborah Murrell
Audiobook Narration by Lisa Negrón
Cover Design by Story Wrappers, Artist K.D. Ritchie
The *Witch's Songbook* contributed by Purple Toad, streaming everywhere on the web.
Typesetting by Colleen Sheehan, Ampersand Bookery

AMPERSAND
BOOKERY

ISBN:
978-1-956189-24-7 (Paperback ISBN)
978-1-956189 09-4 (Hardcover ISBN)
978-1-956189-10-0 (Kindle ISBN)
978-1-956189-11-7 (Audiobook ISBN)

First Edition

LYOŃIC BOOKS LLC

THE WORLD SETTING

ONLINE VIEW OF MAP:

Map of Odessa—Astar's Blade

(astarsblade.com)

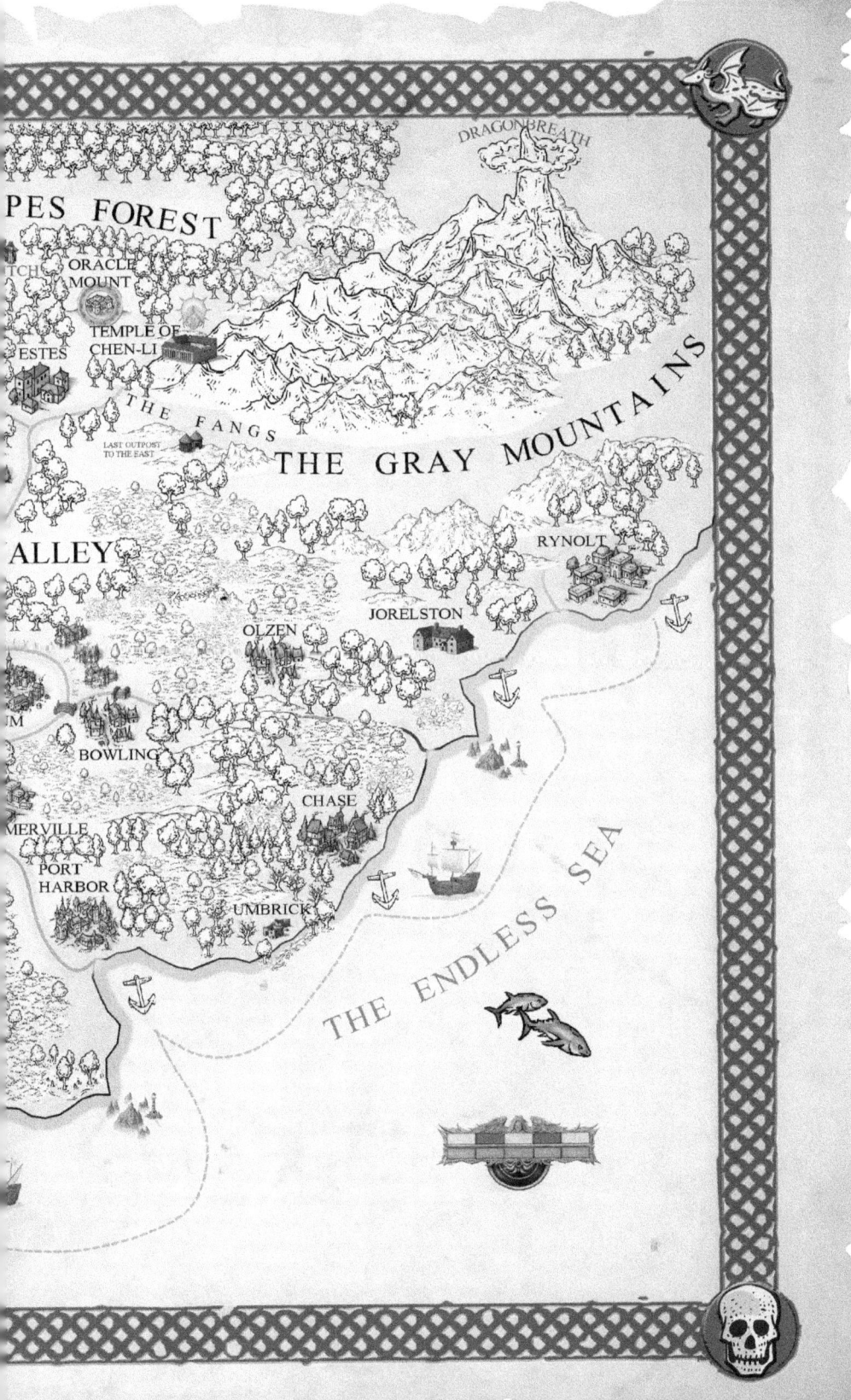

THE FOLLOWING EVENTS OCCURED IN THE YEAR

862 Human Recorded Time (HRT)

THE VILLAGE OF
HOMESTEAD

Astar's birth had been heralded by the Star of Ehlona, which shone for a year. Now no longer a child, Astar has grown well into his eighteenth year. Since the death of his mother, Gilglad, who perished in a house fire fourteen years ago, Astar has been raised solely by his disabled father.

Amtor, now barely ambulatory, is a far cry from the man he was in his younger days. Once capable of bloody violence as a fierce warrior, he has become a sensitive, patient, and caring single parent. He provided Astar with a good, if not overly protected, childhood.

As for the boy, Astar's rogue memories and strange thoughts had not always been entirely his own. Likewise, over the years, he exhibited strange powers he could not understand or control. Powers that occurred mostly in his dreams.

But times are changing.

Time is the sudden movement of her skin
She turns around to face me with a morning smile

Excerpt from *The Witch's Songbook*

PROLOGUE
Dreams of Astar

The door opened.

What time is it?

Does it matter?

Shh! Quiet. Don't wake the boy.

He heard the whispers. Then silence. Too much silence.

Astar awoke. The clock had stopped ticking, its pendulum defied gravity, impossibly frozen in the upward position. He realized he was observing the clock *and* the door simultaneously. The problem was, they were on opposing walls. When he moved his head, a third perspective came into view. In this one, he was looking down at his body. He could see all of these perspectives, all *three* of them, at the same time.

Looking down, he observed he now possessed five arms: three on the left, two on the right. Farther below, he saw he had three legs, two stretched out straight, while a third bent comfortably in a ninety-degree angle.

He lifted his hand and rubbed his face, and a new sixth arm touched his head—*heads*. There were now three of them. Each head framed a perfect copy of his face, each pointing in a different direction. One face was turned toward the door—the one that had opened its eyes on its own. Another face watched the clock on the south wall, its pendulum frozen. Astar's third face was angled down examining the condition of his body.

All of Astar's extra appendages—the arms, legs, and faces—functioned independently, yet simultaneously, and according to the choices of what he willed them to do. All of his parts were valid personas of himself. All of them made up the whole.

Astar had stopped time again. Realizing what he had done, he started it back up.

As soon as time began once again, the clock started ticking. Its pendulum, unfrozen now, swung back and forth to keep the time current.

Fully awake now, he chose a single persona to merge into. The other forms moved toward the one. His one chosen form accepted the other altered versions of himself. A quick slurping sound followed as all the Astars absorbed into the one likeness of himself like watercolors. What remained was a single Astar, one he decided upon, selected by the will of his own choice. For no particular reason, he selected the aspect of himself facing in the direction of the door.

It was at that moment that he realized the door had not opened on its own. Rather, he had just opened it while in another version of himself. Now that form of himself was gone, merged into the one Astar, along with all the other spare versions. He realized the voices that had awakened him had been his own. He had been talking to other versions of himself.

This was not the first time this phenomenon had happened. He had stopped time before many times over the past eighteen years or so. As he got older, the power to do it increased. When he stopped time, his thoughts became movements; he left traces of these movements behind. Moving from here to there with time stopped resulted in his being in multiple places at once. He was not sure how the phenomenon worked or even whether it was real or not. But to Astar, and all his mysterious perspectives, it seemed real enough.

When Astar was just a young boy, stopping time had only worked while he was dreaming, but that was changing. As he grew, this power, and the control of that power, was increasing. He could stop time even during his waking hours now.

Was that a dream? he thought as he listened to the ticking of the clock. *What was it about this time?*

Before rising from bed, he tried to remember what he had been dreaming about. It must have some significance since he spawned off so many copies of himself. He struggled to remember, as the stoppage of time always distracted him, but then, it all came back.

Oh, yes, he remembered. He was flying. Behind him the darkness followed, and complete impenetrable black slammed the scenery shut as he floated by. As he flew forward, he shone a great beam of colored light in front of him. Under his own control, he levitated along illuminating the trees and hills, making them look surreal and dazzling in colors of red, yellow, and green.

But he was not alone. Menacing shapes propelled by large wings came up from the trees to meet him in the air. These dark creatures hated his light and despised being bathed in the colors. They angrily engaged him. These were frightening creatures, growling in their throats, large snouts and stout, boulder-like bodies, like the very stones of the world had come alive to threaten him.

"Stay away!" Astar warned with an outstretched palm. "Don't you know I could destroy you with a wave of my hand?"

But they did not listen. Instead, the creatures circled him. Astar frowned to think he may have to destroy such incredible creatures. He warned them again.

"You are being far too aggressive. Look, I'll let you live, just leave me alone."

But they kept pressing. They continued to fly around him, swiping so close Astar had to duck to avoid being hit. They would not stop on their own. They only wanted to hurt him. As bad as he didn't want to do it, Astar waved his hand, just as he had warned he would. The shapes began to burn like embers of charcoal. They burned and they blurred, until ultimately, they dissipated into wispy clouds of black smoke.

"See what you made me do?" Astar said. "I really would have quite liked your company, and to spend some time with you. But look at you now. You made me kill you all and now I am alone."

As he thought more about the dream, he remembered hearing a loud boom. He could not tell if this was part of the dream or if the noise had been real. Then he remembered hearing more booms but not understanding if they were real or imaginary. That was when he stopped time and multiplied himself to go see. More booms came. They got louder and nearer…until they were gone.

Maybe it was the demons again, he thought.

Over the course of his childhood, the demons had come for him before. But his father, Amtor, always the fearless warrior, managed to keep them away.

As the memories of the dream faded away, the real world returned. He was left with a new threat.

Something was under the ground—something menacing, moving closer and coming to the surface. Something that would soon be revealed.

ACT I

What Comes Out
Under the Ground

I can feel the world tearing apart

Yes, I can feel it

It is breaking my heart

Tear it apart

<hr/>

Excerpt from *The Witch's Songbook*

The Skeletal King had been waiting for him to return.
Now, he stepped closer.
— Excerpt from *Kilmer's Ghost* (Chapter 1)

THE NIGHT OF THE DEVOURERS

GREAT MAPES FOREST

A heavy boom disrupted the serenity of the Great Mapes Forest. The sudden noise sent birds flying from treetops. Deer lifted their heads, rabbits rose on hind legs, all scanning the landscape for signs of danger. Then another boom sounded, louder this time. This one rattled the ground, swaying the trees. The woodland creatures scurried away.

More booms followed. They were coming from underground. A steady pounding against the ceiling of the world below. They were getting louder. The hammering more forceful. Something, it seemed, was moving closer to the surface.

The first fractures of stone formed from a central point, appearing suddenly like a spider's web of cracked ground. Yellow-and-red steam hissed out, venting from the molten underground. Fragmented rocks collapsed under their own weight down into the depths below.

The smoldering hole formed a glowing cavity, a steamy portal into the underworld. Casting shadows across the forest, the glowing vapors exhaled and gave the branches a sinister appearance in flickering light. The hole itself looked like a breathing monster with a noxious mouth completely opened.

Then the pounding stopped.

Deep within the pit something stirred. Movements disturbed the smoky beams of uplifting light. A three-fingered hand, black as the darkest shadow, reached out of the pit and struck the ground, clamping down hard outside the rim. The other hand followed, trailing with it a fleshy purple forearm and elbow. Leveraging against the ridge, the beast endeavored to lift itself out.

The creature came out of the pit and firmly stood on legs of wrinkly flabby skin. The beast, silhouetted against the yellow glow, hissed steam and lifted its head. The motion revealed two round eyes, black as obsidian. Its snout, upturned and rodent-like, jutted up above the thing's shiny eyes. Out of its nostrils came a snort of warm vapors in twin columns. Below its snout, and across the entirety of its body, its enormous mouth stretched in a wide downward frown that ran down in a great arc, nearly touching the ground at its lowest point on either side.

The creature, lumbering slowly, stepped away from the rim of the pit with pounding steps. With another snort of hot air, the massive colossus shook its bulbous head, again exhaling vapors in the cold night air.

Behind the first creature, another pair of dark arms reached out of the pit. A second huge Devourer began climbing out of the steaming crevasse. The second one was an exact duplicate of the first. The thing rose out of the hole and stood beside the first, silhouetted in billowing yellow-and-orange fumes.

The first Devourer leaned back and lifted its arms to stretch. As it did, it untucked a pair of veiny, leathery wings and opened them fully. The wings were connected in segments, sealed over, and supported by spindly rods. They resembled long smooth shields accentuated by sharp edges like unforgiving sharpened knives. Swinging its wings out quickly with only the slightest flap, it hurtled dirt and leaves off the ground back into the ashes. Then once stretched, it neatly compacted its wings, folding them under and away. The creature turned and considered its twin. Then they both paused and waited for yet another to climb its way out.

The second Devourer yawned, exposing a wide gaping mouth that opened the entirety of its body. After a series of smacks with a purplish tongue, thick and covered with sticky clear slime, it closed its mouth into a morose frown. It watched the third shape rising from the steamy underground. Just as the other two had, the new creature labored to climb its way up to the top of the hole. Finally, the third Devourer was born.

Three Devourers stood in front of the glowing billowing steam. Their eyes shimmered like wet obsidian with the slickness of the oiliest black. Upon instinct, they opened their wings and turned into the wind. One by one they took to the sky. With their massive wings pumping the air, they gradually rose in incremental flaps. Soon they were riding the air currents above the trees of the Great Mapes Forest. Into the night they rose, becoming nearly invisible as black on black in the darkness. Reaching the extent of their elevation, they effortlessly moved through the night. They followed one another circling overhead into a triangular pattern. They were scanning the Mid-Run Valley below. The land stretched out before them, revealing its secrets to their unique vision. Nothing escaped their sight in any direction.

They glided down now. The ancient trees were thick and strong enough to support their weight. They silently came to a rest with a gentle, but heavy, landing on some low-hanging branches. There, they sat motionless for a long time, using all their senses, driven by an instinctive need to feed.

A pair of young lovers had stolen away from the watchful eyes of their parents. They rolled in an adolescent embrace, kissing and laughing softly—tempting targets to the Devourers. But the young lovers were not what they scanned for and not what they craved. So, the lovers went about their lovemaking, unaware they had been passed over.

The Devourers looked beyond. A glen appealed to them, a distant cow pasture, where a herd of animals lay asleep. One by one, the living wood sprang away, as the Devourers pushed off the branches. Catching the air in a mighty pull of their wings the creatures rose into the night again. After climbing high and gaining the desired elevation, they dived in unison, reaching incredible speed, soaring toward the ground, toward their unsuspecting prey.

The Devourers struck with taloned feet, and three cows let out startled screams. The surviving bovines scattered as quickly as they could, running for their lives.

The Devourers opened wide yawning mouths, revealing row upon row of triangular teeth that spiraled in circles down deep purple throats. Each monster, in turn, enveloped half of their animal with the elastic skin of their enormous mouths. Then they tightened, and with a series of jerking, crunchy bites, the cows were severed in half—the uneaten half falling to the ground like a wet bag of sand from a single lethal bite.

The black creatures munched until the meat was gone. Afterward, they remained silently still in the darkness, like giant insentient monoliths. There, they waited for their meal to settle and digest. As the hazy dawn blended orange light through the dark blue, they waited.

The hours passed. Then, the Devourers started to stir again. One lifted a wing and preened underneath with a claw, satisfying an itch that disturbed it. Then, each in turn rose on their three-toed feet, unfolded their wings, and took to the skies. They glided back to the waiting branches of the Great Mapes Forest.

The dawn did not bother them. As the sun rose, they remained perched upon the high branches of the great trees. No observer would be able to recognize them from some distant shadow in the branches. Here, they could watch, invisible in the treetops. The only suggestion they were there was the ever unblinking, ever watchful orbs of their greasy black eyes.

The surrounding lands had brightened into a new day. The lovers had gone long ago, never knowing how close they had come to death. But the Devourers were not sent up from below to punish the wicked. They had another purpose entirely, one even more sinister.

Finally, the dew burned away, and the day revealed hazy shapes in the village below. The townsfolk started to move about in the open, intent upon doing their business, unaware of the danger lurking above.

When I came home yesterday
I saw trouble coming our way
I should've left, but I stayed
Feeling inside

Excerpt from *The Witch's Songbook*

Still warm from their beds, people started to stir,
dressed in layers of itchy wool and cold, stiff boots.
— Excerpt from *Kilmer's Ghost* (Chapter 2)

THE SITE OF THE PIT

VILLAGE OF HOMESTEAD

T*ink! Tink! Tink!*

The hammer struck the hot metal in the blacksmith's shop. Gensen stopped long enough to look. Then the hammer repeated.

Tink! Tink! Tink!

The blacksmith's shop was owned by Gensen of the Jeter clan and was comprised of a thatched roof with a narrow chimney that puffed out white smoke. The shop was conveniently located where two roads converged. One road led east to the nearby village of Estes. The other road ran for hundreds of miles west, all the way to the coast of the Endless Sea and beyond to the village of St. Ehlona's; there, the road would turn south and continue on to The Wilds. The sides of Gensen's shop facing the two streets were open without any walls. This allowed the air to flow through the shop, providing adequate ventilation from the furnace's carbon. In front of the shop a large black warhorse was tied to a wooden post. In the backdrop, the sun rose over the village of Homestead, and the morning dawn was breaking in dazzling colors of red and orange.

Tink! Tink! Tink!

Gensen's hammer fell repeatedly, shaping the glowing red metal. He struck the horseshoe on the anvil, shaping it while Amtor and his son watched him work. Gensen hummed a little tune so the others could hear.

Oh, I remember still, sitting on my windowsill
Looking down at that little green place that I used to call
    home.

He rotated the red-hot shoe on the anvil's horn with the dexterity of a man who knew his craft well. He measured the length and width of it time and again.

And I wonder when, if I could return again
Or if I ever really recall, ever looking down there at all.

Once satisfied of the fit, he dipped the horseshoe in a wooden barrel of ice-cold rainwater, creating billows of steam.

Oh, I wonder, does it all come back again?
Yes, I wonder…

"You expect an early winter this year, Amtor?" Gensen continued whistling while searching for any defects in the fit of the horseshoe. Gensen wore a large leather apron, smudged in black carbon. His forearms, thick and muscular, creased while his strong hands worked the red-hot tongs. Despite having a rotund belly, thick barrel chest, and bald-shaven head, his features were sharp and delicate with a pointy nose and thin lips.

Amtor responded while chewing on a couple of sunflower seeds he picked from his own garden before leaving home. "Daylight's winding down, the day's becoming short. Mornings, cold and foggy. The wind, strong and crisp…"

As Amtor continued, Gensen took off his leather gloves. He transferred the shoe to a thick wooden block. Then, he held it close to his face and inspected it carefully, turning it this way and that.

Amtor continued his reply, "Ran into a woolly worm yesterday. Told me as much. So, probably going to be an early winter, I think."

"A woolly worm told you that, did he?" Gensen turned his attention away from his metal work. "Oh? Was his coat more black or brown?"

"More black than brown, I suppose."

"That fellow would know best. So, the cold is coming all right, that settles it, then," Gensen replied and nodded in agreement while turning his attention back to the horseshoe. "Hope you are you ready for a long winter, Astar."

Astar looked at his father. "A woolly worm told you?"

Amtor smiled at his son. "You might be eighteen now, but I would wager, you didn't know I could speak to woolly worms, did you?"

Astar, uninterested in the foolishness, stared starry-eyed at the wall, absentmindedly, at nothing in particular. Gensen smiled and turned his back, wiping his hands on his apron.

"Will you teach Astar to speak in woolly worm?" Gensen asked Amtor with a chuckle.

"Someday, when he is older like me," Amtor said, ruffling the boy's hair. "That, and so much more."

Gensen chuckled. "A wise plan. Now let's go see about getting this shoe on ole Mandrake out there."

Mandrake, Amtor's large black warhorse, waited outside patiently with one foot drawn up as they walked out with the new shoe.

"Now, look there, that's an intelligent gentleman," Gensen said patting the horse. "That's a good boy, Mandrake."

"Ah! Mandrake and I go way back," Amtor said petting the horse's neck. "Way back to the very start of things in Hammerville. Long before that nasty business in Bowling. The massacre they called it. All the way through the war, and up to Mauveguard Pass. Yes, sir. We've been through a lot together. Haven't we, boy?"

Micah, Gensen's eighteen-year-old son, burst onto the scene at that moment, poking his head around the corner of the shop. "Hey, Astar! Come here, I want to show you something."

Micah was only three months older than Astar and being from a small village like Homestead, boys did not have a lot of choice when it came to making friends. These boys were fortunate they had each other; even more fortunate that they genuinely liked each other. Micah's mother had died years ago when Micah was only three; and Astar's mother died when he turned four. It was one of the things the boys had in common.

"What do you want?" Astar asked, then ran after Micah.

"Would you look at all that hair," The bald Gensen said as he and Amtor watched the boys go. "It's so blond."

"Unnatural, isn't it?" Amtor remarked. "I have the blackest hair, his mother's hair was brown. Yet the boy was born with the mark of Ehlona the Goddess, with blond hair and blue eyes."

"Micah's is so dark," Gensen said. "Probably the same color mine would be. Or the best I can remember it."

"I wonder where they are going," Amtor said.

"Up to no good for sure," Gensen replied.

Micah ran down the side of the long row of shops and stopped when he reached the end of the block. Racing ahead and leaving his friend behind, Micah startled when he spotted Astar already in the middle of the road, waiting for him.

How does he do that? Micah thought.

Micah shook his head and ran across the dirt road. They came together in the shade of an ancient tree, thick and tall, which was the start of the Great Mapes Forest. As the boys entered the forest, the distant cottages of Homestead faded away into a distant blur behind them.

"Where are we going?" Astar picked up a short stick and swung it at some weeds. Then swung it at Micah like a sword. Micah picked up a stick too and so commenced the battle.

"I found something you got to see," Micah said in between his lunges.

THE PIT SITE

They traveled into the dark hollow of the Great Mapes Forest. The air was significantly cooler as light barely penetrated through the thick canopy overhead. After a while, they came to a little clearing.

"There it is," Micah said, pointing.

Ahead, a rocky crevasse lay open and exposed. Coming from its center, yellowish fumes swirled out. The boys approached cautiously, eyes widened, to investigate how far down the pit went. Into the darkness below the pit seemingly had no end.

"What is this?" Micah held his nose. "What's that smell?"

"I don't know," Astar replied. "Smells like the world farted."

Both of them laughed.

"There's an underground cavern down there," Micah said.

"The lower side of the rim seems accessible enough," Astar said. "The rocks are not too hot to touch, but what did this?"

Deep marks pressed into the ground around the hole.

"Something's been here," Micah said. His black hair was still a mess from the early morning. "Something big."

"Something with only three toes," Astar added. There was a moment of silence as Astar watched Micah investigate. "Go ahead, Micah, go inside."

"I'm not going down there." Micah backed away. "You can't be serious!"

"I'm not scared." Astar shook his head, then pushed past his friend. Astar had to take a moment to acclimate to the heat. His cheeks ballooned out as he blew on his palms to cool them.

"I don't think it's a good idea, Astar."

But despite Micah's persistence, Astar leaned on the little ridge, climbed over, lowered himself down, and then dropped over the edge, down into the hole, and out of sight.

"Come on, Astar," Micah shouted down into the hole. "Let's get out of here!"

No sound came back from Astar.

"Astar?" Micah crawled up to the pit's rim and looked in but could not see Astar. He felt himself starting to panic, waiting for a reply that seemed too long.

At last, Astar said, "Come on down! There's a ledge. It's safe."

Micah peered over the rim. At that moment, a billowing cloud drifted across his face. When the stinky yellow mist parted, he could see Astar standing on a ledge farther down. The sulfuric smell was horrible, and it was everywhere. The yellow vapor reflected the red light emanating from molten lava deep below. But with Astar encouraging him, Micah reluctantly climbed over the rim and dropped down to the ledge where Astar stood.

"How far does it go down?" Micah asked.

"There's a path, look!" Astar pointed. "Come on, we can go down there."

Micah tried to protest. "I don't know, this doesn't feel right, bad idea."

"Of course, it's a bad idea, Micah. Now, come on, let's go!"

The boys draped their legs over the ledge and dropped to the path below. The gray morning light from the opening above gave way to the cavern's steamy darkness. The boys stood shoulder to shoulder on the narrow ledge until it bottlenecked to fit only one boy at a time. Following the ledge, the broken pathway took them farther below.

"We can go deeper," Astar said. "Let's go."

They continued walking single file down the narrow overhang. They hugged the side of the cavern as it spiraled down like a corkscrew. Through billowing clouds of steam from the center of the hole, they descended, following the passageway farther down into the smelly depths.

"What is this place?" Micah asked. "What's down here?"

"Whatever it is, it's been here a long time," Astar said.

Micah followed Astar. "It must have just opened to the surface recently."

"Think of it, Micah, we've been walking over this thing for years and never knew it. And now you discovered it. Maybe you will get to name it."

The ledge continued down hundreds of feet until, at last, the path leveled off to a rocky landing, a larger enclave carved in the rock. Into the far edge of the landing a passage existed that looked as if it had been drilled out. The boys looked down the round tube of a passage, and darkness stretched before them. A warm, smelly wind emanated out. The stale stench blew Astar's delicate blond curls. Through the long darkness, a speck of light shone in the distance, a faint light at the end of a long stretch of impenetrable darkness.

"There's a light down there, look!" Astar started to go into the passage.

But Micah grabbed his arm.

"No," Micah said. "No farther. Let's go back."

Astar turned to Micah. "Why?"

"Because. It's not a good idea," Micah told him. "I'm going back and you're coming with me."

Astar turned to give another look down the dark passageway. He nodded his head. "We'll need some light anyway. Let's go home, get some torches, and then come back."

"Yeah, maybe," Micah said. "Some other day when we are better prepared. Come on, let's go back up."

Turning and staying in single file, Micah led the way up now. They followed the ridge back up toward the light. Just as they started, Astar kicked something. The object he kicked spun and came close to falling in the pit. Fortunately, the thing came to a precarious rest, teetering on the edge of the abyss.

"Wait, look! What is this?" Astar knelt and picked up an ivory-colored stone that looked out of place among all the black-and-red rocks.

"Don't touch it," Micah said, bending down to examine it too.

"I've never seen anything like this," Astar said. "I think this is a tooth!"

"A tooth? Leave it be, let's get out of here," Micah said. "Whatever dropped it might come back looking for it."

"No way, it's mine now." Astar put it in his pocket.

The two boys continued walking back up toward the light outside the pit. Along the way, they turned around to see if anything followed them, but they saw nothing. When they reached the top of the lip, Micah spit on his hands, jumped up, and grasped the warm rocks. He flipped his leg over the rim, and soon he crawled up and over. He crashed over outside the hole, then scrambled to his feet to help Astar. But by the time Micah looked over the edge of the rim, Astar was not there.

Micah scanned the mouth of the pit. He waved his hand through the fog, and thought he saw a face below in the darkness. A face not Astar's, but a snarling yellow-and-brown spotted beast.

"Watch out!" Micah shouted down into the pit. "What's behind you?"

Just then, a puff of sulfuric steam blew across Micah's face, causing him to wince. Once it cleared, Astar was out of the pit standing behind Micah.

"What's wrong? What did you see down there?" Astar asked.

Micah looked down into the hole, then back at Astar. "How did you get out so fast?" Micah blinked his eyes. "Nothing, just my imagination, I guess. This nasty-smelling steam is getting to me. This place gives me a real bad feeling. Come on, let's go home."

As the boys walked away, a pair of red eyes peered out from the pit. Micah had not been wrong. He had seen a strange face. Its skin was yellow and brown, covered in spots. With fiery eyes, the demon watched them.

This was the demon Monticello. He was adorned in luxurious clothes, a wide-brimmed hat, and an orange jacket with a frilled shirt underneath. He carried a black cane, only as a suitable striking convenience, not an ambulatory one. Monticello smiled broadly and revealed his sharp teeth.

He knew just where to look to find the three Devourers in the distant treetops. He prepared to give the command to attack. But as Monticello started to climb out of the pit, he had to stop short. A surge of flying golden orbs rushed over and around him and the steaming hole. The swarm headed fast for the two boys.

Concerned about the orbs' sudden appearance, Monticello lowered himself back into the pit. From the sulfuric depths below, there he would wait and watch what happened next.

GREAT MAPES FOREST

The boys continued walking in the direction of home, though they didn't get far from the steaming pit. After only a short distance, a multitude of small flying gold orbs caught them unaware. Hundreds, if not thousands, of the little streaming orbs surrounded them in a small hurricane of streaming illuminations.

"By the Gods, what are these things?" Micah shouted swatting at them. "They are going to kill us!"

"No, don't swat at them!" Astar said. "If they wanted to hurt us, they would have done it already."

Though not harmed, the boys were trapped by the spinning lights. The orbs grew thicker around them.

Then, approaching voices called out, "Astar! Micah! Boys, where are you?"

Gensen arrived to see it first. When he saw the boys surrounded by orbs, he stopped short. Limping behind Gensen, grimacing with every step, Amtor came, barely able to keep up due to his old war wounds.

"Stay calm." Gensen knelt, shouting to the boys. "Try to come to me but do it slowly. No sudden moves. Don't anger them."

Micah was first to act. He started to walk out of the circle and toward Gensen. Surprisingly, the orbs created a gap of space sufficient to let him leave. The little orbs did not follow him or move in any way to cause him harm. Once clear of the orbs, he ran to his father. Once Micah was free of the orbs, they closed the circle and came together. In the relative safety, Micah, along with Amtor and Gensen, watched as the growing circle of lights grew larger and spun faster around Astar.

The rotation of the lights started to form a shape—the shape of a woman. The lights moved in perfect unison with precise timing, as if by one collective mind. Through their synchronicity, the form of the woman animated. She spread her arms open and lifted her face up to the heavens.

Amtor gasped. He recognized the form. He had seen the image before.

"By the Gods, it is the great Goddess of Love and Beauty," Amtor said. "Ehlona."

It was the Goddess Ehlona. Visions of the Goddess had come to him decades earlier when he lay injured, so close to death himself in the pit of Mauveguard Pass. Gazing upon the golden orbs, Amtor whispered to himself, *So beautiful she is!*

Astar stood in the middle of the form of Ehlona. The orbs moved the Goddess, raising her illusionary hands. More orbs formed a dagger in her palm.

The vision made Amtor immediately remember the golden dagger he had found at the bottom of the pit of death; the one he had buried behind his house and covered with a large stone almost twenty years ago. The dagger he had found radiated sinister magic, as if the blade wanted to feed upon living souls. It filled him with an overwhelming desire to kill. Not being able to control the dagger, he buried it so many years ago.

In the meantime, the form of Ehlona swept her arm in a motion that caused all the orbs to scatter in different directions. The blade dissipated its orbs back throughout the Great Mapes Forest. Afterward, the image of the goddess spun in a rapid counterclockwise circle, then it was gone too with all the orbs retreating away. Once the air had cleared of the orbs, Astar stood frowning.

"We have just encountered the Timmutes." Amtor stood up too with a grimace. He limped over to his son. "Are either of you boys injured?"

The boys shook their heads.

"I was not harmed by them," Astar said. "They were wonderful, these Timmutes."

"The legends must be true," Gensen said. "I heard Timmutes might be in this forest, but I have never seen them before today. Hardly any have survived such an encounter, so the legends tell. By the Gods! The Timmutes?"

"A strange thing indeed," Amtor said. "And they did not want to harm the boys, nor did they harm us either. They seemed to appear just to show us this image of the Goddess Ehlona."

Turning now to the boys, Amtor glared at them. "What were you doing out here so far? You know better, don't you? Get back to the house! Both of you!"

Gensen assisted Amtor, who limped gingerly on his sore knee. The boys ran ahead but did not get too much ahead of their fathers, afraid of getting too far out in front. They didn't want to rouse any more anger than they already had.

"I told you, you would want to see what I found in the forest," Micah whispered.

"The pit site was strange," Astar said. "But the Timmutes even stranger. Did you see how they were flying all around me?"

"Do you think the two are related, you know, the opening of the pit and the appearance of the Timmutes?" Micah asked.

"I don't know," Astar said. He turned to look behind them one last time. The forest stretched infinitely behind them in the darkness.

Back near the hole, Monticello stood in his fancy clothes, partially obscured in the swirl of yellow fog. Now that the excitement of the Timmutes was over, the demon started walking slowly, through the fallen wet leaves, toward the home of Astar in the village of Homestead.

Streaming pictured lights
Floral queen of our doom
Hoping virgin eyes
Will save me from your tomb

Excerpt from *The Witch's Songbook*

Once out here on the Green, the heights were impossible to ignore.
Some were prone to bouts of paralyzing vertigo.
— Excerpt from *Kilmer's Ghost* (Chapter 3)

THE TEMPLE OF VALOR

ORACLE MOUNT

The new morning found Pirchald under a flannel blanket in the back of a wagon. The wagon rocked along a rutted path, away from the village of Estes, where the family decided they could afford to stop for one night's rest. Every hard bounce aggravated Pirchald; his hand reached for his chest each time the wagon hit a bump in the road. A solitary horse pulled the wagon's wheels splashing through dirty puddles. The route north of the village had long fallen into disrepair, from either overuse or underuse, though which one was not immediately apparent.

Pirchald and his family were traveling to see a new healer. One with the powers of the old ancient ways that had appeared at the Temple of Valor. The Lady Valen was the healer's name, and she was the embodiment of prophecy foretold. Her healing powers were miraculous and becoming legendary. Stories of her healing illness, disease, and injury caused her to be sought out both far and wide throughout the Mid-Run Valley.

Lately a strange sickness had overcome scores of people in the Mid-Run Valley. Rumor had it that the Temple of Valor had swelled in numbers, as many sought out the Lady Valen's healing powers. Pirchald's family was well aware of the rumors, and if they were true, they were prepared to have to camp out along the hills of the Oracle Mount and wait for Pirchald's chance of Valen's healing restoration.

Ahead in the distance the road ran up a hill between featureless fields of emerald grasslands where no trees grew. The wagon rolled up a slight rise then over a break in the ridge. Over the top of the crest, they could finally see the Temple of Valor—a most welcome and long-awaited sight.

"Just look at it, Pirchald, the Temple of Valor," said the gray-haired lady in back with Pirchald. Edith was the wife and attended to her husband, as the old man tried his best to twist around and steal a brief glance.

Pirchald's son, Jerid, saw his father struggle and so described to him what he saw while driving the wagon. "A ridge surrounds its central point in a perfect circle. It looks like the Gods dropped a marble in the sand and froze it midway in its back splash."

"Please, please, Jerid," Pirchald moaned. "Don't stop. I haven't much time."

Jerid looked at his mother. "Yes, of course, Father. Forgive me."

Pirchald and his family were Nomads of Spiron of the Wellish clan. The Wellish had been blessed, as their family always selected the white stone, the benevolent stone. Meaning their clan was exempt from providing the monthly sacrifice of flesh; a condition of the pact between Nadya, the leader of the Nomads of Spiron, and the alliance of the flesh-eaters. Had Pirchald been with anther Nomadic clan that selected the black stone, the sacrificial stone, Pirchald's failing health condition would have most certainly resulted in the old man being selected to provide the demon feast with his flesh.

Unsure if he could even survive the trip, they had traveled nine days from their ancestral home on the southern coast. But Pirchald did survive, and now his eyes beheld the destination they had journeyed so far to see. Finally, the Temple of Valor loomed before them. Here, the priestess Lady Valen could heal his disease. She must. No one else in this world could possibly do it.

"Hold on, Pirchald," Edith reassured her ailing husband. "We are almost there, my dear."

"Just over this next ridge, and on to see the lady of mercy," Jerid said, looking back at him in the bed of the wagon.

"Thank the Gods, not a moment too soon," Pirchald whispered to Edith.

"I'm not sure how much more he can take," Edith whispered to Jerid.

The path on top of the grassy ridge descended through a draw and on to a flat valley. Across the grassland the ground rose to form the ascendant slope of Oracle Mount, a single dramatic rise that lifted gently to a flat round platform. On top of that shelf sat the circular Temple of Valor.

Amid the marbled archways, another sight came into view, most unexpected and very much discouraging. On the grounds outside the temple, hundreds of people gathered in small camps in and around it. A sea of infirmed, injured people, all waiting for the same thing as Pirchald—the healing touch of the Lady Valen.

"Oh no," Edith said. "Look at all the people."

"We are a like a drop of rain in the Endless Sea," Jerid said.

"I have no fear the Lady Valen will let me die here," Pirchald told them. "We have come too far. We are too close to a cure."

They pulled the wagon to a stop and got settled as best they could. Jerid and Edith wondered if Pirchald would be able to hold on long enough, or if he would die with a cure so close in reach. But Pirchald did hold on, and Edith and Jerid had no choice but to wait. And wait they did. Twenty-seven days and nights they waited. Night after night, they camped as all their hopes seemed to dwindle away.

Then one morning, a beautiful female acolyte of Lady Valen unexpectedly came to them. The acolyte was wearing simple robes of clean white linens.

"Come with me," the acolyte told Pirchald and held out her hand. "Your time has come to enter the Temple of Valor and see Lady Valen for yourself. She has asked for you by name, Pirchald. Please. Come with me."

"Wait, he will need for us to carry him, he cannot walk or—" Edith started to say, but she was interrupted, as Pirchald stood on his own.

"You stay here," the acolyte told them. "All we need is Pirchald, as finally his time has come."

The acolyte helped the old man, but Pirchald padded away under his own power. Together the two shuffled up to the Temple of Valor.

"How did she know his name?" Edith asked Jerid watching Pirchald leave them.

"I don't know," Jerid said as he watched the old man leave. "I wonder if we will ever see him again."

When Pirchald entered the Temple of Valor, he was met by another beautiful acolyte dressed in flowing white robes to escort him to his assigned place.

"You are welcome here, Pirchald," she said taking him by the hand and guiding him along the stone pathway. "Please come. Just a few more steps."

Pirchald continued lightly upon the stones, marveling through the palms and tall brass columns that twisted up with the incense smoke to the ceiling. The old man gazed at the round opening above, how it allowed the incense smoke out and beams of dusty light in. The acolyte led him to a smooth white walkway that took them over a stone bridge. The rippling water below reflected the bridge that carried them over the small pond.

They came to his assigned place, which was the stone slab at the back of the third pond. Pleasant sounds of running water accentuated soft harp strings and wind chimes. Plumes of spiraling smoke drifted upward filling the air with an aroma of sandalwood.

Pirchald suddenly felt unsuitable meeting Lady Valen wearing only the simple clothes of a farmer. He was unaware of his moaning or his soft whimpers of pain. Lying on his side, he lay back and clutched his chest.

"Quiet your spirit, Pirchald." The acolyte watched him carefully, consoling him, moving her fingers through his hair. "Our lady is coming. She can make your pain go away. She will restore your hope, your health. Our lady makes all whole again. Now, here she comes."

* * *

Behold, Lady Valen appeared. As sure and flowing as the sunrise, she gradually emerged unexpectedly from the incense smoke. Her auburn hair tumbled down in long curls past her shoulders. She sparkled like a living dream adorned in luxurious textures. She wore a soft emerald gown that clung delicately to the features of her long body.

As she approached Pirchald, reeds of living bamboo swayed toward her. She moved past the crystal pools and the waters rippled from underneath, as the fish lifted adoring eyes out of the water to gaze upon her. In the branches of the palms, colorful birds accompanied her, although none were so bold as to encroach upon her.

As Valen approached, the acolyte moved away. The acolyte bowed, her white overgarment slipping off her shoulder briefly to reveal her naked breast. She raised a hand to cover herself and backed away from the pedestal. Valen replaced her to sit beside the dying man.

"Oh, beautiful Valen, my heart. I am dying of this sickness," the farmer said, clutching his chest. The man strained to look at her through bloodshot eyes. "But at least I can say I died a fortunate man. Now that my eyes have beheld yours."

"Calm yourself, my dear Pirchald. Just breathe." Valen's bright blue eyes looked upon him. Her voice was soft, like the sound of the water rushing by. Valen touched his forehead with her left hand, his shoulder with her right. "For nothing, not even the icy chill of death will ever separate you from our love now. Pirchald, my love. My dear Pirchald. Sweet man, oh Pirchald."

Over and over, Valen whispered the man's name. She breathed on his face and a deep sleep overwhelmed him. Pirchald let out a moan as his eyes rolled back.

From a place hidden in her belt, she produced a small golden knife. Gently, she took the knife between two fingers and a thumb with dainty precision. She lifted Pirchald's left arm and in one smooth gliding motion cut him under his armpit, down along his side. After a slight delay, blood rose out of the wound.

The acolyte brought Valen a fresh cloth. Valen covered the blood with linen, and without another word, inserted her hand into the cut. Into Pirchald's flesh, she reached deep into his back. After the initial push, she paused briefly. Then, she pushed farther into the man. Deeper under his skin. Once she had pushed her arm up to her elbow, she breathed deeply. Then with another deliberate force, she pushed more. At last, she had her arm in Pirchald up to her shoulder. Inside the body, her fingers delicately searched his ribs for an adequate path to glide her hand through. She found her way and inserted the flat of her palm to the edge of his lungs. She held the left lung in her palm feeling the expanding, then contracting of the rising and falling of Pirchald's breath. Waiting for an exhale, her hand reached farther, until she found and held the bouncing sporadic leaps of his heart in her hand.

Pirchald slept deeply while Valen's arm explored inside him. Holding his heart, she closed her eyes and meditated, whispering a chant. The surrounding acolytes sang out loud what Valen chanted.

> *Begone, Oh! The illness that darkens your face.*
> *This sickness, this disease of your heart, begone!*
> *Our love can beat as one, our hearts beat as one.*
> *I absorb the uncleanliness of death, remove your icy grip!*
> *Begone devils, you destroyers.*
> *Angel of our love, make us whole again.*

Then Valen alone spoke the last part of the spell.

"Return, my love. Return to me with your beloved grace."

She stopped the soft chant. Now with a strong aggressive voice she shouted, "Through the power of Valen, I command thee! Begone death!"

Then Valen cried. When she cried, the whole Temple of Valor, all the life contained within, became dark in her mood. The leaves wilted. A dark cloud obscured the sun, blocking the beams of light. A cold and sharp gust of wind whipped through the dome and rang the chimes rapidly, almost violently. The feeling reached its darkest period, and just when the entire structure of the temple seemed as if it could take no more, Valen raised her head and opened her eyes.

The sun returned, shining its brightness once more. The plants that appeared to be dying, so close to death, suddenly greened and brightened with life. The chill left the temple, as the air warmed. The wind felt gentle again, and the harp's slow plucky sounds returned. Through the darkness and horror, beauty and warmth returned to everything under the Temple of Valor...including Pirchald.

She slowly extracted her arm from Pirchald in a careful but steady motion. As her arm retracted, there was no blood, no gore, no residue; her arm came out clean. With her arm removed, Pirchald's flesh began to seal itself. The wound continued to close over, leaving a small blemish but no blood.

She rolled Pirchald over, her left hand resting on his forehead, her right hand on his shoulder. It was precisely the position Pirchald remembered before he fell into the trance.

"Pirchald?" she whispered. "Rise, my beloved."

Pirchald's eyes rolled back and returned to their normal place. He blinked. "What happened?"

"Love has set you free," Valen whispered. "You are a whole man again. Free to live and love once more."

She bent down and kissed him on the lips for several moments. The acolyte came to the man's side. Then the Lady Valen slowly walked backward, away from Pirchald. Another acolyte came. The acolytes helped Pirchald to his feet, where he stood wearily in an uncertain balance. Alternately, his gaze shifted from the acolytes, then back to Valen. The acolytes slowly released him, as he could stand solidly on his own.

"Lady Valen. Oh, my Valen!" Pirchald said in amazement. "My pain, it is gone! My heart feels young again! How can I repay you?"

"Go home, Pirchald, go back to your farm," Valen said. "Live your life as completely as you can. Share your love of the Goddess Ehlona that has made you whole this day. Love everyone, all you meet. This is the only way you can repay me."

The acolytes took Pirchald by the arm and strolled with him toward the Temple of Valor's front arches. Pirchald went gently with them but kept turning his head back to get one more glimpse.

Valen stood glowing in the beams of light, backdropped by the bluish plumes of sweet-smelling incense. She patiently watched him go. Pirchald saw that Valen was crying.

As she took a moment to regain her composure, an acolyte came and attended to her. Once Pirchald left, Valen burst out sobbing. She laid her head on the temple maiden's shoulder. The acolyte comforted her, accustomed to the reaction. Lady Valen's emotive power was great, but every time she performed a healing, the feeling of love overwhelmed her. Her sadness lasted only a few moments, and when she was back in control of the heartbreak, she wiped away the tears from her eyes. She progressed forward through the Temple of Valor.

There were many sick people lying, moaning, in their assigned areas inside the temple, waiting for her. The sick were everywhere. She turned to the acolyte and whispered, "I need a breath of air."

Valen walked past the multitude of hands reaching up to her, pleading for her healing. She stood in the archway looking out. When she walked into the sunlight, the sick waiting out on the lawn could see her. A mix of loud cheers and groans erupted. As far as she could see, people were bringing their sick and wounded. They lay on the grass, in the fields, they covered the steps of the temple and lined the grounds. Valen spread her arms, welcoming those who came from so far away in search of her miracles.

She released an energy of healing power that rippled from her. The wave encompassed all of them. Just a pulse, a fraction, of the healing they would need. Still, enough to refresh them and dull some of their pain.

Valen looked at the sky and allowed the sunshine to dry her eyes; so rarely she saw it these days. To her left, she could see the Temple of Chen-Li. Its white marble columns glistened on the summit of the first of the mountaintops called the Fangs. Valen scanned the grounds of the Oracle Mount. So many people. She breathed deeply as the cheers for her continued. All of them calling to her, pleading, trying to capture her attention. She turned to go back inside the Temple of Valor.

She walked past the blue ponds, past the tall columns with clinging ivy. As she entered into the sounds of rushing waters, moans of people called out in pain in every direction. All of them insistent on the urgency of her help.

An acolyte extended her hand and Valen took it. The acolyte led her to a woman who was bleeding under some bandages. Valen kneeled and kissed her.

"Calm yourself, dear Hela." Valen touched her forehead with her left hand, her shoulder with her right. "Nothing, not even the icy touch of death itself will separate you from our love now."

Hela's eyes gradually rolled back; her body relaxed. Once Hela was under Valen's spell, Valen slowly lifted the golden knife from her belt.

Yet Valen hesitated to make the cut, as just then a strange breeze blew through the temple. A wind gentle and warm, yet Valen thought she heard a voice in it. Not the voice of a person, not one of the sick in the temple. No. Maybe not a voice at all but something familiar to her. Something in that wind tugged at her, reminding her of something long ago. But what that was, she could not remember.

"Do you hear that?" Valen asked her acolyte. "Can you hear that in the wind?"

"Hear what, my lady?" the acolyte asked. "All I hear are the chimes."

"The wind whispered to me just now," Valen said. "I heard something in it."

"What did it say to you, my lady?"

"It spoke a name to me. One that I have not heard for a long time. But now, I cannot remember what it was."

Valen searched the wind for answers. Finding none, she turned back to Hela and made a long cut.

I had a vision just the other day

I saw the whole world in its evil way

I looked to the sky, and Lord! What did I see?

I saw pain and misery

Excerpt from *The Witch's Songbook*

They are killing people, burning them alive.
— Excerpt from *Kilmer's Ghost* (Chapter 4)

THE FOOT OF THE DREADFUL BEAST

VILLAGE OF HOMESTEAD

After the appearance of the Timmutes, Amtor and Astar, along with Gensen and Micah, went back to Homestead.

"What were you boys thinking going out that far?" Amtor continued to scold them. "This forest is dangerous. Astar, you know that."

"We were just exploring," Astar said.

"You are very lucky to be alive, and the Timmutes didn't kill you both," Gensen said. "Not many have survived a Timmute swarm."

"Some have been horribly disfigured," Amtor added.

"I said we're sorry," Micah said. "Aren't we, Astar?"

"We won't do it again," Astar promised but knew it probably wasn't true.

Feeling the heat of his father's gaze, Astar said he was sorry too.

Upon reaching the village, the boys ran back to the blacksmith's shop to sit and wait for their fathers, who lagged behind.

"I wish we could go back in time and avoid that pit altogether," Micah told Astar.

Astar tilted his head to the side. He knew better. "No one can go back in time."

"Our fathers are right, you know," Micah said. "That was stupid and dangerous. Then the Timmutes showed up."

"I know, I know, but weren't they wonderful?" Astar said, still absorbing the experience.

"I mean, the whole thing was strange," Micah reflected. "First a pit opens to the deep. Then, the secretive Timmutes reveal themselves to us. I wonder if one had anything to do with the other."

Coming into sight of the shop, Gensen helped Amtor limp along.

"I don't know what I would do if anything happened to those boys." Amtor winced as he spoke. "Ever since their mothers died, I may have been a little overprotective. But I can't help it. Those boys are all we have left."

"Did you ever think you, of all people, would admit such a thing?" Gensen asked. "You were King Leopold's minister of war, commanding tens of thousands of men. With all you've been through, the armed combat, having to face death all around you. Did you ever think your heart would be held captive by an eighteen-year-old boy?"

"Aye, it's true, Gensen. But eighteen or eighty, Astar will always be my boy. The son Gilglad gave me. Oh, how I miss her still, Gensen." Amtor put his large hand on Gensen's broad shoulders.

The two men looked at each other in silence. Finally, Amtor spoke. "What do I owe you for Mandrake's shoe?"

"You don't owe me anything," Gensen said. "It's an honor to serve the one and only celebrity of the village of Homestead."

They arrived back in the village. There, they found the boys siting on tree stumps talking.

"I'm appreciative of that, Gensen, I am. No, now see here, I will pay you for the shoe." Amtor's face darkened. "But this pit puts me in mind of the one that I fell into. That one, hurt me really bad. And the Timmutes too? Makes me think. Can't help feeling my past is catching up to me, Gensen."

Amtor approached Mandrake and made a quick adjustment of the saddle. Then, he tried to mount up, but Mandrake was on edge. Amtor tried to mount him again, but once again, the horse moved away. It was not like old Mandrake to keep turning in a circle like this, making it difficult. Mandrake had been through the worst of savage wars in the Mid-Run Valley. Yet, he had never behaved in such a flighty manner. Still, Amtor was a skilled horseman, and managed to mount up and get himself settled. Once in the saddle, Mandrake continued with the fidgety and nervous behavior.

"I hope that shoe fits right." Gensen saw what was happening and returned to check if something was wrong with the fitting.

"What's wrong, old boy?" Amtor said, patting the horse's neck. "Calm now, steady boy."

Without further warning, Mandrake reared against a violent gust of wind that rushed past Amtor. Unprepared for Mandrake's sudden lurch, Amtor tumbled backward and off Mandrake, falling directly onto Gensen, knocking him over.

The two men received a thick splash of warm blood across their faces, causing them to shield their eyes. A winged black shape had attached itself to the back of Mandrake. Sharp claws pierced the horse's flesh that now sprayed out blood. The creature opened its mouth and stretched its skin over Mandrake's front half, inserting the animal's entire head, neck, and front legs inside it. Then it tightened around Mandrake. With a single terrible crunch, the bottom half of the horse separated from the rest. The remains of Mandrake fell out of the Devourer's mouth. The rear of the horse fell upon Amtor, crushing his legs and pinning Gensen underneath the weight of both.

A second black creature swooped down on top of Micah, making him fall in the dust. With large leathery wings and clawed feet, the second Devourer held Micah firmly in its grasp.

A third beast came. This Devourer rolled Astar, holding the boy fast in its taloned clutches.

Once the Devourers had their prey, the creatures spun. With powerful wing strokes, all three lifted high in the air. The dark creatures pumped their wings, flying higher and farther away. Two Devourers held the boys and the remaining Devourer carried the remains of Mandrake's carcass to eat later.

The boys struggled for their freedom, pounding with fists against their captors' claws. But the grip of the Devourer's talons held them fast. And after reaching a certain height, instead of struggling for freedom, the boys held on tightly in fear of being dropped. From this height, a fall would mean their death.

Amtor and Gensen sustained no serious damage in the attack, and got to their feet quickly, although covered in horse blood.

"Micah! Astar!" they screamed after the boys being carried away. In vain, the men ran after their sons, but the winged beasts carried them higher and farther off into the distance.

As they flew higher and farther away, just then a steady stream of orbs, colored in tones of fiery red, spun up from the ground like beads of blood. The Timmutes formed a funnel, like an upside-down tornado, wide at its lower base, but reaching up like a finger into the sky and chasing after the Devourers. The red orbs swirled and swarmed in pursuit of the captors.

The red swarm rapidly closed the distance, catching the unsuspecting Devourer holding Astar from behind. The Timmutes spun around the creature, creating a vortex of air. The vortex was sufficient to alter the flight of the great beast. Hundreds, if not thousands, of tiny swarming crimson Timmutes spun around the clawed foot of the beast. Spinning in a rapid circular motion they began attacking. They were sawing at the Devourer's flesh. A fine mist of dark purple, the creature's blood, and fleshy debris spun off the leg that held Astar fast. Then, even more Timmutes came. They continued spinning around the foot of the dreadful beast. The Devourer struggled to fly in the Timmute vortex as more of its foot disappeared.

The monster let out a painful scream. Then, with a crunch, Astar felt himself drifting down and away from the Devourer, riding alone on the smooth air current. Astar's hair whirled in the vortex as he watched the one-footed Devourer fly off without him. The beast did not care about Astar anymore. It only wanted to save itself from the red orbs attacking it. The creature's only instinct was to get away.

Astar was still wrapped and held firm inside the creature's amputated foot. Now, he began falling.

The red orbs pursued the Devourer to kill it, but instead they were forced to abandon the beast to save Astar. They came together with their color changing from red to gold. They swarmed, swirling tightly together to form a cushion of air around Astar and underneath him. They created a vortex like they did to hamper the flight of the Devourer, but this vortex was under Astar to reduce the downward velocity. The Timmutes created a cushion to his fall. Instead of smashing violently, Astar and the severed foot were placed safely on the ground. Afterward, the Timmutes dispersed, flying off in different directions. Soon they had scattered completely away back into the trees and were gone.

Not too far away, Amtor and Gensen came running.

Overhead, the three Devourers flew away. One with Micah, one with half of Mandrake, and one maimed and wounded, empty-handed. Obscured by the forest, the beasts eventually disappeared from view.

Amtor and Gensen rushed to Astar. Tears, dirt, and blood stained their faces. Gensen dropped to his knees. He clutched at his heart, crying out repeatedly, "Oh no! No, no!"

Amtor raced to his son, who was still clutched in the severed foot's claws. Astar's head had landed in a puddle of dark purple blood that continued leaking out of the Devourer's amputated stump.

They worked together to open the claws that held the boy. Eventually, with the men's help, Astar rolled out from the piercing claws. Once Astar was out, the severed foot had a mindless reflex and fully closed in on itself. Then the foot was still, except for the blood that seeped out of it.

Astar, now freed, tore away at his shirt, revealing the slices and puncture holes made through his skin. His skin was pierced and bleeding, but though the wounds were sore and red, they did not run deep. The Devourers wanted only to capture Astar and carry him away, not kill him.

"What were those things?" Gensen began raving while searching Amtor's eyes. "Why did they take Micah? I must go after them, get him back!"

"They came out from under the ground," Astar spoke and both men turned. "Out of a hole Micah found, not too far from here. I bet they took Micah back into that pit."

"I have to go after him. I must find my son," Gensen said.

"The Timmutes…" Astar said, looking behind him, searching for any sign of them, but they were gone. The Devourers, the Timmutes, and Micah—all gone now. All that remained was the severed stump of the Devourer's foot on the ground.

Monticello had watched the attack unseen from the tree line. Satis-fied, he quietly returned to the pit to receive the Devourers and the prisoner they would be bringing.

HOUSE OF AMTOR

Amtor dropped the heavy foot on his dining room table, and a light stream of purple blood dripped onto the floor. With Gensen's assis-tance, they led Astar to his bed and gently laid him upon it.

"What are you going to do?" Amtor asked Gensen.

"I have to go after him," Gensen loudly declared his intentions as if his son could still somehow hear his words.

Amtor went to find a jar of medicinal ointment. While he did this, he talked to Gensen, who kept staring at the Devourer's severed foot.

"I will come with you, Gensen," Amtor said. He dabbed at Astar's wounds, applying the ointment.

"You can't, Amtor. Astar needs you." Gensen watched Amtor limp. "Plus, you cannot even walk. You can barely limp."

Gensen quickly turned his attention to the boy. "Astar, you said Micah discovered a hole?"

"Yes, a place close to where you found us, where the Timmutes appeared. Maybe their appearance was a warning about the pit. There's something else, something we did not tell you earlier."

"What is it?" Gensen asked. "Tell us now."

"We went into the hole."

"You went inside?" Amtor said. "Astar, you put yourself in danger. You put Micah in danger with you."

Astar began to cry. "I'm sorry. I wanted to tell you, but then the Timmutes came, and…"

"What was down there, Astar?" Gensen got close to Astar's face. "What did you see?"

"Nothing, really. There's nothing," Astar sniffed. Wiping his tears away, he collected himself. "A lot of yellow steam with a sulfur smell. It stinks bad, makes it hard to breathe. The sides of the hole, the rocks, they were hot to the touch, but not so hot that it burned our hands. I lowered myself in first by dropping to a ledge that ran along its sides. Then Micah followed. The middle, the-the center, was very deep, endless it seemed. That's where the steam was coming from, way down, far below."

"You dropped to a ledge?" Amtor paused, standing over Astar. "You had no idea if that ledge would hold your weight, did you? Do you know what would have happened if it collapsed?"

Astar burst out. "We weren't thinking. It was a stupid thing to do. We wanted to investigate it."

Amtor shot Astar a stern look.

"What else did you see?" Gensen asked.

"Tracks—there were tracks around the hole." Astar pointed to the severed foot. "Deep, three-toed ones, like the claws on that thing. These things must have come out of it. We followed the ledge—it goes down like a corkscrew—to an opening, a large cavern cut out of the rock. There was a perfectly round tunnel, a passage, going farther down under the ground. It was man-size, but it was dark, too dark to follow. I wanted to go deeper, but Micah stopped me. He insisted we stop. So, we went no farther, climbed back up, and left to go back home. Then, the Timmutes found us and surrounded us."

"Thank the Gods for that." Amtor purposely dabbed the medicine on Astar's wounds a little bit harder this time.

Astar winced.

"I found this." Astar reached into his pocket and pulled out the triangular tooth. He handed it to Gensen.

Gensen looked it over, then handed it to Amtor. "Looks like a tooth."

"No tooth the likes that I ever seen," Amtor said. "But big enough to be one from those creatures. If this is a tooth, whatever mouth it came out of is probably still down there. There might even be more of them."

"If that is true, Amtor, Micah is down there alone with them." Gensen took the tooth back from Amtor. "He is only an eighteen-year-old boy. Trapped with those demons all by himself! If I can go down there…"

"You can't go down there, Gensen," Amtor said. "Not by yourself."

"Are you suggesting I should just leave my son? Leave Micah? To the mercy of those things? You want me to just…give up, accept my son is dead?"

A silence fell upon them. Then Amtor spoke again. "I'm afraid I have brought this calamity upon us, Gensen."

"Nonsense," Gensen said. "Why would you say something like that?"

"Gensen," Amtor started. "I have been pursued. They have followed me ever since I escaped that pit of death in the Mauveguard Pass. There have been demons here before. They've been watching us, lurking just on the other side of the tree line. I think they've been watching us here for years."

"But now the story's different, Father. Now they have taken Micah," Astar said, lying back.

"There is no way you could have known this was going to happen," Gensen said. Then he slowly looked back at Amtor.

An awkward silence followed. "No, of course not. Certainly not anything like this. But it is not their first contact."

Gensen asked, "You know something about these things, don't you?"

"Aye, my friend," Amtor said. "More than I should."

"Demon's fool!" Gensen exclaimed. "Are you in league with these things?"

"Get ahold of yourself man, I am not the enemy," Amtor shouted back. Then with an uncomfortable look at Astar, he began again, "In the darkest of nights, she has come to me. She appeared in what I thought were dreams. But aye, these were very strange dreams. For when I would awake, the dream would continue. I would find her there with me, as real as any woman I have ever known. But more, more than just being there with me. She has…fed on me."

"By the Gods, Amtor! You allowed a demon to feed on you?" Gensen shouted.

"You speak of it as if it was some choice of mine. I had no say in it. I thought she was merely some kind of erotic fantasy. But then, she touched me, crawled on me, beguiling me into her. And at some point, I knew, she was *not* a dream, she was real."

"You keep saying 'she'?" Gensen asked. "That she fed on you? Who is she?"

"The Zorn's concubine, Langula the demon." Amtor hesitated. "Fear excites her. She feeds on blood; and she has tasted mine, always wanting more. And when she came back for more, she took more from me, more than just blood."

Gensen asked, "Has this demon…Langula…does she…give birth to other demons?"

There was another long pause from Amtor as he looked at Astar.

"Father?" Astar asked, holding his bandages in place. "Father?"

"I'm so ashamed… I lack the virtue your mother had," Amtor said to his son. "I fear she may be the mother of all demons."

"I have heard enough," Gensen declared. He handed the tooth back to Astar. "I'm going home now. I'm getting my sword, then I'm going down into that pit to get my son back. You can't help me, Amtor. Just don't try to stop me."

"Gensen, wait. The pit of death in the Mauveguard Pass almost killed me. I was lucky to survive it. If you insist on going down into that pit voluntarily…" Amtor stopped briefly reflecting on his own experience. Then he saw the resolve on Gensen's face. "Then I will send as much help to follow you as I can."

"If not for your wounds, I know you would lead the way, Amtor. If the Gods bless me, then we will see each other again. If we never do, know this: I considered you a good friend. Take care and good luck. That goes for you too, Astar."

"Oh, Gensen." Astar hugged Gensen around his waist. "I am so sorry, for all of this."

"Do not blame yourself, Astar, this was not your fault." Gensen looked at Amtor. "It was nobody's fault."

"Good hunting, Gensen," Amtor gave him a sincere blessing. "Make those damnable demons squeal under the sting of your steel. Bring your son back home where he belongs."

"So be it," whispered Gensen, nodding at them.

Amtor looked down and repeated softly, "Yes, so be it, Gensen, my friend."

Once the blacksmith was gone, Amtor and Astar shared a look of concern. Amtor was unable to look his son in the eyes. Instead, he dropped his head, and without a further word, he walked out of the door.

So be it, Astar whispered to himself and lay back to rest.

We drift apart
And so, drift away
Now you're out somewhere
And somewhere you'll stay

Excerpt from *The Witch's Songbook*

The memories of war stood like ghosts
in a multitude of granite statues of the men who fell here.
— Excerpt from *Kilmer's Ghost* (Chapter 5)

DESCENT INTO DARKNESS

VILLAGE OF HOMESTEAD

Shadows grew long across the hardened roads of Homestead. Inside the back chamber of the blacksmith's shop, Gensen watched the washed-out sky through a dirty window. Dark clouds descended on the little village as the sun went down. The colors from the earlier day had been stolen away; stolen away, just like his son. Today had been the worst day of all his years. Worse, even, than when his wife had died long ago. Now night had come, and Micah was still out there somewhere.

Fires around the edge of town cast an orange glow in the branches of the trees. Gensen listened for Micah's voice but heard only unfamiliar bursts of laughter that occasionally rose above the din.

I will never laugh again, Gensen thought. Just one more thing stolen from him today.

He turned away from the window. Beyond the door, in the darkened blacksmith's shop, the quarry fires steamed. Iron ingots lay cold on the bricks. The hammer had gone idle. Growing darkness permeated everything, subdued into blue-and-black shadows.

Back in his chamber, sitting beside a cold fireplace, Gensen cried alone. A steady stream of tears ran down his face.

"Micah is alive," he pleaded to the empty room. "Please don't be dead."

The bottle clinked hard against his front teeth. Gensen took another drink. The whiskey warmed him.

The sword by the window had never been used before, never swung in battle, never held by any hand other than his. He spent weeks forging it, refining it, and shaping it. It had been some his finest work. Afterward, he honed its edge to an ultra-sharpness.

He knew Amtor was right. Going down into that pit alone was suicide.

Gensen pulled the sword across the floor. Trailing behind him, it scraped against the stones, creating sparks of blue. He placed it upside down, the point in front of him. Holding the hilt with his feet and the flat of the blade between his hands, he adjusted the angle. The pummel found a seam along the stone floor and wedged perfectly there. Maneuvering the point of the blade to the soft part of his belly, just below the breastbone, he leaned forward a few degrees. The hilt found a secure purchase solid against the floor as the point pressed into him. His tunic gave way, stretching to the point of tearing. The sharp pointed tip of the sword pressed deeply into the unprotected soft spot of his stomach.

Almost, he thought. *Just a little more.*

He held his breath. Then burst out crying before holding his breath longer this time. He let out a scream, a loud howl of determination. Intent to send the weight of his body falling forward. *Oh, sword do your dirty work!*

But he could not do it. Finally, he stopped and sat heavily back in the chair. The sword fell to the floor, reverberating sharply as it ricocheted harmlessly away. He could not take his own life.

He tipped the chair and threw the bottle, shattering it. Lifting the sword, he called upon it for another purpose. "Speak to me," he commanded its reflective surface. In the metal, his own bloodshot eyes peered back at him. The blade seemed to transform in his view. Its cold indifference gone. Gensen snarled a word through clenched teeth. *Vengeance!*

THE PIT SITE

Gensen did not remember leaving his shop, but now the pit lay fuming before him. The hole was precisely where Astar said it would be. Gensen gripped and regripped the sword he named Vengeance, eager to put it to use. Instead, he secured it in a scabbard on his pack.

He stretched his neck to look deeper into the hole. A ridge of broken stones ringed the pit and were still warm when he touched them. Lowering himself over the ledge, wisps of foul steam blew into his face. He climbed over the top with burning nostrils and stinging lungs. He hung over a ledge momentarily, then dropped. He landed, scattering dusty cinders off the first landing. A rocky ledge spiraled downward forming a little path of jagged broken rocks. He carefully bounded over the zigzagging cracks where hot steam hissed through. The steam refracted the fires deep below and lit his face in a glow of red and yellow. Gensen took a moment to wipe his brow and to look into the center of the hot pit.

"I can't believe the boys came this way," Gensen said, choking. "Micah, you knew better. Such a stupid, unnecessary risk. If I ever find you…I'll… Oh, I would love to find you again. I would take you in my arms, and kiss you, and never let you go. Oh! Where are you?"

He took a few more steps, then arrived at the wide cavern Astar had told him about. Gensen saw the shaft, drilled into the back of the cavern, leading into the darkness. He looked down the dark passage. The tunnel led away from the sulfuric hole, down a dark incline, and deeper into the ground. A slight rancid wind of heat blew from out of the tunnel, it carried with it a dank and moldy smell. The darkness was oppressive. Yet he stepped into it and began following it down.

Just a few feet into the passage, the light diminished behind him. If there was a crevasse, or opening before him, he could not see it; he would not be able to see it until it was too late. Gensen had packed a torch with him, but he was more afraid of what was in the dark than the dark itself. So, he did not light it, for fear of revealing his presence. He would manage to carry on without it. He kept moving in the dark, pressing his hands against the walls, inching farther along.

He whispered to himself to find more courage. "What's a little darkness to me? I put my life in the hands of the Gods. If darkness overtakes me, I would be no worse than when I was pressing the sword against my belly."

Gensen continued to follow the passage, encountering no holes to fall into. The path and the walls were smooth and round. The creatures he feared the most never appeared to him. Instead, he experienced the opposite, the soul-crushing isolation of being alone in the dark. That was the fear he least expected.

He came to a place where a single beam of light, no bigger than a finger, shone in from somewhere above. The thin beam of light cast a small circle on the wall of the cavern. Gensen experienced a mild relief from the slightest return of his vision. For a short while, he found some minor comfort in the light, but it was short-lived for he discovered evidence of where someone else had once stood here before him.

The small circle of light revealed a symbol drawn on the wall. The symbol, smeared there, looked to be drawn in blood. It was in the shape of an arrow and pointed back in the direction he just came. A foreboding omen, one that seemed to be put there to discourage him, or anyone else, from going forward. The arrow seemed to beckon him to go back. *But I'm not going back*, he thought. Disregarding the sign, Gensen continued down the shaft, and ever deeper into the darkness.

As he descended, he encountered a myriad of other tunnels that forced him to decide to turn left or right, to go up or down. As more time passed, he came across more clearings, more cavern walls illuminated with small beams of light, and more arrows drawn in blood. The arrows always discouraged him, pointing back the same way he just came. Gensen continued to ignore them all.

Still, he traveled deeper, and the air grew warmer. The damp humidity clung to him, sucking the hydration out of his body. The farther down he went, the warmer it got, the more he sweat, and the thirstier he became. At one point, he took off his shirt and wrapped it around his head to keep the salty sweat from his eyes.

How long he had been down here was anybody's guess. It seemed there was no way to determine how long for sure. Time was an unknown factor to him. He had long lost any reference of day or night, and lost track of the hours.

Once while feeling his way along the walls an opening appeared off to the right. Extending his hands in the darkness he progressed blindly forward. This opening was larger than the ones he had encountered before. Carefully feeling the floor in front of him by using his toes, he discovered that the cavern had a solid flooring surface that did not drop out. Feeling his way inside, he found himself standing in complete darkness in a void of nothingness. He decided to find out what this place was. He risked lighting the torch. After a couple of bright sparks from his flint box a warm glow from the torch illuminated the space. Gensen was standing in a room full of spiderwebs. Black spiders crawled upon every web hanging from the cavern's walls. In the middle of the room lay the bones of long-dead adventurers who perished here.

Gensen frantically waved his torch, and despite the flames, the spiders attacked. They converged on him and crawled up his legs. They dropped from the ceiling onto his head. Spiders, ranging from small to large ones, jumped from their webs to crawl on his back and run across his face. Some of the spiders crept slowly, while others darted so swiftly his eyes could not follow.

He dropped the torch in the middle of the cavern. At the same time, he pulled the shirt off his head, threw it into the room, and ran back out into the corridor of the tunnel. The torchlight behind him revealed a gathering wave of spiders following him, covering the floors, walls, and ceiling in a moving black mass. They trailed out in waves from the cavern's opening. Gensen moved along, as quick as he could, farther down the tunnel, shaking, swatting, and swiping the spiders off him. He kept moving, staying just ahead of the determined wave. Gensen did not stop, yet the spiders followed him for what seemed like hours. Eventually, the spiders gave up and he pressed on.

After more time, the signs of the arrows he had been passing finally flipped direction. The blood-smeared arrow now pointed in the direction he was going. A strange change, Gensen thought. First the arrows beckoned him to go back. Now they seemed to encourage him to go forward. Maybe the arrows had more in their meaning than just being an ominous sign.

As he pressed on farther, he found even more blood-drawn arrows pointing forward. But the heat continued to get worse. Gensen found pockets of condensation where he could press his mouth to the side of the wall and moisten his tongue. The moisture was a sour liquid and tasted like rotten eggs, but it cooled his mouth.

Over a vast distance, he wandered until it seemed like many more days and nights passed. The devastating isolation was broken only by creeping things that brushed against his face, or the growl of beasts that stalked him. Occasionally he was bit by something that made him bleed, but what it might have been he did not know. It didn't seem to matter anymore. He bled all the same. Carefully, he crept past.

At times he crawled along the floor. Sometimes he ran with some kind of creature in pursuit. His time was spent either groping in the darkness or sleeping in solitary beams of light. The sharp slopes pulled him farther downward. High rock formations presented him with impassible obstacles. He drank dirty water from the puddles he found on the tunnel floor. He ate what food he had brought with him until it was gone. Then, he ate whatever creeping proteins he could find. They never seemed in short supply.

After all this time, Gensen saw no signs of his son. He finally realized he had made a mistake coming down here. He had become hopelessly lost in the underground. By the time he decided to search for a way out, it was too late. His hope, along with his strength, had drained away. Soon, he could go no farther. He had lost his way. At last, he fell upon the path exhausted.

"I am sorry," Gensen said, closing his eyes to die. "I tried, but I failed. Please forgive me."

The next thing he remembered was hearing his name softly being spoken to him.

Gensen? Gensen? The voice sounded familiar.

It took all his remaining strength, but he managed to open his eyes. At first, he could see no one. Yet the voice spoke to him again.

"Take heart, Gensen, I am here with you now."

Emerging from a small beam of dusty light, someone wearing a green cloak knelt in front of him. Gensen thought he might be imagining it. Then, the mysterious stranger reassured him.

"Gensen," the voice said, "I am going to get you out of here."

I can still remember walking out my front door
I can see the faces of those that came before.
Hot under the spotlight all the pressure's more
But I came through it. Yeah, you can do it.
It could be you.

Excerpt from *The Witch's Songbook*

In the middle of the fire stood the vengeful, bloodthirsty soldiers.
They were laughing.
— Excerpt from *Kilmer's Ghost* (Chapter 6)

THE MYSTERIOUS SCHOLAR

VILLAGE OF ESTES

Throughout the Mid-Run Valley, rumors spread about an abduction of a teenage boy and the demonic attacks in the village of Homestead. The rumors swirled through a web of intrigue until they reached the village of Estes. Eventually they found the ears of a man sitting in a library there, reading a stack of dusty volumes of ancient lore.

Aberfell, the Supreme Historian—the boy that cannot forget— sat reading the book *The Cult of Horrors* when he heard a commotion outside the walls of the library. What he heard piqued his interest enough to close the book in a cloud of dust. As the dust moved, a studious librarian carried a stack of books past him. Aberfell shifted in his seat to keep his face hidden within his hood.

"Excuse me, sir." Another patron of the library approached him. "I see you have been reading *The Cult of Horrors*. Are you finished with it?"

Without looking at him, Aberfell handed over the book.

"Thank you," the man said, taking the book, giving Aberfell a slight nod.

"Uh-hum," Aberfell grunted from underneath the hood.

"Excuse me? What was that, sir?"

"Humph," Aberfell grumbled, motioning for the man to go away. Aberfell's impossibly blue eyes shifted to a multitude of books piled in leaning stacks before him. He had already read all of them, and once read, they could never be forgotten.

Aberfell had long become disenchanted with the throngs of people. Those clinging townsfolk wanting to whisper their secrets to him, just as they had done ever since the day he was born. He felt no remorse or responsibility in denying these people access to himself—no matter how well-intentioned they were—or access to his never-failing memory. Listening to their dull stories, their petty little white lies, it all grew burdensome to Aberfell. He was weary of the fanfare. But the rumors of the abduction and attack at Homestead… now that was something of great interest to him.

THE MARKET DISTRICT

Passing the thatched-roof houses that lined the streets, with their smoking chimneys and stone pathways, Aberfell walked along the little northern hamlet of Estes. He carefully maneuvered to remain anonymous on his way to the market district.

In the market, the smells of baking bread and the daily catch of fresh fish wafted through the streets. Aberfell was not there for bread or fish but to eavesdrop on the many private conversations around him. He pretended to shop for fresh fruit while listening for news. The results were immediate.

"Yes, it's true. A demon carried the boy away on the wings of a bat," a man told two ladies at the market stall.

"No! On the wings of a bat?" a lady asked. "You're making that up."

"Took the boy right up, it did. Never even saw it coming," another man said.

"What a horrible shame," said another. "And how terrifying!"

"Could that happen here?" the lady asked. "To us?"

"Why not?" came the reply. "It could happen anywhere, to anyone."

The first man added to his story. "I heard the boy's father followed those monsters down into that demon pit."

"Threw his life away, he did," another man said. "Any fool knows that."

"A demon's pit?" The ladies gasped. "Bat wings? All of this is just unreal."

"Did the monster have a large mouth?" Aberfell asked from under his hood, not looking at them, pretending to focus on choosing the right apple out of the bunch.

"Did he have a large mouth? Oh, on your life it did. The thing had a monstrous mouth! Such a creature! Why, I'm told the mouth of the demon took up nearly the whole of its body."

Upon hearing the information, Aberfell noticeably turned his head slightly from under the hood. He flipped a metro toward the merchant and walked away with an apple. He moved through the backstreets, avoiding people and hiding in the shadows. He had to be careful. If he was discovered, his cover would be blown and he would be surrounded by a mob of people frantic to tell him their secrets. His memories were already filled with petty and stupid things he had been forced to remember.

Aberfell had been on his own for some time now, leaving his home in Conner years ago. His parents, Norwa and Barclay, stayed in their little home in the village. Aberfell loved them both, so much so that his goal was to relieve them of his celebrity. It seemed to have worked. Aberfell had heard that they were relatively free from the crowds now. It was too much for any of them. The glory seekers searched for Aberfell alone, not them. Neither Norwa nor Barclay had any idea where their son had gone. Aberfell meant to keep it that way.

He adhered to the shadows, moving tactically between the darkness. Methodically he made progress and moved down the road that gave way to the horse trails leading out of Estes. The path would lead him through the southern half of the Great Mapes Forest. There were several paths, but he knew just which one to take, for he had memorized many maps. His never-fading memory guided him in the right direction. It would take him the better part of a whole day to walk to the village of Homestead. So, he continued making his way through a maze of paths that would get him to where he wanted to go in the quickest possible way.

GREAT MAPES FOREST

As Aberfell made his way through the wilderness, the ancient trees provided him with the safety of concealment but also presented many dangers contained within the darkness. Soon those dangers became apparent, as up ahead in the distance a man blocked the way with his horse. He wore a brown cloak and casually held it open, exposing a sizeable dagger in his belt. Aberfell approached him.

"Good day," Aberfell said, pulling the hood off his head, revealing his face, his blue eyes, thin trimmings of a hardscrabble beard, and a head of dark unruly hair. "Your name is Chaney, is it not?"

"I am called Abott. And you can stop right there," the man said, holding his dagger out to stop Aberfell. "That is close enough."

Aberfell stopped more than an arm's reach away.

"What do you want, Abott?" Aberfell asked "If that is who you want to be?"

"Your money," Abott told him. "I'll be taking all of it."

"Sure, sure, if that's what you want, Chaney." Aberfell started to dig in his pockets. "Oh, good heavens! Did I do it again? Did I call you by your *real* name?"

"How do you... Have we met before?" The robber squinted his eyes at Aberfell.

"Oh goodness no. We have never met. If we had, I would remember it."

"Why do you call me Chaney, then?"

"Because that is your name," Aberfell said.

A quiet passed between them. Finally, the robber said, "My name is Abott."

"Of course, of course it is." Aberfell took his hand out of his robes. "Goodness me, I do not seem to have any money to give you, Abott."

"That is very unfortunate for you," the man said and took a step closer. "Can't let you pass without paying the toll."

"The Abott toll, eh? Well, do you know who I am? I mean, I know you. The least you could do is know who you are robbing."

"Why would I care?"

"Because you are not Abott, you are Chaney. So, think on this. If I remembered your real name from the criminal log in the village of Estes, don't you think Aberfell, the Supreme Historian, might know other things too? Like for example, the location of a very large treasure not far from here."

The robber looked at him rather skeptically. "*You* are Aberfell? The Supreme Historian?"

"One and the same." Aberfell bowed low. "Pleasure to make your acquaintance, Chaney—I'm sorry, Abott. Now, are you interested in retrieving a treasure and sharing it with me, or will you want the murder of the Supreme Historian on your head for absolutely nothing?"

The highway robber thought for a moment. "Where is it?"

"I will draw you a map."

"How do I know you are not lying? Or that you are not who you claim to be."

"Well, I knew your name was Chaney. And if it is not, or you don't believe me, then I guess you are going to have to kill me. But then, that would be a lot of work, and no one will ever collect the treasure. I mean, what do you have to lose?"

"Draw the map," the robber said and sheathed the dagger.

Aberfell drew on a page of parchment with a piece of charcoal. He took his time drawing an elaborate map, full of landmarks easily identifiable. During the production of the map, Aberfell made sure to ask Chaney questions as he drew, making sure the man understood exactly the directions into the Great Mapes Forest. It took Aberfell a while to explain them to Chaney, for the man was slightly denser than Aberfell would have preferred. But soon the map was produced, and the directions understood.

"Remember," Aberfell told him. "Next time we meet, don't forget to share the treasure with me. Can I have your word, sir?"

"If there is treasure, or if there is none, the next time we meet I will give you exactly what you deserve."

"Very well," Aberfell said. "Be careful then, Chaney, and good luck."

Chaney watched Aberfell whistle away, while he was left holding Aberfell's map to the secret treasure.

Chaney, or Abott he preferred to be called, followed Aberfell's instructions precisely. For two hours he trudged through the bush and found all the landmarks just as Aberfell described them. Maybe this man was indeed Aberfell and actually knew what he was talking about. Finally, Chaney came to the spot marked X on the map. The spot where Aberfell said the treasure was hidden was in a tree.

Taking out an ax. Cheney spit on his hands and reached back to make the chop.

But before he could swing, the entire tree collapsed in a flourish of red orbs. The entirety of all the trees in the forest collapsed like-wise. Soon the trees were gone and a swarm of red orbs filled the air like a million mad hornets. A red swarm of angry Timmutes spun around Cheney, turning him in every direction. There was nowhere he could run, nowhere to hide. The red swarm spun rapidly in circles, and began tearing through his flesh, sawing it up and spitting out a fine pink mist that permeated the spot where he helplessly screamed. Chaney's bones were soon exposed in ever-widening wounds of disappearing flesh. He dropped the ax, but his knees hit the ground before it did. Rips in his face exposed his skull underneath. By the time the rest of his body had a chance to obey gravity and fall, nothing was left of the man except the bones.

Aberfell strolled along eating the apple he had paid for back in Estes. He took great interest in talking to others that passed him on the road regarding the abduction of the boy in Homestead. He was col-lecting and confirming all the information he could. Once down to the apple's core, he threw it away in the tree line.

After a journey of over six hours, Aberfell reached Homestead. He took the path straight into the village and stopped in front of Amtor's little home. The cottage looked quiet and unassuming, but Aberfell knew who and what waited for him inside. He would help them understand. It was time to make introductions and bring the circle to full.

All the hidden things she kept

I found a picture of you

When everything was new

In a broken heart on a dusty shelf

Excerpt from *The Witch's Songbook*

Some light was coming through the trees, casting shadows.
But they were all mixed up, all of them pointing in different directions.
— Excerpt from *Kilmer's Ghost* (Chapter 7)

WHAT LIES UNDER
THE STONE

Village Of Homestead

Astar had fallen asleep after his ordeal with the Devourers. Amtor looked in on him. The boy lay in his bed, a wrapping of linen around his stomach. Stains of blood seeped through where the Devourers had cut him.

He sleeps so peaceful, Amtor thought. *Now I can do it—I can unbury the stone.*

Astar was not only sleeping but dreaming. In his dreams, he had stopped time again. The pendulum's motion halted inside the clock as before. Amtor watched him, frozen in time, standing there in the doorway without moving. Astar could exist in multiple places at once. One of his personas slept at home while another traveled back to the site of the pit. That other aspect climbed over the rim and descended back into the demon's hole.

Astar crawled down the ledge as before, but this time, he continued farther along the dark passageway. There he found more tunnels. He generated more personas of himself, duplicating further into more aspects, over and over again. Now he could investigate many paths simultaneously.

As Astar explored the underground, his father watched him sleep at home.

Far from the pit, in real time, Amtor turned away from the sleeping Astar. His thoughts raced thinking about how the Devourers carried both of the boys away. Then, the Timmute swarm. Watching helplessly as Astar fell, clutched in the foot of the dreadful beast. Gensen had been gone for over a day now. Amtor wondered what had become of him and his quest to save Micah. Had he found his boy? Or did Gensen only find death in the underground?

Maybe no one will never know, he thought.

Amtor's thoughts turned, as they often did, to Gilglad. He wondered how many things would have been different if she had not died in that fire. How he missed her. He missed loving her. Amtor had to raise Astar on his own, without the boy's mother. But now Astar had grown to adulthood. All the while, the power inside of Astar...well, that was starting to grow too. His powers were starting to come out.

Amtor knew that Astar's power was the Goddess Ehlona inside him.

Ehlona had appeared in a vision to Amtor nearly twenty years ago. During that vision the Goddess told him she had a plan for Amtor. But after all that time, Amtor could not see the plan.

Was this the life she promised me? Was this her plan? If so, he thought it would have been something far more worth waiting for.

Amtor walked out of the house. The long-dreaded moment had finally come. He seemed automated, almost in a trance. He found the shovel and, lifting the spade upon his shoulder, carried it to the back of the house. He searched the grounds for the large stone, long covered over by dirt and leaves. Twenty years had aided the stone to nestle deeper into the ground. Remembering about where he buried it so long ago, he used the iron spade to probe from memory.

Thunk! Thunk! Thunk! He hit the stone with the shovel.

Clearing away the dirt, there it was! Just the way he had left it. Undisturbed for almost two decades. Gingerly on wounded knees, he knelt and traced the corners by hand out of the dirt. The stone had been heavy when he first put it here, now it seemed heavier. The shovel leveraged the stone up and little by little, he loosened it from the ground. Ultimately, leaning into it with his good shoulder, he heaved the stone upright. Then tipped it from the spot he would dig.

Once the rock was removed, he examined the ground. For a time, he wondered if maybe the demons might have found a way to tunnel under the rock, but no such signs of disturbance were apparent. The ground remained unmolested.

He began to dig. The ground was not easy to work, but soon he had a significant hole. Had he buried it this deep? He couldn't remember for sure.

Just then, the shovel struck something in the dirt that rang with the sound of metal on metal. Again, he knelt and used his hands to find the edges of a metal box. Once found, he cleared away the dirt with a sweeping motion. The handle appeared. He managed to wiggle the box in its tight spot. Eventually Amtor worked it loose enough to pull it out of the ground. The box was finally freed and exposed to the light of day again for the first time in twenty years.

Amtor stood straight grimacing in pain. He dusted himself off, while scanning the horizon and the tree line, searching for any movement. He saw nothing, but that did not mean eyes were not watching him anyway. There were powerful forces that had been looking desperately for what he just uncovered—why he had buried it so deep.

He filled the hole back in. The last remaining dirt was tamped back in with a couple of downward pats. Then, leveraging the large stone back into its place, he returned the site to its natural state as best he could. Short of breath, he took the box and limped to the front door.

He stopped at the door, looking at his reflection. He thought about how he used to wash his hands and wipe his feet before entering the house. Gilglad kept things clean and tracking in dirt caused her more work. He loved her so. He took pride in lightening her load, not increasing it through thoughtlessness. But she never got angry at him when he was careless. She only laughed at him, saying what a hard worker he was, and never complained about a little dirt. But Gilglad was gone now. She had been gone for almost fourteen years and he never wiped his feet anymore. He simply did not care about tidiness the way he did with her. Even so, seeing his reflection and the dirt on him gave him pause. Despite himself, he wiped his feet and shook off the dust before walking through the door with the box.

Now inside he saw, as if seeing it for the first time, just how messy the house was. It was always dirty and messy these days, always dark, always gloomy. Never the same since Gilglad's death.

Carrying the metal box, he checked on Astar. The boy was still asleep from his ordeal with the Devourers earlier. Amtor let him sleep in peace and trod lightly not to wake him.

Amtor carried the box under his arm into the kitchen. He put it on the table next to the amputated foot. Pulling a chain from under his shirt, he produced the key, where it was kept safe all these years. He was somewhat surprised when the lock unlatched easily. Yet it took an effort to pry the lid up, as the hinges had rusted.

A small puff of air vented out from the box. Instinctively, Amtor leaned down and breathed in the release of air from days past. He thought he detected a faint hint of honeysuckle, reminding him of the way Gilglad was, and the way he used to be. That puff of air was over two decades old and had come from a simpler, happier time. But just like everything else, his past glory, his love, his health, merely vapors lasting only a moment. Then, it was gone, mixing with the common air of the current time.

Inside the metal box was another smaller box, this one short and oblong. Amtor lifted it carefully. It was lighter than he remembered. He lifted it close to his eyes and opened the lid slightly. When he did a golden yellow glow poured out, illuminating that part of his face. Gold sparkled in his eyes. Observing the treasure, he was unable to avert his gaze from the golden blade that lay inside. His gaze lingered upon it. He found it hard to separate himself from the blade and did not want to stop looking at it. It had been so long. He had forgotten how beautiful it was.

Finally, he forced himself to close the lid with a snap. He returned it to the metal box, then turned his back on it. After stepping away, he meant to walk out of the kitchen and leave the room, but instead, it stopped him as with an unseen hand. The image of it lingered in his mind and hung heavy upon him. Forced to turn and face it once again, he slowly backed away. He could feel the blade working on him.

Walking through the rooms of the house, he tried to focus on something, anything else. The state of the unkept house, the messy floor, the dirty dishes, the unwashed clothes, the foot on the table, all the things Gilglad used to give her time and attention to. He found they were all harder now than before. He had to take care of the house alone. He had to take care of himself alone. Raise Astar, all alone. Even his physical recovery had stalled since Gilglad died. He had his limitations. That, he had to accept. Things would never be the same. As all this went through his mind, he did not even realize he had picked up the box and was once again looking at the golden blade. As soon as he realized it, it scared him. Slamming the lid shut, he dropped the box on the table and painfully limped outside.

The power of the blade was beginning to overwhelm him. Once Amtor was out of the house, he reached for his battle-ax and held it close to his chest. He did not know exactly why, but he pulled it even closer and held it a bit tighter. Holding the battle-ax made him felt better, more reassured. Gripping its long solid handle produced in him a relaxing, calming effect. He walked farther from the cottage, limping to the grindstone to sharpen the axe.

From this moment on, he could trust no one.

Not even himself.

I know the sun will shine on me no more
I know that knock is heartache at the door
And I know just what you came here looking for.
But you can send it all in a letter through the door.

Excerpt from *The Witch's Songbook*

Watching her stumble out with her crooked spine into the night
was the saddest thing that ever happened. Until now.
— Excerpt from *Kilmer's Ghost* (Chapter 8)

STRANGER AT THE DOOR

VILLAGE OF HOMESTEAD

As the door swung open, Aberfell lifted his head underneath his hood, revealing bright blue eyes. He considered Amtor who had just opened the door. Aberfell did not mince words.

"What have I missed? Have you given it to him yet?"

Amtor looked wearily at him. "And just who are you?"

"Well, I am Aberfell, of course." The small-statured young man removed his hood and boldly breezed past Amtor, the largest of all warriors. Aberfell pushed his way uninvited into the home, as the stocky warrior, sensing no danger from the young man, stood back and allowed it.

"Aberfell?" Amtor asked. "The *real* Aberfell?"

Seeing Astar asleep, Aberfell paused for just a moment. Then he turned back to make eye contact with Amtor. "So...you have not given it to him yet. What are you waiting for?"

"Excuse me sir, but—" Amtor started to say that whatever he was referring to was none of his business. But he did not get the chance.

"Aberfell, call me Aberfell. Or the Supreme Historian, if you must. But please, do not call me 'the boy who cannot forget,'" the eighteen-year-old said. "I hate that one the most."

"What are you talking about?" Amtor asked him.

Aberfell immediately saw the problem: denial. "Amtor, come now. I am not going to ask you where it is, but I am sure it is close by. I can wait. If that is what you plan to do. But I would advise you not to wait too long. Things are in motion now. Have you any food? I am quite hungry. The last thing I ate was an apple, but that was a long time ago. On my way here from Estes."

Aberfell casually made himself at home, strolling through the rooms searching for food. Entering the kitchen, he stopped in his tracks seeing the severed foot. It had been there for days leaking purple blood all over the table. "Say now, what is this?"

"A demon's foot." Amtor strode to the counter with a limp. He retrieved a tray of potato bread. Aberfell pulled out a chair and sat at the table. Holding his nose, he began studying the demon foot. Amtor offered the bread to Aberfell. "Smells, doesn't it?"

"Very interesting," Aberfell said despite the odorous stench of the amputated foot. He rolled up his sleeves and started to chew on the bread as Amtor brought over a glass and a pitcher of water. Aberfell helped himself, poured water into the glass, and drank from it. He swallowed hard. Aberfell turned from the foot, gave Amtor a cross look, and then spoke while chewing. "You know what I am talking about, don't you?"

"Aye," Amtor said in a low voice. "I know."

"Good, then let us call it what it is." Aberfell examined the foot again.

Amtor was silent.

"Soothsayer." Aberfell turned, looking at him again. "Come now, is it really that hard to do? You haven't seen it in almost twenty years.

What kind of hold could it realistically have on you?" Aberfell tapped the stinking foot with the bread knife. "So many rumors about this. Who was taken by the Devourers if it was not Astar?"

"Astar's friend Micah. The son of Gensen the blacksmith," Amtor said taking a seat at the table. "Gensen, I'm afraid, has gone looking for his son."

Aberfell thought about it for a moment. "I suspect some kind of pit or hole, I suppose?"

Amtor gave Aberfell a sharp look. "Yes, one nearby. A new crack, a pit, or some kind of opening in the ground back there in the Great Mapes Forest. How did you know that?"

"You weren't intending on following him, were you?" Aberfell asked but did not wait for a reply. "You can't do that. It would only get you killed."

"I fear Micah and Gensen are both lost," Amtor said.

"Probably. I would imagine so," Aberfell said, tapping at the foot again. "Who knows what else is down there?"

"Micah found the pit. Both he and Astar foolishly went inside. They found this." Amtor produced the large ivory tooth and handed it to Aberfell. Aberfell stopped chewing, took the tooth, and examined it.

"Fascinating." Aberfell nodded. "Do you know what this is?"

"A tooth, but from what I do not know," Amtor said sitting down.

"Ever heard of Rock Larvae? Terrifying creatures but quite extinct. I've seen one before, well, pictures and descriptions of it. Not in person, of course."

"Rock Larvae?" Amtor asked, rubbing his sore knee.

"Ancient subterranean creatures of voracious hunger." Aberfell stood and began rummaging through Amtor's kitchen cabinets while he continued, "In his book, *The Cult of Horrors*, the high priest of that order confirmed the existence of the Rock Larvae. That was over three hundred and fifty years ago."

Aberfell found some cheese in the cabinet, then turned back to the table.

"Created by Hexor, the God of Darkness, the Rock Larvae's purpose was to burrow deep underground. Feeding on bedrock, they survived by eating minerals out of the stone. Fitted with powerful teeth, like these, here. *The Cult of Horrors* considered it very good luck to find one of them."

Aberfell returned the tooth to Amtor.

"These Rock Larvae made tunnels underground for hundreds of years. The tunnels go on endlessly in an extensive labyrinth. That's where Gensen went. You see, your chances of finding either of them now that they have entered that abyss are dismal at best. That's why you just can't go down there. You can't follow your friend Gensen. It would be the equivalent of throwing away your life."

"I can't just abandon them," Amtor insisted. "Gensen and Micah."

"Look, if the boy—if Micah—survives, if fortune smiles on them, they will come up to the surface. Then you can help them but not before. For the time being, you must consider both of them lost, until you hear otherwise. Do you have any honey I can put on this bread?"

Amtor stood up, limped to one of the cabinets Aberfell failed to open, and took out a jar of honey.

Aberfell chewed the honey-bread, looking at the foot. "I don't believe they exist anymore, at least not for the purpose for which they were created. But from the looks of this, I'd say they have changed. Evolved, if you will. That tooth Astar found might be all that remains of the old Rock Larvae. Or maybe, it's one of the first artifacts of the newer race of Devourers."

"So, the Devourers are these Rock Larvae things evolved?" Amtor asked sitting again, relieved to take the weight off his aching knee.

"Well, I am not entirely sure. But most likely," Aberfell thought out loud while he chewed. "I would say yes. It's highly probable."

"You are a hard man to follow," Amtor said.

Aberfell slurped down a gulp of water. He burped after finishing. "Do you have any wine?"

Amtor stood wearily again, limped to the cupboard, and produced a dusty bottle.

Aberfell accepted the bottle of wine, then paused. "So, that leaves the original question, Amtor. With these Devourers flying around, causing havoc, when do you intend to stop this charade, and finally join together what is destined to be joined?"

"Well." Amtor took the bottle from Aberfell and poured a glass full of wine. After which, he gave the glass to Aberfell. "We have not had that discussion yet. I'm not sure how to go about doing that right now."

Amtor sat once again and took a long drink directly from the bottle. "It's a hard conversation to have."

"Most things worth doing are," Aberfell said, sipping from his glass, eyeing Amtor sympathetically.

"You seem to know a lot, Aberfell," Amtor said.

"Well, it is my purpose to know a lot," Aberfell said. "But I do not know everything. I do not know what is to happen in the future. I just never forget the past, that's all."

"For the first time, in a long time," Amtor told him, "I feel like getting drunk."

"Have another drink, Amtor. Then another. But then after that, I suggest we get events moving, before it's too late. For somewhere under this roof sits Soothsayer, the world's most powerful weapon, exposed to the open. So, getting too drunk will not solve anything, and most definitely just make matters worse."

Amtor's little cottage had just turned into the center of the universe.

Some say I like it this way
Poor, poor pitiful me
But oh! I feel like crying sometimes
Please, please! Have mercy on me.

Excerpt from *The Witch's Songbook*

The weathering of his face made his skin look like
the cracked leather of alligator hide.
— Excerpt from *Kilmer's Ghost* (Chapter 9)

FRESH MEAT

Deep Underground

Micah felt his head hitting the ground with a dull thump. Dimly he became aware that his head had been bouncing off a series of stairs. The last step was the worst drop and the one that revived him with a white flash. He felt himself moving but not under his own power. The ground was moving under him, his back, and his shoulder blades. His arms dragged free behind him. Slowly regaining consciousness, he was gaining some control of his extremities again. His legs were hoisted up and dragged by powerful pressure that held him tight around his ankles.

He did not know how long he had been held knocked out. The last thing he remembered was being squeezed in Langula's coils until he couldn't breathe. But before he passed out, Langula's face got very close to his, watching him slip out of consciousness.

"Now we got you, Astar. Now, you will belong to us," Micah heard Langula say with a laugh.

"No, wait," Micah pleaded. "You've got the wrong... I am not..."

Micah dimly remembered that she raised her tail, and he could see a dripping barb on the end. Then he felt a sharp stab in his neck, followed by a warm painful feeling under his skin. Then darkness overwhelmed him.

That was the last thing he remembered. Until now. He could still feel her sting in his neck, unshakable blurriness in his vision, and a numbness throughout his body. As he came to, he felt more than just a little sick.

Micah blinked. The dark world around him danced in his blurred vision. He could see only the feet of others, walking along sideways, as he was being dragged. He focused on the black heels clicking in time upon the hard surface. He remembered the Devourers now; he had been taken against his will. He was being held captive, dragged through puddles of water and muck and who knows what else.

"Ah! Astar is waking up," a voice said with a snakelike hiss. It was Langula, the demon, half woman, half serpent.

"Good," a deep voice said. "Because we have arrived."

Micah's feet came crashing down as the motion of his body stopped.

Eerie shapes moved in front of him. Flashes of vague figures and faces he did not recognize. These people looked foreign and unfamiliar to him. At first, they appeared somewhat human but not quite right. Micah thought they were wearing masks. They had stretched skin, oddly colored faces, and weird eyes that sparkled in eerie luminescence, reddened with blood. They were human in basic form only. But not like any human the boy had ever seen before.

"Are you sure this is Astar, Langula?" a deep voice asked.

"I am not completely sure, Grim," Langula said. "There were two boys in the village."

"If this is Astar, it was too easy," Grim, the red demon speculated. "I thought it would be harder than this."

"I agree with Grim," a blue demon now spoke. "Nothing is ever that easy."

"Tender young flesh is always the best," Langula said ignoring them both. "I want to know what he tastes like."

As fast as a cobra can strike, Langula slithered across the chamber and struck Micah. His entire mouth was enclosed inside her black lips. For long seconds, she held him there under a powerful force. He could not breathe. She continued her long demon kiss until Micah started to pass out again. This time from his life force being drained from him.

"Langula, enough!" the deep voice of the spotted demon spoke.

"I can't help myself. He tastes so good!" Langula laughed. She released him.

Micah's head hit the ground, too weak to support himself. Lying on his back with his eyes closed, Micah could hear laughter all around him. When he opened his eyes again, the darkened chamber returned to him in a kaleidoscope vision. He sensed others in the distance, watching him, mocking him.

Langula had casually slithered away on her serpent-tailed lower half. Micah found himself admiring her womanly features as she withdrew from him. Strangely, he wanted more. Even in his predicament, he desired more of her still. He reached up for her, only to grasp at empty air.

More laughter burst forth at his spell-induced passion. A pathetic attempt to possess something that cannot be possessed.

"This is Monticello, first of the Demonic." Langula slithered around a throne and touched the spotted demon beside her. He constantly smiled and bared his fangs, looking at Micah from under the brim of his hat.

"And this is Grim, the baby of the family, the third and last of the Demonic," Langula ran her hands over the red demon standing on her other side. Grim stood growling at Micah. Shorter and stockier than Monticello, his brow wrinkled in a perpetual downward scowl.

The last demon was introduced. He had eyes of silver and hair of flowing white that rolled upward and was taller and leaner than the other demons. His skin was blue just like Langula's. "And this magnificent one is Frost, born between Monticello and Grim."

"Tell me." Grim knelt before Micah. "Do you know where you are?"

Silence filled the chamber. Micah had no answer, as Grim studied him. At last, Micah sat up and spoke. "I want to go home," Micah said.

Frost joined Grim, kneeling to examine Micah. His silver eyes darted all over him.

"What is your name, boy?" Frost asked, gently reaching out and stroking the boy's hair. "Are you Astar?"

Grim's red eyes remained fixed on Micah. "Well, are you?" His voice had a deep growl.

Micah made a sour face. This place had a foul odor of rot and was partially obscured by shadows. "I am Micah."

"Micah?" Monticello asked. "Not Astar?"

"Great," Grim said, throwing his arms up and pacing away. "The Devourers picked up the wrong child."

Frost said, "This is what they brought us."

"It was too easy," Grim said.

"Not everything goes as planned." Frost rose. "Some plans are more difficult than others."

"What do you know about it?" Grim looked annoyed. "Difficulties, Frost? You are Langula's favorite, what do you know about difficulties?"

"Silence!" Langula circled behind the throne. "That's enough out of both of you. This is who the Devourers brought us. We will have to make do."

"I instructed the Devourers to bring us Astar. There were two boys in the village, both the same age," Monticello said. "In the confusion the Devourers grabbed both."

Frost asked, "Then where's the other one? Where's Astar?"

Monticello pointed to the Devourers. They were in the darkness finishing up the half of the horse carcass. One of them licked his wounds, the festering stump where his clawed foot used to be.

"He got away. That one had him, but was attacked by the Timmutes. Obviously, they got the wrong one."

"Yes, obviously," Frost agreed. "The wrong one."

"Does it really matter?" The red demon paced the darkened chamber pursing his blackened lips over razor-sharp fangs. "I say we eat him. Let us dine tonight!"

"You express yourself in very few words," Frost told Grim. "You have too much rage for any practical meaning, no tact, no touch, and even less talent for big picture strategy."

"I am not like you, Frost. I would never hide my true identity behind a disguise of human weakness, the way you have," Grim said.

Frost answered, "Say what you will about my methods, Grim—if you control the king, you control the entire civilized world."

"Come now, Grim," Monticello said. "You know the only reason Frost disguises himself as Brother Barker is to masquerade as one of the king's advisors."

"You make me so proud, Frost." Langula wrapped her coils around her favored son lovingly. "My beautiful blue-skinned demon."

Grim shook his head and turned back to Micah. "Enough discussion! Time to feast."

"Grim's only politics is driven by hunger and violence," Monticello said. "He asks only after he acts. But by then it's too late."

"Yes, no one does violence better than Grim," Frost said. "That's a compliment to you, my scarlet brother."

Monticello stared, coldly stroking his chin. After a consideration, he spoke, "I think we can use this boy. What do you think?"

"Or we could taste new meat," Grim interjected.

"Perhaps," Frost said. "Maybe he could be useful. He could help us identify the real Astar. Now that he's one of us."

The demons watched as Micah struggled to his feet. "I don't want to be here. I want to go home, back to my father."

"You can't leave. We're your family now," Langula said with a pout, eyebrows raised.

"I still say we feed on him," Grim said, stepping closer.

"Wait! No please! You are vampires!" Micah stepped back, and in doing so, noticed the human bones, scattered among the chamber—skulls, spines, and femurs.

"No, hardly! We are not blood-drinkers. We are flesh-eaters." Monticello sat back laughing. "An important distinction, you must understand."

Micah put his hand on his face and began to sob.

"Micah." Langula slithered toward him.

Micah, still under her seduction spell, felt the pull of her attraction.

She delicately put her hand on his back and spoke in gentle tones. "Everything feeds on something. No one is exempt from eating to survive. The Gods have determined it such that your kind is weak, and our kind is stronger than you. But I know what you need. You lust for power and strength. Why shouldn't you want to be stronger than you are?"

Langula intimately pressed her lips to his ear and whispered, "You dream of having lovers the way you want them. But when you wake, you watch them come for more powerful men, never to the sons of blacksmiths. We can change all that. You will never want for any of them ever again."

Langula paused and kissed his ear. Micah slowly turned to stare into her eyes. They held the moment, closing the distance between their open mouths.

Then she burst out in playful laughter as her tail uncoiled around him. "What if I gave you all this, the beauty of the world? Would you bow down and worship me? Think of it, Micah, to have power over others, forever?"

"What do you want from me?" Micah asked.

Monticello walked closer to them. "You are asking the wrong question, for we can take whatever we want from you and leave you an empty husk. You are a scared little rabbit surrounded by ravenous wolves. You should be asking yourself, why have you been in our company this long and are still alive? Why have the wolves not killed you?"

"Nothing seems right here in this place," Micah said. "I just want to go home."

"He doesn't seem to grasp what is happening to him," Grim said.

Monticello caressed Langula's breasts in front of the boy. "Being a part of our family—now that would not be so bad, would it? Choose life with us or choose death. It is entirely up to you."

"Oh, not to worry," Langula said, moving away from Monticello's pleasures. "I can tell by the look in his eyes—he wants it. His desire is to become one of us."

"I feel very dizzy," Micah said. "Something inside me is wrong, has changed."

"You have already begun your evolution," Monticello said. "Langula's serpent venom is coursing through your veins."

Micah reached up and touched his throat, now aware of the source of pain. When he withdrew his hand, he saw it was bloody, mingled with the purple oil of Langula's venom.

"It is done," Frost said. "It is already done. We thought you were Astar."

Grim looked at Frost. "See? I told you this was too easy. Now what do we do? I say we go ahead and kill him and eat him. I'm hungry."

"You can feel it, can't you?" Monticello asked Micah. "Your body is dying from Langula's venom. The only question is whether we allow you to complete the transformation to an immortal...or not."

Grim interrupted with a shrug. "Then, we eat what's left."

"I do not want to die," Micah said, falling to his knees, as the weakness consumed him. "I want the power to live as you promised."

Frost waved his finger at Micah. "The boy may yet surprise us, Monticello."

"Maybe..." Monticello looked over at Langula. "What do you think?"

Langula rushed in and cradled Micah's head as he swooned. She coiled around him, just in time to gently lay him flat on the ground unconscious.

"We must wake the master," Langula said.

"Why?" Monticello asked.

"He needs to be aware of these new developments," Langula said. "Monticello, you and I will go. Frost, you return to King Leopold as Brother Barker, continue your influence over the Kingdom of Odessa. Do not rest until they commit a glorious self-destruction."

"What shall I do?" Grim asked.

Langula considered the red demon. "Go kill something. But do not touch the boy here. Instead, watch over him, make sure nothing happens to him. I feel we can use Micah in the days ahead."

"Come, Monticello, the master awaits," Langula said.

Monticello took a torch off the wall and disappeared down a darkened tunnel with Langula following.

I've scribbled through the lines of a hundred paper faces
I've stolen the hearts from some rose-colored aces.
And I've found God in a starry oasis.
I'd do most anything just to be with you.

Excerpt from *The Witch's Songbook*

The man only had time to widen his eyes to see death coming.
— Excerpt from *Kilmer's Ghost* (Chapter 10)

TEARING THE COSMIC FABRIC

VILLAGE OF HOMESTEAD

Astar wandered through the depths using many copies of himself. Materializing from one place to another in the labyrinth, he investigated many tunnels in many forms. He created additional copies of himself upon encountering crossroads, then merged those copies back when the path led to nothing of interest. He was getting better at this and grew a level of proficiency in his multiplicity. He could do it now whether asleep or awake. Exploring the tunnels using multiple forms, he eventually located what he had been searching for: the cavern where the Devourers had taken Micah. In the torchlit cavern, the Demonic surrounded his friend. Astar stayed in the shadows and peered in the cavern of the Demonic, watching and listening.

He heard Monticello say, "Maybe. What do you think?"

Then Langula replied, "We must wake the master."

They were indoctrinating Micah into their ranks. Unfortunately, Astar could only watch from the shadows. Then, Astar was interrupted by another voice, in another place.

"Astar?" He heard his father whisper far from the Demonic voices in the pit. "Are you asleep?"

Astar began to stir back in the house in Homestead. He merged all his other forms back to this one, the original copy of himself. He was no longer watching the indoctrination of Micah, instead he opened his eyes to see his father standing over him with a golden dagger. A blade that sparked and hummed in Amtor's hand, emitting colors in waves of electric particles, crackling and casting swirling shadows on Astar's face.

"Father?" Astar called out once. "What are you doing? Why are you holding that knife? And why is it glowing like that?"

"This blade is alive," Amtor said, struggling with Soothsayer. "It is reacting to you, Astar, reaching out to you."

Aberfell said, "It's displaying its excitement to be rejoined."

"Who are you?" Astar looked beyond his father at the young man with the blue eyes.

"Well, I am Aberfell, of course."

Astar sat up. "*The* Aberfell, the boy who cannot forget?"

"One and the same." Aberfell smiled and nodded despite hating that moniker.

"You are from the stars like me," Astar said.

"My static sign, the blue comet, was foretold six months before yours, the Star of Ehlona." Aberfell put his hands on Amtor to support him. "I suppose you could say, in that respect, we are like brothers...like star brothers...or star twins...star orphans?"

"Not the time, Aberfell, not the time!" Amtor gave Aberfell an awkward sideways glance, as he continued his urgent fight with the vibrating blade. Soothsayer was becoming hard to handle now with an increased frequency of powerful vibration.

Aberfell shrugged, then cleared his throat. "The real question is, Astar, who are you and what must you become?"

"I tried to protect you from this, Astar." Amtor held the shaking golden dagger. "But …I…could not resist digging the dagger out of the ground. It compelled me here to your room with it just now. I am losing control over it. It is taking control. *You* are what it wants."

"Me? The dagger wants me?" Astar looked at the glowing blade. "I have never seen that dagger or one like it before in my life."

"It's the first time it has been out in the open since before you were born!" Amtor shouted over the electrical buzz from the blade getting louder every second.

Aberfell said, "This is magic Soothsayer, the golden dagger. I am not sure what is going to happen, or what will become of you, or any of us for that matter. But it must be something wonderful as it has been foretold since the era of the Gods! Prophecy is about to come true! Let it be, Amtor! Give him the blade!"

Amtor placed the glowing dagger on the small table near Astar's bed. Then, he and Aberfell backed away, unsure of what would happen.

The dagger spun itself around, offering itself hilt-first to Astar.

Astar sat up from his bed, looking at the blade vibrating on the table. The dagger emitted tiny ripples of energy across its surface. Astar started to reach for it. When his fingers came near to it, the energy began reaching out. Sparks connected with his fingertips in arcs of blue static electricity. The dagger moved on its own, vibrating across the table.

"Is it dangerous?" Astar asked, as the blade's energy turned the entire room blue. "Will it hurt me?"

"It is the most dangerous weapon in the known world," Aberfell said as an unseen wind whipped around them. "Only you can control it."

Amtor became dizzy and put his hand to his forehead. "It wants you, Astar. Only you."

"Soothsayer?" Astar reached closer. He did not grab the blade from the table. He did not have to. Suddenly, it was in his hand.

There came a rush of sound, accompanied by a flash of blinding light. The dagger unleashed a force of energy so strong it lifted Amtor and Aberfell away and pushed them against the wall.

As Astar held the blade, time stopped. Amtor and Aberfell froze in midair against the wall. Debris churned up from the force of the blast hung in the room.

A memory came to Astar. The memory was of another place and another time. He remembered the memory as if it were his own, but it was not one of his own. The memory was from the Goddess Ehlona, sixty years earlier.

"I will live forever." Ehlona smiled.

With the four blessings complete, Ehlona's beauty had abandoned her. Her spine twisted into a large hump. All the sparkle drained from her eyes and darkness obscured her once brilliantly blue eyes, turning them bloodshot. Her hands wrinkled into pockmarked gray flesh.

Coming upon a grassy opening in a glen, she found a freshwater spring to drink from. Falling upon her knees, she saw her reflection in the still waters for the first time. A slow and growing bitterness filled her eyes. Her lips trembled; then, like a wailing siren, she let out a long howl of despair. It gathered in intensity and carried through the woods. Making a shaking fist, she struck the water with a hateful splash.

"Let the name of the Goddess Ehlona be no longer spoken! Let the word go forth from this time forward that the Goddess of Beauty is dead! All that remains is the Witch of the Great Mapes Forest!"

Back in Amtor's little Homestead cottage, he and Aberfell lay collapsed on the floor from the force.

"By the Gods!" Amtor exclaimed. "Did that come from Astar or Astar's Blade?"

"I could not see." Aberfell picked himself up. "The light blinded me."

Time flickered in involuntary spurts of awkward stopping and starting. Astar received more memories from the Goddess. Now Astar found himself deep in memory, deep in the ancient Great Mapes Forest. Astar recalled the memory that was not his.

The Master Tree slowly turned and spread his branches apart in a sweeping motion, revealing a light shining outwardly through a large open knothole in his trunk.

The witch bowed her head, rolling up her left sleeve. She shuffled closer to Master Tree, rubbing the flesh of her left arm. "With this arm, I once embraced the Gods. Now, I sacrifice it for compensation to the Great Mapes Forest in a continuance of our pledge. With this action, may we have peace for a thousand years."

The witch slowly inserted her arm into the knothole. Gradually the hole squeezed until it tightened, compressing her flesh. A numbness spread in her arm. Master Tree waited for a moment, then the cut was swift. The witch fell backward, dropping to the ground, her left arm missing.

In present time, Amtor rose. He watched Astar and saw his head shaking rapidly, until the boy's face was just a blur. Vibrating left and right, up and down, Astar was leaving traces of his face, his head, his neck, in every direction.

"What is happening to him?" Amtor shouted and reached out. "Astar!"

But before he or Aberfell could do anything, another blinding light flashed again. Amtor and Aberfell shielded their eyes.

Time stopped once more. Another alien memory came to Astar. For this one, he was being transported to the Zorn's castle in the Sanguine Forest. Astar found himself in the furnace room, deep below Castle Orlo. A large master smelter stood with a dirty smock, a glowing red forge behind him. Hazor, the well-groomed son of Hexor the God of Darkness was there, a handsome man with crazy yellow eyes. This was the Zorn!

"Did you get it?" the Zorn asked.

"Yes, Your Excellency, I have it here." The master smelter held up the petrified arm of the witch.

"It must be gold," the Zorn told him. "It must be pure."

"Yes, Your Excellency," the master smelter said, flipping a tarp from a wheelbarrow, exposing a stack of gold nuggets. "I have more than what is needed."

Back in Homestead, Amtor shouted, "Enough!" He grabbed Astar by the shoulders and tried to save him from convulsing. Aberfell tried in vain to wrestle the big man away from Astar.

"What are you doing?" Amtor shouted. "Get off me!"

"No, do not interfere!" Aberfell shouted back. The two men continued to struggle with each other.

A fourth and final memory came to Astar.

To bind her spell to her, the witch pricked her finger and dripped blood into a small bowl. She added just the right amount to her

magic recipe, then poured the entirety of the potion into her caul-
dron. She rotated the big iron pot over the flame, and the whole con-
coction simmered to a boil.

Scanning the room, she noticed several orbs dancing inside the
house. The tiny orbs could fly or float, as if they were lighter than air.
Most impressively, they possessed the ability to change their appear-
ance and form, as golden orbs or tiny humanoids, and to camou-
flage themselves and blend in with any surface. When they came to
rest on the table, they became indistinguishable from it. When they
came to rest on a rock, they became the rock.

The next morning, the witch observed they could change color.
They were turning red and swarming something in the forest in a
dense intensity. The next day, the witch found the body of man, a
hunter whom the orbs had swarmed and killed.

Several of the magnificent white oaks in her immediate view
came tumbling down, collapsing into fragments, tumbling down
into millions of tiny particles; they had all been comprised by colonies
of Timmutes. An incredibly loud crashing sound echoed throughout
the forest as more and more of the forest collapsed in Timmute col-
onies. This fragmentation of the forest went on for several minutes
as the Timmutes expressed their joy.

Then, after collapsing the forest, the celebration subsided. The
Timmutes began reconstructing themselves from the ground up to
form the multitude of white oak trees once again.

The witch feared for her life, seeing their great power. Then the
Timmutes spoke to her. At first, the voice was too loud, an over-
whelming boom. The witch winced as the Timmutes shouted in one
voice, "Creator, we honor thee!"

"Do you seek to consume the world?" the witch asked the Tim-
mutes.

"We wish to be a part of this world, not destroy it."

Astar stopped shaking with his head bowed. He lifted his face to Amtor. His eyes possessed no pupils.

Then another wave of power flashed, and Amtor and Aberfell were thrown against the wall again. A series of popping sounds came as Astar began to duplicate himself. Five, ten, fifteen Astars filled the room. Each of the Astars moved independently, facing in their own direction, and all of them were talking at once. They spoke loudly, pontificating on different topics, laughing in varying tones, and one was crying. The noise made Amtor and Aberfell raise their hands to their ears.

Without warning, all the Astars stopped talking at the same time. The silence was so abrupt, it felt jarring. Working in unison, different Astars began speaking different words to form a single coherent sentence.

What. Is. Happening. To. Me? Just five Astars said in turn.

Each of Astar's personas held a copy of Soothsayer, the golden dagger, as it had also been copied with his power of multiplicity. The Astars merged into one but only momentarily. Then, Astar split into even more versions of himself again, filling the entire room with dozens of copies. They all looked to be in pain from overcrowding. They moaned loudly and flashes of light pulsed around them. The energy crackled like lightning inside Amtor's living room.

Amtor labored against them all, but Aberfell stopped him.

"No, wait! Can't you see?" Aberfell said. "He and the blade are becoming one! Soothsayer will not harm him!"

"You'd better be right!" Amtor shouted over the weird noise that had been growing.

"In Homestead, of all places!" Aberfell laughed. "A ripping of the cosmic fabric! The last remnants of Goddess Ehlona, her melted arm in Soothsayer, reunited with her recycled spirit in Astar. We are witnessing the rebirth of the Goddess, a joining of power from the last era to this one! Inserted into your son. Right here in your home, Amtor!"

"Oh, that noise!" Amtor shouted, covering his ears.

"Noise? What noise?" Aberfell shouted back. "Harmonic feedback! I am sure it will pass."

"If you're wrong, Aberfell"—Amtor gripped his battle-ax— "I swear by thunder, I'll kill you for not allowing me to stop it!"

"You can't stop it!" Aberfell shouted.

They continued to watch Astar's transformation. Still, Aberfell looked nervously at Amtor's battle-ax. He swallowed hard and took a step away, just in case he was wrong.

Then the multiple Astars groaned, arching their backs in agony. Astar's multiplicity was happening uncontrollably, in random spasms. New versions of himself flared in sporadic flashes. No sooner would one appear than two would disappear out of existence. Finally, in a flurry of quick slurping sounds, all of them absorbed back into a single form.

For a moment, all was quiet and still. The flashing lights and duplicating Astars were replaced by a steady and rising warm glow. Astar emerged from the fantastic light with aftershocks of electrical energy sparking upon his body. He stood alone, light radiating from his one solitary form. He marveled at the glowing blade in his left hand with a widening grin. Something had changed. Something was different about Astar.

"Look, Amtor! The transformation is complete," Aberfell shouted even though the harmonic feedback had faded away and he did not need to. "The blade is now part of him, and he is part of the blade!"

"Part of the blade?" Amtor did not understand.

"See, I told you, Amtor," Aberfell exhaled and rested his head against the doorway wiping the nervous sweat from his brow. "Nothing to fear."

Astar looked up with eyes of pure gold. "I understand it fully now."

"Understand what?" Amtor asked. "What has happened to your eyes?"

"Can you articulate it?" Aberfell asked, wiping his brow.

"I can feel the entire universe. The mysteries of who we are, where we came from, where we go to," Astar said. "The fabric of the Cosmic Creation. Each of the individual threads of the whole of humanity."

"Your eyes—you have power reflecting in them," Aberfell said, looking upon Astar's face in wonder.

Amtor said, "There were copies of you everywhere. You were everywhere at the same time."

"Like this?" The voice was Astar's but came from behind them.

They turned to see another Astar in the doorway to their rear.

The second Astar spoke to them, "I used to have to sleep to do this. Now I can do it anytime. Like this."

Now another version of Astar appeared to their left and spoke, "This era has been reunited with the previous era. Through the flesh that has been dissolved in Soothsayer..."

A fourth Astar appeared and finished the thought, "...a barrier has ripped space and time." Copies of Astar surrounded Amtor and Aberfell, one in each direction.

Astar converged back to the single form in front. He lifted the blade. A radiant golden sheen came upon him as he inherited the physical characteristics of Soothsayer. Astar's skin shone as brilliantly as the gold in the blade.

In pure golden form, Astar spoke in a voice like that of the rushing wind. "Ehlona the Goddess of Beauty! I remain Astar, yet I am also she that has come back into the world. Together we will usher in the third era! A new era free of Gods and magic, for this will be the era of men and mortals. The power of the blade, the power of the Cosmic Creation, I am now…both! I am the one true God in this world. The one all will fear!"

The walls are thick and they're rich

In the palace of love

Swift dance of time

Stole the hand off your glove

Excerpt from *The Witch's Songbook*

They violated him again, repeatedly and at will,
inhabiting his humanity
just to briefly feel the warmth of living flesh once more.
— Excerpt from *Kilmer's Ghost* (Chapter 11)

COLUMNS OF STONE

Deep Underground

Monticello and Langula made their way through the drippy darkness of the underworld. Monticello carried the torch, as flames illuminated his fancy adornments and the yellow-and-brown spots on his skin. Darkened in shadow, Langula slithered behind, riding on top of her giant serpentine tail. They knew where the Zorn could be located and soon, they reached the only way in.

The opening was a tunnel, a long and dark narrow entrance to the cavernous subterranean chamber beyond. Monticello extended the torch into the tunnel and looked within. Beyond the passage, lights flashed in colors inside a distant cavern. A subdued sound like the fluttering of wings reverberated in the distance ahead.

"Hear that?" Monticello whispered. "What's that sound?"

Langula answered, "Probably guardians of the Zorn."

"Then, this must be the place?" Monticello stopped and turned to her.

"Go on, go inside," commanded Langula with a nod.

The spotted demon squinted a final look down the tunnel. Then, he lowered his head and entered the passageway. Langula followed close behind. The torch led the way as one in front of the other they crept through the roughly hewn passage of oily puddles. They were getting ever closer toward the strobing lights and constant sound of fluttering.

Entering the cavern, Monticello stood fully upright. He paused to absorb the sight. From the ceiling, sharp rocks dripped with milky minerals, resembling hardened icicles. The place was filled with large moths. Scattered like a thick carpet before him, the moths crawled over the multicolored stalagmites that pointed up like jagged fingers. Clinging to the walls and fluttering in the air, the moths whirled around the cavern like tiny tornados, rising and falling in thick swarms.

Langula entered the cavern next and pushed past Monticello. As the demons walked and slithered through them, the moths took wing, obscuring their vision, and confusing the depth of the place.

"I did not expect it to be like this." Monticello scanned the darkness of the cavern with his torch.

"Be happy it was not scorpions he conjured," Langula said, searching.

"All these moths," Monticello said. "They are annoying."

"They are supposed to be."

They searched the cavern. The torch revealed the shadows. Finally, they found what they were looking for. A tall stalagmite held a body within it. This was the body of the Skeletal King, the Zorn himself.

"There he is." Langula placed her hand on Monticello, moving his arm, shifting the torchlight to shine on the stone pillar. "Look there."

"I see him," Monticello said.

The Zorn had become like the rock itself, growing into, and becoming part of the world. Inside the stone, pulses of energy rippled, illuminating the cavern in light resembling flashes of lightning. Each purple bolt of lightning crackled in a loud buzz.

"Is he asleep?" Monticello asked.

"No, he is very awake."

"What is he doing?" Monticello watched the purple energy rippling within the stone.

"Generating sickness, disease, madness," Langula said without any inflection of interest.

"Why is he melded into this ancient stone?"

"He is using it to amplify his magic," she said. "And send it to the world above."

"You mean he is now actively manipulating the minds of the villagers?"

"Turning their thoughts into his own," Langula said. "Turning mortals into murderers. Killers that bring the balance back and correct the numerous blessings bestowed by the Gods before. But now we must interrupt him at his most magnificent work."

"Go on and summon him, then." Monticello squinted and held the torch high as a cloud of moths swarmed around him. "And let's leave this place as fast as we can."

Langula touched the stone. For a moment the pulsating lights flashed faster. She embraced the stone and the Zorn inside it. Warming the stalagmite with her hands and scaly underbelly, the flashes of light slowed and changed in color from purple to red. After a moment the flashing ceased altogether. The work of the Zorn stopped, and he emitted his magic no more.

The chamber plunged into darkness except for Monticello's torch. All at once the moths dropped and burned away in a fog of blue sparks.

Under the milky surface of the stone, two yellow eyes opened.

Langula whispered, "Come to me, my love, Hazor the Scorned."

"What is it? Why have you disturbed my work? What do you desire?" The hollow voice of the Zorn spoke more into their minds than in their ears.

Just then, a blue apparition of the Zorn appeared behind Monticello. The spirit of Hazor the Zorn appeared and gazed upon his physical body still in the stone. Langula and Monticello turned away from the glassy stalagmite to face the spirit of the Zorn.

"Our ancient game begins once again," Langula said. "There have been some developments."

The Zorn's yellow eyes sparkled in rapid movement. "I can feel Soothsayer. It is out in the open. The blood in its metal cries out to me. Where is it?"

"It is revealing itself now, my darling one," Langula said.

"It is…in the village of Homestead," the Zorn said, looking up at her.

"It is where you suspected it would be," Langula said.

"And in what form has she appeared?"

"In female form as a healer named Valen. And in male form as a boy named Astar."

"She has come back in multiple forms? Once again, the Cosmic Creator tries to confuse me," the blue apparition spoke. "What about the Rock Larvae? Have they finished their metamorphosis?"

"It took them over ten years, but finally they have emerged from their cocoons," Langula said.

"They have completed their change into the Devourers," Monticello said.

"What have you done with them?" the Zorn asked.

"There was a problem."

"Of course there was a problem or you wouldn't have woken me. What kind of problem?"

"We sent the Devourers to capture Astar, but there were two boys in the village," Monticello said. "Unable to determine which one was Astar, they abducted both."

"Sounds reasonable. So, we have them both, then?"

"No, my liege, that's the problem," Monticello said. "We only have one: the son of a blacksmith."

"The real Astar was protected by the Timmutes," Langula said.

"The Timmutes? I had almost forgotten about them," the Zorn said.

Monticello continued, "The Timmute swarm, well…maimed one of the Devourers. They cut off his foot to free Astar."

"We had him in our grasp, but he is still alive and free," Langula said.

The manifestation of the Zorn stared at Monticello for what seemed like a long time. Monticello could not look the Zorn in the eyes and averted his gaze.

"We failed you, my lord," Monticello dared to say. "Our efforts to capture Astar have been in vain."

"But we have turned the other boy," Langula added. "He is Astar's friend. He will be useful to take us to the real Astar. I have a familiar connection with him, this blacksmith's son. I can see what his eyes see."

"We are ready to strike the Temple of Valor, my lord," Monticello said. "And commence our capture of the second of Ehlona's form."

"This healer named Valen?"

"Yes, Scorned One," Langula answered. "We aim to kill her to solve at least half of our problems."

Without another word, the blue spirit of the Zorn faded away. Langula and Monticello turned to the milky stalagmite encasing the Zorn's physical body. The rock in front of his yellow eyes began to crack. Then, the stone spider-webbed in cracks forming from his jade-colored skull. The column of stone, along with the adjoining wall, even the ceiling of the cavern started to rumble, as the Zorn began breaking out from inside the pillar of ancient stone. All at once, the icicle-like stalactites broke from the ceiling, raining down into splintered pieces.

As the shaking continued, rocks crumbled from above, and Langula and Monticello covered their heads to protect themselves. Energy crackled all around him. The vibrations reached a crescendo. An explosion shattered stone fragments through the cave.

Monticello dropped to the ground. As he fell the torch went out. The cavern was bathed in utter darkness. After a moment, the eruptions ceased, replaced by sounds of settling rocks. Then all was quiet.

Langula and Monticello uncovered their heads, searching for any sign of the Zorn. Through the pale mist a single dim light emerged from a dusty darkness. It was the Zorn's yellow eyes that slowly appeared. He was freed from the stone now. The Zorn approached the demons in the darkness. His gaze darted rapidly over them within his moldy green skull. As the dust settled, and as their eyes adjusted to the darkness, they could see more of him. They heard his boots move to pick the unlit torch off the floor. With a whoosh, the torch flamed back to life. The firelight's glow revealed the Zorn in a faded and torn gray uniform. His clothes had ripped sleeves and broken gold buttons. His appearance had gotten ghastlier over the past ten years. There was no flesh left to decay. His brow was low, pressing down on the top of his eye sockets. His teeth were flat and exposed inside a gaping jaw amid a wide chin.

"My beauty, my mistress of demons, and my flesh-eating first-born son, hungry for power," the Zorn said. "I fear the years have taken their toll on me."

"We await your commands." Monticello bowed his head.

The Zorn patted Monticello on the back, examining him carefully. The Zorn's eyes darted over the yellow-and-brown spots on the demon's face and neck.

The Zorn reached out for Langula next. He cupped her chin with a bony hand and gently lifted it. "And you, my love, are still superb. Unchanged after all these years."

Langula exposed her neck to him, accepting his kiss upon it. Her serpent tail coiled around his waist, pulling her closer to him.

The Zorn whispered in her ear, "Bring me a fresh uniform, won't you, my dear?"

Langula gently kissed him, biting the bottom of his withered lip. "Yes, I am ready to serve you."

"Ah! You will strike fear in the mortals again," the Zorn said. "Although they have never stopped fearing you."

"Give the order," the Zorn said. "Commence the attack against the Temple of Valor immediately. Put the foolishness of this great Mother Goddess to an end, once and for all."

ACT II

With Joined Hands

We Die

I've been kicked around and been held down

I've been hypnotized by eyes so brown

I've been paralyzed by a thin disguise

Now I'm watching those embers rise.

Excerpt from *The Witch's Songbook*

Suddenly the rotten hand of the dead priest clutched his wrist,

reluctant to give up the dagger.

— Excerpt from *Kilmer's Ghost* (Chapter 12)

A PULLING ON THE WIND

TEMPLE OF CHEN-LI

Chen-Li could sense the magic of Soothsayer out in the open. Fully exposed to the light, the blood of his mother called to him. He knew his brother, Hazor the Zorn, could feel it too. Chen-Li turned to the northwest, in the direction he felt it pull. This pull was the magic of the blade; it would be felt by immortals and demons alike.

Chen-Li padded down the shadowy hallway of his mountain home. Along the way, he looked out the windows as he passed. When he stopped, his reflection came into view. He was over sixty now. His topknot of banded hair, once red like his father's, grew longer and grayer with every passing year. Beyond his reflection, the Temple of Chen-Li sat below. Several pinpoints of light illuminated it from the torches and fire braziers. The warrior-priests of the White Eminence remained on guard, ready to defend the Mid-Run Valley at a moment's notice.

Tyla came down the hall and Myra followed, stirring his attention away from the window.

"We've received a message from the Temple of Valor," Myra told him.

"The Lady Valen is requesting your help," Tyla said with a worried expression.

"This sickness," Chen-Li said, "it's spreading across the land. Those infected are going mad."

"Also, we've received reports from our spies," Myra said, then looked at Tyla.

Tyla continued, "Reports of flying demons in the village of Homestead. They abducted two boys and killed livestock."

"Soothsayer is pulling that way," Chen-Li said. "Can you feel it? Something has changed."

"We cannot feel what is only in your blood," Myra told him. "But the children are restless tonight."

Chen-Li nodded and turned to look out the window again. "The children can feel it in their blood too. Soothsayer is back."

"What are you going to do?" Tyla asked.

"Go to the village of Homestead, the house of Amtor. There, his son, Astar, is the recycled soul of the Goddess Ehlona. The renewed soul of…my mother." Chen-Li stared at the Temple of Chen-Li below. "It confirms our suspicions. The blade was right where we thought it was. The Zorn knows it. Why else would he send Langula and her demons to attack there? They know where it is, and they want it."

"Soothsayer will never allow demons to control it," Myra said.

"Hazor tried and failed to control the magic in the blade," Tyla said.

"Look what it did to him," Myra added. "The blade ate his flesh away."

Chen-Li reflected for a moment. "My mother once told me that no one can wield Soothsayer. It is too powerful. That it will find its champion among the people."

"Will you ride to Homestead?" Tyla asked. "Or travel there through your Li?"

"I will go investigate in physical form," Chen-Li told them. "I need to find out who has it. What they are trying to do with it. All I can do is keep watch—I must not try to possess it or alter the path. I will stop below and put the White Eminence on high alert. Then, I will ride through the Temple of Valor on my way to Homestead."

Chen-Li thought about the Lady Valen's request for help at the Temple of Valor. "Can you take a dozen of our best healers and escort them to the Lady Valen? This should provide the help she requested. It would be gratefully received."

"It is more than duty," Tyla said. "It is our pleasure to help."

Myra added, "We will gladly help bring comfort to these people in their sufferings."

"Be careful with what you find in Homestead." Myra kissed him. "We will take care of things here."

Chen-Li smiled at them. "Do you know how proud I am of both of you?" He kissed them gently. "How could one man be so blessed?"

After kissing Tyla and Myra, he opened the window. The night air rushed in cool and quiet. He stepped upon the open threshold and looked down. The dizzying space below dropped sharply down a long sheer cliff face. A narrow waterfall majestically sprayed mists of water into the air, splitting the cliff in two equal halves.

Chen-Li smiled at his First Wives. "I'll see you soon."

He stood there a moment letting the cool wind blow on him. He listened to the rushing waters falling to the lower reaches. The lights of the temple sparkled far below. He took out the feather he kept around his neck on a chain. Then, with a bend of his knees, he pushed off, and leaped into the emptiness of the void with confidence.

Chen-Li always wore the gift his mother gave him. The magic feather gave him the ability to become as light as the air. He sped down the cliff in free fall, with the confidence of knowing the feather would do its magic this time, like it had the times before.

His First Wives peered out after him, watched him briefly, then closed the window, sealing themselves off from the cold wind.

As Chen-Li continued to plummet, the cold wind rushed across his face. He nose-dived down the cliff, picking up speed as the temple rushed to meet him. Prepared to come in for a landing, he swung down in a wide pattern resembling a fishhook. He glided to a stop just in time to rest upon a branch of a waiting tree. His landing was as graceful as a sparrow's.

From this high vantage point, Chen-Li could observe the warriors training. Training like this went on day and night here. In one area they practiced advanced, elaborate fighting routines, involving wide sweeps, followed by sharp punches, and finishing in a furious shout. Looking over another area, a group of priests stayed in a circle of deep meditation, while their spirits, glowing in unique colors, levitated outside of their bodies. Some of the spirits took to the air to circle. On command, they slowed to a stop. On another command they accelerated to form multicolored rings.

Chen-Li was pleased to see how committed the White Eminence were in their training. They were showing signs of self-sufficiency and hardly needed him anymore. It filled him with pride. These warrior-priests had turned into a fierce but dedicated order. Still, as fierce as they could be, they were priests of peace. None of them hoped for battle, but if battle were to come, they would be prepared.

Chen-Li leaped from the branch and glided down to the training area. Recognizing their master's presence, the training halted, as they recognized Chen-Li with a hearty cry.

"Body and soul!" the priests shouted in unison—a recognition of their creed.

"White Eminence! Send the word," Chen-Li commanded. "Demons have been spotted to the west. The enemy has sent them to attack innocent children in the village of Homestead! What's more, the magic of the golden dagger Soothsayer has been revealed! After twenty years, it is back, out in the open! This comes at a time when the Lady Valen from the Temple of Valor requests our help to comfort the afflicted, the ones stricken by this mysterious sickness throughout the Mid-Run Valley. These are strange times, my priests. There is danger in the air. Stay alert and ever watchful. Be prepared for anything. Body and soul!"

"Body and soul!" hundreds of priests replied in unison.

"Body and soul," Chen-Li said quietly with a nod. Then he shouted again, "Now I am off to the Temple of Valor."

"Body and soul!" the priests responded again.

TEMPLE OF VALOR

Chen-Li found a horse waiting for him at the stable. He mounted up and rode out of the temple, down the zigzagging limestone paths that took him down the Fangs. When rounding the western side of the path, the Temple of Valor came into his view below. He continued down the rocky slopes below his temple until he reached the flat grasslands of the Mid-Run Valley.

Once on level ground, Chen-Li brought his horse to a gallop as the Oracle Mount became larger in his view. He charged up and over the ridge that separated the high lands from the Oracle Mount. Coming to a trot through the valley, along the way, Chen-Li passed many injured people lying in the field, camping under the stars.

He carefully navigated around the sick people in the fields and wound his way through them, up to the base of the Oracle Mount. He dismounted and climbed to the steps of the Temple of Valor. In the temple, aromatic incense burned in fire braziers that illuminated the night with a flickering orange glow. Reaching the top of the stairs, the incense smoke swirled around his shaved head and long topknot. Chen-Li was glad to be in his physical form and paused to take in the pleasant sensations he could not experience while traveling in his Li form. The incense carried prayers to the Gods, while the fire provided light for the hundreds in the field. Everywhere he looked, he saw the infirmed, moaning for help.

It is enough to drive a person mad, he thought.

On the temple steps there was a flurry of activity, unusual at any time, but especially at this late hour. Acolytes were coming and going, rushing up and down the temple stairs. The acolytes were busy attending to the sick around the clock without rest.

The sick had crawled up the steps, wailing for help, crying out for healing. They tried desperately to get inside the temple. But the Lady Valen could not help all of them at once. They had to wait their turn. The sick did not notice Chen-Li, too absorbed in their personal sufferings to care that the famous master priest was among them. Yet there was one old man who reached up and latched on to the hem of his pants.

"I am sick, in need of a cure," the old man desperately choked out. "Please, please help me."

"I'm sorry, but I'm afraid I can't help you," Chen-Li said. He reached down and removed the old man's fingers from him.

A weary acolyte finally acknowledged Chen-Li and begged him for pardon. She announced she would take him to the Lady Valen. Together they entered the Temple of Valor. The scene was the same on the inside as it was on the outside. A great many people despaired with agonizing wounds and sickness. The living moaned in pain. The dead were silent, carried out wrapped in human-shaped bags. These had once been elderly men, women, children—none were spared the pain of the recent sickness. Death was all around them and it did not discriminate.

The acolytes tended to the living, and the dead, as best they could. But the real healing came from her, Lady Valen. Chen-Li finally saw her. She was kneeling behind a twisted pillar that stretched to the open-domed ceiling. She was caring for a small child that she had just healed.

"Our love has set you free," she said. Her voice meant more than words. She embodied love and trembled when she spoke. When the Lady Valen told a patient she loved them, she felt it, they felt it, and they believed it. It was sufficient to heal their afflictions.

An acolyte saw Chen-Li standing nearby. She whispered into the Lady Valen's ear. Valen looked over and saw Chen-Li standing there. Her eyes sparkled and she smiled in acknowledgement of seeing her longtime friend. She stood and wiped her hands on a clean linen.

"Oh, Chen-Li, thank the Gods you are here," Lady Valen said. "We are overwhelmed with this sickness."

Chen-Li bowed his head. "My lady Valen, so very nice to see you again."

Valen continued, "You are always welcome, Chen-Li. Please stay a while."

Chen-Li watched how her long auburn hair fell gracefully past her shoulders. She was adorned in a luxurious wrap woven from delicate emerald fabric, held together with straps of gold that clung to her idyllic form. There were golden bracelets on her arms and wrists, and an elaborate necklace of golden leaves graced her neck. Her amber eyes penetrated secrets, captivating any who gazed into them, making ordinary mortals unable to turn away. But as in the present case, neither could Chen-Li. Far from being an ordinary mortal, he was the offspring of Heironomus, the God of Light and Ehlona, the Goddess of Beauty. Yet the pull of Lady Valen's eyes, her beauty, and healing love were legendary. It took every bit of willpower he had to resist her charms and not make a fool of himself.

"There are so many sick and wounded," Chen-Li remarked. "I've never seen so many here before."

"Every day there are still more that come, I'm afraid," Valen said. "This sickness spreads so quickly. We wouldn't have called you, Chen-Li, but we have been seeing the sickness escalate into madness."

"What form of madness?" he asked.

"The madness of cannibalism," Lady Valen answered. "There seems to be no end."

"There is something else, Lady Valen," Chen-Li said. "Something else you need to know about."

"That the most powerful weapon in the world is out in the open?" Lady Valen's expression turned to worry. "I know, because I can feel it too. The ancient relic, Soothsayer, is revealing itself? The arm of the goddess?"

Chen-Li said, "There was a demon attack in the village of Homestead."

"So, it is true, then?" She put her hand over her mouth. "We've heard rumors about the attack."

"No rumor," Chen-Li told her. "They are demons called Devourers. They abducted a boy from the village. His father went looking for him in the underground tunnels."

"They took which boy?" she repeated softly to herself. "Do you know the name of this boy or the father?"

"No, I don't, not yet anyway." Chen-Li looked out of the archway at all the sick people camped out in the fields surrounding the temple. "Look at all of them."

"The sick, the injured, the mad," Lady Valen said. "We've never had so many. We do not have enough room. So, they camp and wait their turn outside. It seems like it will never end."

Chen-Li was quiet for a moment looking out at all the campfires dotting the landscape. "I fear the Demonic."

"What was that, Chen-Li?" Valen asked.

"I'm sorry." He realized he had not finished his thought. "I fear the Demonic are responsible for this. This sickness is not natural. I fear the Zorn has put a curse upon this land and these people."

"The Zorn?" Valen started to say. "Chen-Li? ...Never mind."

Chen-Li faced her. "What were you going to say, my lady?"

"I was going to say, the pull of Soothsayer..." Lady Valen began. "Something is pulling me that way, toward Homestead. I feel as if...I should be there. But oh, Chen-Li, I am so conflicted. I am desperately needed here to heal these people. But, if these were ordinary times, I would go there with you. When you told me a boy was taken and that the father went underground, I had the strangest feeling." Valen hesitated.

"Of what?"

"Something familiar is pulling on me. Isn't it strange? As if someone needs me there. Even more there than I am needed here. The Mother Goddess has always guided me, putting me wherever I need to be. Is this any different, that I should ignore the call now?"

"My lady, if you feel the need to go, you should go," Chen-Li said. "For the Gods are directing you."

"But..." Valen motioned with her hand. "What about...these hurting and sick people?"

"Distractions. If you feel the Goddess pulling you, then I believe you should go," Chen-Li interrupted her. "Trust your instincts."

"But I can't." Valen started to cry. "Many will die."

"None of these people will die needlessly. I have already instructed the First Wives; they are coming in the morning with a dozen healers. They can fill in for you, help care for these people until your return. Tyla and Myra are quite accomplished healers."

"Maybe you are right." Valen looked out over the sea of moaning humanity. "Something bad is going on. It doesn't feel right to leave. It doesn't feel right to stay."

"Ehlona was always mysterious in her ways," Chen-Li said about his mother. "I did not always understand her. But I knew one thing for certain. When the Goddess speaks prophecy, you would be wise to listen. I'll take you with me to Homestead, Lady Valen. Let's see what she wants to show you. Then, I'll get you back safely if that be her will."

Lady Valen looked out over the people coughing, bleeding, and moaning for help. "Many of these people will not survive the night. Will any of them know comfort again before they take their last breath?"

"Whether you are here or not, the Cosmic Creation will take what is due them. It is true, I see people close to death here, but I also see women in labor. They will be giving birth to new life soon. The Cosmic Creation is a never-ending cycle of life and death."

"New lives replacing old lives," Valen murmured. "With all this hanging in the balance, who are we to decide who lives and who dies? Sometimes I think we insult the Gods."

"We all must choose a path to walk, Valen," Chen-Li said. "None are free from risks or dangers. But along the way, there will be beauty in it too."

"Thank you for reminding me of beauty, Chen-Li. It has been so hard to see of late." Valen turned to an acolyte. "Can you please bring my emerald cloak?"

The acolyte asked, "Are you cold, my lady?"

"No," she told him. "I am leaving with Chen-Li."

"You are leaving us?" The acolyte took a moment to look at her through the top of his eyelids.

"I'm afraid I must for a little while," Lady Valen said. "In the morning, the First Wives from the Temple of Chen-Li will be coming with additional healers. In the meantime, I must go to the village of Homestead on business most urgent."

"Yes, my lady, as you wish." The acolyte turned to go.

"When the Goddess calls, I must go," Lady Valen said, trying to convince herself that she was doing the right thing. "It will be an honor to ride with you, Chen-Li."

The acolyte returned with her cloak. The acolyte fastened it for her with a golden clasp in the form of a tree. There was something different about her now, something more, as if she glowed with an energy by putting on the emerald cloak. She was more beautiful than ever. It was all Chen-Li could do to tear himself away from her gaze.

Chen-Li extended his hand, and together arm in arm, they stepped down the steps. Along the way, Lady Valen touched the wounded. By touching the hands that reached for her some healing magic flowed to them as she passed.

Chen-Li came to his horse and mounted it. Lady Valen took her time and continued making her way through the campfires. She attended to as many groups of the sick as she dared to do.

Two male acolytes waited for her and stood by a small wagon. They bridled two horses—one to drive the wagon, the other a riding horse to ride along for protection.

Chen-Li joined them. Soon Lady Valen and her two acolytes rode from the temple. They were on their way to the village of Homestead.

Won't you show me a sign or lend me a hand to give me courage

Sometimes I cry, in the night from all my fury

Please don't forsake me for the things I feel inside

Cause I'd do most anything, just to be by your side

Excerpt from *The Witch's Songbook*

The boldness of your spirit favors you.
Even as tedious as I may find it.
— Excerpt from *Kilmer's Ghost* (Chapter 13)

ASTAR'S BLADE

VILLAGE OF HOMESTEAD

"You have to be careful with the blade," Amtor told his son. "It filled my heart with a murderous desire. While I held it, I had an overwhelming urge to take a life with it."

"Soothsayer is extremely dangerous," Aberfell said. "When the Zorn forged it, he could not control its magic. Instead, Soothsayer destroyed his flesh because of his vanity. It made you want to kill because of your military background. The magic in its gold, which was the physical arm of the witch, ensured that no one other than the spirit of Ehlona could wield the blade."

"Does it fill your heart so, Astar?" Amtor asked his son.

"No, but the blade needs to feed, and very soon," Astar said. By now, his skin had settled back to its regular color. His pupils returned to normal.

"On what does it feed?" Amtor asked. "Or on who?"

"Don't you know what?" Astar said. "It feeds on the energy of souls."

"Isn't there any other way of satisfying it?" Amtor said.

"Don't worry about what the blade will feed upon," Astar said. "There is no reason for it. Ehlona, in her life, saw to it to provide everything the blade needs. Just no one knew how, or why, or what it wanted."

"What do you mean?" Amtor asked. "She provided everything the blade needs?"

"Come with me," Astar said. "And I will show you."

They walked outside. Astar reached the middle of the road and turned back to the group. A few curious villagers shuffled by and stopped to watch what was happening in front of Amtor's house. Astar lifted Soothsayer over his head with both hands. He began to shout, "Come to Soothsayer! The Goddess Ehlona calls for your service!"

Astar's voice echoed through the nearby forest. After a moment, Amtor and Aberfell gave Astar a little shrug.

"Well, that was embarrassing." Aberfell looked at the watchful neighbors, as they turned and went about their business.

"Nothing happened," Amtor said.

"Just a moment," Astar told them. "Here they come."

A building vibration could be felt under their feet. A soft hum followed, disrupting the sounds of the natural forest. The trees began to shake and rumble. It sounded and felt like the approach of some heavy animal.

The ancient trees collapsed and dismantled. They burst apart, crumbling into thousands of golden particles. Timmute orbs, hundreds of thousands of Timmute orbs, began bursting out of every tree, stone, and shrub. Everywhere they looked, the Great Mapes Forest came alive with scores of Timmutes, multitudes of them. They came together streaming in golden swarms. Then, twisting through the air like funnel clouds they came to Astar. Circling in a swarm around him, Soothsayer was the center point of the Timmute storm.

"Mighty Timmutes! Come to the creation of the Mother Goddess. Fill her blade with the might of your numbers! Bring the feast to feed hungry Soothsayer!"

The first of the orbs absorbed into Soothsayer. The proud Timmutes were becoming part of the blade. The dagger recoiled, causing it to glow a neon blue. More of them came, and Soothsayer accepted them all.

With each soul absorbed, the dagger erupted in a shower of blue sparks, as the metal began to grow. Thousands of Timmutes came and sacrificed themselves to the blade. The blade gobbled them up, satisfying its voracious need to feed upon a life force.

Whomp! Whomp! Whomp! The blade produced vibrations and loud reverberating sounds. As it grew, the speed of the sounds increased.

Whomp! Whomp! Whomp! Whomp! Whomp! Whomp! The blade roared to life like a mighty engine. It was all Astar could do to keep ahold of Soothsayer.

The blade stretched to a mighty length, as large as his entire body. Yet as it grew, the lighter it became.

When Soothsayer was as big as it could get, the sound changed as if the machinery was powering down.

Whomp…whomp…whomp! The sound of it slowed.

It had reached its capacity. Soothsayer had evolved into a massive golden sword. Multiplying in size, it weighed the same, perhaps even less, than the original blade.

The remaining Timmute horde raced away. They returned to the forest to re-form the landscape. As they did, the trees reassembled and rose again from the ground up. Until, at last, stillness and quiet settled over the Great Mapes Forest that had been made whole once again.

All eyes were now on Astar, as he held giant Soothsayer over his head.

"Thank you, proud and mighty Timmutes," Astar said. "You have greatly pleased your creator this day."

"No one could have accomplished that but the one true spirit of the Goddess Ehlona," Aberfell whispered to Amtor. "Nobody."

"You have become the most powerful creature in the universe," Amtor said. Then he asked, "Astar, what will you do now?"

Astar crackled with new and immense power. Yet he smiled as warm and youthful as his age. He looked at Amtor and Aberfell. "Let's eat. I'm hungry."

"Lunch?" Aberfell asked.

Astar put the blade down. "We cannot change the world on an empty stomach."

HOUSE OF AMTOR

Back in the house, Aberfell demonstrated his studied culinary expertise. He toasted slices of bread, and garnished it with a garlic, parsley, and herbed butter spread. Upon which, he applied thinly sliced venison. The sandwiches were on par with the finest gourmet chefs in the Mid-Run Valley. It was a result of Aberfell's unfailing memory and insatiable reading of recipe books, but through it all he continued to watch Astar.

Astar was busy affixing a strap of leather around Soothsayer's handle. No small dagger anymore, it would be harder to wield. He adjusted the strap for size. With it, he could carry the massive Soothsayer on his back.

Amtor watched him too. As powerful as Astar was now, Amtor still saw his boy, the one he had raised all these years.

"Astar?" Amtor asked. "How do you feel?"

Astar paused to take inventory of himself. "Good, I feel good. Still myself, but...changed, in a good way."

Aberfell prepared the sandwiches on plates and carried them to the table. As he placed them on the table, Amtor nodded at him. Aberfell took a seat across from them but did not eat yet. He merely picked at the crust.

"This power you have, the ability to duplicate yourself," Amtor said. "This is a fantastic power, yet it is so strange. How can you ever get used to it?"

"Can you see through all the eyes of the copies you make? Two of them? Ten? A hundred?" Aberfell asked.

"Depends on what I want to focus on," Astar said. "I can see everything through my peripheral vision. Some things are far away, while other things can remain near. But always everything is within my sight if I want."

"Are you afraid one of your copies will be killed?" Aberfell asked to the shock of Amtor. "I mean, would the death of one kill all the others?"

"I can stop time, so I would be hard to kill," Astar answered. "But no, the more of me there are, the more I can lose. The more diluted I become."

"What about food?" Aberfell asked. "Can you eat a whole banquet of pies with a room full of Astars? What about alcohol? Would you even get drunk after a hundred Astars had a hundred pints?"

"That's not important, really doesn't matter," Astar said. "What I want to know is what is Micah eating with those demons in the dark underground."

"Astar?" Aberfell said. "You said you have...have received the memories of Ehlona. What do you remember about that past life?"

Astar answered, "Only certain things."

"Can you tell us?" Aberfell asked.

"Well, I know about the making of the Timmutes. I have memories of Ehlona blessing all her beauty away. How the Zorn destroyed Ulrig, the Master Tree."

Astar took off Soothsayer, hung it on a nail on the wall, and walked back to the table. Amtor and Aberfell pulled out chairs and joined him.

"And other things, like how her left arm became Soothsayer." Astar took a bite of the venison sandwich. As he chewed, he looked at the stump, the demon's foot, still resting upon the table. He rocked the foot this way, then that way, examining it more closely. Then he continued speaking, "I cannot remember it all. I'm not like you, Aberfell. But I feel there is more to be uncovered. Her memories are like a painting under a veil. Sometimes I can see them, other times I cannot. They come to me, like, paper unburning, in reverse; I see them unfolding, then scorching into my brain. Sometimes I hear them like whispers in the dark."

"Do you still possess your own memories?" Amtor asked. "Of your mother, when you were a child?"

"I still have those of you and Mother, of Gensen and Micah. I remember them dearly. I also remember scenes of the fire. That awful night when Mother died. But try as I may, I can't seem to recall anything before the fire though."

"Astar, I need to tell something of your mother..." Amtor whispered. "Oh, where do I start?"

Aberfell looked at him sideways. "The beginning, I would start there."

Astar stopped eating. "What of Mother?"

"The night of that fire," Amtor said. "The truth, I have concealed from you."

"What truth?" Astar asked. "What have you concealed?"

Amtor started to hesitate and waiver.

"Go on, Amtor," Aberfell encouraged him with a whisper. "Go on."

"I don't know...so, I'll just...say it." He hesitated again. "Gilglad did not perish that night of the fire."

Astar furrowed his brow. "What are you saying?"

"Gilglad *was* the fire."

"My mother did not perish; she is still alive?"

"No, no...let me try to explain," Amtor said. "After all these years, it's still hard for me to trust what my own eyes saw."

"Try harder," Astar said.

"Gilglad was consumed by flames but flames of her own making. Flames that...came out of her, maybe through her. I'm still not completely sure. It's hard for me to describe it, even after seeing it."

"Exactly what did you see?" Astar demanded. "Did you see her die or not?"

"Gilglad did burn in a fire and Gilglad ceased to exist after that," Amtor told him. "I did not watch her die though. I saw her change."

"Change?" Astar asked. "Change into what?"

"Instead of Gilglad, there was another in her place."

"Another in her place? Another what? Another person?" Astar was reeling now.

"Yes," Amtor answered.

"Another person?"

"You know of her," Amtor said. "You have heard of her. She is famous throughout these lands."

"What are you telling me?"

"Lady Valen, the priestess of the Temple of Valor. Your mother, Gilglad, and Lady Valen are one and the same."

"Valen!" exclaimed Astar. "Lady Valen? *The* Lady Valen? From the Temple of Valor? How can this be? It's impossible!"

Astar searched Amtor's eyes.

"Come now," Aberfell said, patting Amtor's back. "Don't stop now. You have more to say, don't you? It is time you came clean of everything."

"It is impossible. For most," Amtor whispered. "It was you, Astar. You endowed your mother with the healing spirit of the Goddess Ehlona. It was this transition that caused the flames. You brought the Emerald Fire that changed her."

"I did what?" Astar now stood, his face getting red. "You are saying I am responsible for the death of my mother?"

"She loved you very much. She used to watch you while you slept. You were just four years old when you granted her what she prayed to you for—Ehlona's healing powers."

"She prayed to me?' Astar asked. "Why?"

"She knew the spirit of Ehlona had come back through you," Amtor said.

"How did she know?" Astar asked.

"A messenger came to her. The messenger told her she would be blessed for being the vessel that brought the Goddess's spirit back."

"The vessel of the Mother Goddess?" Astar asked.

"Fourteen years ago, your blessing turned Gilglad into Valen. That transference of magic and energy caused the Emerald Fire. It was not a consuming fire but pure magical energy that caused a tremendous release of force when your mother transformed into Valen."

"I was responsible for that?"

Amtor took another deep breath. "After the fire, we went back inside the house. You noticed your straw bed had not burned. I remember this because you asked about it. Your straw bed had only been pushed up against the wall by the force. We came in and straightened it. You saw it had not burned at all. You questioned it, but after a while, the questions...just seemed to fade away. I never wanted to bring it back up after that. I'm sorry, my son. I should have had more courage."

Astar sat thinking about what Amtor told him. More questionable things came flooding to him from the past. His memories, not memories of the Goddess. "Yes, I remember. That old straw bed. There was no fire damage, none anywhere. That always disturbed me. I mean, I'm sure I had my doubts. But I convinced myself into believing. I thought I was just not remembering it right. Now I am questioning all my memories about that night…"

"You were not remembering anything incorrectly," Amtor said. "You're right, nothing had burned. There had been no fire at all. But Gilglad, your mother, was gone just the same."

"I remember seeing you and Mother inside the house during the fire," Astar said. "The flames were all around you. You were struggling against each other, you were fighting."

"Not fighting, Astar. I was trying to save her from making the transformation. But to no avail."

"You could not stop her from becoming Valen, could you?" Astar searched his father's face.

Amtor hung his head. "I was terribly afraid, Astar. I did not understand what was happening. I loved her more than I loved anything in my life. And she loved me. But she was becoming what she always desired, above me, above all other things. The demons that came to me, fed upon me, used me to breed the Demonic…she knew all about them. She helped me resist, the late-night beguiling of Langula. In the end, she did help me, but I think the whole affair broke her spirit."

"She knew about the demon?" Aberfell asked Amtor.

"Of course, she knew and it took the greatest toll on her." Amtor took a long breath, then continued. "Four years had passed since the Star of Ehlona had announced your birth, Astar. The whole world saw it. Everyone in the Mid-Run Valley knew Ehlona's spirit had returned to the world, but nobody knew for certain who or where. But Gilglad and I knew. We both knew that you were the recycled spirit of Ehlona. Once she became Lady Valen, she left for the Temple of Valor. You and I had to carry on without her. You without your mother, me without a wife. She belongs to the world now."

"But why?" Astar asked with tear-dimmed eyes.

"For no other reason than she asked you for it," Amtor said. "You loved her enough to give her what her heart desired."

Astar was beginning to understand. "All of this seems so familiar to me now. Even as more memories are waking inside me. I cannot tell if they are Ehlona's or my own."

"Maybe a little of both?" Aberfell said.

"Where is Valen? I need to see her," Astar said.

Just then, Astar and Amtor heard a loud crunch. They looked at Aberfell, who had taken a huge bite and chewed enthusiastically.

"I worked hard on these." Aberfell shrugged with his mouth full.

Way up in the sky
I see her white face glowing
I never knew why
I felt the bad wind blowing

Excerpt from *The Witch's Songbook*

Visions of the Goddess Ehlona intermingled with
strange swirling yellow eyes,
black raven-like priests, and bright glowing priests with
shaved heads and banded red topknots.
— Excerpt from *Kilmer's Ghost* (Chapter 14)

NO MERCY FOR THE FALLEN

TEMPLE OF VALOR

Tyla and Myra rode onto the grounds of the Temple of Valor on chestnut horses. They came down from the heights of the Temple of Chen-Li the morning after Valen left. A dozen healers accompanied the First Wives and guided extra ponies that were carrying shifting loads of supplies on their backs. They came with ample stacks of fresh linens, ointments, medicine, food, and water. As their caravan neared the Oracle Mount, signs of the sick were everywhere they looked, huddled around the grounds.

"This sickness has spread beyond control," Myra said.

Tyla agreed, "Look at them all, they're everywhere."

The First Wives and healers were immediately welcomed. Grateful acolytes received the generous supplies and began to immediately distribute them.

"This will accommodate this significant influx of people stricken with this sickness," an acolyte told them.

"We should have come sooner," Tyla apologized. "Please forgive us, we had no idea of the extent of your need."

"No need to apologize," an acolyte said. "You are here now and bless the Gods you are. Bless the wisdom of Chen-Li for sending you to us."

The healers immediately went to work. They began healing the sick inside the Temple of Valor and outside throughout the grounds, rendering aid to the sick and the dying. The day was long and the work never-ending.

They all worked until the sun went down and another cold night began. There was no more space in the Temple. So, people huddled together to keep warm outside. As darkness descended all around them, campfires began dotting the landscape, indicating where the sick would spend the night. The stars twinkled above, while below the sounds of coughing and moaning echoed across the fields.

Unseen and unnoticed far away in the distant valley, blood-red eyes appeared in the tall grass. A group of predators watched and stalked the grounds of the Temple of Valor. A voice spoke out in a serpent's hiss.

"Go to the east and wait for my signal," Langula whispered to Monticello.

Monticello, barely visible in the dark, moved silently away, creeping to the east just as Langula instructed.

Next, Langula gave orders to Grim. "Go south."

Grim revealed his sharp ivory fangs, then maneuvered into the valley. He slipped undetected among the sick and despondent.

Langula watched the two demons take their places in the field. Her silver eyes were perfectly adjusted to the darkness. She scanned across the fields and the fires of the huddled camps. Looking across the valley, she saw Monticello on the farthest eastern slope. He gave the signal.

"That's good," Langula said. "One in place."

She watched Grim settle to the south. Looking back, he gave the sign.

"Simply delicious!" she whispered.

The Zorn stood behind Langula and whispered in her ear, "You know what to do. I will wait for you here and watch."

She whispered to him, "Tonight, we strike at this reincarnation of Ehlona. Tonight, we will kill this, Lady Valen."

Langula rose on her serpent's tail. With a wave of her hand, the Demonic commenced the attack.

The demons rushed out of their concealed positions from three directions. A scream pierced the night as Grim struck first blood. Followed by another scream, then yet another. More screams followed as the full panic of what was happening set in. Many people were too weak to run. These people could only pray fervently to the Goddess Ehlona for protection.

Ruthless murder swept through the grounds. The demons tore through flesh with sharp claws and biting fangs.

Everyone heard the screams as chaos erupted across the camps. The First Wives appeared in the temple's archways.

"Come inside!" Tyla shouted. "No harm will befall you here!"

Myra also called out, "Come into the safety of the blessed Temple of Valor."

A rush of people came running from the massacre to crowd inside the temple. Yet many did not make it. Their screams echoed through the night.

The wailing of the dying could be heard all the way to the Temple of Chen-Li. The White Eminence responded immediately. It did not take long before the skies were filled with multicolored plumes of spirits rocketing from the Temple of Chen-Li above. The warrior-priests had been put on high alert by Chen-Li. Their spirits separated from their bodies; they came flying down the mountain heights to the Oracle Mount below.

Langula dragged a bloodied woman along with her, but finally tossed her aside after cutting her throat. Langula searched for Lady Valen but could not find her. Instead, she saw the spirits of the White Eminence speeding toward her from the Temple of Chen-Li.

"Monticello, the White Eminence!" Langula shouted the retreat over the screams of the suffering. "Grim, they are almost upon us! Back to the hilltop."

Langula disappeared into wispy black vapor.

Monticello was busy slicing throats when he saw the spirits. Grim looked up, entrails hanging from his mouth, and was surprised to see the spirits too. They both raced to get to the top of the hill with blinding speed, moving so fast that the incoming spirits seemed to slow.

Without warning, the wispy black vapor swirled in front of the Temple of Valor. Langula materialized on the steps of the temple, in front of Tyla and Myra.

Langula's claws slashed at them, just as the spirits of the White Eminence struck into her violently. Langula screamed and rolled backward. The spirits were landing hit upon hit to the serpent demoness. Already struck by several spirits, and seeing more about to hit her, she vanished again into a cloud of black vapor. Just as she transported away, several spirits reached her, but instead of striking her, they passed harmlessly through the black smoke, ricocheting off the marble steps. The second wave of spirits succeeded in striking nothing but her remaining vapors and scattering them.

Tyla's and Myra's eyes burst open wide as they grabbed their throats. Blood started to pour out of their necks. Tyla fell first. Myra followed. They collapsed on the stairs. Their bodies slowly slid down the marble steps slick with oily blood.

Monticello and Grim stood on the hilltop with the Zorn. They waited for Langula, calmly watching the incoming spirits draw closer. Langula finally appeared with a burst of smoke. After she appeared, the demons clasped hands. The spirits of the White Eminence were right upon them now and dangerously close. Then with a cloud of sulfuric black steam, they all vanished into the night. The spirits passed harmlessly through the smoke without striking any of the demons on the now empty ridge.

The spirits of the White Eminence looked for signs of the demons. The people on the temple grounds, who were just attacked, were not accustomed to such sights. They had never seen spiritual Lis before. They screamed. Seeing what they thought were ghosts, they were hysterical. As the Lis moved through the grounds of the Temple of Valor, people ran wildly in chaos. Most of the sick never saw the demons and blamed the attack on the spirits. The presence of the spirits of the White Eminence created a sense of fear. Soon the people started to spread rumors throughout the camps. It was not demons who were responsible for the murders, but the spirits of the White Eminence.

Back at the Temple of Valor, the acolytes worked frantically to save Tyla and Myra. Their throats were slit, cut by the claws of Langula, and the wounds were just too deep. The acolytes did what they could, but they did not possess the healing power of Lady Valen.

The First Wives continued to drain out and blood cascaded down the steps of the Temple of Valor like two crimson waterfalls. As they fought for life, Myra and Tyla reached out for each other—one trying to save the other. In the end, they interlocked their hands, and holding hands they died.

In shock and in anger, the spirits retreated back to the Temple of Chen-Li. They rejoined with their physical bodies, then the White Eminence returned on horses. They came immediately to aid those wounded and collect the dead. Valen's acolytes provided clean linens from the Temple of Chen-Li to cover the remains of their most honored dead, the bodies of Tyla and Myra.

After the attack, the dead and dying littered the grasslands. There were panicked, wide-eyed people, filled with terror and shock.

Ghosts! We were attacked by ghosts!

Not ghosts, vampires!

Not vampires, demons!

Not demons, ghosts!

The sun was now rising and the Demonic rematerialized far away.

"I can't believe it!" Langula said, rubbing away the pain where she took direct hits. "I think I may have gotten Chen-Li's First Wives! I think I may have killed them!"

They could still see the Temple of Valor sitting in the distance to the east. The Demonic watched the remaining spirits streak back home to the Temple of Chen-Li. Through the stillness of the morning, they listened, and could hear the rising and falling screams in the distance.

"Do you hear that?" Grim asked. "They are screaming in agony."

"Your attack was a real success," the Zorn said. "But Chen-Li will react to the murder of his First Wives with rage and expected vengeance. You may have gone too far."

"I thought we were going to kill Valen?" Grim asked.

"We have disrupted the Temple of Valor," Langula said.

"Valen was not there," Monticello said. "She still lives."

"Let's come back tomorrow night," Grim said, eager to have his way with them again. "They cannot stop us."

"Why would we do something so stupid?" the Zorn asked. "Right now, they are paralyzed with fear. We have put them on the defensive. They will have heightened security. It will stay that way for months. It would be nearly impossible to attack them again and get away with it."

"Maybe Frost will deliver us a distraction," Langula said. "You worry too much about the mortals, Zorn."

The Zorn looked at Langula. "Don't be foolish."

"We will go back for more blood," Monticello said. "When the time is right."

Langula added more of her thoughts, "Your sickness overloaded the temple. It is impossible for them to defend against it. It made them easy prey for us. Even so, I can't believe I killed the First Wives. That is just as good as Valen, maybe even better."

"You speak nonsense," the Zorn said. "Rousing the fury of Chen-Li only makes things considerably harder and much more dangerous. Do not forget, the real power is with Soothsayer. Chen-Li can give us problems. Now his anger will burn hotter than ever before for revenge."

Langula rolled her eyes. "They are just as dead, aren't they?"

"Let us go back and attend to the new boy," Monticello said. "Micah will attack with us next time."

"Will he be ready?" Grim asked.

"We will see," Langula said. "Now, give me your hand."

The demons joined hands again. Langula's spell transported them back to the underworld in a puff of sulfuric vapors. As they left the wispy black smoke behind, her maniacal laughter filled the morning air.

ROAD TO HOMESTEAD

"Stop the wagon! Stop!" Valen exclaimed to her horsemen. She was nearly delirious from some unseen pain, as if shot from an invisible arrow. Chen-Li felt it too. He reined in his horse, as he distantly observed the death of his First Wives.

"Lady Valen? Are you hurt?" one of the acolytes asked.

"No, not me," Valen said.

"There has been an attack on the Temple of Valor," Chen-Li said to the acolytes without looking at them. "She is in pain, as she senses many deaths."

"Pain is everywhere," Valen said, touching her forehead. "Oh, I'm so sorry, Chen-Li. I am so very sorry."

"Myra and Tyla, they are...dead," Chen-Li said.

"You should go back," Valen told him. "We should all go back. You are needed at your temple, and I am needed at mine. It was a mistake to leave. If we had stayed..."

"Then you would be dead too, and it would have been much worse," Chen-Li said. "The pulling of the Goddess has saved you. No, we have come too far, we must continue on, we are so close."

"I can go no farther," she said through tear-rimmed eyes.

"There is only death is behind us." Chen-Li choked back tears. "An attempt to distract us from our destination. Don't you see that? The Demonic are trying to separate us, keep us from uniting. Keep us from completing the circle between you and Soothsayer. No, we must continue forward not backward."

"It will only get harder," she cried. "So many have already died."

"We knew that before we left. There is something moving in the Cosmic Creation," Chen-Li told her. "We can do nothing for the dead anymore. Tyla and Myra must not have died in vain. They understood the dangers of the blade, and what it meant. They would want us to continue. But if you can go no farther, Lady Valen, I will not let anything happen to you. There is too much at stake. I will stay with you. Escort you back to the Temple of Valor. If that is what you wish."

"My heart aches," Valen said. "I will try to go on, for those lost at the Temple of Valor, and your First Wives, I will go on. But I am so very sorry, Chen-Li. So sorry."

"I am sorry too," he said. "More than you could possibly know."

They continued riding quietly for a time. The acolytes steered the wagon through the bumps and ruts in the worn road.

Chen-Li broke the silence. "Hazor hurt my mother once. He visited her in the Great Mapes Forest. He could not hurt her physically, so instead he hurt someone she cared for."

"You mean, Ulrig, the great white oak." Valen nodded. "She called him Master Tree. I can remember that memory of Ehlona."

Chen-Li looked at Valen. "Your connection with the Mother Goddess?"

Valen nodded again. "Hazor killed Ulrig just to steal the arm of the witch and use her magic to create Soothsayer."

"That is how he operates," Chen-Li said as the horse clomped along. "He hurts the ones you love. This time, my brother has the blood of Tyla and Myra on his hands. He will answer to me for that!"

"For all of them," Valen vowed. She looked down after speaking. "But my sadness...for the love that was lost..."

"I know." Chen-Li choked back tears. "Oh, I know."

"Through his wounds you will find strength," Valen suddenly said.

"What was that you said, my lady?" Chen-Li asked.

"I remembered something the Goddess once told me. She said, *Through his wounds you will find strength.*'"

"What does it mean?" Chen-Li asked.

"I am not sure. The words just came back to me. *Through his wounds you will find strength.*' Gives me a strange comfort."

At that moment, the acolyte turned and told her, "The village of Homestead is approaching, my lady."

"Good, just a little way farther," Chen-Li said. "We are almost there."

No more time spent, wasting all my energies

On worthless mind games, played upon my jealousies

If you can't take it, don't try to trace it

Don't try to trace it back to me.

Excerpt from *The Witch's Songbook*

Maybe being alone in the dark was better than the alternative.
— Excerpt from *Kilmer's Ghost* (Chapter 15)

THE FULL CIRCLE

VILLAGE OF HOMESTEAD

Chen-Li rode beside Valen's wagon toward Homestead. Valen's green cloak ruffled in the breeze. Outlines of the first distant houses appeared. They found the one house they were looking for and came to an abrupt stop. Chen-Li dismounted and rushed to the Lady Valen's sideboards as a cloud of following dust swept through them.

"The house of Amtor, my lady," the acolyte turned to say.

Chen-Li helped her out of the wagon.

Lady Valen stepped down and looked over the quaint little cottage. "What a beautiful home," she said, removing the hood of her emerald cloak.

"I have been here a few times myself," Chen-Li said, also looking over the place. "But always in my Li form, and never let Amtor see me."

As they watched the cottage, the door opened to reveal Amtor. The large, bearded warrior took a few steps outside. Amtor froze at the sight of Lady Valen and Chen-Li. Before the door could close,

Aberfell followed holding his sandwich and chewing. Then Astar walked out of the house next, Soothsayer strapped to his back.

Aberfell whispered to Astar with his mouth full, "You said you needed to speak with Lady Valen. You got your wish. Here she is."

"Greetings, Amtor." Chen-Li made the introductions. "I am Chen-Li. And this, of course is the Lady Valen accompanied by two of her acolytes. We have come from the Temple of Valor on a matter most urgent."

"Lady Valen, after all these years, you have returned," Amtor said, remembering his love and life with the former Gilglad. "I thought my eyes would never again behold you. No, not in this life."

"Greetings and love to you. Have I been to your home before, Amtor?" Lady Valen asked, stepping down from the wagon. "Everything seems oddly familiar to me. Yet I do not remember being here."

"My lady, excuse me." Amtor stared deeply at her. "Please look deep at my face, then tell me, do you have any memory of me?"

Lady Valen studied him as he asked. "We have met before?"

"Do you not remember?" Amtor asked.

"Maybe so." Valen searched the large warrior's face. "You look very familiar. Where would we have—?"

"You must remember this one?" Amtor put his arm around Astar, pulling him closer.

"You…do look…so…" Valen searched the faces of Amtor and Astar. "It is very strange. Familiar, yet I cannot seem to remember."

Aberfell wiped his hands on his shirt and stepped forward to continue with the awkward introductions. "We, uh, welcome you, Lady Valen, the most honorable Chen-Li, to this house of, uh, Amtor's, the first Minister of War of His Majesty, King Leopold. I would like to introduce you to, uh, his son, Astar. I am Aberfell, no doubt you have heard of me…probably."

"Of course, the Supreme Historian," Chen-Li said. "It has been a long time since I last saw you though. Please tell me about that meeting so we can be sure you are who you say you are."

"I was aged three years. It was in the year 855," Aberfell recalled. "At the wedding of Gia and Glover, the Star Prophets, at the Southern Star Observatory. The night of the Emerald Fire."

At hearing this, Lady Valen sharply returned her gaze to Amtor.

"Perfectly correct, Aberfell," Chen-Li said. "You have grown to manhood. It is very good to see you again. And about you, Amtor, I have heard so much already. The king's minister of war. I am glad to finally get to meet you."

Amtor mumbled something in response to Chen-Li. No one heard it clearly. He remained transfixed on Lady Valen.

Aberfell asked, "Something has happened, hasn't it?"

"Always perceptive, Aberfell. The Lady Valen and I are here because we felt a pulling on the wind that led us here. We both felt the last remnant of the Goddess Ehlona's magic exposed in Soothsayer, out in the open. But after we left, tragedy struck the Temple of Valor. Last night it was attacked by the Zorn's demons," Chen-Li said, finding it hard to contain his mournful emotions.

"There were many serious losses..." Lady Valen choked on the words, and only gave a sad glance to Chen-Li.

"We are very sorry to hear this very troubling news," Astar said. "We suffered two losses ourselves in an attack of three gruesome Devourers."

Chen-Li lifted his face up, out of his grief, and was drawn to Astar. "That golden sword on your back. It has all the markings of, could it be..."

Aberfell spoke while patting Astar on the back. "The golden dagger you speak of. Behold! You have found the very thing that you sought. Soothsayer, forged from the very left arm of the Goddess.

Now the last physical remnant of that era is joined through her renewed soul. Now it is Astar's Blade, engorged by thousands of Timmute souls."

"Looking upon it now," Chen-Li said. "I do not see a weapon forged in gold but feel the power of my mother. It has found its champion."

"We came immediately. The spirit within called us," Lady Valen said. "So, it is you, Astar, that we have come to see."

"Please, please," Amtor said, coming to his senses, disappointed it was not him Lady Valen came searching for. "Won't you please come inside?"

HOUSE OF AMTOR

The party went inside. There, they saw the foot of the Devourer sitting on the table.

"Devourers, they are called—products of Hexor's Rock Larvae. Sawed clean off by a swarm of red Timmutes." Aberfell picked up a piece of chalk and pointed to the foot. "Now, if you look right here at this line of rolling fat. Right here, see it? This indicates it exists on a diet of—"

"Lady Valen, maybe you knew my wife?" Amtor interrupted to probe Valen's memory. "Her name was Gilglad."

"Gilglad?" Valen looked at him with curious eyes. "I have heard that name before."

"Gilglad was Astar's mother," Amtor said. "Astar's mother and Gilglad, they were one and the same."

"Gilglad? Why does that name..." Lady Valen took a moment searching Amtor's eyes. "I was Gilglad, wasn't I? In a life before Valen."

Lady Valen looked back at Chen-Li, who gave her a shrug.

"I have no knowledge of that," Chen-Li said.

Amtor searched her, trying to find any familiarity in her face. But it was not just her mind that had changed dramatically. Her appearance was nothing like the Gilglad he remembered.

"Forgive me for saying so, my lady. Your hair has changed. It is different than Gilglad's," Amtor said, still examining her. "Hers was brown and straight, not the reddish auburn curls you have."

"Any woman easily could have changed her hair, Amtor, using a dye," Aberfell said, a bit rudely. "Sorry, my lady. But I mean, common women do it all the time,"

"Yes, I know, but I do not dye my hair," Valen said, motioning with her hand. "This is the natural color."

"But Gilglad had green eyes." Amtor observed the eyes of Valen and their magnificent sparkle. "Yours are light brown."

"Yes, they are almost reddish, to perfectly match the highlights of her hair, absolutely brilliant." Aberfell's face flushed a brighter pink. He found himself starting to reach out for her, but then forced himself to stop short. With some embarrassment, he cleared his throat harshly. "Well, uh, we can all agree. A dye to change the color of the eyes would be most impossible."

"I do not wish to embarrass you, Lady Valen," Amtor spoke again in a whisper. "Yet I realize even more upon looking at you there are changes other than hair and eye color. It is your facial structure itself. Your face, as lovely as it is, bears no resemblance to Gilglad. The shape of your nose, the curvature of the lips. So different. Yet I can be sure because I was there. I saw the change. Even though that was a very long time ago."

"There is a tug of something familiar, like waking from a dream." Valen searched his face. "And you, Amtor, your hair is grayer than

I remember. But I do remember. We have history, you and I, don't we, Amtor? Your face was the last one Gilglad ever saw and the first one for Valen. It was your face. It was your love I remember."

"You became a new creation on that night of the Emerald Fire," Amtor again spoke softly. "I watched it happen, the transformation, into what you became after the fire."

"Yes, of course, there was a fire. Wasn't there?" Lady Valen remembered. "Tell me what happened in the fire."

"You were Gilglad. You were my wife, and I was your husband. I loved you more than anything. More than myself."

"I am remembering." Valen touched his face. "Cold winter nights. You kept me warm, kept me safe. The memories of Gilglad are coming back to me now. How could I have forgotten them? I do remember you, Amtor."

"Lady Valen?" Astar approached her now. "Gilglad was my mother."

She now turned to face Astar and looked into his eyes. She could detect the recycled spirit of the Goddess Ehlona in him. Yet, the Goddess was in the form of a young man. A young man that possessed the massive sword of Soothsayer.

"Astar is my son." She touched him. "This is very overwhelming."

She had to turn away. She pulled the emerald hood over her head and closed her eyes briefly, letting the memories return. The others watched her, unsure what to do. Lady Valen was an emotive healer and learned long ago how to control strong emotions. At last, she turned quickly, returning to Astar's blue eyes.

"Yes, the Emerald Fire was the Goddess's magic power radiating from your eyes, Astar. A pure energy that transformed my old life and body of Gilglad to Valen. Yes. Yes, I do remember it now. For me, such a feeling of righteous joy! A strong emotion, so strong that it made me forget everything. The change carried me away from this place—from you, Amtor, from this life. Still the energy sustains me to this day, giving me the power of healing."

"I have no memory of it at all," Astar said, holding back tears. "I never knew the things I did, I'm sorry."

"No, you were just a small child." Lady Valen touched his cheek. "You were born with great power. That night the magic pulsed from you, from your eyes. It came out of you, a tremendous force of emerald energy."

"Your static sign, Lady Valen," the Supreme Historian interjected. "The prophecy of the great Emerald Fire, long awaited for by generations of Star Prophets. Its sign signaled the coming of the great healer. All foretold since the dawn of time."

"Really, Aberfell, must you?" Amtor looked at Aberfell.

The Supreme Historian shrugged. He really couldn't help himself.

"I remember one night, when I was still Gilglad," Lady Valen addressed Astar again. "The spirit of the Goddess Ehlona appeared to me. She told me that in your fourth year, she would grant me a great blessing, for being the vessel to return her spirit back into the world. She could only give me this blessing through you, Astar."

"I don't understand it." Astar shook his head. "Why were you blessed by being taken away?"

"The Goddess Ehlona has always been mysterious in her ways," Chen-Li told them. "In time, you will see the wisdom. But, at the time, everything she did seemed strange."

"Amtor, you were chosen too and have had your own struggles, with men of war, and the very real demons that came to you. Yes, I remember them, the demons too, the sacrifice you were forced to make against your will. The Goddess told me something else too, something about you."

"What did she tell you?" Amtor asked.

"The Goddess said, *'Through his wounds you will find strength.'* She knew the blessing that took me away would exact a great toll on you. Amtor, you are to receive a great blessing too. Not by any one of us, but by the creation of a new power, one greater than Ehlona herself. We are being compelled to join the circle and close it."

"Join the circle—what does that mean?" Amtor asked.

"*'Through your wounds you will find strength.'* The Goddess Ehlona selected you, Amtor, because of your legendary strength. No man could have endured the pain that you have." Lady Valen lifted her hand and touched his face. "You are as much a part of this destiny as we are. And, behold, your blessing is now at hand."

"Blessing?" Amtor asked. "What blessing?"

"Astar's Blade," Lady Valen said. "Join hands with me and let the magic of the circle be joined."

Astar removed Soothsayer from his back. The massive blade weighed nothing in his hand. When he touched Lady Valen's hand, an unexpected wind swirled around them, lifting their hair on an unseen force.

"The blade is reacting to our touch," Astar said.

"Now, you take my hand, Amtor."

When he grasped Lady Valen's hand another surge of energy swept over them.

"Aye, something is happening. It is strange to feel." Amtor lifted his voice over a growing crackling.

Aberfell and Chen-Li shielded their eyes. Bright flashing blue lightning sparked in long arcs throughout the room.

"Now to complete it and join the circle," Valen shouted over the noise, her emerald cloak whipping in the unexpected wind. "Amtor! Now touch Astar's Blade."

Amtor reached out. Careful to touch the flat surface of the sword with his outstretched palm, the circle became joined.

Throom! A powerful boom sounded, a bright flash of light. A single jolt of energy connected through all three of them. Erupting outward from Soothsayer, rippling energy encompassed them, surging from the tops of their heads, down to their feet. The blinding waves of pulsating energy ascended, then descended over them repeatedly.

The doors and shutters of Amtor's house flew open. After the house opened, wave upon wave of the tiny golden Timmutes made their appearance again. A cyclone of a thousand Timmutes stretched throughout and around the house of Amtor. Their ever-widening, whirling swarm reached up to the very heavens. Those Timmutes rose above the gathering clouds, calling down conductive lightning that flashed in crackling spiderwebs across the sky.

Phoom! A burst of energy pulsed outwardly again. Lady Valen was knocked backward. She was thrown out of the circle, breaking the connection. Astar likewise was hurtled off his feet and landed on his back. Soothsayer continued to float on his own, flat against Amtor's palm.

Aberfell and Chen-Li were momentarily blinded by the flash. When the bright light faded away, gradually their sight returned. The Timmutes were gone, and Astar and Valen lay on the ground, separated, no longer holding hands. Soothsayer lay on the ground in the middle of where the circle had been.

Standing over Soothsayer, in the center, the old decrepit warrior that had been Amtor was changed. In their midst now a significantly strengthened warrior stood firmly. Amtor had not just been healed—he had been reborn, set free from all maladies. The injuries he had sustained in the Mauveguard Pass were now all gone. He stood youthful and confident in boots made from soft leather and soft new fur inlays, in a new chest plate of hardened steel and blackened armor. Underneath, his biceps rippled with fresh muscles. His waist was lean and girdled in a belt of vertically aligned flexible steel segments. He looked up with a smile appearing unblemished, polished, and reflecting the rays of the sun upon a new body.

Amtor examined himself. "My wounds! They are gone! Look at me! They are gone!"

"You have been blessed by the Goddess." Aberfell could not help himself. Knowing he was in the company of Gods, he fell on his knees. "Praise be to the Goddess! This is a blessing that has been long overdue."

"It is true, Aberfell, I have been greatly blessed by the Goddess, still…" Amtor looked at Lady Valen. He asked her the only question that still mattered to him. "Will I ever be loved by Gilglad again?"

The question made Chen-Li look away. Astar and Aberfell too stared down at the ground. Lady Valen carefully searched Amtor's face.

Then she smiled at him. "You are a good man, Amtor. You have been given a great gift by the Gods. You have been blessed more than any man in the world. I will always love you as I have love for the world, but Gilglad is gone. I cannot go back in time. But if I could, I would find her and bring her back to you."

"Then I must share you with the world," Amtor said, touching her face. "But I will never forget Gilglad, and the love we had."

"Astar," Lady Valen said, turning to him. "As the vessel that brought you into this world, I was once your mother. But now, as Valen, I am servant to that aspect of you that is the Mother Goddess. So, I will follow you, Astar. Wherever you would go, I will go too."

Lady Valen dipped into a bow, dropping to her knees in front of him.

"Aye, my son, likewise as your father," Amtor, said with a deep breath and a clear strong voice. He took a knee. "As will I follow you."

"As do I." Chen-Li also took a knee. "In body and soul."

Aberfell, already on the ground kneeling, looked at the rest awkwardly. He bowed his head instead. "Uh, wherever you would lead me...Astar...I will, uh...take with me my memory...uh, to go with you...when you go...you know what I mean."

"Forgive me, I hate to interrupt, but I have to impose upon you all now," Chen-Li told them, standing. "I need some time. I need to travel, in my spiritual form, to the Temple of Chen-Li. I must see for myself the damage to the Temple of Valor. But mostly I must pay respects to the lives of my First Wives. Will you mind watching over my physical body while I am gone?"

"I'm so very sorry, Chen-Li," Astar told him. "Of course, we will."

Chen-Li thanked them. Then, he walked to a corner of the house and began to meditate. It did not take long, as Chen-Li was a master of his body of spirit, for his body to begin levitating. There was an audible pop when his Li left his body. Then a translucent white copy of Chen-Li appeared over his body. His Li took a final look at the situation he was leaving his body to, then dematerialized through the ceiling. His spirit flashed overhead and like lightning he returned to the Temple of Valor.

They watched Chen-Li go in spirit form. Seeing his body levitating without a spirit in the corner was unnerving, but at length they turned from it.

TEMPLE OF CHEN-LI

The mood was mournful. Chen-Li had traveled, as fast as the wind, in his Li form to the Temple of Chen-Li. There, in the inner sanctum, a great multitude of the White Eminence gathered in silence. Chen-Li floated like a ghost down the center aisleway. Heads turned from their prayers as the master priest passed through. In spiritual form, he could feel nothing. But not just in this nonphysical form, at this moment, he was empty and numb. Thousands of priests watched Chen-Li in silence.

His spirit approached the single casket alone. They lay side by side, holding hands in death as they did so often in life. Tyla and Myra, together in repose. Even now in death they radiated great beauty. Their eyes were closed, and they appeared as if they were merely asleep. Their robes were of the finest silk, Tyla in blue, Myra in gold. Chen-Li noticed the fabric wrapped all the way to their chins to conceal the awful wounds, the damage inflicted upon them by the claws of Langula.

He studied their faces, looking upon them for the last time, remembering more cheerful days. They looked so peaceful, no trouble or pain anymore. Fresh flowers were woven into their hair and graced their heads. Chen-Li noticed that when the soft wind blew, the petals moved slightly, giving an illusion of movement. But it was only that, just an illusion, and Chen-Li knew it. They would never move again.

He let a long moment pass before he eventually faced the throngs of the White Eminence. The inner sanctum was solemnly silent. All eyes watched Chen-Li in front.

"We once knew angels. They lived in our presence. Once we were blessed. Angels who we will never see again, nor will we ever forget. The gold and blue colors fade. We are so much less without them. My eyes will never see those two colors again. Tyla and Myra were the original First Wives before there was a Chen-Li. They helped make me who I am. They made us who we are, and what we have become. But so much more, they made us happy. They made us feel good. It is impossible to believe that they have been taken for no reason. Certainly, their lives could not have been taken in vain. It has to be because of something. Some work of the Gods that will justify their loss. But to what purpose is this tragedy? I cannot see it right now. I hope it will be made right someday, somehow. Right now, there are only dark storm clouds. Right now, the metal feels like it is hot, waiting for the hammer, poised to strike. Whatever purpose is coming to us, our purpose must be one. War is coming. It is looming closer. In this generation, in our near future, long prophesized by the Gods, it has been marked in the signs of the celestial bodies! It has all been foretold. I am ready! We will be victorious! Our destiny is at hand. Vengeance will be ours for the taking!"

For a moment no one spoke. Chen-Li had wild determination in his eyes that seemed to blind them.

Finally, a lone voice shouted out, "They will be avenged, Chen-Li!"

Then another, and another, then more voices cried out. Like a wave, a building rush, it came out in shouts for revenge. The entire inner sanctum loudly burst forth in an echoing repetitive stomp and clapping of thousands of hands and feet. A great cacophony, so loud, no single voice could be heard. Chen-Li levitated higher, so the whole assembly could see him.

Chen-Li focused his energy on his hands, and they erupted in two balls of fire. What Chen-Li did next had never been done before. Through the heightened emotions of his murdered First Wives, Chen-Li ignited. His entire form burst into flames. He had turned himself into embers of fire. Soaring through the inner sanctum, Chen-Li left a vapor trail of superheated gases behind him. All the priests were shocked by his newly found lethal power.

Rallied, his priests broke into a wild crescendo, cheering him as he glided over their heads, crackling in flames. Other spirits joined to fly with him. Soon, the entire sanctum became alive with the flying spirits of the White Eminence. But only Chen-Li burned with raging fire.

VILLAGE OF HOMESTEAD

No horse could ever take the place of faithful Mandrake. Mandrake had been the best warhorse Amtor ever had. Unfortunately, Mandrake was gone now. So, Amtor purchased a new chestnut horse at the local trader for a fair price.

"Where do we go first?" Amtor asked, adjusting himself in his new saddle.

"The Temple of Valor, if no objections," Astar said. "We can help the injured and use that location as a meeting place. As for me, I will go with you, while other aspects of myself will go to other places. For instance, I'll want to go to talk to the Zorn alone."

"Talk to the Zorn? Alone, Astar?" Chen-Li asked. "Isn't that dangerous?"

"Not for me," Astar said. "I do not fear Hazor the Scorned. As long as I can stop time and multiply myself, I am never truly alone. Plus, where I go, I take the power of the Goddess with me in Soothsayer."

"For years, Hazor the Zorn lived in the Sanguine Forest, inside Castle Orlo," Aberfell told the group.

"Doesn't he live there now?" Amtor asked.

"No, apparently not. He abandoned it a few years ago in favor of going underground," Aberfell said. "No one knows why. Since then, the castle has been inhabited by a band of outlaws."

"I will go there and talk to him in his underground lair," Astar told them, adjusting the massive sword on his back. "I will go to the Sanguine Forest and see what kind of outlaws are living at the Zorn's old castle."

"Astar, I want you to have this," Lady Valen said, taking off her emerald cloak and wrapping it around him. "A special gift—this emerald cloak was the original cloak the Goddess Ehlona wore.

More than just a piece of history though, it was blessed by her, and so, is magical. It will aid you in your journeys to come."

"It is beautiful. Thank you, my Lady Valen," Astar said.

Valen helped secure it around his shoulders.

Valen nodded her approval. "The cloak strengthens the power you already have. Use it well, Mother Goddess."

Adorned with the new cloak, Astar climbed into the wagon. He gave Valen an uncomfortable look. "I'm not sure I like being called 'Mother Goddess.'"

"Just Astar, then?" Lady Valen smiled.

The boy smiled back and pulled the cloak around him. "Yes, that's much better, thank you."

Valen shifted her head to look at Astar. "The cloak will keep you safe when you do not want to be seen."

"It is kind of hard not to be seen with a sword as big as Sooth-sayer on his back," Aberfell remarked.

"This is true," Chen-Li said, riding up on his own horse. "Nothing at all like the dagger we searched for twenty years ago."

"Ready now, let's go home," Valen told her acolyte driver.

With a snap of the reins on the backs of the horses, the wagon started to move down the path and away from Amtor's home. After immediately hitting a large bump in the road that rocked the passengers in the wagon, they settled down into a smoother ride. The two acolytes sat up front to drive the two-horse-drawn wagon. Valen, Aberfell, and Astar sat in the back. On the left flank of the wagon Chen-Li and Amtor rode along with single mounts.

Amtor looked back at the little cottage, his home for many years. He wondered if he would ever see it again. "This is the first time I've been able to leave my home in years. Feels good to have my strength back. I am ready to leave. Still hard though."

"Funny, isn't it?" Valen said.

"What is?" Astar asked.

"In a former life I was your mother. But because of the renewed spirit of the Goddess Ehlona inside you, all this time you have been the Mother Goddess I prayed to."

Aberfell shifted in the wagon. "That must be why it was necessary to change you. It eliminated the paradox."

"Perhaps so, Aberfell." Valen turned to Astar. "But losing your mother like that, Astar, and at such a young age too must have been awful for you. All those years, enduring the thought that your mother died in a fire."

"It was hard on all of us," Astar said with a yawn.

"Are you tired, Astar?" Valen asked. "Maybe you should get some sleep."

"Would you mind?" he said.

"Not at all," Valen said.

"The Temple of Valor is a whole day's ride," Aberfell added. "We have a long trip ahead of us."

"I wonder how Micah sleeps," Astar said, his eyes half closing. "On the cold damp stone floor in that dreadful place in the underground? With demons all around him? How could I possibly sleep, knowing he is going through so much? Such a terrible thing for him to have to endure. How can I sleep? It would be shameful of me."

Within minutes, Astar was asleep in the back of the wagon. Soon, he was dreaming. He no longer needed to be asleep, and dreaming, to stop time. But he slept anyway, as the troop rolled away the miles.

He looked asleep but was actually hard at work. He stopped time and multiplied copies of himself. Soon, different Astars started popping up in multiple places across the Mid-Run Valley.

His first stop was under the ground.

Hey, Mama, what's going on?
How come I seem to do everything wrong?
I see the rain, it's coming tonight
Stab me in the back with all your might.

Excerpt from *The Witch's Songbook*

There are many enemies, and you have strength like no other.
— Excerpt from *Kilmer's Ghost* (Chapter 16)

A BRIEF INTERMISSION: THE DAY BEFORE LAST

VILLAGE OF HAVERHILL

"If it pleases the court," Talbot said, giving a bow to the bench. "This case is just one of dozens this year since the sickness first spread to the Kingdom of Odessa."

Talbot took a small drink, then adjusted his glasses.

"As we all know, the sickness strikes indiscriminately, infecting people at random. No one can tell where, or who, or how the sickness will strike next. The sickness either attacks the body, or the mind. Some get physically ill. While in others, it produces a homicidal madness. The worst? Cannibalistic rages. Either way, without treatment, it will ultimately kill them.

"However, as a matter of law, throughout these cases, the court of King Leopold has upheld innocence, if the accused 'lacks a willingness to commit the crime, sufficient to demonstrate a diminished mental capacity.' By our understanding of prior rulings in these cases, regarding the sickness and the effect of the resulting madness, we feel we can clearly demonstrate beyond any doubt, in the court's judgment, the innocence of the accused sitting here before you today.

As such we will be asking the court to return a not guilty verdict associated with this man's alleged crimes regarding the fate of the missing death warden."

The judge motioned with his grizzled hand, long and dark in the fingernails.

Talbot gave the judge an uncomfortable look. He swallowed another sip of water, then continued speaking.

"Very well, Your Honor. Will the defendant please state your name and profession?"

"My name is Tullis. I am a woodsman by trade; some call me a lumberjack."

"Where do you reside?"

"I have a home on the outskirts of Haverhill. Near the forest where I work. I can easily walk there. The hardened trails lead into the woods."

"Thank you for that. Now, tell me, Tullis, would you say you were happy in your home in Haverhill?"

"I lived a good life with my family, yes, sir."

"Now day before yesterday, uh, did you work that day?"

"Yes, spent the day felling trees, sawing lumber, and such, yes, sir."

"You have a contract, paid in advance, to construct a home for a customer. Is that right?"

"Yes, sir. A good and decent family who wanted to move into the area here."

"Good. Now, on any ordinary day, you would characterize your workday as doing what?"

"I might be sawing down a tree or two. I might be nailing the frame, laying a floor, putting on a roof. Yes, sir, almost anything related to building a house on any given day."

"But the day before yesterday was far from an ordinary day. Wasn't it? Please explain to the court how the incident started."

"No, sir, not an ordinary day at all. That was a day that everything changed. Well, for me, the incident started after I came home from work. I was hot and tired. I just wanted to get home, just wanted to get out of my work boots. Change my dirty clothes. Wash the grit off my face and neck."

"Yes, of course. You longed for the comforts of home, didn't you? The familiar surroundings, seeing your wife and children. Would this be a fair characterization?"

"Yes, sir."

"Do you drink, Tullis?"

"Sometimes."

"Were you drunk the day in question? The day before last?"

"No."

"Had you been drinking?"

"Just water."

"Please continue."

"As I approached the house, I saw a large man there on my porch. Dressed all in black, he was leaning against the railing. He was watching me, as if he had been waiting for me to come."

"Did you recognize this man?"

"Well, sir, I could not remember his name. But yes, I did recognize him though. I had seen him before. I finally did recall. He was one of the death wardens from the village of Haverhill."

"What was he doing?"

"He saw me coming and stopped leaning on the railing. He straightened his vest and turned to face me square. Like I said, he was all in black. I couldn't help thinking he had to have been hot. Black? On a day like that? Yet he was dressed in a black shirt and pants, a black hat, and he had a-a black cloak draped over his shoulders. I remember seeing him fidget with a pair of gloves, black ones, of course. The shadows on the porch protected him from the full brunt of the sun. I guess in retrospect, he looked a little nervous to me. That's when I noticed four horses were tied to the tree. Yes, sir, there were other horses there too."

"What went through your mind at that time, when you saw this man standing on the porch of your house?"

"I thought, my God! Why is a death warden here? I worried that, like an accident or something, may have gone wrong. I-I didn't know what to think. I guess I was getting a little nervous, myself."

"The death warden was not alone? You mentioned the horses tied to the tree."

"You see, sir, as I got closer, a bunch of soldiers holding spears made themselves known. They came from around the house. I think they were also standing in the shade, waiting around on the far side, just to keep themselves out of the sun. But as I approached, they moved out of the shade and into my view. As if they had been waiting for me all along."

"Did they say anything to you?"

"Yes, sir, they asked me my name. But I didn't need to tell them. They already knew it. They asked if I was Tullis, the owner of the house. I told them that I was."

"Then what happened?"

"Well...then, the death warden said he wanted to talk to me. So, he walked off the porch, and—"

"Were you holding the ax at this time?"

"I held the ax, yes, sir."

"Please continue."

"The soldiers with the spears started to walk around me, surround me. They did so real slow, as to not risk any quick movements."

"You had no idea why they were there?"

"No, sir, I didn't, not at the time."

"Now take us back to when the death warden wanted to speak to you."

"The death warden tells me, he says, 'How casual you are, woodsman.'"

Talbot asked, "Did you know what he was talking about?"

"No, sir. I thought that was an odd way to start a conversation. But then I asked him, I said, 'Sir, I do not recall your name.' But he never volunteered his name. He only acknowledged that we had indeed met a few times before, mostly in passing, back in Haverhill. He never did give me his name."

"Can you please tell the judge and this court, in your own words, what transpired next?" Talbot asked Tullis.

"Yes, sir. Well, the death warden sort of pointed to the door and asked, 'Do you know what is beyond that door?' I told him, 'No, sir.' And he says, 'Go see for yourself.' So, I walked up to the door and opened it. And my God! What lay beyond... My poor wife was on the floor lying in a puddle of blood. My two small children, the same way, collapsed on the floor. Just lying there like lifeless dolls. Blood everywhere! They were all dead. My whole family!"

Tullis started to cry. Talbot let him go for minute, then asked him to continue.

"Then the death warden came up behind me and asked, 'Where were you today?' The death warden sort of turned me from the door. Leading me away, see? Well, I had been crying pretty hard by then. We walked off the porch. And I asked, 'Certainly you do not suspect me?' I could not believe he would think I could do this to my own family.

"He asked me again, what I did that day and where had I been. I told him I had been chopping down trees in the forest. He sort of turns his nose up at me, like this, and asks, 'What kind of trees were you cutting down?'

"I said sycamores. I asked, 'Why ask me a question like that? Why would it matter about what kind of trees?' Then he answers me. He says, 'Because I never knew sycamores to bleed.' That's when I noticed what I hadn't noticed before. My ax was covered in blood. I'd been holding that ax all day long. I never noticed all the blood, but I was drenched in it. Blood on my shirt, my pants. Everything I had was covered in blood. As I was making the realization that I had all this blood on me, he reached for my ax, real slow and gentle. I gave it to him. I didn't put up no fight. He took it, then handed it to some soldiers standing there. I never saw the ax again. Until right now."

Tullis pointed to the ax, now clean, on Talbot's table. After this, Tullis looked down and stopped talking.

"What do you remember about the murders?"

At first, Tullis just stared blankly. Then he said, "The night before last, I had a dream. This shadow woman appeared in my dream. The shadow woman was pressing her hand against the glass of my windowpane. Her hand was blue and had these terrible claws. She slid the window open, and a snake slithered in. Only the snake had the likeness of a woman on top of it. Impossible I know, but in my dream, *that* is what slithered in. Even in the dream my eyes were fixed on this thing. I-I could not even blink. Once it was inside, the...this serpent lady, rose again, and stood at the foot of my bed. The creature had animal horns on its head, like a goat or something. And its eyes glowed silver.

"Well, the dream never ended. I kept dreaming it was in the morning now. My wife and children were awake. We were preparing for the day. But then, without a word, I walked out to the woodpile and grabbed my ax. I remember there was a lot of screaming. Blood was spraying all over the place. But I just kept swinging the ax over and over again. Blood kept getting in my eyes and in my mouth.

"It seemed so real and so unreal at the same time. It took me all day to wake from the dream. And when I did, I could still taste the copper in my mouth from all the blood. But I guess that is not how it happened. The death warden told me that I had never gone to work that day, never went to the forest at all. I never went anywhere except I just kept walking in circles outside. In my mind, I thought I had been chopping down trees in the forest. But then, all was quiet...and he found me just lingering there. But that was not me. I loved them. It was not me. I promise you. It-it was somebody else, not me." Tullis cupped his hand over his mouth.

The judge leaned forward to ask a question. "What happened to the death warden? Did you kill him?"

Tullis looked up from the stand with watery eyes. He insisted he was innocent. "No, no, no. I don't know what happened to him."

After Tullis's testimony there was absolute quiet in the court, except for the squeak of the judge's rickety old chair as he sat back.

The judge cleared his throat. "In light of these...circumstances, I agree this sickness is a plague of madness across the land. This is not the first case the court has heard where the defendant has no memory of the crime. Unfortunately, I am afraid it will not be the last. Quite frankly, Tullis, I find your story simply not believable. Your confession about killing your wife and children is foundational enough to warrant a pardon due to this sickness. But lying about killing the death warden to cover up your crimes demonstrates a predisposition toward murder. This deception indicates a willful act, demonstrating full mental capacities, not caused by the recent sickness."

"Objection, Your Honor!" Talbot said, coming out of his chair. "Tullis was taken away from his house by a unit of soldiers. Then incarcerated under the care of the state, while the death warden was still alive. There is no possible way that he—"

"Overruled, counselor. Therefore, by the authority of King Leopold, the decision of this court is that the defendant is found guilty of the murder of his wife and two of his own children. As well as the murder of the death warden. Hereby, this defendant, Tullis the woodsman of Haverhill, is sentenced to death. The accused shall hang by the neck until dead. Sentence will be carried out the day after tomorrow. May the Gods have mercy upon your soul, Tullis. Next case, please."

WHAT HAPPENED EARLIER

The day before last, after the discovery of the grisly murders inside his house, Tullis was taken away by the four soldiers. The death warden watched them go, then stood alone assessing the situation.

He complained to himself, after the men left with Tullis. He mumbled, "What a job to have. You'd think any death warden would be used to it by now. But one just cannot ever get used to this."

The death warden took off his black cloak and hung it on a fence post. He rolled up his black sleeves and unbuttoned his black vest. He picked up a wooden bucket and took it around the back of the house to the well. There, he found the spigot and primed the pump. After a few gargled pumps, a steady stream of water flowed.

While he waited for the bucket to fill, he considered the back of Tullis's house. There he saw the window Tullis claimed the serpent woman came through. The death warden squinted at the mud at the bottom of the window. There he found large deep ruts. Something big had come dragging through here. Was it something dragged, or did it slither under its own power? A deep channel left in the mud led from the window to the not-so-distant tree line of the woods. If something did come here, if Tullis was telling the truth, then maybe this was the evidence. Might there be some truth in Tullis's story? If so, he needed to present this evidence to the court, when Tullis came to trial.

The death warden let the bucket fill, and he walked closer to investigate the mysterious tracks in the mud. As he contemplated the scene, a strong clawed hand covered his mouth from behind. At the same time, an equally powerful elbow clutched his throat. His eyes were wide as a large serpent's tail wrapped around his body. The death warden kicked and struggled trying to resist, but to no avail. He was dragged against his will to the tree line.

The bucket overflowed with water until the pressure from the pump released and closed the water's flow.

EXECUTION DAY

A day after his trial, the sentence was to be carried out. Tullis walked out of the soldiers' barracks and the bright light hurt his eyes. Beyond the glare of the sun, flashes of the high wooden gallows came into his view. He came out of his cell with his hands tied behind his back. He was led like a lamb up thirteen creaky steps to the waiting platform above. A hooded executioner waited patiently for him on top of the gallows. Beside the executioner, a priest of Heironomus recited a poem.

Tullis squinted in the light. From this vantage point, he could see the faces of the crowd gathered to mock him in his final hour. The scratchy rope was placed around his neck. The executioner produced from behind his back a burlap sack that would go over Tullis's head but not before the priest's signal.

"Do you have any last words, Tullis?" the priest asked after reading the poem and closing his book.

Tullis spoke, "Beware! All of you! Hear my words and beware! An ancient evil walks among you. Stalking you. It feeds upon the mind as well as the flesh. May the Gods be with you, and may they forgive me that I was not strong enough."

Then, Tullis went silent.

The sackcloth was placed over his head. The executioner gave a tug on the rope, tightening the noose. The priest nodded to the executioner. Taking the signal, he pulled a lever that released the crossbeam below the platform's trapdoor. The platform under Tullis opened, and he fell. Quickly, the end of the rope snapped, twisting above the full weight of the lumberjack's body.

A collective gasp went up, as the crowd watched the sudden jolt and jerk of the rope. The dead man swung under the gallows. After a few minutes of excited whispers, the crowd dispersed.

DEEP UNDERGROUND

As Tullis was being hanged, another scene was taking shape deep underground. The prisoner of the demoness Langula, fastened in chains, had been beaten bloody. This was the death warden, and he watched with horror as the demons dined on the bodies of the wife and children from the house of Tullis. The demons picked through the bones, then flipped them to the Devourers who fought over what was left.

The death warden learned too late that Tullis had been telling the truth. He watched wide-eyed, as the demons now started to creep his way. He screamed as the first of them ripped into his flesh.

ACT III

Out of One

There Are Many

Horns rang out, signaling the beginning of the king's celebration on the
Green of Castle Odessa.
— Excerpt from *Kilmer's Ghost* (Chapter 17)

AN UNPROVOKED ATTACK

CASTLE ODESSA

A red velvet curtain parted slightly, and a pair of silver eyes peered through. King Leopold sat on his throne. The king was adorned in a red cloak, blue military uniform, and bejeweled golden crown. Behind the king the curtain shut.

The blue-skinned demon Frost could not afford to be seen in his true form. He had invoked a spell to manipulate the shadows of his face. The magic mingled with the contours and colors of his appearance, rearranging them. Neither he, nor anyone else, would be able to immediately perceive his true, sinister identity. Instead of the demon Frost, the mortal face of Brother Barker emerged.

When the curtain opened, it was Brother Barker who breezed into the council chamber. Arriving late as usual, his terse lips curled into a familiar yet disturbing grin. The other members of the council, already seated, had been waiting for him. These were noblemen of the kingdom. Present were Lord Whitney, Lord Rhodes, and ten others. One lord was conspicuously missing: Lord Plum-Kilmer.

As Brother Barker entered, the others shifted uneasily in their seats. Whispered murmurs followed, along with several stern looks.

"Thank you for joining us, Brother Barker," King Leopold said without a hint of sarcasm. The king motioned for Brother Barker to begin.

"Apologies, Your Majesty. This council is called to order," Brother Barker announced to the dour faces around at the table. "Our agenda: to discuss the recent attack on the Temple of Valor and to determine the king's response, if any. The people of Odessa demand to have an actionable plan by the end of this meeting."

"Your Highness." Lord Whitney stood and faced the king with a stately bow. "Refugees from the Temple of Valor are streaming into Castle Odessa now. These people are wounded, hungry, scared, and they need a place to—"

"Brother Barker," King Leopold interrupted Lord Whitney. "What is your assessment of this situation?"

Brother Barker glared at Lord Whitney with a wry smile. The priest was a tall, lean man with long flat hair of black. His face, faded and pallid, bore the most unusual skin tone, with more than just a hint of being unnatural. A long black goatee framed his sardonic smile and came to a point well below his chin. Motioning with his long bony hand, Brother Barker seemed to take great pleasure instructing Lord Whitney to return to his seat.

After a heated glare to Brother Barker, Lord Whitney slowly, reluctantly sat back down. As he sat, Lord Whitney turned to whisper in Lord Rhodes's ear, "Why does the king allow this?"

Barker, the tall priest, was now the only council member standing. He turned to the king, flashing a toothy grin. "As previously mentioned, we have heard reports about these refugees." Barker barely motioned in Lord Whitney's direction. "Through them, we have eyewitness accounts, witnesses, to an attack on the Temple of Valor. Situated outside Valen's temple, sick and defenseless people waited for Valen's healing, while unexpectedly the spirits of the

White Eminence mercilessly attacked them. Frightening ghostlike spirits ravaged those that waited outside on the Oracle Mount. The night of the attack, men, women, and children were brutally murdered by the priests of the White Eminence. Reportedly, even the First Wives of Chen-Li were deliberately murdered in cold blood, that Chen-Li might be rid of them. As a result, innocent people died as the White Eminence did for him what he himself did not have the courage to do."

The chamber erupted, murmuring, in chaos.

"These defenseless people," Barker had to shout now. "Already helpless! Already woefully vulnerable! The White Eminence and the Temple of Chen-Li are to blame! This was clearly an attack on the Temple of Valor by the White Eminence to eliminate the First Wives and grant Chen-Li the divorce he wanted but could not have!"

"Barker, to what extent are we to believe what you say?" Lord Whitney sat back in his chair. "For what purpose would the White Eminence attack?"

"Because, my friend—" Barker said.

"I am *not* your friend," Lord Whitney cut in.

"A pity then," Barker continued, "The people who follow Chen-Li are ambitious, aggressive, and malevolently evil."

Once again, the council room erupted. Brother Barker only spoke louder, ignoring all of them. "They have never adhered to or acknowledged the sovereignty of King Leopold or the Kingdom of Odessa! They claim their own dominion! They have laid designs on conquering the entire Mid-Run Valley for themselves, starting with the Oracle Mount and the Temple of Valor! Chen-Li wants to control every village, every peasant, every nobleman for service in his temple. Why, Chen-Li would have you all practicing kicks and perfecting some ritual spiritual deviation outside your own physical bodies if we did not prevent him from doing so!"

Barker pounded his fist on the table, while pointing at the other council members. "Mark my words! If allowed to continue unchecked, if we do not address their aggressive, belligerent, and destructive behavior, in the most militant way at our disposal, they will rule over us some day!"

Lord Whitney laughed. "A preposterous notion! Chen-Li was given a golden plaque of undying friendship from the king for saving the lives of those who fell under the possession of the demon Langula. Why would he break that faith?"

"A ruse, Lord Whitney. That's all it was. Twenty years ago. A whole lifetime for people who change. Since you brought it up, take Kilmer for example."

"That's Lord Plum-Kilmer," Lord Rhodes interjected.

"Not anymore, Lord Rhodes. Once a hero to this realm, the court found the previous man named Kilmer guilty of treason to the crown! The titles and privileges of traitors to this kingdom are revoked!"

There was more grumbling from the council. This did not stop Brother Barker.

"He was tried! Tried and convicted and sentenced to death. But executed? No. I fear not. Did he do his duty and swing from the gallows as directed by this council? He did not. Instead, he convinced others—others more traitorous than himself—to help him escape the noose of the king's justice. I submit this to you all now: a sickness of treachery has pervaded this kingdom! Even in this council! And Chen-Li is the latest manifestation of this disease!"

"Come now, high priest," Lord Whitney asked, searching the faces around the table. "When is it any man's duty to hang from the gallows? Is it not in every man's nature to want to live? Consider this—what if our friend Brother Barker here was captured by the enemy? May the Gods forbid it—but what if this enemy so ordered that he should roast his skin off, then roll in a bed of salt?"

The council laughed, much to the chagrin of Brother Barker.

Lord Whitney chuckled himself. "Would you expect that our pale Brother Barker's duty would be to obediently submit to this abuse solely for duty to the state? Or rather, would it be expected, and far more reasonable, for him to wish to attempt an escape, to evade capture of these evil men, and not be so willing to go quietly to be…now what did I say? Oh yes. Roasted alive."

"Careful, Lord Whitney," Barker stated, looking down at him. "One might confuse your words with sedition."

"Enough of this talk!" King Leopold commanded. "I want to consider this matter of the Temple of Valor. Based on what we have heard here already today, would it not be reasonable to send ten thousand of the Red and Blue to the Temple of Valor?"

Barker folded his arms and smiled. The rest of the council became quiet.

Lord Rhodes, the hero of the Sanguine Forest, stood up and addressed the king: "Your Majesty, the Temple of Valor is very close in proximity to the Temple of Chen-Li. What would be the objectives in sending the Red and Blue? What mission would they accomplish with the mobilization of ten thousand of our forces?"

It was Brother Barker who responded, "The Red and Blue would not be there to *invade* the Temple of Valor, it would be there to *protect* them."

Seizing Lord Rhodes's logic, Lord Whitney now stood. "Your Majesty, Lord Rhodes brings up a good point. A troop movement of that size may be perceived as an offensive force. The message could easily be mistaken as this kingdom's aggression toward the Temple of Chen-Li. Our intentions to protect the Temple of Valor might be better understood if we sent a message to the White Eminence. Would it be wise to open diplomatic channels with Chen-Li? Tell him our intentions?"

"Treason, Lord Whitney," Brother Barker said. "We do not inform our enemies of our intentions. King Leopold commands the Red and Blue, not Chen-Li."

"We project a force of nearly fifty thousand warrior-priests within the defenses of the Temple of Chen-Li. To provoke military power of that scale is careless to the point of recklessness. It could drag this kingdom into an unnecessary and unwanted war."

"Why, Lord Whitney, I had long heard of your heroism at Mauveguard Pass. Have you lost your courage and conviction?"

"Have a care, Barker," Lord Whitney warned him. "You would be wise not to find out for yourself."

King Leopold continued, "We have two avenues of action. Lord Whitney and Brother Barker have laid them out before us. Lord Whitney favors a more humanitarian, diplomatic approach. While Brother Barker would prefer—"

King Leopold was interrupted by a tremendous boom that shook the very foundations of Castle Odessa. The sound of breaking glass followed. The king held tightly to the arms of his throne, while Barker was thrown against the wall and grasped the curtains. The table lurched under movement of the stone floor. Paintings and wall sconces rocked from the heaving walls, propelled to the floor along with other debris. Then, another equally strong, loud boom followed. Chairs were knocked over. Stone fragments started to fall from the walls and sheets of plaster dropped from the ceiling.

"By the Gods!" King Leopold said. "What is this?"

"A preemptive attack!" Barker shouted, "Chen-Li has attacked us first! He attacks King Leopold!"

A third tumultuous boom rocked the castle. More debris fell to litter the dusty chamber, and this time the cabinets overturned.

The council members struggled to their feet. Soldiers came stumbling into the council hall. Reports started to stream in to the king:

"Creatures have landed on the Green!"

"We are under attack!"

"Mobilize the Red and Blue!" King Leopold commanded. Just then the entire castle rocked again, sending the men reeling.

ON THE GREEN

Three massive shapes landed in the middle of the Green, the highly polished limestone overhang serving as the grand balcony of Castle Odessa. Black creatures screamed in furious anger as their mouths yawned open, encompassing most of their oily black bodies. They landed in the exact center of the Green, upon the small Red and Blue symbol inlaid upon it. Using that symbol as a center marker to strike, their fists slammed upon its surface. The creatures raged with giant hammer-like fists pounding on the limestone surface.

The king and the council members rushed through the green doors to see the Devourers. Unleashed again, released from the depths of their fiery pit, and hungry for more devastation. They took turns hammering the Green's surface. With each strike, the behemoths rattled the foundations of Castle Odessa. Stones worked loose and fell, wooden beams splintered, the plaster casing cracked, and terra-cotta tiles ejected from the parapets and tumbled down from the swaying spires of the high towers. Soon the entire castle grounds were littered with fallen debris.

Many people were running, screaming, wounded, and bloodied. More people lay dead, crushed under the falling stones.

From the ground level, the doors and the windows above were filled with archers of the Red and Blue. Warriors appeared, firing arrows into the three fearsome creatures, but many of the missiles ricocheted off their thick flabby hides. The arrows that did stick protruded out of their skin like quills. Unabated by archers, the Devourers continued their agonized screams and vicious pounding on the Green's surface. Bent on its destruction, they continued to carry out the attack.

Soldiers rushed out of the castle to attack with long spears. Others came and struck them with swords, attacking the dreadful beasts up close. Brave men were sent tumbling back with a sweep of the demons' arms. Sent flying over the railing, they met their fates by tumbling down the heights of the Blue Mountains. Still more fearless men came, some unarmed. They rushed to leap upon the creatures, holding fast to the creatures' backs, onto their arms, weighing them down to burden their movements. Some stung the creatures with only their knives. Others helplessly hung on, swinging along with the Devourers' swatting arms.

Seeing this courage inspired others to rush the beasts, joining the mass to weigh down and overwhelm the creatures. An ever-growing number of men found courage, while others found death. Still the Red and Blue tried to defend against the attack. Despite their growing number, the dead increased disproportionately to those who tried to save them.

The Devourers continued hammering away, producing a rhythm of fists. Hairline cracks appeared under the stress, splintering, growing, breaking from one side of the Green to the other. The exposed area under the stone started to show, as the balcony was being blasted apart by force. Gravity and the distant weight of the Green did the rest. The heaviness of the Devourers, along with the growing numbers of fighting men, only made it worse, hastening the inevitable.

A shifting quake was followed by the sound of a loud rumble. A decisive crack split the floor open under them, and the surface tilted sharply downward. At first the descent was almost imperceptible as the overhang cracked away from the castle. Breaking in jagged ruptures, the Green floor rapidly found its momentum, falling downward and away from the castle. Hundreds of tons of limestone fell at the same time, taking a wash of men with it. Finally, it crumbled down in fragments from the high mountain peak.

Two of the Devourers, still covered with clinging defenders, rode the balcony's motion down for an instant. As the Green continued downward, each of the monsters flipped, shifted their weight, and caught the wind on their mighty wings, dipping and rising. Unable to hold on, the clinging soldiers lost their purchase and fell kicking and screaming down the lofty mountain heights.

The third Devourer teetered precariously over the broken ledge, on the precipice of a three-thousand-foot drop. Trying not to lose its balance, made more difficult with only a stump of one missing foot, it waved its flabby arms and extended its wings. Eventually the last Devourer took to the air. All of them lifted higher, covered in arrows, dropping men from them as they flew away.

The massive limestone balcony broke apart as it plummeted down the mountain face. Finally, it struck the bottom, smashing into pieces, killing the men trapped underneath, and destroying the ceremonial markers placed there to honor the dead.

The sound of its fall echoed like thunder across the Mid-Run Valley. The collapse could be heard all the way to the Gray Mountains in the east. Pieces of green rock tumbled down the long three-mile ramp of the Mauveguard Pass. A cloud of thick dust filled the empty vacuum and lifted back up the heights. A bitter taste of limestone filled the mouths and stung the eyes of those still left, staring in shock over the fractured ledge. In the shadows of the dust cloud, King Leopold emerged to assess the damage. Working his way through the crowd, just as all the other bystanders did, the king approached as close as he dared to the broken chasm. The survivors coughed and put their hands over their mouths in a vain attempt to rid their faces of the dust particles, and to hide their shock. All were quickly covered in a thin layer of sickly yellowish dust.

Brother Barker pleaded with the king. "Can there be any doubt now? We must take action against the White Eminence, Your Majesty."

"Your Majesty, please," Lord Whitney pleaded between coughs. "We do not know this attack came from Chen-Li. We must not make a rash decision."

"I disagree, my lord. The warrior-priest is responsible for this," Brother Barker said. "And not just the attack on the Temple of Valor, but the recent sickness of madness as well."

"How is that possible?" Lord Rhodes asked. "What does the recent sickness have to do with Chen-Li?"

"King Leopold understands Chen-Li's abilities well," Brother Barker said. "And those of his priests of the White Eminence to spiritually possess unsuspecting people against their will. Why, they train incessantly to do just that at the Temple of Chen-Li. Once inside a body and commanding it, they commit the most outrageous acts against the will of their hosts. Things they would never do if not possessed. Just last week, for example, a lumberjack murdered his whole family. A beautiful wife and two small children. Later, and still out of his mind with spiritual possession, he killed the death warden while he was preparing the poor man's murdered family for burial. Even though this lumberjack was innocent, he was found guilty of these crimes. Yesterday, he was executed. Hanged in Haverhill. This is but one of many similar cases of madness brought about by possession of Chen-Li's spiritual priests. King Leopold understands this dilemma more than most. For it was Chen-Li himself who tried to possess His Highness in Umbrick many years ago. If the White Eminence and Chen-Li go unchecked, if this council does nothing, the Mid-Run Valley can expect more possessions, more deaths, more murders and executions. We must act now. We must march against Chen-Li. The sooner the better!"

"Your Majesty, a direct assault upon the Temple of Chen-Li would require over a hundred thousand soldiers, maybe more," Lord Whitney said.

"Mobilize fifty thousand," King Leopold ordered. "Prepare to march on the Oracle Mount. We will take the high ridge and surround the Temple of Valor. We will draw out the White Eminence and make them come to us. If they do, then we will destroy them out in the open."

"March on the Temple of Valor?" Lord Whitney asked. "Your Majesty, do you mean to attack them?"

King Leopold looked at Lord Whitney with stern eyes. "We will do everything to defend ourselves against further attacks from these demons."

"Very good, Your Majesty." Barker turned to go.

"Brother Barker!" King Leopold called before he could walk away. "If you want a war with Chen-Li, I will give you your damned war."

There was a moment of silence from Lords Whitney and Rhodes.

"Your Highness," Brother Barker responded with a bow.

The Kingdom of Odessa was now at war with the Temple of Chen-Li.

CASTLE ODESSA

Brother Barker faded away through the crowd pleased. Scores of people rushed by him to get a better look at what was done to the Green. But the Green was gone. Shock and panic filled the people with fear. Barker walked back into the council room again; everything was in disorder. He passed the king's throne, then went beyond, through the parted curtain.

Once there, Brother Barker dispelled his magic. Frost appeared in his natural form, a handsome blue-skinned demon, born from the queen of demons, Langula the serpent. Gone was Barker's straight black hair, replaced by Frost's wild uplifting white hair. His silver Demonic eyes sparkled, quite pleased with how the day had turned out. In his guise as Brother Barker the long-awaited project he had labored hard to achieve was finally delivering the desired results. The Kingdom of Odessa was going to war with the Temple of Chen-Li, while the Temple of Valor was marked ready for its destruction. All the Zorn's enemies were now at war with each other. This outcome was simply too ticklish for Frost to bear alone. He had to tell his masters.

"A most wonderful self-destruction on the scale of empire," Frost mused to himself. "I must congratulate Monticello. The Devourers could not have attacked at a better moment."

MAUVEGUARD PASS

About an hour later, Rhodes came along beside Lord Whitney. Both men wore iron-banded breastplates separated into four squares in colors of alternating red and blue. Upon them gold eagles were emblazoned to identify their status as lords.

They both directed a flurry of battle preparations. Thousands of troops. Supplies, catapults, siege equipment, weapons, armor, horses, transports—everything was a flurry of activity.

The men spoke of losing the Green, the attack of the Devourers, and the lives already lost. Revenge permeated through them. The target of that revenge was Chen-Li and his warrior-priests of the White Eminence.

Rhodes watched all the activity, then questioned Lord Whitney. "What do you make of this? An attack upon the Temple of Valor? This cannot be right."

"It is what the king has decided," Lord Whitney said.

"The king or Brother Barker? These days they are one and the same."

"I have never known King Leopold to take any man's counsel. Moreover, a man as treacherous as Brother Barker," Whitney said.

"The king does not seem to be himself," Lord Rhodes said.

"And Barker has no honor," Lord Whitney said. "Not the kind of man the king would ever have listened to in the past."

"Like the way he did in the persecution of Lord Plum-Kilmer?" Lord Rhodes added with a sideways glance.

"Treason by Lord Plum-Kilmer? For fighting as an Amalgam-ate?" Lord Whitney said. "King Leopold already knew about that and dismissed that charge after the Sanguine Forest incident."

"Yeah, Barker still got the king to sign Kilmer's death order though." Lord Rhodes looked at the sea of soldiers, fifty thousand of them, working in the Mauveguard Pass. They were preparing siege equipment for deployment.

"Catapults?" Lord Rhodes asked. "Really?"

The wind blew cold and crisp. The collapsed remnants of the Green lay in heaps all around. Looking up at Castle Odessa, high upon the mountain peak, the front of the castle now bore a raw scar where the Green had broken off, altering its once grand appearance.

"Sure looks weird without the Green," Lord Rhodes said. "Looks like a kid who just had his front teeth punched out."

"That is what this is all about, you know?" Lord Whitney said, pointing at where the Green used to be. "Finding someone to blame that on. The Temple of Valor is the most vulnerable. But mark my words, Lord Rhodes, Chen-Li had nothing to do with this."

"So, what do we do?" Lord Rhodes asked.

"We follow orders. Try not to invoke the king's wrath, at least for now," Lord Whitney said. "We need some time to figure this thing out."

Rhodes nodded, thinking on the situation. "Lord Whitney, when we get to the Temple of Valor, what if the order is given to attack wounded, unarmed civilians, consisting of women and children?"

"Let's hope it does not come to that," Lord Whitney said. "In the end, be true to your conscience, Rhodes, just as you were in the Sanguine Forest. I foresee troubling days ahead."

"We are in troubling times now."

Lord Whitney bent close. "Keep an eye on Brother Barker, Rhodes, a close eye."

"I'll keep an eye on him all right," Rhodes said. "Maybe even a bit more than that."

Then Lord Whitney straightened in the saddle and trotted off to give orders to his division commanders for an orderly deployment.

Keep an eye on him, Lord Rhodes thought. He scanned the area and saw no presence of Brother Barker anywhere. *Keep an eye on him? I can't even find him.*

You've got to take your chances

You open up your mind

Throw off your circumstances

Make it yours this time

Make it yours this time

Excerpt from *The Witch's Songbook*

Between the cold and her nervousness, her hands were shaking,
and she had trouble working the flint tinder.
— Excerpt from *Kilmer's Ghost* (Chapter 18)

THE CELEBRATION OF LIFE

Deep Underground

Gensen was close to death in the underground, yet he felt he was not alone. Wearily he thought he heard someone and looked up but could see no one, just the endless darkness of the tunnels. At first, the sound was low, then it grew, forming into a soft voice that spoke his name.

"Gensen, Gensen?" the voice said. "Wake up, Gensen."

Gradually, a person, partially hidden in shadow, approached through small dusty beams of light. Coming forward in a green cloak and hood, the person knelt beside him. As the hood was pulled back, Astar's face emerged, his blond curls spilling down.

"I am here with you now, Gensen," Astar said.

"Is that you…Astar? But how did you…"

"Shh, save your energy, Gensen." Astar seemed very different now to the blacksmith. Astar wore a massive golden sword across his back. The sword looked too big and too heavy for the boy, but Astar carried it as if it was nothing. There was more though, Astar seemed to possess a heightened mature confidence, far beyond his years. It sparkled from his eyes, made him appear to be more than a young man of eighteen. Something about his sudden appearance did not sit well with Gensen.

"Liar! You are not truly Astar." Gensen questioned him, "What is your father's name?"

"I am Astar, and my father is Amtor. He is safe at home in Homestead," Astar said.

"Too easy an answer for you, wasn't it?" Gensen put his hand on his sword. "I know you are not Astar. You are an only an illusion of the boy. Just a magic spell cast on the face and body of a demon." He pulled his sword free from its scabbard.

"Don't do that," Astar said.

"Why don't you fear?"

"Try as you will, you cannot harm me, Gensen."

Gensen's heartbeat and breathing grew rapid. There were tears welling up in his eyes.

"A powerful illusion!" Gensen shouted now. "Stand back, you demon! Or I swear by my only son, I will strike you dead." Gensen worried he might be wrong. But if this really was Astar, the son of Amtor, what was he doing all the way down here in this labyrinth? It couldn't be him. But the illusion was convincing. The demon looked real enough, just like the real Astar. It would be hard for Gensen to kill a likeness of Astar, but he resolved to do it if he came any closer despite the warning.

Astar approached anyway. "Strike me down if you wish. Let me show you."

"I mean it! I'm warning you!" Gensen's lips quivered in fear. "I will strike you down!"

The threat did not deter Astar. He came closer still.

"I warned you! Forgive me, Amtor!" Gensen attacked Astar with a sudden thrust of his sword.

Gensen's sword bit into the side of the green cloak. But he swung through empty air, the form of Astar was gone. There was no sign of him anywhere. Gensen was alone in the dark again, as if no one was ever there to begin with.

"I've gone mad," Gensen cried.

"I am here to help you, not hurt you, Gensen," Astar's voice called out to him from the darkness. The green-hooded figure appeared again, standing away in the dusty beams of the tunnel, carrying the large golden sword like before. Once again, Astar knelt and pulled the hood off his head, blond curls spilling out. "I am Astar. I am really here with you, and we really don't have time for this. You are burning up. Here, eat this."

Astar reached in the cloak and pulled out one of Aberfell's sandwiches. Gensen examined it with hungry eyes. He could smell the buttered herbs, bread, and tender venison. The rotund man grabbed the food and ate it in large bites. Then, Astar produced a skin of fresh water still cold from the well. Gensen put the sandwich on the ground and greedily drank.

"There, now do you believe I am real?"

Gensen's eyes widened, staring at Astar. "Am I dreaming? What are you?"

"I told you, I am Astar. You are not going to strike me again, are you?" Astar asked. "I want to get you out of this place. Don't you want to see Micah again? Come, follow me. I will take you back to the upper world again. There I can reunite you with Micah. But you can't stay here in this place of death any longer."

"Are you tricking me?" Gensen said. "Deceiving me, to lead me to my death?"

"Come along, now." Astar stood, pulled his hood up and started to walk away. Then he stopped to look back. "You coming?"

"Oh, what do I care?" Gensen struggled to his feet. "I think I have gone utterly mad in this place. It's finally taken its toll on me. My mind is obviously having visions, seeing specters. But I will follow you, spirit of Astar, even if it is just to put me out of my misery."

"I am real. I have already told you. No harm will come to you now." Astar turned. "Just follow me."

Gensen sheathed his sword and stepped forward, letting Astar lead the way.

"Much has happened since you left the village, Gensen," Astar said, walking through the short tunnels in a stoop. Gensen thought he saw another Astar up ahead that gave directions to the one Astar he followed. But when they neared that apparition, it got sucked into the one Astar as they passed. Gensen had to blink his eyes several times.

"I do not understand," Gensen said. "How did you find me?"

As they walked through the darkness, Astar spoke, "Do you remember, eighteen years ago, the Star of Ehlona shone to announce the recycled spirit of the Goddess?"

"Yes, yes, I remember, of course," Gensen said.

"Ehlona's Star was real. She did return to the world," Astar continued.

"There could only be one person born of this spirit of Ehlona," Gensen said. "Do you know who it was?"

"It was me. I am that person, Gensen," Astar told him.

"You?"

"I received the spirit eighteen years ago. Since then, the universe has been beckoning, revealing itself to me a little at a time." Astar continued to navigate through the myriad of dark humid tunnels.

"Where did you get that sword upon your back?" Gensen asked.

"Its name is Soothsayer." Astar climbed over a large step. Gensen followed with Astar's help. "Amtor found it in the pit of death when he was trapped in the Mauveguard Pass. It was merely a dagger then, but more than just any dagger. This blade was forged with the left arm of the Goddess Ehlona cast into its gold."

Astar turned to the side to slide through a tight fissure. Gensen needed help to pull his fat belly through. "This blade has bestowed me with great power. I can stop time...and more important...I know where Micah is."

"Wait!" Gensen stopped and spun Astar around. "You know where Micah is? Take me to him."

"No, I can't. Not yet."

"What are you talking about?" Gensen demanded. "Where is he? I need to see him."

"He is as safe as he can be for now. But where he is and what he has become is not for your eyes yet. To get to Micah, we must first defeat his captors. When the time is right, I will take you to him. But for now, we must get you out of here."

"Micah is alive?" Gensen said. "But..."

"I told you he is as safe as he can be," Astar said, avoiding the question. "I will lead you out."

Micah is alive, Gensen thought. *Micah is alive.*

Gensen followed the green-cloaked figure along in the darkness, hardly believing what he saw was real. Their trek was long, but eventually Gensen saw a glow in the distance. He could smell cool wind freshening the dank air. Seeing the way out, Gensen climbed faster now.

At last, he emerged out the dark hole. Standing in the midday rain with cool wind blowing in his face, he took deep satisfying breaths that filled his lungs with sweet clean air. He let the rain fall directly into his mouth. He wiped his face and looked around for Astar. Refreshed in the moment, he had not even noticed Astar was not with him anymore. He wondered if the person in the green cloak with the big golden sword was ever there in the first place.

Gensen turned to look at the mouth of the labyrinth behind him. Unlike the pit opening in the Great Mapes Forest, this one was significantly subdued and hidden. There was no sulfuric steam or dramatic broken stones to distinguish it. This was just a hole hidden by tall grass in an anonymous field. A casual observer would never know it was there. But this was no ordinary hole. This hole was an ancient one. A disaster waiting to happen for anyone or anything that could fall into it. Gensen wondered just how many like this there were in the Mid-Run Valley.

He turned and took a few steps away from the hole, searching for landmarks to orient himself. He could see mountains. By the shape and look of them, he determined them to be the Blue Mountains. They would be situated on the western horizon of the Mid-Run Valley. In front of them was the Sanguine Forest, a forest of sick-looking trees. To the south there was a multitude of plumes of smoke in the distance. These were cooking fires from a gathering of wagons. Even farther south, beyond the wagons, the beginnings of the Endless Sea stretched to the razor-thin horizon.

Gensen chose. He began walking south toward the wagons. He wanted to see what he could find there. Maybe they would know something about the whereabouts of his son.

THE NOMAD CAMP

No one dreaded this night more than the clan of the Gellers. Over the past year, the Geller family had selected the black sacrificial stone three times. *Three times*, they had selected that accursed stone! A high price to pay for any family. But the safety of the Nomads of Spiron had to be preserved from the Demonic with a fresh sacrifice of flesh every month, as the alliance had specified.

Of the twelve families, four of them—the Onedas, the Fulmers, the Wellish, and the Hadleys—had not pulled a single black stone or had to sacrifice a single family member to the demons all year. These families were as blessed as the Gellers were cursed. Selecting the white benevolent stones meant, for that family, that they were exempt from providing the sacrificial flesh for the unholy feast of the Demonic. At least for that month. Until the next cycle of the new moon and the new selection of the stones.

But the Gellers had pulled the black rock three times this past year alone. Some families, like the Oparks and the Edmans, had selected the black rock twice. Overall, seven of the twelve clans had pulled the black stone at least once in a year. Pulling the black stone meant these clans had to make painful decisions as to which family member they would give up to be consumed by the Demonic.

Now, the period of the new moon was upon them. Again, that dark time, when the dreaded black satin bag was brought out. Representatives from all the families came together to pull the stones again: eleven white ones, along with one accursed black one. The black one indicated which family had to supply the sacrifice. All the stones had been freshly washed in salt water from the shores of the Endless Seas to purify them, then laid out for display on a silver tray. The stones were displayed for the sake of honor and fairness before being put into the bag for all to see.

This was not a dour event; it was a celebration of life. Laughter and singing rang out. A party-like atmosphere revolved around the stones. Each family took turns dancing around them. Each approached and blew their smoke upon the stones to request favor with the Gods, and not judgment. This was the Nomads celebration of life.

The celebration brought out the old as well as the young. They ate, laughed, drank, and danced with exuberant energy. Musicians played the drums with lively beats. Scantily dressed women danced around the fire with their perspiring wiggling midriffs keeping time with the exotic rhythm. Laughter and liquor dripped off the bushy mustaches of the men. All of them let their hair down, earrings dangling underneath elaborate scarves.

The camp was demarcated by a circle of wagons. Nearby, unhitched horses grazed in the firelight's shadows as the constant sound of harps, singing, jingles, and clapping filled the camp indicating that in just a short while the selection would take place.

Suddenly, a dead body came launching over the wagons, thrown into their midst, landing hard in a cloud of dust. The girls screamed and ran. The music stopped, as the musicians scattered.

Boldo, the biggest of the Nomad men, appeared from on high. He stood on top of one of the wagons, looking down upon the celebration, his face red and brow burrowed. He had thrown the dead body into the camp. Now, he jumped down off the top of the wagon. He landed in a cloud of dust, next to the dead body.

"Do you *see*?" Boldo shouted. "Do you see what has become of Turkos, my brother? Murdered on the road...like a pig. While you dance, and laugh, and celebrate! What are you celebrating, you stupid fools? What has become of us? What has become of our honor? Turkos died all alone. When we agreed to the Alliance of the Flesh-Eaters, we agreed for the safety of our survival. Yet look at the marks upon his throat! See the mark of the Demonic upon him. There is no safe place in this alliance, not here, not with them. Despite our sacrifice, despite our pain, the Demonic feed on us whenever they want. And you? You dance? Look at Turkos! Take a good long look at him. This is your future. Ever since these dark strangers came to rule over us. Ever since Nadya began to—"

"Have a care with your words, Boldo." Nadya appeared from out of the shadows to interrupt him. "Be careful what you are about to say, my brother. There are children here. You should not scare them unnecessarily. Watch that you do not go too far."

"Why should I?" Boldo said with a tear forming in his eye. "I'm not afraid."

"Aren't you?" Nadya asked. "You're not afraid to die?"

"This is not living," Boldo said, pulling the scarf from around his neck to reveal the blood marks on his neck.

"But yet you still you live, don't you?" Nadya bent down and returned his scarf, tying it carefully back around his neck. Now she turned and addressed them all. "And so shall the tribe continue to live. You can understand that, can't you?"

Boldo dropped to his knees crying. Nadya lovingly placed her hands on his head, stroking it, comforting him in front of the others. Turkos lay on the ground dead before them.

"No more children!" a voice rang out from the assembly.

"Yes, of course, and the children too," Nadya said. "But understand this: Turkos was an outcast, acting in rebellion from his family. Upset and disagreeable with my rule, Turkos left the safety of the tribe. I tried to convince him not to go but could not. He wanted to strike out on his own and as far as I know, he was making his way work. As I hoped he could. Yet once separated from his family, he died alone. The price he had to pay, for his way was a foolish way. Our strength is in our numbers. The Nomads of Spiron stay together. Or, like Boldo so dramatically demonstrated, *this* happens. There is only death to those who strike out without the family. Thank you for reminding us of such an important lesson, Boldo."

"But what about these outsiders?" another voice shouted from the crowd.

"The demons are our salvation. Their power protects us," Nadya said.

But the crowd began shouting again.

"Only God brings salvation."

"What if they turn on us?"

"We cannot protect ourselves!"

"Behold!" Nadya suddenly shouted, pointing into the tree line. "Langula is coming!"

All the tribe screamed and fell upon the ground to protect themselves.

Nadya laughed.

"Look at you." Nadya continued to laugh. "Pathetic. When you talk of power you speak of things you know nothing about. The names of Langula, Monticello, Frost, Grim, and yes even Nadya, make you tremble, make you wet your pants. Those names keep you awake at night. They are the only ones you need to know."

Nadya took a long last look at her dead older brother Turkos. He had dared challenge her. Only she knew that the demon's attack upon him was no accident. She had ordered it herself. Now that it was done, she was full of regrets but could show no signs of weakness.

"Get this stinking dead man out of my sight. Throw his rotten carcass in a ditch far away from here before he offends my senses. And as for the rest of you—drink wine, dance, dance, and beat the drum like you never have before. Like your life depended on it. Rejoice in what life is left! Celebrate this moment! Do not worry about things you do not understand. Dance! And don't think twice about what is out there beyond the darkness."

Slowly the drum beat back to life. Cymbals tinged together and laughter lifted once more. The party continued. Boldo continued kneeling in the dirt over the body of his dead brother. He suspected Nadya had something to do with his murder but could prove nothing.

Nobody saw Gensen in the dark tree line. His eyes reflected the red light of the bonfire. He had been concealed in the bushes, watching, waiting, and listening. If he had crawled away, nobody would have been any wiser. But he had nowhere to go. His only thought was to prepare for his bloody vengeance.

"Langula!" Gensen spoke the demon's name softly to himself. That must be the one Amtor told him about. The one that had stalked Amtor, came to him in the middle of the night. The one that fed on him, bleeding him dry. Langula had to be the name of the demon responsible for Micah's abduction. The one he vowed to find.

"The Nomads will take me to Langula," Gensen whispered to himself. "Langula will take me to Micah."

Gensen emerged from the bush and walked directly into the Nomad camp. The women dancing around the stones saw him first and gathered dancing around him. The men watched the stranger advance with suspicion in their eyes and strong drink on their breath. Nadya saw him too. She followed the man across the flames on the other side of the fire. Mirroring his steps, they came together and stood face-to-face.

"I am a lost traveler. Would it be possible to share in some of your food please?" Gensen asked over the music. Even though he had eaten what Astar had given him a little while ago, he made up a story. "I am very hungry and thirsty and have not eaten for several days."

"Of course, of course, come, stranger," Nadya said with a kind smile. "The Nomads of Spiron are friends to any in need."

About this time, Nadya was brought the empty black satin bag ready to be filled with the sacrificial stones. Without giving them a look, she quickly pushed them away. The other Nomads noticed the stranger's presence and continued to celebrate. This time with a little extra vigor.

"Bring this man some food," Nadya commanded. Quickly, platters of bread and oil, fish and red meat, milk and cheese were placed before him. "Would you enjoy some wine?"

"Very much so." Gensen sat cross-legged on the ground. Young daughters of the Gellers, Oparks, and Edmans came to him under the watchful encouragement from their fathers. The girls sat so close to the stranger they nearly sat on top of him. They smiled at him seductively, touching his arms, and running their fingers along his bald head. He ate their food heartily while trying not to seem greedy.

"Thank you," he said.

Nadya did not ask the man for his name. She did not care about knowing it. She rose and retrieved a wineglass. She gave a long stare to the Gellers, the unfortunate family that had selected the black stone three times; they gave her an affirmative nod. Then Nadya gave a glance over to Boldo. He had stopped sobbing and had covered the body of Turkos out of sight with a nearby blanket. He too gave a quiet nod. Walking to the silver tray where the sacrificial stones were kept, she retrieved a small vial of purple liquid. The sedative prepared for the sacrifice. It had long been established that the demons did not mind. The sedative deadened the nerves of the living when being consumed by the demons.

Nadya twisted the container's seal and poured the contents into the wineglass. She filled the glass with red wine. Then, she returned to the stranger. The man took the glass, and with a thankful nod, drank it all down.

Gensen stuffed bread, then some fish, in his mouth. He watched the attractive girls talk and twirl their hair. They helped take his attention away from the light-headedness. They giggled to one another as the music started. They jumped up to dance in time with the psychotic drums. Frantically the music pounded out rhythm upon quickening rhythm. The entire Nomad camp was now watching Gensen. Waiting for the drug to take effect.

The girls continued spinning with laughter. Gensen felt the eyes upon him but had no concern. The red-orange flame of the bonfire changed in his sight to a blue-violet one. The dancers spun in the night, disappearing in the fire's glow.

Gensen fell over and his chin hit the ground. By now whether he kept his eyes open or closed did not matter. The fire continued to burn in his visions.

"Do you realize how well you have fulfilled my will?" the crow asked.
— Excerpt from *Kilmer's Ghost* (Chapter 19)

A GHOST FOR GRIM

DEEP UNDERGROUND

After their attack on the Temple of Valor, Monticello and Grim followed Langula through the vast complex of passageways underground. Navigating through these ancient tunnels was accomplished by looking for the signs. The signs were simple. Previously put there by the Demonic, they were arrows marked on the walls in blood, which there always seemed to be plenty of blood. The arrows always pointed in the closest direction to the surface. So, by going in the direction of a blood arrow meant a navigation to the top. Going against the arrow meant going deeper underground. Navigation in the tunnels depended on how many exit arrows they must pass before descending farther down into the depths and finding any certain location. This was the system the demons used to help guide them through the tunnels to the right places. The same system Gensen mistook as a bad ominous sign.

On this day, they found themselves counting arrows, navigating to where their lord and master, Hazor the Scorned, was to be found.

While walking along with the others, Grim glanced down a side passage, a darkened tunnel not marked by any arrows or signs.

Grim! He thought he heard a low voice call out to him.

He sensed movement down the unmarked tunnel. He stopped to look down the dark passage as Monticello and Langula continued on without him.

Grim! There it was again.

"Hello? Who's there?" Grim spoke into the darkness. His demon eyes detected no heat radiating any signs of life. Yet there was a low voice, calling his name, he had to investigate. He took a turn into the darkness.

Walking through the tunnel alone, with a constant sound of water dripping, Grim splashed through puddles. He could see nothing so far. There was nothing living in the tunnel.

Grim came to a sudden stop, startled at the presence of a hooded man who stood directly in front of him. The man radiated no heat. He stood in robes of gray with his adornments moving on their own, as if carried upon currents of an unseen ocean. Grim scrutinized the man closely. The figure had its deep hood pulled over his head so his face could not be seen.

Grim questioned, "Who are you? What do you want?"

The hooded man made no reply.

"What are you doing here?"

Sympathy, the low voice said. The hooded man reached out and touched Grim on the arm.

Grim felt his blood freeze inside his veins. He could not move anymore and his mind hummed. Just then a vision penetrated Grim's mind.

The vision was of some distant scene long ago. A man screamed burning in a fire, skin roasting, turning black to burst open in the licking flames. Yet the man lived and continued a long agonizing scream. Grim could feel it, the emotion of it; he felt as if he were dying himself watching this pitiful creature burning to death in his mind. Grim felt life slipping away from him. He felt weak, fully feeling the emotions of what it was like to die. Then the vision was gone.

"What did you do to me?" Grim touched his head for relief.

But before he could recover, the hooded man placed his hand on Grim's shoulder.

Plum, the voice said, as another vision forced its way into his mind.

This time, Grim experienced a woman gasping for breath. A sword had pierced her stomach, eviscerating her. Grim struggled to breathe, reeling in a moment of death, as if he was there and it was happening to him.

"Stop killing me!" The red demon shook his head trying to clear his thoughts.

More, the voice said. The next vision slammed into him.

A terrified girl appeared, and Grim could feel her fear, her rapid heartbeat, the anxiety of her desperation. She tried to run and Grim felt he could get away. But then her neck was cut open and Grim felt the sharp edge cutting his throat. The girl suddenly had warm blood pouring from her throat. When she failed to breathe, neither could Grim. With her strength gone, the girl collapsed and died. Grim fell to the floor, powerless and weak.

"Why these?" Grim mumbled. "Why did they die?"

A new vision came, one without a name attached. A man floated in an endless universe. In a place without form, without matter, without light. Grim felt crushing isolation. The man tumbled lengthways in absolute desolation, utter loneliness. Grim felt panic to be in a place of absolute nothingness. As he kept tumbling into the dark void, Grim felt that the solitude and the loneliness would never end.

Then the universe faded away, leaving Grim grateful to be back in the world once again.

One last vision came to Grim. There was a boy with curly red hair. Before Grim's eyes, he grew to be a man. Scenes of war, heartbreak, and loneliness pervaded Grim's mind. He watched the man being restrained in chains inside a dark dungeon. His stomach was slashed, causing his blood to flow into onto a large demonic egg. Grim could feel the wound to his stomach and rolled to the fetal position in front of the hooded man.

"Father?" Grim heard himself say. "This is my father?"

Grim knew that he was observing his own Demonic egg, and inside it, he lay in the fetal position. Still incubating, not ready to be born into this strange new world, the blood of the redheaded man fertilized the egg. But the blood was infected with an ancient curse. The hooded man showed Grim that he came from that same tainted blood. Grim was a part of that curse. This man shackled to the wall of the dungeon, bleeding out over this Demonic egg, must somehow be Grim's father. He and the tortured man in his vision were linked together somehow, by the same family curse.

The curse, the voice suddenly said. *I am the ghost. I will be with you forever.*

After this, the ghost released him, and then disappeared. Grim was left on the wet floor in the fetal position. He looked around the cavern for any sign of the spirit.

"Why did you do this to me?" Grim shouted. "Where did you go?"

With the disappearance of this ghost, his own thoughts and actions returned. Grim stood up and splashed out of there. He returned along the corridors of the dripping tunnel. He stumbled down the same passageway he left Monticello and Langula to go down earlier. Along the way he fell several times and needed more than once to lean against the walls to support his weight. Finally, he entered a long passageway that opened to an enormous cavern.

By this time, Monticello was the only one present, except for the recently turned Micah, who lay motionless on the floor. Monticello was shirtless and busy rustling through a wardrobe looking for clothes. The spotted demon did not even consider Grim when he entered, but Monticello spoke to him without looking his way.

"Langula is busy escorting her favorite son to the Castle of Odessa. Frost the blue devil. He has persuaded King Leopold to go to war with the Temple of Valor. Of course, without my Devourers showing up when they did, he would not have gotten so far. But what thanks do I get? No recognition for me at all," Monticello said, giving a pair of pants the flip. "I am bored with these clothes; they bore me now. I need something new, something colorful and fresh."

Grim ignored Monticello and knelt beside Micah. The boy was living out his last moments as his body died. He would continue to live but would be permanently changed. Remembering the vision the ghost showed him, he could now feel what the boy was going through.

Monticello rested an elbow on his bureau. "Before she left with Frost, Langula said that the king might need a little help. What that meant, I have no idea."

He noticed Grim watching over the boy. The red demon was uncharacteristically quiet.

"The boy is dying," Monticello said. Monticello gave Grim a curious look, then returned to searching through the clothes. "It will be over soon."

Micah was on the floor, lips blue, skin pallid yellow, black circles around his eyes. He crawled forward on his fingernails that were caked with dirt, cracked, and broken. He scratched along, crawling slowly toward the last remnant of the previous Demonic feast, an old thighbone, moldering and maggot-ridden.

"Everyone feeds on something, don't they?" Grim softly repeated what Langula told Micah earlier. Grim pushed the bone toward Micah.

Micah laid his face upon the stinking bone. Working over the rancid purple cartilage of the bone's end, he searched with his mouth for a remnant of putrefied flesh. Micah found a stringy sinewy muscle and stripped it off the bone. With some effort, he tugged at the flesh with tears in his eyes. Finally, he chewed the human meat.

Grim watched. "You will gain more strength, the more you eat."

Micah continued to gnaw at the red bone.

"Why this boy?" Grim asked Monticello. "Why do this to him?

"Why not?" Monticello, still rifling through his wardrobe, picked out a green shirt and tried it on. He spoke to Grim as he looked in the mirror. "Tomorrow marks the cycle of the new moon, when the Nomads sacrifice for our feast. Why don't you take the boy up to see Nadya and what kind of monthly sacrifice they have selected for our feast?"

"I will do that," Grim said, looking back at Micah. "I will take you with me up and out. And introduce you to the Nomads of Spiron."

Grim's response made Monticello take notice. Grim was not talking to him, he was talking to Micah. Monticello set down the hangers and the clothes he had been rummaging through.

"Are you feeling unwell?" Monticello asked. "You seem...different. Not nearly the Grim you usually are."

"You are not nearly as spotted as usual," Grim said to Monticello without looking at him. "Leave me alone."

Monticello guffawed, took off the green shirt, and turned back to selecting clothes.

Later, Grim escorted Micah through the dark passageways. Unknown to anybody else but Grim, the ghost followed. Grim kept turning to see if it was keeping up with them. The spirit drifted along following, without any noticeable contact to the ground. The ghost was still adorned in a luminescent robe that moved around the edges in the perpetual motion of the sea. The specter obscured its face inside a deep hood, making Grim wonder if the ghost even had a face.

"Why are you following me?" Grim asked the spirit. But the ghost made no sound.

"You told me to follow you," Micah said.

"No, not you," Grim snarled. "That blasted hooded man behind you."

Micah turned to look behind him. "No one is there."

Micah had changed completely now. His skin was pale to the point of radiating a dull ivory glow from under his face. The pupils of his eyes had turned milky gray. They were embedded into the deep sockets of his skull.

"You can't see it?" Grim stopped and pointed directly at the ghost. The ghost had stopped with them. His finger reached out and practically touched the spirit.

"There is only darkness," Micah told him. "Darkness everywhere."

Grim sneered at the ghost. "Why do you haunt only me? Why only me?"

They continued walking silently down the dark cave, Grim, Micah, and the ghost. Grim kept turning to see if the ghost was still following them; every time he turned, the ghost was still there.

"My teeth hurt," Micah moaned, rubbing his gums. His fangs were coming in, causing him great discomfort.

"They won't for long," Grim said.

"But they hurt now, and I'm getting hungry again."

"Shut up," Grim told him. "We're almost there."

They traveled past wispy silks of spiders, past dripping water falling overhead into milky pools. They passed the last sign now, an arrow drawn in blood on the cavern wall.

Grim pointed at the arrow. "This way to the top."

They continued through the tunnel. It turned into a steep incline. After a few more minutes, they approached a dim blue light glowing from the darkness outside. The way had led them to the top, where the air changed gradually to a fresh crispness.

NEAR THE NOMAD ENCAMPMENT

Grim and Micah emerged from the underground. This was the night of the feast and Nadya had been waiting for them. In accordance with the Demonic agreement, she was here to give the demons their monthly sacrifice. She sat on a bundle on the ground, a burlap bag from which two legs were sticking out. This was the sacrifice offered by the Nomads, knocked unconscious from a dose of sedative.

"The lunar phase of the new moon shines above," Nadya addressed them, tapping the bundle. "Another sacrifice from the Nomads of Spiron. Flesh for your monthly feast. You have brought someone new with you. A fifth member of the Demonic?"

Grim turned in Micah's direction to see the ghost standing near him. "Do you mean the boy?"

"This pale guest you brought with you tonight," Nadya told him. "Will this boyish-demon come to collect our sacrifice in the future?"

Grim motioned impatiently to the package on the ground. "Wake the sacrifice. I don't intend on carrying them."

"As you wish." Nadya took her waterskin and knelt beside the bundle. She pulled back the burlap bag revealing Gensen's face. Nadya pulled the cork on her waterskin, preparing to splash water on his face. But a man in a flowing green cloak and an unusually large sword walked up in front of her. Nadya stopped short with a start. "Who are you? Where did you come from?"

The green-cloaked figure stood by the sacrifice, staring under his hood at the two demons.

Grim let out a shout as he lashed out at the emerald-clad stranger. He sailed right through where the person stood, who was not there any longer. The ferocious momentum of the attack carried Grim until he fell on the ground. Having attacked and connected with nothing, from the ground Grim turned to see the cloaked stranger in a completely different place. Now the man stood next to Micah.

The figure pulled back his hood. It was Astar. "Micah, it is me."

"Astar?" Micah said. He had been rubbing his gums prior to the stranger's appearance but now looked up in surprise. "Is it really you, Astar?"

Grim breathed heavy from the ground. "You know this person?"

Nadya wisely backed away, anxious to have the business of demons done for another month.

Astar spoke again, "Micah, I am sorry for what they have done to you."

"Don't look at me, Astar." Micah shielded his face with his elbow.

"Micah, I already know what they have done," Astar said. "There is no need to hide it from me now."

"Astar." Micah slowly dropped his elbow. "I thought I would never see you again."

"What's going on here?" Grim stood up, dusting himself off. "I demand to know."

"Silence, demon!" a second Astar said, appearing seemingly out of nowhere and surprising Grim.

Seeing a second apparition of Astar, Grim stepped backward. "Ah yes, I know you. You must be Astar."

"You did this to him?" the second Astar asked Grim.

The first Astar put his arm around Micah's shoulder.

Just then a third, then a fourth version of Astar appeared—all in green cloaks and each with a copy of the large Soothsayer on his back. All of them were hooded and surrounded the red demon to keep him in check.

Grim lashed out impulsively in anger. But the more he tried to slash Astar with his sharp claws, the more he fell on the ground, and the more energy it took him to continue with his attacks. Copies of Astar kept appearing and disappearing only to reappear. Facing these multiple personas of Astar, Grim was quickly tiring himself out. Finally, he became too exhausted to continue.

"You cannot hurt me in that way," Astar told Grim who lay on the ground. "You can hurt me only by telling me the truth. Now tell me, what did you do to Micah?"

"Astar," Grim ceased to struggle. He bent with his hands on his knees, breathing heavily, and realizing he had been subdued by these replicating Astars. He grumbled between breaths. "What marvelous magic you have."

"Magic of the ancients," one of the Astars said. "In which you are greatly outmatched!"

"We do not wish to hurt you," another Astar told Grim. "Will you answer the question please—what have you done to Micah?"

The third Astar asked, "Do we have to start showing you what our fists can do to you? Or would you rather have a taste of mighty Soothsayer?"

Grim looked around. He was surrounded and powerless.

"Boy's been infected by Langula's poison," Grim said, noticing the ghost still lingering, a witness to all of what was happening.

"What kind of poison?" a fourth Astar asked Grim.

"Demon's venom. From the poison sacs of Langula's serpent glands." Grim stood up straight looking at all the Astars around him. "She wanted you, Astar. Wanted to turn you to the side of the Demonic. The Devourers brought the wrong boy."

"You need help," Astar told Micah. "Lady Valen can help you. She can heal you."

"It is too late," Micah told Astar. "There is no help for me."

The body of the sacrifice started to stir.

"We will go to Valen. I will take you there," Astar said. "She possesses the healing power of the Mother Goddess. If anybody can restore you, she can."

Micah did not answer Astar.

"He says it is too late," Grim said. "Because he knows his body has been dying over the past few days. The change is complete."

"Well, we must do something," Astar said as the extra versions of himself absorbed back into the one.

"Micah?" a soft voice said from the ground. It was Gensen, who rose unsteadily. As the burlap bag slipped off his head, he repeated, "Micah?"

"Father?" Micah, surprised to see his father, rushed to Gensen and embraced him. "Oh, Father!"

"Father? Now, wait just a minute," Grim said. "This is the ceremonial sacrifice for the feast of the Demonic!"

"*No!* This is my father!" Micah turned to shield Gensen from
Grim. "Don't touch him!"

Micah helped Gensen back down to the ground.

"You demons will have to go hungry," Astar laughed at Grim.
"No one lays a finger on this man."

"You don't understand, I can't go back empty-handed. You!" Grim
pointed at Nadya. "We reject this month's sacrifice. Bring us another
or the Demonic will ravage your whole tribe!"

Grim moved toward Nadya but found another Astar standing
in his way.

"Get out of my way, Astar," Grim said. "A contract has been
breached."

"You will not harm the woman either," the second Astar said.
Grim watched Nadya flee. She ran away as fast as she could, down the
hill, and back toward the lights of the Nomad camp in the distance.

"They will never be free from the Demonic," Grim sneered.

Micah knelt beside Gensen. "Are you hurt?"

"Oh, Micah, I have found you," Gensen told Micah. "We can
go home."

Micah looked up at Astar. And Astar frowned.

"You can't take Micah home just yet," Astar told Gensen.

"Astar, is that you again?" Gensen blinked at him.

"We must get Micah to the Temple of Valor," Astar told Gensen.
"He needs Valen's healing. Then we can all go home together."

Gensen looked at his pale son. He could see the death on his face.
"Yes, yes, the Lady Valen will surely help us."

Grim stood looking at the ghost. After Nadya's escape, there
would be severe consequences for the Nomads of Spiron. Once the

others heard about the Nomads' disobedience, there would be punishment for them all.

But just as Grim thought this, he looked down and saw the ghost's skeletal hand on his arm again. Another vision penetrated Grim's mind. This vision was of his own death at the hands of Langula, ordered by the Zorn, and assisted by Monticello and Frost. The Demonic would soon turn on him; and if the current events remained on the same line of fate, he would soon be betrayed and murdered by his own.

As the ghost released him, Grim could feel the divisiveness of the Demonic. After his own death, the Demonic would erupt into a war of betrayal. It was coming. And the Zorn would do anything to save himself at the expense of the others.

The ghost slowly lifted a finger and pointed to the Endless Sea. The visions stopped and the ghost faded away. For Grim, there would be no turning back. His own life was on the line now. He had to save himself.

Without saying a word, Grim turned and used his speed to disappear down the little hill where he faded into the darkness. He raced toward the sound of the crashing waves.

With Grim gone, Micah, Gensen, and Astar all knelt together on the ground.

Micah whispered to his father and Astar. "I have become like them. I'm afraid there is no going back for me. I must feed. I need human flesh."

Ripples on the lake,
Like time that slowly passes.

Excerpt from *The Witch's Songbook*

He entered the observation platform by
materializing through the stone wall.
— Excerpt from *Kilmer's Ghost* (Chapter 20)

A THOUGHT-PROVOKING PROPOSITION

Deep Underground

The Zorn had not fully integrated back into the stone and the stalagmite only partially covered him. A milky substance trickled over his face and body, as the minerals were beginning to fuse him back into the stone formation.

The Zorn opened his eyes. He was startled to see a person standing in front of him. The man who stood before him wore an emerald cloak and carried a massive golden sword on his back. He made no movement toward the Zorn to threaten him, just stood quietly looking at him. For a moment, they continued to consider one another, neither saying a word. The Zorn studied the large golden sword strapped against the man's back. It was a larger but exact replica of the smaller dagger, Soothsayer.

"I suppose your presence is why my blood has been tingling." The Zorn looked down upon Astar. "Why do you have my sword strapped upon your back? Have you come to return it?"

"You fuse yourself into the rock," Astar said under his hood, examining his progress. "You are using them as a force amplifier to the world. They are providing you with additional harmonics to enhance the power of your magic spells. I'm impressed, very resourceful. You always were the clever one."

The Zorn spoke, "I do not need your flattery. I know how clever I am. What I need is my property. Now give it back to me!"

Astar pulled the emerald hood down, his long blond curls spilling out. "So, you can see me. I want you to know who I am."

"I know who you are," the Zorn said. "Even better, I know who you *were*. Through the years you have been a great many things. A Goddess, a witch, now a boy. But I never took you for a thief."

"Don't forget, I was the Goddess of Beauty, painter of sunrises and sunsets," Astar said. "The wife of the God of Light, Heironomus. Lover of Hexor, the God of Darkness, your father. Champion and defender of the living things of the Great Mapes Forest. I am creator of the Timmutes. And…of course…your mother."

"Yet here you stand as Astar the thief."

"Don't you mean, Astar the holder of Soothsayer?" Astar held out his hand as a single moth landed on it. Then, Astar looked back with raised his eyebrows and smiled. "See that?"

"Add liar to the list," the Zorn said with no amusement. It did concern him though, how the moths did not react to Astar's presence with the agitation they had when Langula and Monticello entered his lair. With Astar they continued flitting around the cavern as if everything was normal.

Astar shrugged turning again to the moths. "I did not want to disturb them."

"Yet you disturb me. How did you find me?"

"You are not hard to find," Astar said. "I can be clever too. As you are drawn to Soothsayer, it is drawn to you. I let the blade lead. Took me right to you on the first try."

"That's not clever, just lucky for you."

"Why do all this, Hazor? Why spread this madness?"

The Zorn chuckled, then shut his eyes. "Go away. I do not want to disturb the delicate connections. The crystals break easily."

"Your power is growing far beyond your reach." Astar watched the Zorn's face, hideous as it was, accept the mineral milk oozing over him in rivulets.

Astar flung back his cloak to take a seat on a flat stone. He produced Soothsayer effortlessly from his back, hanging it from the strap on a nearby stone. Astar turned his head to watch how the Zorn's tiny yellow eyes darted rapidly over the length of the golden sword, as it hung in front of him, just a little over an arm's length away.

"Come down from your rock and get it, if you want it so bad," Astar teased him. "But because you are no fool, you will not take up a challenge you are certain to lose. Judging from your face, the last time you possessed it, I don't think you really want it."

The Zorn did not answer.

Astar continued, "This scorn of yours, Hazor, has twisted your purpose."

"If it has, it has only been because of you," the Zorn said. "Take a good look. You did this to me. And so, *you* are responsible for my scorn, for this sickness, all the madness, all the death and suffering. It is all your fault, you see. If you want it stopped, I will make you a deal. Go kill yourself again, just like you have before, and I will gladly stop. No? You're unwilling? You see, your hands have the blood of this humanity on them. *Tsk, tsk, tsk.* How can you continue to live with such guilt?" The Zorn chuckled, amused with himself.

But to the Zorn's surprise, Astar laughed as well. "I suppose you are right, Hazor. I never have been an innocent player in these things. I gave you an impossible challenge, you gave one right back to me. My compliments. But tell me this, is there no way to repair the damage I have done to you?"

"What are you talking about? What do you mean?"

Astar stood and came closer. Soothsayer stayed behind. "Look at what have you become, Hazor. The damage this scorn has done to you. Your flesh has been completely destroyed by it, hasn't it?"

"You have made me as you see me," the Zorn said with an angry look. His vanity had always been fragile at best.

"You do realize, don't you? That is because my power was, and still is, greater than yours," Astar said. "I think you would kill me if you could."

"I cannot kill you," the Zorn said. "I have eyes everywhere and heard what you did to help the blacksmith. He could not lay a finger on you when he struck out with his sword. Neither will I be able to."

"But if you could…you would, wouldn't you? I do not wish to kill you. You might think that is a weakness on my part. But I feel only pity for you, because of your weakness, of how this vanity of yours has consumed you. My desire is to help you. I have come here to ask if I may serve you."

"*You* serve *me*?" The Zorn laughed. "That will be the day."

"Serve you by saving you," Astar said.

"Save me from what?" the Zorn asked. "More of this boring conversation? Do you intend to stand there all night long bothering me? Is that your clever plan? Oh, the endless torments of Astar the thief!"

"I have always had the gift of prophecy, my son," Astar said.

"Don't call me *son*," the Zorn said, moving slightly, putting fresh cracks in the meld between him and the stone. "Now look what you made me do."

"My apologies. The truth is, I see many threads in the fabric of this destiny. I have seen the end of your thread. I think you have seen it too. Yours is a chilling, bitter ending."

The Zorn's tongue, purple and sticky, ran across his wide front teeth. "How very interesting. Why don't you go away now and leave me alone?"

"What if I told you I could restore your flesh? Back to the way it used to be. Before the Zorn, before the Skeletal King. Bring Hazor back to the world again."

The Zorn said, "Why do you torment me?"

"I have already stated why. You are a tree of many roots. You sicken so many, faster than I can save them. But I could save them all just by saving you. That is something I am quite prepared to do. All I ask is this—is it too late for us? I admit, so much has happened. I can only stop time; I cannot go back in it and fix what has already happened. Are things so far out of reach that we cannot be saved from this bitter ending?"

"The end will be bitter no matter how it comes," the Zorn said comfortably within the stone. "Now go, I have business to do."

He began his vibrations, resonating again, as his spell amplified through the stone. With every pulse, the sickness lifted to the surface. Astar returned and sat upon the flat stone.

"Your father and I," Astar mused, "used to enjoy the beauty of the night together. Purple evenings, where we would watch the shadows grow across the mountains. The darkness, so beautiful, I remember tiny lights from the villages appeared as stars in the sky. Your father and I used to watch them. The ripples on the lake, moving on the waters like black mirrors. Beautiful nights those were in the darkness with Hexor and me. You see, we both understood that death for these mortals is as necessary and equal as their births. Your father also knew the mortals should not be made to suffer in death, any more than they should suffer in birth. It was always important to him. They should not fear the balance of life and death. Yet the balance had to be maintained. The problem was with all these blessings of long life, the curses of death. It perverts the purpose of our powers. When these are given, something is taken, stolen from these mortals. Your father knew this better than Heironomus. I only want to give life and death back their dignity and give them beauty."

Astar tapped his palm on Soothsayer. "It is in its major form now. You know why it is so powerful, don't you? The spirit of the Goddess present in me has been reunited with the arm in Soothsayer. The arm you stole when you killed Ulrig the Master Tree. The action that cursed your flesh to turn green and fall away from your bones. You call me a thief and say you want it back, but we both know better. You don't really want it back. You know you cannot wield it. The blade cursed you. But in my hands, the blade could restore you."

"Restore me? You offer me restoration of my flesh?" The Zorn searched Astar's young face.

"We could make you whole again," Astar told him.

"Who is *we*?" the Zorn asked. "A collection of your aspects?"

"I control the blade and Lady Valen controls the healing power of the Mother Goddess. Together, we can join the circle, and by completing it, with you in it, we can heal you back to Hazor, again and forever. You could put the Skeletal King away."

"Why would you do that for me?" the Zorn asked.

"Because only you can stop this sickness."

"And you think I would do that in return?"

"If you don't, you'll forever remain the Skeletal King. This era, your era, is coming to an end soon; it is nearly gone already. You sense it, I know it. The door is closing. Another door—my door, my era—is beginning to open. Yes, you could be restored. You need to decide what you are willing to do, if you could be Hazor again, if it is not too late."

Astar rose. "This is the primary purpose I came to talk to you about. But I also wanted to confess, admit, that many mistakes have been made. I was wrong not to have loved you, Hazor. I should have. From the very beginning, you deserved love. You never had a chance to be the son of Ehlona and Hexor. You never had a chance to be anything before you were filled with this scorn and became what you became. For what it is worth, I'm sorry. You should have been loved. Maybe if I can help you find a part of what you lost, help you break away from this scorn, you can enter the new era a different person. A full and complete person. This is what I wish for you in your journey to come."

After a long pause, the Zorn spoke, "This is the most hateful, cruelest thing ever done to me."

Astar pulled his hood back up and turned. He walked through the moths without disturbing them. Before he took his leave, he looked over his shoulder to say one more thing. "If being the Zorn, if hating all humanity, is something you desire above all things, I will leave you to it, then. But if you desire to be restored to your former self, you have to tell me and say so. I will no longer make you anything you do not wish to be. The greatest sin is the one repeated."

The Zorn watched Astar leave. His emerald cloak breezed through the stalagmites and the moths. Finally, he disappeared into the darkness and the Zorn was alone. A quiet filled the cavern.

The Zorn felt the tension in his shoulders. He tried to relax himself back into the place where the rock had cracked. He closed his eyes to get comfortable. But now it was no good. It didn't feel right. It was ruined. He could not seem to find the right place. Opening his eyes, he watched the moths flitting around throughout the chamber.

"So many lives," the Zorn whispered, looking at the moths. With an electric buzz, he began pulsating, emitting the madness of his sickness spell through the rock and onto the world again. After a while, the Zorn chuckled, thinking of Astar's words.

We watched the ripples moving on the waters like black mirrors.

His chuckle grew until laughter echoed loudly off the cavern walls. "Clever, very clever, indeed."

Oh, you left me hurting
Left me feeling quite uncertain
You care for nobody
But yourself

Excerpt from *The Witch's Songbook*

Bump! Bump! His left boot hit the wall occasionally
as his body twisted on the frayed rope. Bump! Bump!
— Excerpt from *Kilmer's Ghost* (Chapter 21)

FALLING WHITE PETALS

SANGUINE FOREST

Warning!
You Are Now Entering the Sanguine Forest
Forbidden by Order of King Leopold
Do Not Enter!

Astar read the sign. Despite what it said, he entered the forest anyway. After a few steps, the forest blotted out the light of the day, darkness descended, and the temperature dropped.

Astar saw the bones in the dirt as he passed. Human skulls stared empty-eyed at him. Long hollow rib bones gave way to crooked twisting spines. He stepped over them as best he could. But some he had to crunch through. It turned his stomach to feel them break under his boots.

As he continued walking, a loud scream filled the air. Then a second one came from farther away, echoing in the distance. He stopped, and a brief silence followed. Astar wearily looked in all directions before continuing. Unexpectedly, there was a sudden rush of more screams, many more of them. The screams surrounded him in every direction.

The screaming continued as Astar caught glimpses of movement. Shadows darted behind the trees. There, to the front of him, off to the side, then behind him. He felt a multitude of eyes upon him. Taking a moment to moisten his dry lips, he continued through the darkness. Turning to look behind him, he did not see the way out of the forest anymore.

A wisp of blue vapor floated through the trees and then was gone. He stopped in his tracks. Even more blue wisps materialized, making their presence known. They came racing to him, dancing around his head. He had to avoid the orbs that sailed too close. As they traveled, they left trails of dissipating blue vapor behind them. An orb passed, circled around, then came back to Astar. As it came closer, the sphere of blue altered its smooth surface, taking shape, forming into a human face. For a moment, Astar stared into the face. The round orb now resembled a man's head weathered by age with sad upturned eyes. Astar and the orb gazed at each other. For a moment they seemed to connect like two neighbors passing on the street. Then the orb shook, furrowed its brow, and let out a tremendously loud screech. The orb then shot through Astar. It entered Astar's body from the front and exited through his back.

Even in all his many aspects, Astar was still flesh and blood and not spirit. When the orb sailed through him, his stomach immediately turned sour. He suddenly felt he could vomit. Just then, another orb shot through him, then another and another. The spiritual invaders penetrated him, then darted away, floating back through the shadows of the Sanguine Forest. But as some of them floated away, a multitude of others came rushing in.

Astar looked up to see more of them coming. Through the darkness of the sickly trees, they appeared to rise from the long-dead bones Astar had been walking on.

"Oh, help me!" Astar moaned as they surrounded him.

These were the ghosts of the Vengeful Spirits and they numbered in the thousands. Vengeful, because in life they belonged to the Zornastic Order, dark priests of the Zorn who commanded them to destroy themselves. Since then, the long-dead priests were forever cursed to remain and haunt the Sanguine Forest.

But now, as the few spirits that had penetrated him learned of his intentions, word of Astar must have spread through the Vengeful Spirits. For they did not attack him anymore, nor did they move to harm him in any way. They simply spun around him, eventually opening to reveal a path for him to take.

Astar went on, letting the blue orbs guide him. He was being led through the Sanguine Forest. Soon a castle, with seven spiraling towers above a central dome, loomed ahead of him.

The Vengeful Spirits had taken him to the legendary Castle Orlo in the center of the Sanguine Forest. Once this had been the home of the Demonic. The Zorn and Langula had abandoned the castle years ago in favor of the underground. It would have remained deserted too, if not for some outlaws that used it as a hideout now.

Having revealed Castle Orlo to Astar, the Vengeful Spirits took their leave of the place. They scattered back to the bones where they came from. Astar watched them all go for a moment. Then he was all alone.

All around the front of the castle, Astar could see traps consisting of bottles, bones, and other pieces of metal strung up with low-hanging strings. Astar immediately knew what they were. This was a warning mechanism put there by the outlaws to sound an alarm against trespassers. With these hanging devices surrounding the entrance, it would be impossible to get near the castle walls or doors without invoking the alarm.

Regardless, Astar ducked under the wire. As he did, it produced a series of rattling noises. As an alarm system, it was not sophisticated but effective. No matter. He approached the thick double doors. First, he tried to open them, but they were locked from the inside. Next, he pounded upon them with his fist.

"Hey in there, hello," Astar shouted. "Is anybody in the castle?"

There was no answer.

Again, he pounded on the doors. Still no answer.

But then, he heard a noise from inside. A winding gear started to whirl. He could hear the locks starting to spin, followed by the sound of a heavy latch falling into place. Then, the mechanism became silent again. The door did not open. Nothing at all seemed to happen.

That's when Astar heard noises behind him followed by a harsh voice.

"Just hold it right there! Don't move and don't turn around," a man's voice said. "I have the point of my sword at the back of your neck. No sudden moves. Just stay still. We are going to search you."

There was more than one of them. Astar heard several more footsteps joining whoever was already behind him. He had fallen into a trap laid by the outlaws.

"Slowly! Slowly," another man's voice called out. "Let me see your hands. If I see any conjuring, I'll run you through, right here. Now, do you have any weapons?"

"A dagger," Astar said, holding up his hands. "In my belt."

"Go ahead, search him," another voice said. Astar felt a pair of hands search over him for the dagger.

"Would you look at this?" They found and took his golden dagger. "Pure gold."

"Its name is Soothsayer," he said. "Mine is Astar. But you might know me by my former name. The Goddess Ehlona."

There was a brief chuckle behind him.

"Don't know of any Astar," one of them said. "And you are definitely not a goddess. Watch out with this one. He is probably mad with the sickness."

"Did you see my star eighteen years ago?" Astar said. "I am not sick but have come to cleanse this forest of its sickness. I am going to make it whole again."

"The Star of Ehlona, you say?" another one asked. "You say you're the Goddess Ehlona?"

"I said I was Astar first, which I am. But since that meant nothing to you… Look, if you are going to kill me, can you please get it over with? I have another version of myself riding in a wagon with Lady Valen and Aberfell right now. I would like to get back to them, and I don't have time to waste. I have a lot of work to do. So, if you don't mind, can we rush this thing along?"

"You should not joke about killing," a man said. "Whether you are Ehlona, or Astar, or whoever you are, remember, I'm the one with the sword."

In a flash, Astar reversed the situation. Where he stood a moment ago was now just empty space. The man holding the sword to Astar's neck had now lost his sword and held only the thin air. Now it was Astar who held that sword to the neck of the man who once held it against his.

Astar was amused and could not help but laugh. "Now who is the one with the sword? You would rob me, but now you have become the one who holds nothing but a handful of empty air. Would you like to hear another joke about killing or are you the one in a hurry now?"

The other outlaws started to move into action, but Astar quickly shot them a glance. "Nobody move! I'm the one with the sword now," Astar told the one in front him. "Kindly lift your hands where I can see them."

"Please don't kill me," the man said, slowly lifting his hands. "I do not conjure. I have a family."

He got a clear look at them now. There were five outlaws in total, the one in front of him, one on the left, one on the right, and standing off to the rear, an unarmed woman with a small child.

"You are unusually adorned for outlaws," Astar remarked. All of them wore expensive armor with King Leopold's colors emblazoned in red and blue upon the Odessa coat of arms. These people were from the kingdom.

One of them, a tall lanky man, had not found it necessary to even draw his weapon during the ambush. But now he gradually lowered his hand toward the hilt of his sword.

"Uh-uh." Astar shook his head. "Let's not bother dying today."

The lanky one moved away from his hanging sword and extended his hands out in front of him. "No need for that."

Astar then turned to the woman. "What's your name, my lady?"

"Darla," she said. She wore a thick leather corset without royal colors or a coat of arms. Still, Astar could tell from where he was, the leather of her armor was of the highest quality and worth a small fortune, made from the best cured leather, luxuriously light, colored in shades of dark browns. Her hair was thick and black. She had been blessed with oversize brown eyes. Behind her left leg, she protected a young boy. Obviously, probably, her son. The boy looked to be about five. "Our son, Kory."

"Glad to meet you, both of you," Astar nodded toward Darla. Still directing the conversation to Darla, Astar turned and referenced the tall lanky man, the one who had just about gone for his sword. "What's his name?"

"That is our friend Oaks," she said. Oaks had been the one who put his hands on Astar and searched him.

Astar addressed Oaks now. "Just seconds ago, Oaks, you had in your possession Soothsayer, the most powerful magic weapon in the world. But before you could realize you had more than just gold in your hand, I took it back from you. Now you hold nothing, and Soothsayer is safely back in my belt. It's my pleasure to meet you."

Astar dipped his head. Oaks grimaced and bowed slightly back at him.

"You're very fast," Oaks conceded to Astar.

"You have no idea," Astar said.

He turned to the other one, a wide-bodied soldier, thick in the neck and chest. He dutifully stood as he was told, holding his hands out in front of him. Astar asked, "Who are you?"

"My name's Melvin," he answered, a grim look on his face. "We don't want any trouble."

"I haven't decided yet," Astar said and nodded to him.

Melvin, too shocked to nod back, just stood there with his mouth open.

"Good morning to all of you," Astar said. He jiggled the sword on the back of the man's neck, addressing him next. "I have already told you my name. Now repeat it back to me."

"You said you were the Goddess Ehlona," the man said, holding up his hands. "And you said you were Astar."

"Ah! Now you see, finally, we are getting somewhere," Astar told him. He pressed the sword against the back of his neck again. "Tell me who you are, if it's not too much trouble, sir."

"Always found that question a little hard to answer," the man with the red curls said. "But I shall try."

Astar considered the group one more time. Then he lowered the sword. "Look, I am pretty sure I do not intend to harm any of you. So, unless I've gravely mistaken your character, I don't think you wish me any harm either. Turn around, let me look at you."

The man turned to face Astar, his hands still in the air. He had an tall athletic build, a ruggedly handsome face, and red curls with a touch of gray around the ears. "I am mostly called Lord Plum-Kilmer."

"By the Gods!" Astar declared wide-eyed. "The *real* Kilmer? Why, I can't believe it! My deepest, sincerest, apologies, Lord Kilmer. If I would have known… My father is Amtor."

"Amtor?" Kilmer slowly lowered his hands now. "You are the son of Amtor?"

"Kilmer! I have heard so much, well, just everything about you! How you saved my father's life. By extension, so, you saved my life too! Why, I would not be here today if it were not for you. You are my hero. My father's savior, at the Mauveguard Pass. Here, take your sword. I can't believe it—I'm so embarrassed I was holding it on you. I'm so sorry."

"Forgive me, I do not wish to offend you." Kilmer accepted his sword, eyeing him. "But if what you say is true, my heart is full of happiness to meet the son of Amtor. The thing is, we have been seeing a great degree of madness lately. You have told us you are the Goddess Ehlona. On top of that claim, you say you are the son of Amtor? You sound like…like you may have been touched with the sickness. Are you really who you say you are? Astar, the son of Amtor, and the Goddess Ehlona? How do we know you are not possessed, like so many?"

"Fair question." Astar smiled. When he did, it only made him look more insane. "Here, let me show you so you won't doubt me."

Astar disappeared.

"Where did he go?" Melvin asked.

Astar reappeared, materializing behind Kilmer once again. Back to where he had been standing in the first place. He tapped Kilmer on the shoulder with his own sword again.

"There he is," Melvin pointed out. "Behind you."

"What is this?" Kilmer turned around to look.

"Of course, unless you like me the other way." Another aspect of Astar appeared behind Kilmer at the same time. Now an Astar stood both in front of and behind Kilmer. Each one of the Astars held Kilmer's sword.

"Great Gods! There are two of him!" Melvin said. "He is in two places at once."

"How do *you* know you are not infected by the madness?" Astar asked. "Maybe this sickness has made you mad? How else would this be possible?"

Astar began doubling his personas from two to four in a series of rapid quadruple pops. He paused momentarily, waiting for the effect. Then, he multiplied himself over and over, again and again. Within a span of ten seconds, thirty-two Astars popped into existence in the area in and around Kilmer and his party. All the Astars moved freely and spoke independently with each other. Their talk, in a multitude of thirty-two voices, created a chaos of sound impossible to follow.

"There! Do. You. Believe. Us. Now?" Six of his personas spoke in timed responses to form a single sentence. The voice was Astar's, but it came out of different bodies. Hearing no answer from his stunned onlookers, the six Astars spoke again, "Or. Shall. I. Make. Some. More?"

"No, no, no," Kilmer declared. "Don't make any more! Don't do that! I have not seen magic like this in the Sanguine Forest in years."

All the Astars came together now. Thirty-one of them slurped back into a single being.

"I am sure I am sane," the one Astar told them. "And I believe you are too. It is hard to believe, I know, but everything I told you is the truth. I am Astar, son of Amtor. Also, I am the recycled spirit of the Goddess Ehlona, heralded back to this world by the Star of Ehlona."

"The Star of Ehlona," Kilmer murmured under his breath, looking at Melvin. "I know your sign well. I was leading a search party in the Sanguine Forest when that star first shone. It was a very bad time. The star confused us. We became lost. Not all of us survived."

"Many people died because of that star," Melvin remembered. The others stood in silence.

"Well?" Astar finally said. "Are you going to invite me in?"

Darla answered him, "Please, won't you join us inside the castle? We would be honored if you stayed with us."

"Why, thank you." Astar bowed to Darla. "I would love to join you."

CASTLE ORLO

Kilmer's party had rigged the front doors of Castle Orlo to render them useless. They used the side of the castle, through a small hidden passage, as the main entryway. The oval-shaped passage was nothing more than a hole that had been punched through the stone and concealed by a curtain of vegetation.

Once inside, Astar looked over the interior of the castle. White staircases ascended on both sides of the entryway. Astar watched Melvin and Oaks work to reset the false gears affixed to the inside of the large double doors consisting of counterweights controlled by a wooden lever. This contraption provided an illusion, the sound of the doors opening, even though they were not. This provided an effective distraction to give Kilmer and his party time to slip through the concealed passage, come around behind an intruder, and complete the ambush. Just as they had with Astar.

"The gears were my idea," Oaks said. "Makes a lot of noise, but that's all it does."

"Effective." Astar nodded. "Sure fooled me."

"When we first arrived here," Kilmer said. "This whole area needed to be cleaned of the grime and blood."

"We have spent a lot of time cleaning this place," Darla said. "There is so much more to do, but we cleaned only enough for the small space we needed to live in."

"We only planned to be here a short time," Melvin said.

"Very glamorous having a whole castle to yourself," Astar remarked.

"Not this castle," Melvin said, after resetting the trap. "There's been too much death here."

Kilmer pointed to the stairway. "There used to be a lot of horrible artworks on the walls, I guess that's what you call them. Paintings of death and tragic events used to be here. But we removed those."

The stairs led to a common balcony overhead. The balcony led to four doors.

"All those go to the same place," Oaks said, pointing to the doors. "They lead to the grand auditorium. But we never go in there."

"Why not?" Astar asked.

"Too many bad things in there," Oaks replied.

"Yeah, lot of dead bodies still in there," Melvin added.

"I see," Astar remarked.

Kilmer led Astar under the archway and through a set of double doors until they came to an open room.

"This is the antechamber," Kilmer said with a flourish of his hands. "This is where we stay mostly."

"There are many rooms here in the castle." Darla helped Kory sit on a high-backed chair. "But we never intended to stay this long, and it is not safe to explore."

"So, you keep yourselves situated primarily here in this antechamber?" Astar said, looking over the place.

"We prefer to stay together," Oaks said. "It has been good for us so far."

Darla added to the subject, "We've put in a lot of work to clean this much of it."

"Gives us plenty of space," young Kory said.

"Yet ready to leave at a moment's notice." Kilmer came up and gave Kory's hair a tousle. "In case trouble comes looking for us, we have escape plans."

"How did you come to be here?" Astar asked. "How did you meet?"

"We were orphans," Darla said. "Well, except for Melvin."

"We do not need a lot of space anyway," Oaks told him. "We learned that at St. Ehlona's."

Astar approached Kory. "You have your father's hair, Kory, and your mother's good looks. What of you, Melvin? You were not an orphan?"

Melvin said, "That's right. I came from a good family. It was normal, well, as normal as it could it have been, I guess. My parents did what they could. We were poor. So, I joined the Red and Blue. Lately, I've been sort of an outcast. I've been shunned by them, hunted by the Red and Blue. I've kind of become an orphan too, of sorts."

Darla continued, "Melvin was a loyal soldier in the service of King Leopold. He and Kilmer went through a lot, and they developed strong loyal bonds for each other. Especially when they went into the Sanguine Forest to save Yori, King Leopold's First Archer. Yori had been captured and held captive right here in Castle Orlo. That mission nearly killed them both. Of course, all that was when the Zorn and Langula lived here."

"Melvin is an outlaw too. Just like the rest of us," Oaks told Astar. "He was the one that set Kilmer free, after Kilmer had been condemned to death. They wanted to hang him, but Melvin saved Kilmer's neck from the hangman's noose. For that, now Melvin has a death sentence on him. As we all do."

Kilmer added, "For freeing me, Melvin earned a first-class invitation to the gallows, to stretch his own neck in my noose."

Oaks continued, "My parents were killed by some kind of disease when I was just a baby. I grew up with Kilmer and Darla in St. Ehlona's Orphanage outside the village of Plum. We have all been fugitives of King Leopold's twisted justice ever since. All of us have a price on our heads for desertion and…and I don't know, what else?"

"Treason," Kilmer said in a low voice. "We are traitors to the crown, or so they say."

"Yeah, treason. But it all works out," Oaks said. "I get to be with Kilmer, Darla, and Melvin. I would rather be with them than with any of those ignoramuses in Leopold's Red and Blue."

"Me too, Oaks," Kory added. "Don't forget me too."

"Oh yeah, and little squirt here," Oaks said.

"Kory was named after our friend who was lost in Mauveguard Pass," Kilmer said. "Isn't that right, Kory?'

"Yeah," Kory said with a smile.

"Why are you here in Castle Orlo?" Astar asked. "If this place nearly killed you?"

Kilmer answered, "Because King Leopold ordered it forbidden. Didn't you see the sign? It's off-limits to come here. The Red and Blue once tried to burn the Sanguine Forest down, but they couldn't destroy it. And I just happened to know that the castle had been vacated. Its former occupants gone."

"You see, the Zorn is afraid of Kilmer's ghost," Melvin said. "Hollow Face shows Kilmer things. So, he knows the Demonic won't be back."

"So, for us," Oaks said, "it's safest place to be. It's the last place anyone would dare look for us."

Astar thought out loud for a moment. "Hazor, the Zorn?"

"You've heard of the Zorn?" Kilmer asked.

"Of course," Astar said. "He is my son."

"Your son?" Kilmer dipped his head and asked.

"Hazor was the Goddess's second son." Astar saw the incredulous stares. He laughed. "But that was me in my previous life. At least the spirit inside me. I know it's confusing, but...well, we are trying to work that out."

"Work it out?" Kilmer burst out laughing. "I have to be honest. I don't know what to make of you, Astar. I can tell there is something special and magical about you. That much is clear. I have seen you disappear and make copies of yourself. So, I know there is something incredible about you. But..."

"But you are not helping to convince us that you are sane," Melvin said with a chuckle.

Kilmer sat back in his chair. "These claims, the things you say... well...well, they are outlandish, hard to believe."

"Preposterous is more like it." Oaks also laughed.

"Oaks, don't be mean," Darla pleaded with them. "Astar, please, don't make any more copies of yourself! Just stay together as one person, okay?"

"You do have the magic," Kilmer said. "But to say the Zorn is your son. Why, you can't be a day over twenty, and Chen-Li is what? Over sixty?"

"Well, you do have me there. If it were not happening to me, I would not believe it either." Astar laughed with them. Their laughter ended in an awkward silence. Then, Astar leaned forward. "Kilmer, how long do you and your family intend to stay here in Castle Orlo?"

Kilmer said, "We do not have plans to leave. Why?"

"What would you do if the demons came back?" Astar asked.

"I don't believe they will because of the ghost, Hollow Face," Kilmer answered. "The ghost inhabited the Zorn's body, exposing a weakness he didn't know he had. The Zorn is anxious to avoid the ghost of Fortis Plum."

"What if King Leopold lifted the sanctions into the Sanguine?"

Kilmer said, "They are too scared to come here. It's haunted. Or so they think."

"Where would you go if Castle Orlo wasn't an option any longer?"

"On the run again, I suppose," Kilmer answered. "Why do you ask?"

Astar told him, "Listen to me carefully. I want you to make your way to the Temple of Valor. Things are happening very fast there that will render all this hiding unnecessary. But you have to make your way there."

"It is too dangerous for us. We cannot travel on the roads." Kilmer leaned closer to Astar. "We cannot be seen by Leopold's troops. If we are caught, we will hang."

"Make your way to the southern shore of the Endless Sea. I have spoken to the Nomads of Spiron. They will be expecting you," Astar said. "They are adept at smuggling. You will be safely hidden in their supply wagons. They can carry you northward, unseen along the roads. You will safely reach the Temple of Valor."

"Why would the Nomads of Spiron do that?" Kilmer asked. "They have not left their homeland on the southern coast of the Endless Sea for generations."

"You are a man of destiny," Astar said to Kilmer. "Events are in play once again. The spinning wheel is in motion. It is important you leave this place and get to the Temple of Valor. But don't take my word for it. If you don't believe me, ask him…Hollow Face."

"You can see him?" Kilmer asked, wide-eyed. "Only one other person has been able to see him. That was the Zorn himself."

"He's been standing there ever since I walked in." Astar pointed to the ghost looming over in the corner. He gave the ghost a friendly greeting nod. "Hello, Fortis."

The ghost slightly dipped his hood.

Astar continued, "Hollow Face knows what you should do. I am confident he will help guide you, first to the Nomads of Spiron, then on to the Temple of Valor. Chances are you have already seen visions—haven't you?"

"You are a mystery," Kilmer marveled at Astar. "Hollow Face acknowledged you."

"I am not fearful of the ghost the way the Zorn is," Astar said. "I have my own memories of Fortis Plum in his mortal life, when he was still in his physical body. You must understand, I *am* the spirit of the Goddess. I am not an equal to the Zorn but the procreator of him. While Fortis Plum can possess the Zorn's body, he could never possess mine. In spiritual terms, I outrank him, as one of the original three Gods, the embodiment of Ehlona."

Kilmer nodded to Astar. "I am sorry I doubted you."

"Well now that's settled." Astar rose from his chair. "I do want to thank you for your hospitality. It has been so nice to meet all of you. I so hate to cut our meeting short, but is there anything you need to take out of the castle before I destroy it?"

"Destroy...Castle Orlo?" Kilmer sat up and asked.

"This is the very reason I came."

SANGUINE FOREST

Moments later, Astar paced through the forest while the others followed. Carefully they stepped over, or walked around, the littered bones of the dead Zornastic priests. Hollow Face kept pace with them and floated alongside, not too far behind.

Soon, they walked a fair distance away from the castle. But as they went deeper into the forest, and away from the castle, the Vengeful

Spirits appeared again. Feeling the sweet warmth of living blood among them, the spirits began a cacophony of random screams. Their agony and despair were personified by the pained faces that materialized just under the surface of the orbs.

"Poor spirits." Astar watched them moving about. "I feel sorrow for them. Their torments must finally be at an end."

Kilmer spoke as they walked farther away from Castle Orlo and deeper into the foreboding trees. "Other than these Vengeful Spirits, this forest holds no magic anymore—no ruthless treachery of the Zorn, no more missing time or false direction or impossible landscapes. The hordes of insects are gone. No paralyzing fear anymore. Just these wicked trees, bleached bones, and the blue orbs of the pitiful Vengeful Spirits are all that is left."

"The threat of the forest is just a bad memory, only an illusion," Melvin said. "Ever since the Zorn and Langula's Demonic left this place. They were behind it all."

"They used the forest as their hunting ground, until there was nothing left to hunt. But these trees are nightmarish," Darla said, looking around. "Their dead branches seem to turn into menacing claws."

"No real harm really," Oaks added, looking at the trees. "But they sure are creepy."

"This should be far enough." Astar stopped. He turned toward the castle, then retrieved Soothsayer out of his belt. He lifted the golden blade high over his head. Then, his voice echoed through the Sanguine Forest. "Vengeful Spirits of the Zornastic Order! See the portal of your redemption! Come to Soothsayer, and you will find your reward of eternal rest! Come to me, all of you now!"

At first, nothing happened. Kilmer looked at Oaks. Oaks gave him a shrug back. But Melvin continued watching Astar with heightened interest. Hollow Face, who was there with Kilmer, continued to watch as well. But still, nothing seemed to be happening in the dark forest.

A single blue light came. Then a few more. Soon a steady stream of twenty, thirty, forty. The spirits circled his outstretched blade. Next, all the Vengeful Spirits came. Soon, their numbers swelled to several thousands. They flowed to him from everywhere, from every direction, out of the ground, up from the bones. They streamed out from the castle. Soon the entire surrounding area filled with blue spirits. They surrounded Astar, rotating in a funnel over him. The forest was bathed in blue by the orbs' collective light.

For the first time in decades, the true voices of the orbs rang out. They cried for their freedom, pleading with Astar for release from their eternal torments. These were the original voices of so many villagers, robbed of their own free will, before being taken by Langula as slaves. Their shouts echoed in the common tongue of the ordinary folks they were in life: the children, farmers, painters, builders, soldiers, and Nomads. These were not the oppressed voices they were commanded to be by their consumption of the Zorn's blood. These were prisoners of the Zornastic order, and they hungered to be free. They came to Astar screaming, moaning, crying, and laughing. They started chanting the only praise they knew, the ancient lyric.

Your days are gone never to return! Your days are gone never to return!

Only this time, the song had a different meaning. It was lifting them up in freedom. They were saying goodbye to their eternal torments.

They started circling down, absorbing into Astar's Blade. The blade sparked to life. It grew larger, gorging on the energy of the Vengeful Spirits. The orbs dissipated into Soothsayer like water running into a drain.

"Yes, that's it, that's it," Astar encouraged them. "Come to me, all of you! Power the blade to strike back in vengeance at your tormentors!"

They arrived faster now and entered the blade until the last of them had been absorbed. As the dagger fed upon them, it grew. It became as large as Astar's body. Just like the one still laying on Astar's chest, back where he lay asleep, back in the wagon heading to the Temple of Valor.

After all the spirits had been absorbed by Soothsayer, the Sanguine Forest darkened again. Except for Astar's Blade, which sparked with a lasting electricity. Astar held the massive sword out in front of him with one hand, as if it weighed nothing at all. Then his brow furrowed, and his face changed. It glowed with the collective anger of the Vengeful Spirits the blade had just absorbed. His stature was golden and shone with the supreme confidence that only a God could have.

Oaks could not help himself; he fell upon his knees. Darla embraced her son, Kory. Overwhelmed with emotion, Kilmer and Melvin stood speechless.

"Take cover behind the rocks," Astar turned to say. "There will be an explosion. Prepare yourselves for it."

Kilmer and the others quickly huddled behind boulders and trees, whatever they could. Even Hollow Face backed away.

"Now the vengeance I promised! Behold! Be the first to witness the power of Soothsayer!" Astar lowered the tip and pointed it toward Castle Orlo.

The sword responded. There was an audible rumble felt in the ground as the massive weapon pulsated and swelled. The great sword glowed releasing sparks of concentrated power. *Thoom!* The blade thundered with a blast of energy. Astar's form flashed in white blinding light as he hurled its power forward.

There was a massive eruption, as a great force struck Castle Orlo. The castle bulged for a moment, glowing between the cracks in bright whitish-yellow. The walls heaved as the entire castle exploded outward in a great fireball! The resulting shock wave ripped from the epicenter of the explosion. The ground rumbled beneath their feet.

The wicked trees swayed and bent. Some broke, others became uprooted and tumbled away. Other debris rocketed up, rocks, dirt, sticks, and bones. The force carried past Kilmer and the others as they shielded themselves.

When it was finished, and the explosive force diminished, Kilmer and company cautiously lifted their heads to see what had happened. Where Castle Orlo once stood, only a cratered hole remained.

"He destroyed Castle Orlo!" Kilmer exclaimed.

But soon after Kilmer said that, a rain of debris came peppering the landscape. Fragments of the castle started to fall out of the sky and back down to the ground. The party had to shield themselves with their arms over their heads.

"Blown right out of the forest!" Oaks shouted.

"The spirits got their revenge!" Melvin joined in.

"Back to the clouds where it came from!" Kilmer shouted.

The resulting plume of smoke, fire, and ash rose a mile high. The rolling cloud inverted back upon itself as it rose higher in the atmosphere. While it rose, lights of continued explosions rode up with it. Until, at last, the energy dissipated.

"Are they at peace now?" Darla asked about the Vengeful Spirits.

"Yes, their torments are over," Astar said. "They no longer suffer. They have been released from the curse that oppressed them."

"They are free." Darla embraced Kory tightly again.

And upon experiencing the power of Astar's Blade, Hollow Face faded out of existence.

Kilmer and the others crawled out from behind the cover of the stones. They assessed the condition of the forest. Many trees had been uprooted, especially near the epicenter. Yet many others bent but did not break, and otherwise seemed undamaged.

Astar lowered his arms. The massive sword was gone. He held Soothsayer in its minor form again. It had converted back to the size of the original golden dagger. Now he held just a small blade still smoldering in his hands.

The surviving trees reacted to the removal of their oppressive menace. For all their lives, the trees in the surrounding forest had long been denied a healthy existence. Even the plants, born from the blood of the Zorn's victims, suffered the malady of the curse. Now everything in the forest became free of the Zorn's influence.

As they all watched, the trees started to move. New growth began to form. The trees, once barren and menacing, lifted their branches. Green sprouts appeared and grew upward. New branches extended out to unfurl delicate leaves. New buds appeared and then burst forth in white foliage of the most spectacular round flowers. The entire forest began blooming. White petals fell and floated through the air, giving an illusion of snow.

Tender shoots of green grass thrust upward through the cursed soil. They pushed up soft and lush, swallowing up the dirty bones, carpeting the darkness and despair with new life. In the crater where Castle Orlo once stood, a spring of fresh water rose. A newly formed lake spilled over to form crystal-blue streams that reflected the light of the sun.

Kilmer, like all the rest of them, gaped in awe at the transformation. Everything was fresh and new. The oppressiveness was gone. Darla and Kory could not stop crying, smiling, and brimming with satisfaction, seeing how beautiful and healthy the Sanguine Forest flourished.

Putting his arms around his wife and child, Kilmer reflected, "This Astar is truly what he says he is. The recycled spirit of the Goddess Ehlona. The one foretold by the Star of Ehlona. This will be the era of Astar's Blade." Kilmer continued speaking so the rest could hear, "Astar is the new God of Beauty. Every step he takes, green branches blossom in white petals. We will do as he says. We will seek out the Nomads of Spiron. We will have them take us north to the Temple of Valor."

Astar smiled and tucked the golden dagger into his belt. Then, he walked through the beauty of a new Sanguine Forest. Everywhere he stepped blossomed with new life.

"Papa, what will happen to us there, at the Temple of Valor?" Young Kory looked up and asked his father.

"At the Temple of Valor? I am not sure, Kory," Kilmer said. "But if Astar says that is where we need to be, then that is where we will go."

Ran down to the mountain

Don't fall over the edge

Cause you know it's a razor

And it just stuck in my head

Excerpt from *The Witch's Songbook*

"It does not stink," she said and continued to
wipe away the blood and mucus.
— Excerpt from *Kilmer's Ghost* (Chapter 22)

WHAT LURKS IN THE DARK?

THE ROAD EAST

The wagon swayed over the bumps in the trail. The acolyte guided the horse along, as Aberfell sang a song.

> *The sinking of the ship,* Lusitania
> *Is setting in the sand on the ocean floor*
> *In gleaming beams of light, concealed from human sight*
> *A thousand feet straight down, five miles off the shore*
> *Every time you die, A hero is born*
> *Every night you lie awake, So far from your home*

Just then, the distant sound of a massive explosion interrupted Aberfell's singing.

"Whoa! Would you look at that!" Aberfell pointed behind him. The acolyte pulled the reins and stopped the wagon. Likewise, Amtor and Chen-Li turned their horses and stopped to watch.

First, there came a blinding flash. As the light faded, a rising column of flame and smoke grew larger and reached toward the sky.

"An impact?" Amtor said, gazing at the southern horizon.

"Perhaps. A very big explosion whatever it was," Valen said.

Amtor replied, "What else could have caused an explosion like that, other than a meteorite?"

"Looks to be just southeast of the Mauveguard Pass," Chen-Li said. "That is in the direction of the Sanguine Forest and Castle Orlo."

They watched the column billow up to form a white-and-gray cloud that eventually came apart in the upper wind shear.

Valen turned to ask, "Chen-Li, you've been to the Sanguine Forest before, haven't you?"

"A long time ago. Never want to go back either," Chen-Li said as the cloud drifted higher. He watched and reminisced, "Once, a young priest came to me. He wanted to parlay on behalf of his master. His name was Nantz. He was a young priest of the Zornastic Order. His master was the Zorn. After our parlay, the Zorn had no more use for the boy and tried to kill him by stopping his heart. What the Zorn did not realize is that I had given Nantz a glass of juice that had my blood in it. This inoculated the boy from the Zorn's power. That saved his life. At least for a while."

"I didn't think you could quit the Zorn's service..." Aberfell stopped short, realizing the implication. "Oh, sorry."

"Nantz did not quit the Zorn, Aberfell. He is dead," Chen-Li said.

Lady Valen looked at Aberfell as he spoke, "Chen-Li used Nantz to steal Soothsayer from the Zorn; and through Nantz, Amtor found Soothsayer and brought it out of the pit of death."

Amtor agreed, "Aye. If not for the help of my friend Kilmer, I would have died down in that pit. I would've joined Nantz, like he beckoned me to do in his skeletal form at the bottom of that deep hole. Poor lad. He made a lonesome ghost. Had Kilmer not saved me... I wonder where Kilmer is now. I heard he had become a lord of Odessa. Good for him!"

"Due in part to some adventure he had in the Sanguine Forest," Chen-Li said. "I know because my First Wives and I came to rescue him from a demon. A deadly attachment, a demonic possession, he received in the Zorn's castle, over where that explosion was."

"Soothsayer has taken a fortuitous route to be lying here on Astar's chest," Aberfell said.

"I don't see it as any great prize." Chen-Li gave Aberfell a stern look. "Many have paid an awful price for it."

"True," Aberfell said. "But here we are, on the road to the Temple of Valor, talking about Nantz. If not for the legend of Soothsayer, we never would have known the boy's name. So many have died at the hands of the Zorn, and we will never know their names. Such a common boy like Nantz, now his is a name worth knowing for the price he paid. He may have saved the world a lot of pain and misery disappearing with Soothsayer like he did. He guarded it with his life and kept it safe all these years."

"Aye, the Cosmic Creation does work in mysterious ways," Amtor said.

Lady Valen continued to look at Aberfell. "You have a strange way of looking at things, Supreme Historian. But I can't disagree with your romantic logic."

Chen-Li said, "I sense the Zorn still lives. He was unhurt by the explosion. He will still spread his sickness and his madness to all humanity. Nothing has changed. Nothing ever changes."

The acolyte snapped the reins on the backs of the horses. The wagon started to move again. It rolled down the road leading them to the Temple of Valor.

"How easily he can sleep," Chen-Li said. Astar had covered himself with his emerald cloak. The massive golden sword Soothsayer lay upon his chest. "I have not slept that peacefully in years."

"He has slept nearly the entire way." Lady Valen watched over Astar. Then she tilted her head. "Strange."

"What is it, my lady?" Amtor asked.

"I feel a rush of spiritual energy, the presence of many, many spirits," Lady Valen said. "I have never felt anything like it before. Something has happened."

"Many may have died in that explosion," Amtor said.

"No, this feeling is not death, but a release, somehow," Lady Valen said. "It's like..."

As Valen spoke, Astar woke up and wiped the sleep from his eyes. "What you are feeling are the souls of the Vengeful Spirits. I have released them. The Sanguine Forest has been cleansed. Castle Orlo has been destroyed."

"Did you say Castle Orlo has been destroyed?" Chen-Li asked. The party stopped again. All gathered around Astar in the back of the wagon.

"I destroyed it with Soothsayer," Astar said, looking in the direction of what was left of the explosive cloud. "I have just begun purifying this generation for the new era."

"New era?" Chen-Li asked.

"The first era was the era of the Gods," Aberfell interjected his knowledge. "That era died with the Goddess Ehlona. The second era was marked by you, Chen-Li, and Hazor, the sons of the Gods."

"This is a mystery to me. I do not know of any other era." Chen-Li noticed the distant smoke of the explosion was nearly gone, dissipating into the clear blue sky. "I am unaware—was another era foretold?"

"You would not have known, Chen-Li. No one would have," Astar answered. "The Star of Ehlona was more than a sign of the Goddess's return. It also was the start of another era to come. A third one. An era for the common mortal. They will inherit this world as we will leave it."

"An era for the mortals?" Lady Valen said, reflecting her thoughts out loud.

Astar continued, "These times, the changes, all these conflicts, these were all birthing pains. Everything is being resolved."

Amtor searched the path that lay in front of them. Up ahead, he saw a new sight. "Look! The Oracle Mount lies in the distance. See? Up ahead there, you can see the Temple of Valor. We are getting close."

"Astar?" Lady Valen quietly spoke. "Are you fully with us now? Is this the single form of yourself? Or do you remain copied and divided elsewhere out there?"

"It doesn't much matter now, my lady. Any part of me is still a part of the whole. But to answer your question, I am certainly still out there in more places than one. I will be from now on. I need to be in many places, restoring the balance in one of many forms." Astar turned away from Lady Valen as he looked at Amtor. "I found Gensen and Micah and reunited them."

Amtor rode up beside him. "You found them? Where? Did they make their way out of the underground?"

"Maybe we can help them," Aberfell said.

"Gensen and Micah came out of the tunnels and are at the southern shore of the Endless Sea," Astar said. "They needed help, so I sent Kilmer to them. What a joy it was to meet Kilmer, the man who saved your life!"

"Kilmer?" Amtor asked. "By the Gods! I haven't seen his face in twenty years."

"Kilmer and his party were the outlaws holed up in the Castle Orlo," Astar said.

"Incredible!" Aberfell said with a nod. "Very clever hiding place."

Astar continued, "They are coming with the Nomads of Spiron, who are traveling this way to escape the wrath of the Demonic. They will be at the Temple of Valor in about two days. You will see then. But I must warn you—Micah has changed. He has been turned."

"Turned?" Amtor questioned. "Turned how?"

"I hope that does not mean what I think it means," Aberfell said.

"Is he alive?" Amtor asked. "What do you mean...turned?"

"He is...alive as he can be," Astar replied. "He has been bitten with a powerful serpent's venom...from Langula. He has turned very pale in appearance, and...well, I don't know if he will ever be the same."

"Undead. He is what they call the undead." Aberfell gave Astar a nod of understanding. "At least, that is what I've heard a condition like that has been called. He lives, though his body is actually dead."

"Not Micah," Amtor said, reflecting on the words. "What about Gensen? Is he undead too?"

"No, he's exhausted, but not undead." Astar looked to all of them. "From now on, I must warn you, all of you. Everything is in motion now. From this point on, everything will be rapidly changing."

"Everything," Astar said, looking at Chen-Li. "I hope you're ready for it."

Chen-Li looked away. "I'll go with you to return Lady Valen to the Temple of Valor. But soon after, I need to get back up to my temple. I need to get back and bury my dead."

Astar leaned over and whispered to Valen, "Everything will need to be changed."

Later that evening, the wagon rolled over the top of the last hill. In the dim light of a quarter moon the Temple of Valor came into full view with its marbled archways and glistening bronze pillars. A long and sprawling valley of grassland lay in between the riders and the Oracle Mount. Riding down the ridge, they saw plumes of smoke rising from a number of campfires in the fields. Multitudes of people were already there camping out. They huddled together on the surrounding grounds, awaiting their turn to be escorted inside.

Chen-Li and Amtor galloped ahead of the wagon. The two were riding down the ridge, when they came to a stop. Abruptly, both tensed in their saddles.

"Something's wrong here," Chen-Li said, scanning the fields.

"Aye, you're right, Chen-Li," Amtor said. His battle senses tingling, alerting him to some unsuspecting danger. "Dark shapes seem to be lurking in the dark."

"They move too rapidly for just the sick and infirmed," said Chen-Li.

Aberfell picked up on it too. He quickly told the acolyte to stop the wagon. He reined in the horses, pulling them to a stop. As the dust settled, the acolyte reached down and applied the hand brake.

Aberfell jumped from the wagon. Likewise, out ahead in the dim light, Chen-Li and Amtor had dismounted their horses.

"Listen," Chen-Li said, squatting low in the high grass. They heard growling. The sounds of beasts accompanied by distant screams and shouts for help. "You hear that?"

"Going to be some trouble." Amtor pulled out his battle-ax. Astar, Valen, and the acolytes disembarked from the wagon. "Be on guard, all of you! Beasts are lurking in the dark among the wounded."

Chen-Li cautiously approached the first of the bonfires. The eerie light of the fire revealed an awful sight. The dark shapes were not beasts at all, but people acting like beasts, viciously tearing, ripping, and eating other human flesh. The sickness had evolved into cannibalistic insanity. Those infected with the madness were attacking the noninfected. People were feeding on the flesh of other people.

"By the Gods! What is this?" Amtor said. "Dark magic has befallen the Temple of Valor!"

Astar ran up to look for himself. After seeing the horrific sight, he swung the massive sword from behind his back and donned the hood of his emerald cloak. The others—Valen, Aberfell, and the acolytes—came running up behind. The rustling noise the party made as they maneuvered together gave away their positions to the infected and the mad.

The cannibals stopped their attacks on the hapless sick, and with only a moment's hesitation, they made eye contact with the party. Like a pack of wild animals, a frenzied mob rushed up the hill to attack these new trespassers. In a fit of delirious rage, the first of many cannibals reached the party.

Chen-Li sprang into action. He moved in a blur of rapid motion, punching, kicking, and spinning with overwhelming leverage and force. He sent the first one flying backward. Then two more with a sweep of his leg. Then three of the cannibals tumbled down the hill in a combination. Chen-Li quickly moved back. He had punched and kicked over and over, neutralizing the closest of the attackers. Yet more came. Cannibals ran up the hill like beasts, faster than he could dispatch them. Even those he knocked down the hill recovered quickly and did not stay down for long. Before long, they were wildly scrambling back to their feet and up the hill for another attack.

Amtor lunged forward next. His long-handled battle-ax cleaved into the rushing throng with a wide and lethal arc. He severed the heads off the first few attackers. Amtor turned, sweeping in a circle, he swung his battle-ax through the chests of the next few. Using the sole of his boot to eject them away, he quickly turned in another smooth arc and buried his blade deep into the head of one of the cannibals. With one still stuck to his axe, Amtor swung him around and used him like a human hammer, taking out an entire group of attackers. They tumbled away down the hill.

"Don't hurt them!" Valen pleaded, passing one of the dead men. "They do not realize what they are doing!"

Despite her pleas, more of the attackers flanked them, and Amtor did not know how to make causal war. More of the savages fell to his battle-ax. Even Lady Valen had to concede lethal force was necessary.

Astar jumped into the fray. He swung his golden sword, relieving a man's head from his neck. Astar wielded the massive Soothsayer as easily as slicing through the wind. With each kill, Soothsayer absorbed more of the spiritual energy of the dead. The blade sparked electrically as it fed on the souls dispatched.

A severed head rolled down the hill, past some more campfires. As it rolled, it alerted more of the cannibals, and they reacted. Setting their gaze on the battling newcomers, they rushed to join the growing mob.

"This is getting out of control," Aberfell said and rushed to Lady Valen's side.

Lady Valen used her power to pulse a ring of energy around the party that strengthened and protected them. Then, she shouted, "Run for the Temple of Valor!"

Aberfell repeatedly called out to the others, "Make a break for the temple! Come on!"

The party started to run, down the hill, and through the underbrush. They ran across the valley, until they reached the gentle upward slope of the Oracle Mount. Scrambling up the hill, they ran toward the temple's archways, toward the light of the fire braziers.

But one of the creatures caught Aberfell from behind. The Supreme Historian was pulled off his feet and flung backward. He landed on his back with one of the attackers upon him. Aberfell struggled with the snarling man made wild in madness. He stretched his arms out in defense, trying to keep his hands away from the snapping bite.

Together, the two rolled back down the hill, until they finally came to rest in a cloud of dust. Aberfell held the seething, frothing killer at bay as best he could. But the madness made the attacker beast-like, ten times stronger than a normal man. Other cannibals came now, pouncing on Aberfell. They huddled over him, with snarling, gaping mouths, lowering themselves down toward the Supreme Historian.

A thick spray of warm blood splashed on Aberfell's face. Amtor had come back to save Aberfell. His battle-ax quickly dispatched them. As it cleaved the head off one, the headless body slumped forward to leak blood all over poor Aberfell. Chen-Li followed and struck, removing more of the attacking cannibals from the Supreme Historian. Amtor lifted Aberfell off the ground by his collar and got him up and running toward the Temple of Valor again. Amtor and Chen-Li kept up behind him, guarding the rear as Aberfell scrambled for his life. Giving up on the party after they had reached the confines of the temple, the ravenous mob lumbered away, toward the less protected camps.

Valen and Astar entered the temple at the same time. None of the acolytes nor the people inside had been infected by the insanity.

"This is a blessed place—the madness cannot reach us in here," Lady Valen said as they reached out to help the others.

"We may be free from the madness, but we are not free from the fear," the acolytes said. "We have been surrounded."

"Stay here in the temple where we are protected by the Goddess Ehlona's power," Valen said. As she watched, the mindless cannibals could only wander up to the archways but could not enter. An invisible barrier of the Goddess's blessing prevented them from going any farther.

Amtor and Chen-Li helped Aberfell into the temple. The mob that pursued them could not follow inside. Eventually, they turned and shambled away to find others to terrorize.

"Those poor souls!" Valen exclaimed, knowing those outside had no protection and were too sick to defend themselves. "There is nothing but death all around us."

"Aberfell? You carry no weapon?" Amtor asked him. "Bad idea. Especially when a cannibalistic mob pulls you down from behind. You either need a weapon or learn to run faster."

"I am not a fighter. I am only a watcher." Aberfell huffed for air after running up the Oracle Mount.

"A watcher?" Amtor said, shaking his head incredulously. "Well, that's the damnedest thing I ever heard of, and an occupation with all the intrigue of a short life span."

"Welcome back, Lady Valen."

A flurry of reports started coming from the acolytes, describing the first Demonic attacks and the murders of the sick on the Oracle Mount. Then the sad report came of the murder of Tyla and Myra. Their necks were slit by Langula. Chen-Li listened intently, as the acolytes described it.

"Demon attacks!"

"Vicious! Merciless!"

"Langula's claws cut their throats!"

Chen-Li's rage burned hearing the details. He became very sullen afterward and he would not engage in conversation with anyone. Something in him seemed to have snapped.

"Good heavens!" Aberfell shouted, pointing up the hill. "Our horses!"

A mob of infected madmen attacked their horses. In their insanity, they wrestled the horses down to the ground, then the mob proceeded to slash and eat them.

"Outrageous!" Amtor said. "This is madness!"

"This is the Zorn's doing," Astar told them. "Who else? He is underground using the rock caverns as an amplifier to multiply the force of his spells. This is how he spreads this madness."

Aberfell asked, "How do you know this is the Zorn's doing?"

"I spoke to him," Astar said. "I was there with him while I was here with you."

Aberfell didn't know what to say. "You are more powerful than I ever could have imagined."

At just that moment, Amtor cried out and pointed to the horizon. "Look, there beyond the ridge. Kicking up dust. An army approaches."

"You sure that's an army?" Aberfell asked.

"A familiar sight for me, Aberfell. I've seen many armies," Amtor said. "This is a legion of fighting men. Their feet are kicking up dust as they march through the dirt. There's no mistaking it. An army of men and horses, coming from the west. It could only be the Red and Blue, King Leopold's army. If it is, it's going to take a lot more than a bunch of crazy sleepwalkers to stop them. They will not be as kind to the insanity of these people and show them the mercy we just did."

"Let them come," Astar told them. "The final act is about to begin."

I see the rain

It's coming tonight

Stab me in the back with all your might.

Excerpt from *The Witch's Songbook*

The patrol deliberately stayed on the hilltop silhouetting
themselves as to be more detectable.
— Excerpt from *Kilmer's Ghost* (Chapter 23)

THE HEART OF THE MATTER

DEEP UNDERGROUND

Langula reluctantly entered the Zorn's lair with bad news to tell. Once again, Monticello held the torch for her and led the way. In the moth-filled cavern, the moths reacted when the demons entered, filling the room with darting movements.

Langula searched the place where the Zorn had previously been. But he was not there. All she found was the continuous drip of water into milky white pools.

Drip! Drippity-drip!

He had already broken out of the multicolored stalagmite, leaving only a man-shaped impression on the wall. He sat, greenish skull resting in bony hands. In the darkness, head down, he appeared to be deep in thought.

"Master Zorn?" Langula addressed him in a whisper. "Something has happened."

The Zorn did not acknowledge her.

"There has been a shocking development—" Langula said, as the Zorn interrupted her.

"Do you remember, Langula? How our Zornastic Order used to gather together in our dungeons? How they looked wearing their black robes? And how they used to speak in a single voice? They used to bring sacrifices, offerings of blood to me. That doesn't seem like it was that long ago, but it was so very long ago. I know why you are here."

Langula and Monticello stood in silence.

"Castle Orlo has been destroyed." The Zorn took another deep breath. "The castle of my father. I knew it immediately. I could *feel* it! It disrupted my blood...as soon as it was gone."

"Your beautiful castle, our home, gone." Langula shook her head. "Obliterated. But by what I do not know."

"Astar came to me," the Zorn announced.

"He did? When, where?" Monticello asked.

"Walked right into this very chamber, right here into my lair," the Zorn said.

Langula asked, "Did he say anything?"

Monticello asked, "You didn't kill him?"

"You *still* do not understand, do you?" the Zorn raised his voice. "The boy can stop time. He can take multiple forms. Be in many places at once. He has been learning to walk among us. He has been down here with us before. He can do whatever he wants."

"What did he want to do with you, then?" Monticello asked.

The Zorn looked away. He reflected and sighed. "He wanted to apologize."

"Apologize?" Langula asked. "For what?"

The Zorn continued, "He stood right there in front of me and while he said he was sorry, at the same time, he was also in the Sanguine Forest destroying my castle. Can't you see? He was doing both at the same time!"

Langula creased her forehead. "He apologized for your castle?"

"No, not that." The Zorn was getting flustered. "He apologized for withholding love, in my formative years. He apologized for the scorn he caused me when the soul that is inside him was the Goddess Ehlona. Astar is merely reacting to memories he's, no doubt, been reliving from his former life. He told me that I deserved better. That I deserved to have been loved. That is what he said at least. That is what he claimed he was sorry for."

The Zorn started to laugh, slowly at first. Then his laugh started to grow until it was echoing through the chamber. "And while he was telling me all this, he was busy destroying my castle!"

Langula and Monticello did not find it funny at all.

The Zorn continued to laugh uproariously. "Oh! The marvelous treachery of this boy! He really knows what he is doing. He knows just what to say. Oh, this Astar! He is something completely different and fresh. This recycled version of the Goddess Ehlona, this one is going to be legendary! He is already so much more accomplished than that drab Chen-Li; he was always so boring and predictable. But this Astar—he is really, really good."

"Sounds like he impressed you," Monticello said.

"He truly did." The Zorn stood now. "He is as powerful as he is clever. Two beautiful qualities, a very dangerous combination. He holds Soothsayer, and he can wield it too. He has fed the blade and it has grown. By destroying Castle Orlo, he is demonstrating what he can do, he is communicating with us on a new level, on a grand scale. And I must admit, he is compelling and infinitely entertaining."

Finally, the Zorn turned to look at them. He studied their faces with jittery yellow eyes. "Was there anything else?"

Monticello addressed him now: "The Nomads of Spiron have not met their monthly obligation to provide an adequate sacrifice for the Demonic feast."

"That's nothing to me!" The Zorn guffawed, stood up, and walked away. "That was entirely your deal, Monticello. You handle it. I have more important matters to attend to."

Monticello said nothing, only bowed in capitulation.

The Zorn questioned Langula, "Where are Frost and Grim?"

"Frost is with King Leopold. As Brother Barker, he has successfully influenced Leopold. He is leading the siege upon the Temple of Valor," Langula answered. "They will draw out the enemy of the White Eminence. Then we will launch an attack upon the Temple of Chen-Li. I will see to it, personally."

"Frost has accomplished much in a short amount of time," the Zorn said.

Monticello saw an opportunity. "Of course, he could not have done it without my help of sending in the Devourers to Castle Odessa to destroy the Green."

"Without your help?" The Zorn laughed. "Remember, the Devourers belong to me. I evolved them from my Rock Larvae. Frost's plan is working because I have been wearing down the sensibilities of these mortals. It is because of the sickness I have spread. They are afraid of their own shadows now. The frustration among them is high. They are pointing their fingers, blaming each other for their devastation. Do not get yourselves distracted. The goal is *not* the Temple of Valor. The goal is to collect a blood payment for destroying Castle Orlo. Everything else is merely…a means to that end. Now, where is Grim?"

"We don't know where Grim is," Langula said. "He is missing."

"How can one of our own be missing?" the Zorn asked. "Can we not use the blood connection? Does he still live? Has he been destroyed?"

"No, I don't think so, that's not it." Langula's face contorted into a look of pain. "Something is interfering with our blood connection."

"Interfering with your blood connection?" The Zorn thought about that for a moment. "Remind me, what blood was used to incubate Grim?"

Langula said, "We used the blood of Kilmer."

"Of course! Why did I not think of that before?" The Zorn paced among the stalagmites. "Why did I not see this sooner? The blood with the Plum family curse? Could it be that the ghost of Fortis Plum has been here watching us the entire time through Grim? We can only assume so, we must. So, in order to rid ourselves of this accursed Fortis Plum spying on us, Grim must be destroyed."

"You mean to kill Grim?" Langula asked with considerable shock. "You can't, and I could not possibly kill my own son."

"We have to, my darling, it's the only way." The Zorn kissed her. "We must not allow Kilmer's ghost to live."

Langula was unmoved. "On the same day you lose your castle, and the spirit of your mother apologizes, you want to kill one of our own?"

"Ah, irony, yes," the Zorn realized without much care. "It's as treacherous as you are."

"What shall we do?" Monticello asked.

The Zorn thought about it. "Let current events unfold. Watch and wait for opportunities."

"What are you going to do, Zorn?" Langula asked.

"It might be time for the Skeletal King to ride into the world again," the Zorn said.

"Did Astar say anything else while he was here?" Langula asked.

"Nothing else that matters," the Zorn said, leaning over a water puddle, looking at his reflection in its surface.

Langula and Monticello turned to go, and left the Zorn distracted by his reflection.

Langula whispered to Monticello, "Did you see that, Monticello? He looked at his reflection. After all these years? He has not done that in many years."

Monticello said, "There is something he is not telling us."

TEMPLE OF VALOR

"What are they doing out there?" Aberfell asked, watching the army upon the distant ridge. Across the valley, King Leopold's Red and Blue, some fifty thousand of them, had taken positions overlooking the Oracle Mount.

"They're laying siege," Amtor said, staring up at the ridge. "They will soon surround us."

Aberfell asked, "Why would they lay siege to the Temple of Valor? This is a place to heal the sick. It is no threat to them."

"Holds no strategic value either," Amtor added.

"Do you think they are doing this because they know we are here?" Aberfell said.

"My guess is, not you, but me." Chen-Li had been sitting unseen in the shadows. Now he rose and spoke to them. "My spies tell me Leopold's receiving bad council. He is blaming the attack upon the Temple of Valor on the White Eminence. The king has blamed me for the attack that collapsed the Green. I am blamed for the sickness and the madness too. The Red and Blue hope to draw the White Eminence out into the open. They have no hope of attacking my temple directly. So, they hold a knife to the throat of the Temple of Valor. If the White Eminence does not come down from the Temple of Chen-Li to meet the Red and Blue on the field of battle, they will cut the throat of Lady Valen and destroy the Temple of Valor."

Amtor looked back inside the temple at Lady Valen. "Since getting back here, she has been making up for lost time," Amtor said. "She has been healing as fast and as many people as she can."

"She is an emotive healer," Chen-Li told them. "She can feel and experience the pain of others. In doing so, she can heal their maladies."

"That would have to be a terrible power," Aberfell said, looking at her.

They all looked at her now. Valen was healing an old lady, inserting her hand in the old lady's chest.

"All this death is especially hard on her. Especially after we had to kill several of those sickened people," Chen-Li continued. "She suffers tremendously in her emotive state."

"All these sickened people," Amtor said. "They only came here for a chance to see her. All they wanted was a chance for her healing touch. Not to become victims again."

Chen-Li sympathized, "The Zorn and his infernal sickness. These people were helpless, defenseless. The madness changed them into animals that attacked us last night."

"Is there no place safe anymore?" Aberfell asked. "What is to happen to Lady Valen? I fear it is too much for her. She is in over her head."

Lady Valen kissed the old woman and smiled. The old lady regained enough strength to stand. With her heart repaired, she would live on years longer.

Astar went to Valen. Soothsayer was in its massive form on the back of his emerald cloak.

"There's a hole in my heart, Astar. So many have died, and I blame myself," she said. "If I would have stayed, none of this might have happened, and many more would be alive today. I will always blame myself."

"Lady Valen," Astar said. "This is not your fault."

"I feel I could have prevented it," she said. "Had I not answered the pull of the Goddess."

"But then we never would have come together," Astar said, putting his arm around her. "Have you ever thought the demons might have killed you in their attack? It was you they were after. The pull of the Mother Goddess saved your life. And in saving your life, saved the lives of the many you can still help today."

She touched his face. "Astar, memories of Gilglad have been flooding back to me. I remember sitting in your room when you were a baby. I used to listen to your breathing. A feeling used to come over me. It was peace. A deep sense of overwhelming love. As I listened to you breathe, you would emit an emerald light around you that poured over me, all around me. I would be in the spirit of love from the Goddess Ehlona's healing. The connection between us was so powerful."

"I remember too. I also have memories of being Ehlona. Are these memories not our own?" Astar asked.

"We are reliving the lives of the past," Valen said. "We are being shown the events of what has happened before. It took me fourteen years to know that I even had another life with you. Fourteen years! To remember that before I became Valen, I was first Gilglad. Your mother and wife of Amtor. I was Gilglad. How could I have forgotten such a thing? My memories were pushed aside, out of my mind. I am so sorry that I forgot you and Amtor. You did not deserve that."

"Come now, what's done is done, Lady Valen." Astar gave her a sweet smile. "For all her life, Ehlona wanted to go back in time and fix what she had done. But despite all her powers, she could never do it, and neither can I. Neither can you."

Valen said, "I think it is so we don't make the same mistakes over again."

Astar and Valen embraced and when they came together a great energy crackled from them. An emerald wave rippled through the entire Temple of Valor. The palms, the reeds, the incense smoke, everything bent toward them. The acolytes saw it and fell upon their knees extending their hands to them. The glow captured the attention of the others, Chen-Li, Aberfell, and Amtor, all basking in the feeling. The healing wave went beyond the temple in a jolt. It raced outward, reaching the sick outside on the grounds. For the time being, the madness stopped.

"Look at all these people," Valen said. "If only we could help more of them."

"I will, as best as I can," Astar said. He multiplied himself rapidly with a series of pops and appeared everywhere inside the temple and outside on the grounds. Having created copies of himself, Astar began to help the sick and wounded.

Valen told her shocked acolytes, "Remember well what you see here, for it will not be here forever. Now, take me to those most in need."

Chen-Li stepped through the masses of people. Everywhere he looked, Astars were kneeling by the sick, carrying the wounded, and handing out supplies. All of them wore the green cloak without the massive golden sword.

But there was one that did possess Soothsayer, and this one stepped through the others to speak to Chen-Li. "You are leaving us?"

"I must go to the Temple of Chen-Li," he said. "I have been gone too long and there are many things to do."

"What will you do now?" Astar asked. Then he pointed toward the overlooking ridge. "And what about them?"

"First, I will bury my First Wives." Chen-Li nodded. "After that, I will inspect my forces for battle."

"The Zorn is setting a trap for you, you know?" Astar said. "He wants to draw you out. He is trying to provoke you away from your stronghold."

"When the time comes"—Chen-Li put his hand on Astar's shoulder—"be prepared to use that blade. I'm afraid we are going to need it, and need you too, Astar. What do I intend to do? I intend to exact a payment for what he has done to Tyla and Myra. They will be avenged…in blood, and more than blood."

"May I walk with you?" Astar asked. Then turned to look at all of the copies of himself working. "I think I have things in control here."

They walked among the sick and the multiple Astars moving about. The two walked past the rest of the camp. Several sick people on the farthest outskirts of the Oracle Mount raised their hands to plead for their assistance. As the pair encountered such people, an additional form of Astar would peel off into being, stop, bend down, and offer what help he could provide.

"Now that we are away from the others…" Chen-Li looked back. They had strolled far away from everyone else. "Can you tell me what is going to happen?"

"There is never a certainty. The threads change all the time, but if the current path remains as it is now—"

"Yes, please tell me," Chen-Li said.

"The destruction of your temple."

"Destroy the Temple of Chen-Li?" he repeated in shock.

"The Zorn lacks the power," Astar told him. "So, it will have to be me. *I* will destroy the temple."

Shocked, and without a word, Chen-Li turned away. He turned to look at Astar once more before he lifted into the air. Rising, he left Astar to grow smaller down on the ground. The power of the magic feather the witch gave him long ago lifted him as lightly as the wind.

Approaching the Temple of Chen-Li—the fluted white columns, the polished marble floors, the angled ceiling—he studied it, as if for the first time. The temple was solid, well-constructed, built into the very foundations of the mountain itself. How could what Astar told him be the truth?

Higher up the mountain, he started thinking about the Green and its destruction. The Green was where King Leopold once presented him, and the First Wives, with the golden plaque pledging friendship between them. But now the Green was destroyed, and King Leopold blamed him for it.

Could it be everything he could see would soon be rubble? Chen-Li thought back on what Astar had said. *If the current path remains as it is now.* Could he change destiny? Would there be some way to reverse the threads?

Over the walls of the temple, he came down to a gentle landing in the courtyard. A crowd of priests had been keeping watch for him from a distance. They knew he was approaching and had anxiously waited for him.

"Body and soul!" the White Eminence saluted.

Watching his people gather in the courtyard, in white garments, gave him a chill. A feeling passed through him, a very fulfilling one.

But then, Chen-Li was startled by another's presence, not one of his priests. Of all the people waiting to welcome him home, one single person, standing among them, shocked him the most. It was Astar! He had been there waiting for him ever since Chen-Li lifted and left him back on the ground. Here he was again! Had he just arrived, or had he been there for some time?

The destroyer of the temple? Chen-Li thought. As for Astar, he cheerfully waved at Chen-Li, welcoming him back home with a big smile on his face.

For the first time in his life, Chen-Li felt powerless in the presence of this Astar and his powerful new magic. Chen-Li wondered if anything could stop what was about to happen.

In the meantime, the crowd gathered there insisted on hearing from their master. Chen-Li glided up to the top of a stone pillar, lifting above the crowd, so all could see him.

"White Eminence, I thank you for the warm welcome. My heart rejoices to be rejoined with you again. And to Astar, I say this—welcome to the Temple of Chen-Li."

Chen-Li watched Astar with a sense of dread, as the boy smiled cheerfully under the emerald cloak and waved as if he did not have a care in the world.

I should've been gone you know
I had a feeling that came real slow
It didn't take long for her to go
Feeling inside

Excerpt from *The Witch's Songbook*

This was no ordinary man.
His strength, his speed, and his power
were not possible for something human.
— Excerpt from *Kilmer's Ghost* (Chapter 24)

WATCHING THE FLEETING SPIRITS

ORACLE MOUNT

The catapults were positioned high on the ridge overlooking the Temple of Valor. The fighting men of the Red and Blue waited, tired and dirty from sleeping in the mud.

Over the past few days, there had been some skirmishes with the mad cannibalistic savages who had incurred the sickness. In their madness, they would run headlong into the soldiers attacking them. When the soldiers saw them coming, they could dispatch them easily. But occasionally, an attack would come when the men least expected it and did not see it coming. In those cases, there were injuries, and some soldiers were killed.

Then the numbers of fatalities started to grow worse as the sickness turned to the very soldiers themselves. At night, random screams would disrupt the quiet. Through the night, none of them could sleep, as the soldiers started to attack each other. Infected civilians as well as soldiers could only be put down by the sword.

Lord Rhodes watched Brother Barker. The priest moved from tent to tent. Brother Barker darted into one tent, emerged to give orders, then went into another. Inside, he sent more orders in private, sealing them with his signet ring into red wax.

King Leopold's tent was situated on the highest point on the ridge to give him access to the best view of the valley below. As Rhodes watched, he never saw Barker speak directly with the king. Actually, Rhodes had not seen King Leopold at all since the siege started. Yet his orders kept coming through, by way of Brother Barker, and always without any consultation from either Lord Rhodes or Lord Whitney.

Lord Whitney saw to it that supplies kept coming from Castle Odessa. With Whitney in charge of logistics, the transport wagons reliably came and went. They routinely came back and forth all day long carrying food and supplies to the army. As the transports went back to Odessa, so did the casualties, along with stacks of dead bodies.

Whitney also supplied the Temple of Valor. Leopold, through a reluctant Brother Barker, agreed to supply them to keep up the appearance of protection. When supplies came in from Odessa, they were moved to smaller wagons, and transported down to Lady Valen.

Lord Whitney always sent a letter with the supplies:

Compliments of King Leopold.

Lord Whitney wanted to say more, but he was not making the decisions. He did not know what to tell them anyway. He didn't comprehend the purpose of this siege, why they were here, or how it would end. Questions everybody wanted to know, but nobody had any answers.

"This siege is getting us nowhere," Lord Whitney said to Lord Rhodes. "Every day on this ridge we incur more and more casualties with no discernable progress and no clearly defined objective."

Lord Rhodes replied, "This is not the type of military action I have come to expect from King Leopold. He is not the king I have come to know and respect. The only thing that seems to be working are the supply transports, and those are under your oversight, Lord Whitney."

"This is not like King Leopold at all," Lord Whitney agreed. "This is of the influence of Brother Barker. There's one thing I don't understand."

"What is that?"

"Is Barker this incompetent, or does he know exactly what he is doing?"

"What would he have to gain to put us in this position?" Lord Rhodes asked.

"Now, that is the question, isn't it, Lord Rhodes? Look at him up there."

They watched Brother Barker come out of a tent. As they watched, King Leopold came out of the tent next. He had a chair with him and was taking it out to the ridge. There, the king sat looking overlooking the valley to the Temple of Valor. Brother Barker continued barking orders to the men.

Rhodes commented, "Looks like Brother Barker is the only one doing the talking."

"You expressed it well, Lord Rhodes. This is not the King Leopold we have come to know. Stay alert, Rhodes. At some point, I may need to take some risks. That's all I have to say about that for now. But when the time comes, I could certainly use your help."

Lord Rhodes looked at Whitney. "You'll have it."

Later that night, Rhodes watched Brother Barker mount a horse. Then the priest rode away from the top of the ridge. As Barker rode down the ridge and out of sight alone, Rhodes saw his chance to speak to the king.

That morning it had snowed, and the ground was frozen. By evening his boots squished through mud, heavy and thick. The temperature was dropping again, and his breath turned to vapor in the cold. He walked across the flanks of his line. Stopping occasionally to talk to his men, he kept one eye on the king and another looking for the return of Brother Barker. Eventually he reached the farthest point of his left flank, and Rhodes looked beyond to the king's headquarters.

The king sat ahead on a slight lift of the ridge. Leopold kept himself to a simple tent. The only thing that set it apart was a red-and-blue flag that waved on its highest pinnacle. The area around the king was heavily patrolled by his elite force who constantly guarded him. Rhodes decided to continue anyway.

He struggled through the ruts of mud, until the rise of the hill gave way to some better footing. Here the path was less worn. He moved from mud to the grass, flatly worn, yellow, and slippery.

As Rhodes approached, he was quite aware of being watched by many eyes. Two elite guards approached him. Their hands rested casually on their swords, but that could change at a moment's notice. Behind the two approaching guards, there were four more, who watched with interest as they halted Rhodes.

"I'm here to speak with the king," Lord Rhodes said.

The guards recognized him. "Lord Rhodes, one moment please, sir."

Being recognized could be a good thing, Rhodes thought, *or a bad one.*

One of the soldiers produced a little book. He searched the pages but came up empty.

"Did you make an appointment, sir? Have you gone through Brother Barker?" the guard with the book asked.

"I have not gone through Brother Barker," Lord Rhodes said.

The elite guards hesitated. "Well, it is highly unusual, sir."

"It is not unusual at all for a lord to speak with his king."

The guard gave the other guard a look. He only shrugged. Then the elite guard looked back at Lord Rhodes. There would be a penalty from Barker for allowing Rhodes through. The guard decided that, between the two, Barker presented the greater threat. "Brother Barker is not here at the moment. Can this wait until—"

"Let him through," the king's voice called out. Leopold sat nearby in the chair out in the open, overlooking the valley at night. He did not turn to look at Rhodes and did not need to. He had heard everything.

"Yes, Your Majesty." The guard gave Lord Rhodes a frown. "Well, there you have it."

Lord Rhodes returned his frown with one of his own, and the men reluctantly escorted him through the lines.

The king sat staring at the valley below. The distant campfires glowed like yellow stars.

Without looking at Rhodes, King Leopold spoke: "I had a dog once."

"Yes, Your Majesty, Babbit the Magnificent. I remember him well."

"Ever have a dog, Lord Rhodes?"

"No, Your Majesty, I never had time for one, I'm afraid."

"For some reason I can't explain, dogs love us unconditionally. Even when we are not worthy of it. I miss him, Lord Rhodes."

"We all do, Your Majesty." Rhodes looked at the guards who remained unmoving with him there.

"It must be hell for those people down there," King Leopold said. "First, they suffered some injury that brought them here in the first place. Then the demon attacks. Then the sickness. Then this madness...now us."

"Yes, Your Majesty, it must be terrible," Rhodes said. Lord Rhodes looked down over the valley now. For him, it had been the same view night after night. Yet as the king spoke, he saw it, perhaps for the first time, in terms of the human suffering below.

"Leave us," Leopold told the guards without looking back, knowing they were still there. They acknowledged the king's order and turned to go. Rhodes watched them leave, leaving him alone with the king.

The king said nothing at first. Lord Rhodes stood by his side, looking at the mud caked on his boots. The cold air blew across the ridge.

"Did you know Babbit died?" King Leopold asked. "Several years ago. Passed away peacefully in his sleep. A good way to go for Babbit. I miss him, Lord Rhodes."

"Yes, I know, Your Majesty. Your faithful companion for many years, Your Highness."

"Things haven't seemed the same since Babbit passed. Wonder if anyone passes away peacefully? I don't think we do. Eventually we all fight for our lives, and ultimately, lose the fight." Leopold laughed thinking of that. "I miss him though...Babbit the Magnificent."

After a moment, the king continued, "I have been sitting here watching the Temple of Chen-Li, Lord Rhodes."

Rhodes lifted his gaze. He looked out directly across the valley to the east, past the Oracle Mount and the Temple of Valor, past the sharp uplifting rocks of the Fangs. On top of the distant mountains sat the Temple of Chen-Li. Framed by a purple sky, the temple was a distant gray outline silhouetted in front of a large black mountain—the cloud-draped Dragonbreath Mountain. Lights could be seen from the fire braziers and occasionally they flickered, as some temple guard or a wandering priest passed in front of them.

Lord Rhodes never noticed the detail before that made the Temple of Chen-Li look alive.

The king continued, "I've been watching it for some time now. If you watch long enough, you can catch a fleeting glimpse of an occasional flash. A Li, one of the priests' spirits, separated from out of the body, leaving the temple for parts unknown, performing some covert operation against us."

There was silence that lasted for a long moment.

"There! Did you see it?" The king pointed for Rhodes's benefit. "There goes another one."

Rhodes watched carefully but saw nothing. "Yes, I think I caught a glimpse of it. Yes, Your Majesty."

King Leopold rested back in his chair. "I have always had a gift for strategy, Lord Rhodes."

"Yes, Your Majesty, you have," Rhodes agreed.

"Back in my younger days, in Hammerville, in the fighting ring. Amtor was always too big, too strong. He was too skilled a fighter for me, or anyone for that matter. Yet night after night I went to the fights to observe him. He fought like a grizzly bear in those days. He was undefeated, unbeatable. But I would go to study the man, to see what made him tick. To become anything in this life, I would always have to beat the best. Always. Can you understand that, Lord Rhodes?"

"Yes, Your Majesty, I do," Rhodes said again. Another long pause. "In the war, General Blaize Plum was no match for you either, sire."

"Ah! General Blaize Plum. He was a good man. Lousy general but a very good man. He has been dead for over ten years," King Leopold reflected. "You know, Lord Rhodes, I have read it takes ten years for a body to completely decompose to dust in the grave. I wonder if there is any truth to that. What do you want, Lord Rhodes?"

Distracted by the king's words, Rhodes was caught off guard when suddenly asked.

"Your Majesty, I came here to ask you for strategic counsel. I have been very troubled in my mind of late, and confused about coming up with a successful strategy. I was hoping you could help me understand."

Unaffected by intended flattery, King Leopold did not respond. He merely blew into a steaming cup.

Rhodes continued, "Well, Your Majesty, it is these fleeting spirits you see. How does one combat these Lis of Chen-Li and his White Eminence, if they are like ghosts? How will they fight us? How are we to fight them if attacked? The men, including myself, do not understand how we will defend ourselves if they are merely spirits."

"Tell the men not to worry about that. We can't fight them," the king told him.

"We can't?" Lord Rhodes was again surprised. "We can't fight them, Your Majesty?"

"We can't fight against them. We can't and we won't. These are spiritual forms. Our men will have little hope of defending against their skills at spiritual possession. You will have to wait, Lord Rhodes, until they inhabit the bodies of our troops. Then, as they turn our own men against us, you will be able to kill them. We have provided all the materials they need. Fifty thousand bodies that they can possess."

"I don't understand, Your Majesty."

"Lord Rhodes, do you think I am immune…to the sickness or this madness?"

"You? Your Majesty?"

"This sickness kills in a variety of forms. Some with disease. In others, madness. Some, it turns to eaters of human flesh. But it all comes from the Zorn, and he wants me neither dead nor mad. Actually, he probably thinks I am mad enough already." King Leopold chuckled. "No, not me. When he sent the sickness to me, it came as…compliance, Lord Rhodes. That is my sickness, my madness is compliance."

"Compliance, Your Majesty? Compliance with the Zorn?" Rhodes asked.

The king finally turned to face Lord Rhodes. He considered the man for a moment. "And do you think you are not infected with the madness too, Lord Rhodes?"

"Your Majesty? I-I don't know what to say."

"You have an inquisitive nature," the king said. "Surely you can feel something moving you, guiding you in a very specific way."

"Why, yes. Yes, I think I do, Your Majesty," Rhodes said. "Your Highness, if I may be so bold, I feel this siege is all wrong, Your Majesty. It is just that, Brother Barker—"

King Leopold interrupted him at the mention of that name. "Brother Barker is not one of us. He comes from a darker world. He is one of the Zorn's demons. His name is Frost."

Lord Rhodes hesitated. "By the Gods, my king, then why?"

"This is not the first demon that has come to me in my life." King Leopold breathed vapor in the wind. "Something less obvious is happening here, Lord Rhodes, and I want to find out what it is. Something is changing right before our eyes. Can't you feel it? I do. The whole world can feel it. A shadow is being cast dark and long upon us. Yet through the darkness, there are still remnants of light."

"The explosion from the Sanguine Forest?"

"We will see." King Leopold turned back to the lights of the Temple of Valor. "The light is out there. Soon all mankind will lay its hopes upon it. You are a good man, Lord Rhodes. You and Lord Whitney. Your hearts are good and true and honest. You both have tried to guide this army, this kingdom, into that light, into the right direction. Your efforts have not gone unnoticed. The problem is, Lord Rhodes, you can't defeat what is in the darkness by hiding in the light."

"Your Majesty?" Lord Rhodes said. "I do not understand."

"I have been compliant with Brother Barker, *that* is my madness," the king said. "I am letting him lead the way. I knew all along he takes us closer to the dark face of the real enemy. That is where we fight. This place is where we need to be. All is yet to be revealed."

"The real enemy, Your Majesty?"

"Death, Lord Rhodes," King Leopold told him. "Death is the real enemy."

Rhodes looked up silently now. He joined the king to gaze upon the distant lights in the Temple of Chen-Li.

"Stay true to yourself, Lord Rhodes. In the days that follow, you may have to do a lot of things you do not understand," the king said. "Worry about yourself and your men—have no concern about me."

Lord Rhodes stared silently at the king.

"The change is coming," the king added.

Lord Rhodes considered the king, considered his words with concern. He did not understand and realized he most likely never would. "Do you have any orders for me, Your Majesty?"

"No."

The king's response was a simple one. Lord Rhodes took a moment; he wanted to say more. But after hearing Leopold's words, his mind became distracted. He could not remember why he had even come to talk to him in the first place. At length, he could not think of anything more to say, except to bid a farewell to the king.

"There!" the king abruptly said. "There goes another one. Did you see it?"

Rhodes looked at the Temple of Chen-Li but once again saw nothing.

"They are like shooting stars," the king added.

Lord Rhodes thought the king may have gone mad.

"Yes, Your Majesty," Rhodes told him. "I should get back to the line now. Thank you for your time. Good night, Your Majesty."

Lord Rhodes gave a low bow and left the king in his chair, overlooking the fires in the valley, watching the distant lights of the temple and the phantoms.

"Good night, Lord Rhodes," King Leopold whispered after some delay.

* * *

As the chilly night passed, the wind turned colder and had a bitter bite. Lord Whitney came walking up to Rhodes. Whitney approached blowing into a steaming cup and eating a hardtack biscuit.

"You want one?" Lord Whitney offered a biscuit of hardtack to Rhodes. "You hungry?"

"No thanks. I can't bear eating another one of those."

Lord Whitney took a bite. "You went to see the king?"

Lord Rhodes nodded. "Yeah. I saw him."

"And?"

"I don't know, Oskar," Lord Rhodes said. "I have yet to decide how that meeting went."

"I fear the worst for him, for all of us, really," Lord Whitney said. "There are still three Devourers out there somewhere. Who knows when or where they will strike? The sickness is breaking out even among our own men. And yet, here we are, presenting ourselves out in the open like a big target. Why, I ask?"

"There are no answers. Speaking with the king just made it worse," Rhodes said. "There is a lot of confusion. He talked a lot about his dog. But you were right about Brother Barker. The king admitted as much."

Lord Whitney looked shocked. "He admitted what?"

"Brother Barker is not what he seems, he's more…Demonic." Rhodes looked back at the Temple of Chen-Li. "The king said he knows what is happening. Something about we are in the dark now, and we'll remain in the dark, until we achieve victory, or…death. The king's words, not my own."

"Well, at least that sounds like the old King Leopold I knew." Lord Whitney gnawed the hard biscuit. They both looked at the distant Gray Mountains, as the wind blew cold. "Maybe things aren't as bad as they seem. I don't know, maybe they are worse. Who knows?"

Just then, Lord Rhodes actually saw a wisp of light lift up from Chen-Li's temple.

"Well, I'll be damned," Rhodes said. "He wasn't mad after all."

THE RIDGE

Willard hated latrine duty. He held his breath as he bent over a basin full to the rim of the worst smells imaginable. He dragged the short tub out from beneath the toilets. Then he kept pulling it, sloshing down a pine-straw slope deeper into the woods. At last, he reached a fresh hole he had dug earlier with loose dirt piled beside it.

He made a sour face as he tipped the basin upward. Trying not to look, he could still hear the chunky contents gargle out. He could imagine the scene all too well. The container finally dripped the last remaining liquid into the hole. Once the basin was empty, he set it to the side. Lastly, he picked up the waiting shovel and refilled the hole with dirt. Despite the raunchy work, Willi did it quickly.

Once the task was complete, he was to return to the latrines with the empty basin. Scanning to make sure he was not being followed, Willard walked deeper into the woods. Up ahead, he came to the predetermined meeting place. Once there, he found the translucent spirit of Chen-Li waiting for him.

"Body and soul." Willard bowed to his master.

"Body and soul," Chen-Li gave the response. "Willi, for once in my life I am so glad I do not have the capacity to smell in my Li form."

"My apologies," Willard said.

"No need for that—you are a good spy. Doing the one job in which you are sure to not be followed," Chen-Li said. "Now, is there anything you can tell me about why the Red and Blue occupies this ridge?"

"Master, before I begin, I need to tell you, I am so sorry about the loss of the First Wives. My heart aches for Tyla and Myra. They were very much loved."

"Thank you, Willard. Their absence is felt among all of us."

The spy nodded. "My only desire is to avenge them, master. Maybe what I have to tell you will help in some small way."

"Go ahead," Chen-Li said.

"King Leopold is not himself. Not in control of the Red and Blue. Not their strategic actions or military maneuvers."

Chen-Li leaned closer. "Who is, then?"

"Ever since the presence of the priest, Brother Barker—he is the only one the king takes counsel from. I'm afraid he has poisoned the king's mind."

"I have never known King Leopold to take counsel with anyone, especially a pious priest, such as Brother Barker. What religious order does Brother Barker represent?"

"He says he represents the horn of the ram, the ancient religion of Heironomus, the God of Light. But others say that's merely a ruse, and that he's really a demon in disguise. That is not so hard to believe, even easier to see. His look is pale, unnatural, and artificial."

"You believe Brother Barker is one of the Zorn's demons?" Chen-Li asked Willard. "Have you any evidence of this?"

"One of the servants saw Brother Barker without his disguise. Saw him behind a curtain before he cast an illusionary spell to shadow his face. What the servant saw was not Brother Barker at all, but a blue-skinned demon."

"Blue-skinned? Langula?"

"Just like Langula in color. But in this guise, the demon was male and had two legs instead of a serpent's tail. What's more, the dark hair of Brother Barker was gone, replaced by up-flowing white hair."

"The demon Frost!" Chen-Li said. "The second born to the Demonic. Where is Brother Barker now?"

"Away, on some other business errand or so I heard. He is not on the siege line or on the ridge."

"A business errand? Most likely with his master, the Zorn." Chen-Li thought for moment. "I wonder. If I find any of the Demonic, they could lead me to Brother Barker."

"When you find them," Willard said with a low bow, "make them pay dearly for the lives of the First Wives, my master."

"They will, Willard, that I swear," Chen-Li said. "Anything else you can tell me?"

"Lord Whitney is not involved in any of this. He is a good man you can trust," Willard said. "He constantly breaks Brother Barker's rules, sending supplies to the sick on the grounds of the Temple of Valor. Lord Rhodes can be counted as his trusted ally too. They both speak out against Brother Barker all the time, but the king… he is…too distracted in his mind to listen."

"Good to know. Thank you, Willard. You should go back before anyone realizes you are gone."

"True," Willard said. "Plus, these men would not know what to do without a basin to shit in."

"Next time, Willard, we'll find you a better assignment."

"I serve at your pleasure, my lord," Willard said with a grin. "But I don't think it could get much worse."

"I will be back same time next week. Until then, stay safe, Willard."

The spy watched his master lift into the sky, just a dull ghostly streak. Then Willard turned alone to go back deeper into the woods. He fetched that wretched empty basin and carried it back up the hill.

When he arrived, he slid the basin back under the latrine. Just in time, for as soon as it was in place, he heard the explosive guts of someone above relieving themselves into it. Willard wiped his hands on his shirt with a sour look.

Then, he went to the next latrine, and made his usual sour face again, pulling out another basin full of nasty sloshing.

Oh! The glamorous life of a spy, he mumbled to himself.

As Chen-Li left, he could not just go directly back to his temple without endangering Willi's cover identity as a spy. The Red and Blue would have seen him leave, then know they had a spy in their midst. So instead, Chen-Li flew in a long arc around the ridge. He went west, which was in the opposite direction of the Temple of Chen-Li. After putting a few miles between him and the siege-works on the ridge, he turned north. His trajectory curved in a way that did not reveal where he came from. Avoiding the eyes of the

Red and Blue, he used the Temple of Valor and the Oracle Mount for concealment. Once the roundabout route was done, he was free to sail upward and home.

He was undetectable to all, save one.

"There goes another one," King Leopold said, watching the fleeting spirit return.

ACT IV

When I Take

My Last Breath

Quiet hope and desperation
Reflected through the years.
I can see it clearer
Than the man in the mirror

Excerpt from *The Witch's Songbook*

She had developed a sad look these days
as if all happiness seemed to have abandoned her.
— Excerpt from *Kilmer's Ghost* (Chapter 25)

A MOST EXCELLENT ILLUSION

VILLAGE OF HAVERHILL

The Zorn stood in the middle of a blood-filled room. The house was empty. It had been ransacked. Bloodstains splattered on the floor, on the wall, on the ceiling.

"What happened here?" asked the Zorn, scanning the room.

"A family was murdered last month." Langula sounded a bit bored when she answered him. "Murdered by a woodsman, I think. I heard his name was Tullis or something like that. Whatever his name was, he was under the influence of your sickness spell. It drove him to this madness. But it doesn't matter. He was hanged in Haverhill the day before yesterday."

"The dignity of death was taken from them?" the Zorn whispered looking around.

"What was that?" Langula replied.

But the Zorn did not bother to answer. Instead, he walked to an empty cabinet sitting against the wall.

"Thieves have been here already," Monticello said. "What boldness to loot this place. Most people would think this house to be cursed.

Thieves. I suppose they don't care about losing their lives dying. And that is what would have happened, if we'd walked in on them."

"How delicious would that have been," Langula said.

The Zorn walked farther into the house. He passed an empty dish cabinet and saw his reflection. His skull stared back from the glass's wavy reflection. His face had long been reduced to nothing but bone, discolored, and rotten pale green. Glowing yellow spheres, which were his eyes, rapidly danced in their hollows. His neck had not enough meat on it to support the collar of his uniform, so it sagged low under his chin.

"Your appearance is absolutely Demonic," Langula said with the usual compliment. "When did you start caring about your looks again? Have you finally come to admire the Skeletal King?"

"Do you remember how I used to look?" the Zorn asked her. "Before this malady of my flesh? The curse of the golden dagger?"

"I remember all too well," she said. "You looked like a common man back then, an ordinary man."

"Just an ordinary man." The Zorn continued to look at his reflection. "I could be again."

Langula did not care about the Zorn's musings for now; for just then, Frost entered the house. Langula rushed to her son. She wrapped her tail around his waist, pulling them closer together.

"Frost, my son, you're back! You have been away so long. I am so glad to see you again." Langula touched his face and kissed him deeply on the lips. She ran her fingers through his thick white hair.

Frost wore the priestly robes of Brother Barker, but without his disguise, he looked his normal Demonic self, complete with blue skin, silver eyes, and wild upwardly flowing hair.

"Brother Frost," Monticello welcomed him. "The favored son favors us with his presence."

"Don't be like that, Monticello." Frost released his mother and turned to Monticello. "You will always be the first demon and I the second. While I am always away at Castle Odessa, you are always with Langula and master Zorn. I am gone too much. That is the only reason she holds me so dear."

"Your absence has made their hearts grow fonder," Monticello said. "At least that is the saying the mortals have been known to use."

"It holds true with our kind as well," Frost said.

"Time away is not the only reason they love you more, Frost. Of that I'm sure," Monticello told him. "But I am genuinely glad to see you again, brother."

"How long has it been?" Frost asked his mother.

"Too long," Langula said.

"Two months maybe?" Monticello remarked.

"That is long?" the Zorn asked, returning to the mirror. "My face has been a stranger to me for over twenty-five years. What is two months?"

Frost replied. "Regardless, my work there has just begun."

"What is the news of our good king?" the Zorn asked Frost from the reflection of the mirror.

"My lord Zorn." Frost bowed, then approached him. "Good news. The war between our enemies is about to begin. The military of the Red and Blue surrounds the Temple of Valor. We will soon watch them go to war with the White Eminence of Chen-Li."

"I have a gift for you, master." Frost reached in his cloak and pulled out a rock the size of his hand. He gave it to the Zorn.

"You present your master with a rock?" the Zorn shrugged.

"Not just any rock, my liege. Look on the flat side of this rock. Look, it has a layer of polished green limestone. This, my lord, is a piece of the Green, King Leopold's high balcony. The pride of

Castle Odessa, it now lies in pieces, among the broken ceremonial markers at the bottom of the Mauveguard Pass. A trophy to your power and success."

The underside of the rock was comprised of pale vanilla stone, but the flat side was smooth, highly polished emerald. The Zorn examined the green stone. But as he rubbed the stone, eventually his yellow eyes darted to his pale green skin on the hand that held it. The Zorn rolled the stone in his bony hands.

"Are you not pleased?" Langula asked him. "What is wrong?"

The Zorn could not help looking at his fleshless arms, just empty bones colored in a sickly green.

"Master Zorn, all is ready," Frost said. "The order to attack has already been given. At sunrise, the Red and Blue will attack the Temple of Valor."

The Zorn considered the blue demon as he continued speaking.

"The forces of Chen-Li will come down from their mountain, come down from their stronghold to defend Valen against the attack. Once the White Eminence take the field, the Red and Blue will attack them. That will pit our enemies against each another, Leopold against Chen-Li."

"And while they destroy each other," Langula said, "I will move against the Temple of Valor and kill Lady Valen. Imagine all our enemies destroyed. It is perfect!"

"And at the height of the battle tomorrow," Monticello added, "we will release the Devourers to dominate the field."

"The plan is simply delicious," Langula exclaimed.

"Attack the Temple of Valor? Kill Lady Valen?" the Zorn asked, holding the green stone in his right hand. He turned to look at them. "Kill Lady Valen?"

"Naturally, we plan to kill her," Langula said with some relish.

"No!" The Zorn threw the stone. "I cannot allow that!"

Frost and Langula ducked. The green rock flew by them, busting in pieces against the bloodstained wall. "No one will lay a finger on Valen! She is not to be hurt in any way! Do you understand me?"

"Zorn, this was your goal from the very beginning!" Langula reminded him of the order he gave back in the caverns of stone. "The outcome you asked for…what you demanded from us!"

"Conditions! Conditions!" he screamed, throwing his hands in the air. "Conditions have changed!"

"What conditions have changed?" Langula asked. "How have they changed?"

"You think Lady Valen can heal you?" the ever-perceptive Frost asked. "You don't want her harmed because you are hoping the power of the Goddess can restore your flesh?"

"Is that true, Zorn?" Langula asked.

The Zorn turned to the mirror again. "You always were the smartest of the group, Frost."

Monticello had heard enough. He turned his back, brooding in silence.

"But you can't let Valen live," Langula said. "She has the soul of the Goddess. The spirit of our enemy."

"But is she really our enemy?" the Zorn asked. "I just don't know about that anymore."

"Is healing your flesh something Valen promised you?" Langula asked.

"Once again, you have not been paying attention, my dear," the Zorn said. "Valen is not the recycled soul of Ehlona, Astar is. Valen is the transfer of Ehlona's healing power. That is all I need her for."

"Astar spoke to you?" Frost asked.

Langula answered, "He came to the Zorn and apologized to him."

"Astar? Apologized? To him?" Frost asked. "For what?"

"The scorn of his mother. The scorn that turned the younger Hazor into the old Zorn," Langula laughed. "You cannot trust him. It is preposterous. He has the potential to blow up all of our plans."

"On the contrary, he can be trusted beyond any reproach," the Zorn said. "You see, Astar has power and a lot of it. He is the most powerful creature in the universe right now. So, he has no need to lie. Since he has no reason to lie, whatever he says will then be the truth,"

"Master Zorn, assuming Valen can restore your flesh," Frost asked. "Even if she can do it, will she do it, for you?"

"I don't know if she can or not," the Zorn answered. "But if she is dead, any chance of restoring my flesh dies with her. So, I don't want her damaged by any of you. Not anyone! Not until she restores my flesh. Do you understand?"

"Yes, my liege, the greatness of your flesh must be restored." Frost bowed. "No harm will befall Lady Valen."

"Once my flesh is restored"—the Zorn looked at his reflection again—"then you can kill her."

Frost agreed, "It will not be a problem in giving the order to spare Valen. The soldiers already have a tender spot for her. The order to not harm her will be well received. They will be only too happy to comply."

"In the meantime," Langula said, "instead of killing her, we'll do one even better. We will destroy everything she loves and make her watch."

Before the Zorn could say anything else, Langula escorted Frost out the door. Monticello followed, leaving the Zorn alone. Once outside, Langula turned to Frost, so only he could hear. "Do *not* give that order, the one to protect Valen," Langula whispered.

"But the Zorn said—" Frost started to say.

Langula interrupted him, "No matter what he says, I want Valen dead. Especially if she can restore the Zorn's flesh. I do not want him to turn back to Hazor. I need him to stay the Zorn—as the Skeletal King. There is no room in this world for another ordinary man, like the man the Zorn wants to be. The Demonic needs to be led by a Skeletal King not a Hazor the common."

"This could be a good opportunity for us," Frost whispered. "Maybe our time has come."

"So, you do understand?" She smiled. "After tomorrow night, we might not need him at all—neither as the Zorn nor Hazor."

The more Frost thought it all through, the more broadly he smiled. Finally, he confirmed Langula's treacherous plan with a nod. "Lady Valen is as good as dead."

With a flourish of his hands Frost applied the magic of his disguise. The spell bathed his face in shadow, rearranging how the light reflected. His appearance changed to Brother Barker. He now had dark hair, a pointed goatee, and a permanent smirk.

"A most excellent illusion," Monticello said. "You have returned to the appearance of Brother Barker."

"Thank you, brother," Brother Barker said. "Have the Devourers been instructed?"

Monticello answered, "They are ready. They will be there for the attack as planned."

"I appreciate you, Monticello," Brother Barker said.

Monticello took his leave. He walked into the house. Brother Barker and Langula were left together. She smiled and considered him in his disguise.

"I don't like this look. I like you better the other way," Langula said. "With your wild white hair."

"Maybe so," Brother Barker told her. "But in this disguise, I have gained influence over the king. My orders have already been sealed and given for tomorrow's military operations against the Temple of Valor. Everything has been arranged. Now, as much as it pains me to do so, I must leave you, Mother. I must get back to the Red and Blue to begin the final assault."

"I know you have to go," Langula said. "They are waiting for you, for Brother Barker's leadership. Tomorrow is a big day for us. For everyone. The day we shake the world through you."

Langula came close. She ran her fingers through his dark hair. She gave him a long deep kiss. Then she whispered in his ear, "Remember what we discussed about Lady Valen."

"Of course, Mother," Brother Barker said with a smile. "Valen is as good as—"

Interrupted in midsentence, Brother Barker was violently rolled backward. A strong wind blew past Langula. Barker had been struck and struck so hard and so suddenly that his illusion dissolved. He was back to being Frost.

Frost convulsed on the ground. Langula was knocked to the ground too. She lifted her head and found that Frost had landed in a field. A cloud of dust rose under him. Langula slithered quickly on her tail and raced to him. Frost got unsteadily to his feet.

Langula stopped just short of him. His eyes had no pupils and were like pale white almonds.

"Frost? Be still. Don't move," Langula said. "You have been struck by a ghostly spirit that is trying to inhabit you! You must concentrate! Fight against it for control."

Frost mumbled something as his silver pupils returned. "A spirit possesses me?"

"Not just any," Langula said. "But the master priest himself."

"Chen-Li is inside me?" Frost shouted. He reached out to Langula.

Langula spoke to Chen-Li, "Chen-Li, don't do this."

Frost's eyes rolled back in their sockets again. This time, the real possession began. Frost's body started to shake violently.

Langula screamed to the demons in the house. "Zorn! Monticello! It's Frost! We need help!"

Langula wrapped her tail around Frost's body to hold him up. But just then, a whoosh of flame and heat blasted her away. She was lifted by force and propelled backward. Frost's hands burned with fire. He tried to resist, but it was spreading up his arms.

He opened his eyes momentarily. For a brief minute they were silver again. He had wrestled control of his spirit back from Chen-Li.

He had time to reach out with flaming hands. "It burns!"

Then his eyes rolled up and he shook violently. There was a loud sound, like an ignition of gas flame, and fire burst forth from his entire body. His flesh was roasting. Frost's blue skin burned to black, began to swell, and then split apart in sticky open fissures. Inside of him, the flames burned red and became hot as charcoal.

Langula cried in horror, helplessly watching him burn. She tried to rescue him and fought against the flames. But the intense heat prevented her from getting close enough to do anything.

Frost collapsed to the ground and stopped moving. His flesh continued to burn and billowed up in black smoke.

Chen-Li then emerged from Frost's body. When he exited, he took most of the flames with him. Then, with the damage done, Chen-Li relinquished control back to Frost, leaving him burning in the field.

"Tyla and Myra, dead at your hands," the spirit of Chen-Li mocked Langula. "Now, your most favored demon, Frost is dead! Your Brother Barker destroyed! And next, it will be you. Are you ready to burn too, you demon beast?"

Langula snarled at him with tears in her eyes. But that did not stop the flaming spirit of Chen-Li from entering her body. Langula was knocked backward. But before Chen-Li could take possession of her, she dissipated in a cloud of black smoke. She transported to someplace far enough away that Chen-Li was forcibly ejected out of her body.

"Run, you coward!" Chen-Li laughed maniacally within the flames. When he turned back, he saw the Zorn and Monticello standing there with mouths open. They had run out of the woodsman's house. They could see the burning body of Frost smoldering in the field with the spirit of Chen-Li floating above it.

"Don't make me fight you!" the Zorn warned. "If we do, we will negate each other. We will spend eternity battling each other in the Cosmic Creation."

"We don't know that," Chen-Li said. "Nothing is for certain."

"Do not throw away the future for this vengeance! The death of your First Wives was not my idea. I did not command it, to take their lives. Langula did it on her own. It never should have happened."

Chen-Li increased the heat of his flame. The Zorn had never seen him like this before. Chen-Li was blinded by fury. Chen-Li moved forward and headed right for the Zorn. The Zorn ducked. Chen-Li deliberately passed over the Zorn's head but so close as to leave burning ashes upon him.

"This is the beginning of your end!" Chen-Li glowed as fire. "For you and all your demon born! The end!"

"You've gone mad, Chen-Li!" The Zorn's yellow eyes flashed.

Chen-Li smiled at the smoldering body of Frost. Then, with a final look at the Zorn, he jetted away. A tail of red vapor was left behind.

"He has become frightening and unpredictable." The Zorn exhaled a release of energy.

Langula rematerialized not far from Frost. In a cloud of black smoke, she returned to the field. She held his charred head in her hands.

"Frost?" Langula whispered. "Frost, can you hear me?"

"Mother," he said in a weak voice. "I will give that order…"

"He's still alive!" Langula said, her eyes filling with tears. "Don't worry about that order, not now, my love. Just rest, rest now. We'll make you all better."

"Mother…I…can't…breathe." He spit out some blood. His body slumped.

"Frost? Frost!" she shouted. "Oh, Frost!"

She let out a howling scream and held him closer. As she embraced him, his skin peeled off in gooey layers right in Langula's hands.

"Langula," Monticello said, approaching her. "You are on fire."

She had red coals burning through her hair with trails of smoke rising from her head.

"Oh, leave me to die with him!" she cried. "I do not care. I want to burn with him. I want to feel the pain to override what I feel in my heart."

The Zorn watched Chen-Li's fiery spirit. Just like that, he was back at the Temple of Chen-Li.

"We were so close. So close to victory." The Zorn could smell Frost's body burning, and it disgusted him. He yelled at Langula, "And we would have had it all if not for you. If *you* had not murdered his First Wives, incurring Chen-Li's wrath."

She spun on him and shouted back, "You blame me for this? For the death of Frost? For the loss of victory? Chen-Li incinerated him, my beautiful Frost. Is your brother still a bore to you now? I will never forgive you for this."

The Zorn turned and walked away without waiting for any of them.

"Oh! Those attacks on the Temple of Valor will be executed," Langula vowed with the lifeless body of Frost in her arms. She whispered a silent promise to him. A promise that she would make sure of, with or without the Zorn's help. Despite the outcome, Frost would be avenged. She resolved to do this with every wicked fiber in her being. Frost would have his vengeance.

I want (you)

I want (you called me a lunatic)

I want (you don't know who you've been messing with)

Excerpt from *The Witch's Songbook*

The old man's eyes widened as the feast started.
— Excerpt from *Kilmer's Ghost* (Chapter 26)

THE HERO AND THE HEARTLESS BEAST

SOUTHERN SHORE

The Vengeful Spirits were now at peace and Castle Orlo had been destroyed. The crater that had been the Zorn's castle began rising with fresh water to form a fresh spring. White petals fell. New grass sprouted under their feet. Laughing at the miraculous change, Kilmer, Darla, and Kory walked through the Sanguine Forest. Oaks and Melvin walked not too far behind.

"I can't believe it," Melvin said. "Once this forest nearly killed us. Now it blossoms with new life."

"The darkness has lifted," Kilmer said. "The oppressive heaviness is gone."

"I am happy for the forest," Oaks said. "It is finally at peace."

"Never forget what Astar has done here," Kilmer said, observing all around. "He is the one true remaining God in this world."

"I thought I saw it all with Chen-Li," Oaks said, hardly containing himself. "But Astar! When he blew up the Zorn's castle! That was crazy!"

As the grass covered the last of the bones, Kilmer addressed the group. "Astar told us to go south to the coast and find the Nomads of Spiron. He said they will help us find safe passage to the Temple of Valor. That is where Astar asked us to go. If that is where Astar wants us, that is where we should go. But we must be careful. We are still fugitives from the king's law. The explosion will attract soldiers. Be on the lookout. If we are caught, we will all swing."

Kilmer was relieved that Hollow Face showed up to guide them. The party made their way out of the blooming Sanguine Forest without incident, staying ever watchful for scouts.

"What do you make out of Astar asking us those questions?" Melvin asked Kilmer.

"What questions?" Kilmer asked.

Melvin continued, "He asked, 'What would you do, if the demons came back, if King Leopold lifted the restrictions, and what if Castle Orlo wasn't an option any longer?'"

"I think Astar had all this planned from the very beginning," Kilmer said.

They made their way south, walking below a ridgeline, carefully keeping themselves concealed from open view. Behind them, the Sanguine Forest faded away. Taking advantage of the available foliage, they traversed the foothills of the Blue Mountains. Having to cross in the open areas of the Mid-Run Valley was the most dangerous time. They kept a sharp watch for any approaching soldiers.

Tensions were running high when Kilmer heard a sudden rustle behind them. Kilmer whirled and pulled his sword, ready to defend himself. But it was only Melvin; he had caught a wild rabbit in the bush.

"Anyone hungry?" Melvin proudly held up the animal by the back legs.

They made a small cooking fire and soon Melvin's catch was turning on a spit. While they waited to eat, Oaks spoke to Kory.

"You hungry, little squirt?" Oaks asked Kory as he sat down beside him.

"Very," the five-year-old boy said.

Oaks continued to talk to Kory. "You know, squirt, you are very much like your parents, you know?"

"How so?" Kory played in the fire with a little stick.

"Well, even though you are not an orphan, like the rest of us were, you still live the orphan's life," Oaks said.

"Oaks." Darla tried to stop him.

Melvin, who had been busy roasting the rabbit, decided the meat was done. He took it off the spit, quartered it, and began distributing it to the others. He gave a plate to Darla first, then to Kilmer.

Kilmer accepted the plate from Melvin. "No, please, Oaks, enlighten us. What is the orphan's life?"

Oaks continued, "You are what? Four years old?"

"Five!" Kory corrected him.

"And in all that time, you've been moving from place to place. That has been your life. You've never stayed anywhere long enough you could get accustomed to or call home. Just like the rest of us. Just like an orphan, see?"

Darla watched Kory play in the fire without a care. She did not feel much like eating anymore. She looked at Kilmer. He stopped chewing and met her glance.

Oaks saw Darla's expression too. He immediately regretted what he said. But then, Kory spoke.

"I like it outdoors," Kory said.

"What do you like about it, squirt?" Oaks asked with sympathetic eyes.

Kory knelt beside the fire. "The campfires at night, the stars, the trees, the streams. Being all together. I like it here, especially with you, and Melvin, and Mama and Papa. We got to meet Astar too."

The others all looked at Kory, then to each other.

Kory stared into what was left of the fire. "Maybe we can have a home someday, as long as I know we can still have campfires there."

They marched for over a day. Then they came to a rise in a hill overlooking a long slope on the other side. Random sways of saw grass led down to a sandy beach to the shores of the Endless Sea. Its frothy waves rolled foam up and onto the land. Ahead should have been a packed camp full of people. But the Nomads had abandoned their camp and were already gone. The tracks of their departing wheels ran to the northeast. The trail of rutted tracks would be easy to follow. The only thing left on the beach was some trash the Nomads had left behind.

"Where did they all go?" Oaks asked.

"One's left, look there," Melvin said. He pointed to a lone figure standing on the beach.

A single person stood there, one lonely man. He was looking out over the waves. The foamy sea crashed at his feet. Squawking seagulls circled him overhead.

"Maybe he knows what happened here. Come on." Kilmer led the troop down the hill, through the tall saw grass, past the driftwood, and to the windy sand of the beach.

The closer they got; the more concerned Kilmer became. He considered the lone man carefully. Now, Kilmer slowed, becoming more cautious. Something seemed off.

"Hello there? Excuse me," Kilmer addressed the mysterious figure. But the man did not respond and continued standing with his back to Kilmer. The man was dark and either unaware or uncaring of Kilmer and his party's presence.

"Maybe you did not hear us," Melvin spoke louder to the man.

Just then, Hollow Face appeared. The ghost had visions for Kilmer. Hollow Face's visions told him there was extreme danger here.

"Draw your weapons," Kilmer whispered, withdrawing his own. "Something's not right with this person."

"Not right? On the contrary, it is you I have been waiting for." The man slowly turned to face them. This was no man; this was a demon. The creature made no threatening movements toward them. Instead, the red demon chewed upon the flesh of a bird. Their presence did not stop him from eating. The demon took another bite, swallowed the flesh, then spoke.

"Name's Grim," he said to Kilmer. "Been waiting for Darius Plum. Have you seen him?"

Kilmer recoiled at that name. It was his given one.

"I am the one you seek," Kilmer answered. "I am Darius Plum."

Grim was focused solely on Kilmer. Kilmer slowly walked to Grim's left. He motioned for the others to go right. Slowly they flanked Grim on two sides. The demon would not be able to attack both sides at once. Whichever side he attacked, the other side would be vulnerable. Kilmer held his sword toward Grim.

Oaks and Melvin quietly pulled their swords and drifted to the right of the demon. Darla did not flank the demon. Instead, she backed away and shielded Kory behind her. She pulled out a long knife.

"The Plum family was executed. Murdered by the Red Guard," Kilmer continued. "After, I changed my name to Kilmer. That is who I am now. Where have you heard of Darius Plum? How do you know my real name?"

Grim clicked the seagull meat from his teeth with his tongue. He smiled, and when he did, his fangs appeared.

"You said you have been waiting for me," Kilmer continued to circle to the left of Grim. "How did you know I would be coming here? What do you want?"

"Lot of good questions," Grim said. "But did you know? Hollow Face has been showing me visions. Yes, just like he shows you. Through Hollow Face and the visions, I have learned all about you, Darius Plum, and why you are Kilmer."

Kilmer lowered his sword but quickly raised it again. "Hollow Face has been with me ever since I was a young boy. How do you know Hollow Face?"

"Mama, what's happening?" Kory asked from behind Darla.

"We're just being careful, darling," Darla told him. "Don't worry."

"Your boy?" Grim finished eating. He threw the bird aside. "Does he see the ghost too?"

Kilmer shook his head. Kory had the same blood but had not grown into the curse yet.

Melvin and Oaks both flanked Grim, maneuvering around the demon, swords pointing at him. Melvin saw the remains of the seagull in the surf, bobbing in the water, washing away on the rolling waves; the sight made his stomach turn.

Grim searched Kilmer's face. "We have the mark of Heironomus. The red hair. Just as I see the mark has been burned into yours too. I wasn't born with the mark you know. My hair was once black and stayed that way most of my life. But it turned to red when Hollow Face started coming to me."

"What is it you want, Grim?" Kilmer asked. "If you think you will feed on—"

"As the ghost and I get to understand each other, the more I have changed," Grim interrupted him. "I just needed to see you for myself."

"Now you have seen me, and I have seen you." Kilmer leveled the sword off and pointed it at Grim. "What do you want now?"

"I want to know if this ghost is a blessing or a curse." Grim took a step closer. He walked into the very tip of Kilmer's sword, which pressed deep into his skin. "Don't you know?"

"If you are trying to scare me," Kilmer said, holding the sword tight, watching a trickle of blood coming from Grim's chest, "I am not afraid of you."

"Why would you be?" Grim said, standing firm. "When there is a bond of blood between us?"

Darla retreated; her only concern was Kory. Just then, she felt him tugging on her pants to get her attention. She looked up to see three men on the top of the hill coming toward them. The men were holding each other arm in arm, as if supporting each other. Darla presumed the men were wounded.

Grim paid no attention to Melvin and Oaks who were flanking around behind him. Instead, Grim spoke directly to Kilmer.

"I have seen some of the things you have seen," Grim said. "But the ghost does more than just show me. He makes me *feel*…things— things I have never felt before. Why? Can you help me understand why?"

Kilmer lowered his sword. He gave Melvin and Oaks a shake of his head. The signal not to try anything. "I suppose if you wanted to kill me you would've done it already."

"I do not wish to harm you," Grim said. "On the contrary, I think you are the only man alive that can help me understand. It was your blood that incubated me. The blood made me a part of you, and part of this curse. Making us related, like father and son."

"I am not your father," Kilmer said.

"No, you are not. Not in the mortal sense of the word, I know," Grim said. "Still, a connection is there."

"I never wanted that."

"Of course not. I know you didn't," Grim said. "It was against your will. Still, it happened. I just wanted to meet you before I go."

"You're going somewhere??"

"The Zorn is trying to kill me. Hollow Face showed me that. There is nothing here for me in this land anymore." Grim turned along the sandy beach and looked out over the sea. "I am a being set apart now. Set apart more than anything in this world, I am an outcast." Grim turned to Kilmer. "I must leave this world to find a new one."

Grim and Kilmer turned and walked down the beach together.

"Can this be happening?" Darla watched them walk away. "Is Kilmer really casually speaking to a demon?"

"What should we do?" Oaks asked.

"I don't know," Melvin said. "But let's not let them out of our sight. Keep close."

"But not too close," Darla told them.

⚬ ⸰ ⸺ ⸭⁖❧⊙⊂❧⁖⸺ ⸰ ⚬

"What do you plan to do, Grim?" Kilmer asked. His red curls blew in the wind while Grim watched a sailing vessel on the horizon.

"I will go on the Endless Sea," Grim continued. "Find out if it really is endless, or if something else is out there, some other world of the unknown. If so, I will live there. If not, then I will die adrift."

"Why do that?" Kilmer asked, putting his sword back in his scabbard.

"Hollow Face has been showing visions of the sea, pushing me relentlessly. I cannot tell if the visions are real or not, or if he is leading me to my destruction. Either way, I will find out if the ghost comes with me on this voyage. Will he, Kilmer? Can the ghost exist for both of us?"

"I suppose, if he wanted to." Kilmer stopped. "There is nothing to prevent it. I hope he guides you, for your sake, Grim."

The two of them started walking again. Grim continued speaking, "The Zorn has never feared anyone before, but he fears you, Kilmer. He fears Hollow Face, calls it Kilmer's ghost, the spirit of Fortis Plum. He knows about this blood connection we share. If I stayed, he would try to kill me. Eventually he would succeed."

"That is very strange, since you are his demon born," Kilmer said. "Yet, I am sorry, Grim."

"He wants me dead. The world wants me dead. Everyone wants me dead." Grim looked out at the ship on the horizon. "I cannot survive here. I have nothing left, with few choices. But I have decided my fate will not be in the hands of the Zorn but in the hands of the Gods and the spirit of Fortis Plum. I hope Hollow Face is protecting me and not sending me to die, but I guess it doesn't matter much anymore. We all have to face it, one way or the other."

"Grim, how will you exist out there on the Endless Sea? How will you…eat? I mean, what will you…feed on?"

"I am a flesh-eater, Kilmer. I can eat almost anything. Any flesh will do. I'm sure I'll find something."

"Hollow Face will lead you to somewhere special," Kilmer said. "I know it."

"I wonder if he will reveal anything more to me. Maybe so. But either way, this is the end for me."

Kilmer said, "I believe he will help guide you somewhere out there in those open waters. He has been charged to watch over his family, not to lead them down a path of destruction. With this blood connection, I do not think you are any different from any who have come before. However far you go, his spirit will continue to find you. Warn you of dangers. Show you the opportunities. Take heed, Grim, in what he shows you. I do not doubt him for a second. He has proven to me that I can trust what he shows me."

They listened to the waves crash on the beach.

Grim turned from the sea now. "Oh, one more thing, Kilmer. I need to hand over these others to you, just as I was told to do." He pointed beyond the sand dunes. Dark figures stood on a hill in the distance. As the people approached, they shouted for help, supporting each other as they walked.

"You were told to leave them with me? By Hollow Face?" Kilmer asked, squinting at the approaching distant shapes.

"No, not Hollow Face. It was Astar," Grim said.

At the same time Grim spoke, Kilmer recognized that Astar was walking among the strangers on the hill. "You know Astar too?" Kilmer looked more closely again at the people approaching. Hollow Face was there with them too, standing on the distant hill. "Who are they?"

"A grave mistake I never should have allowed to happen," Grim said. "Just an unfortunate blacksmith and his son. The boy's name is Micah. The other is the father, Gensen. The boy was taken against his will from the village of Homestead. He has been infected by the poison of Langula that is killing him, if he is not dead already. The boy's father went looking for him in the underground. Astar came to his rescue."

"The boy is dying? Is he Demonic?" Kilmer asked.

"Not truly Demonic, but demonly," Grim said. "He's turning undead. He'll hunger for flesh."

"And the father? Is he turning undead as well?" Kilmer said, watching Gensen support his son arm in arm.

"He's just a sentimental old fool," Grim said. "Recklessly heroic, overly passionate, otherwise unharmed."

"And in the green cloak?" Kilmer took a step in that direction. "That is Astar?"

"Yes, he wanted to stay with Micah."

"What do they need from us?" Kilmer asked.

"They need to seek out Lady Valen at the Temple of Valor. They hope to find a cure for his condition and a way back home." Then Grim reflected, "For me, there is no home. Except what waits for me out there."

"I have never known of a home for a very long time, Grim," Kilmer said. "But I have hoped the visions will lead us to one someday. We must believe that."

"Hello? Hello!" Gensen called out. He waved as they came struggling down the hill with his son in tow. "Can you help us? Please!"

With an affirmative nod from Kilmer, Melvin and Oaks rushed to help.

As they went, Grim turned to Kilmer once more. "I feel like this is goodbye."

"It is a strange thing," Kilmer told him. "This blood connection. I feel sad that you have to go. I understand why you must though."

"Something went wrong in this world," Grim said. "I will search for a better one."

"You will be a reluctant explorer of new worlds. I hope you find what you are looking for," Kilmer said. "A world without curses and great blessings."

"Maybe we will meet again in some other world in some other time," Grim said. He gave Kilmer one last look. "Goodbye, Darius Plum."

"Yes, goodbye, Grim," Kilmer said. "I'll see you on the other side."

Grim walked into the sea. Kilmer knelt in the sand to watch him go. Entering the powerful waves, they rocked his body backward. But after a moment of wading through the shallows, he began to swim. Up and down over the foamy swells he swam out to sea.

Out on the horizon, a sailing ship was passing in the distance. Grim swam in that direction making slow progress. But soon, Grim's red curls disappeared below the waterline and did not come back up. Kilmer furrowed his brow and rose to see. A line of frothy bubbles appeared just under the surface. Grim was swimming incredibly fast, speeding like a torpedo toward the ship on the horizon.

THE ENDLESS SEA

Captain Tristen was the skipper of *The Celestial.* He had over twenty-five years' experience navigating through the Endless Sea. He was startled when his first mate, Renaldo, burst into the cabin to give him an astonishing report.

"Captain Tristen, Captain Tristen!" Renaldo shouted.

"What is it, Renaldo?"

"Captain Tristen, we have lost a lifeboat, sir."

"Lost a lifeboat? How is that possible?"

"I don't know, but it is gone just the same!"

"Oh! For the love of… Show me." Captain Tristen walked off the bridge and followed Renaldo. When they got to the side of the ship, the rigging to the lifeboat was untied and dragging its ropes in the water below. Captain Tristen pulled the end of the cord out of the salty water. Once up, he examined them carefully. The ends had been cut clean as with a very sharp knife.

"Who tied these lines off, then?" Captain Tristen asked.

"I tied them off myself," Renaldo said. "Same as I've done a million knots before, captain. Ain't a-one of them ever failed before."

"Aye, yet we lost our lifeboat to the sea just the same?" The captain stormed back to the bridge. "I have never known any of your knots to slip before, Renaldo. Had you been drinking when you tied it?"

"No, sir, I don't drink, remember, Captain?" Renaldo said. "Well, not much anyway. The knots did not slip. I can promise you that." Renaldo held up the cut end of the rope. "They were cut. By a thief or a stowaway, or whatever that thing is out there. Look, Captain."

"Cut? Who would cut the lines to a lifeboat?" Captain Tristen said while searching where Renaldo pointed. "Look, Renaldo, out there! A man in our lifeboat. Who is that out there?"

Grim left in *The Celestial*'s lifeboat and set off over the waves. The farther he paddled, the more he felt the blood connection strengthen between him and Kilmer. Kilmer, the hero, and the heartless beast Grim, had been joined by the blood of an enduring family curse.

Far beyond *The Celestial*, and almost at the horizon, Kilmer watched Grim paddle out to sea. The rowboat broke over the last of the big waves. Grim now rowed for open water.

Darla approached Kilmer and put her hand in his. "What do you think will become of him?"

"I have no idea," Kilmer said. "But I hope he finds what he's looking for, more than what he would find here. Something better than death by the Zorn."

"I hope he never comes back," Micah said, watching with eyes dark and hollow. "I hope he dies out there."

Hollow Face stood silently alongside him. Along with Astar, and the others, they would later find the Nomads of Spiron.

But as for now, Kilmer gave the ocean one last look. Out on the Endless Sea, Grim's rowboat was just a small dot on a vast horizon of water. In the next breath, he was gone. Grim had paddled over that horizon and out of the known world.

She's a dragon breathing fiery coals
A scaley alligator in a sleepy hole.

Excerpt from *The Witch's Songbook*

Opening his eyes, he thought he saw an angel standing over him.
— Excerpt from *Kilmer's Ghost* (Chapter 27)

A BRIEF INTERMISSION:
THE FRACTAL DRAGON

BLUE MOUNTAINS

He wanted to try something new, so Astar went off by himself, but he was never truly alone. Astar had left behind multiple copies of himself to help the sick at the Temple of Valor. Yet this single version of Astar walked alone for many miles, deep into the mountains. There, on a remote and distant hilltop, he found the isolation he needed. Once far away from the others, he duplicated himself to have someone to talk to.

"Do you think this will work?" the first Astar said.

"We will need to try it first," the second one answered. "And we will need many more."

"You make one copy, I'll copy myself three times," said the first. Three more copies of himself popped into being just as he suggested.

The second duplicated into just one more copy. "We want to create fractals, by duplicating in unequal ratios. In this way, we can create building blocks."

"To construct something larger than ourselves. We can become anything with these fractals." The Astars multiplied again and again in unequal ratios. Until there were many groupings small and large.

"I'm not sure I understand it," one of the Astars said.

"I'm not sure if we can do this," another Astar answered.

"How do we connect ourselves?" a distant Astar asked.

"Here, interlock arms," an Astar in the middle said. "Like this."

"Hold the first group," another one spoke. "Secure them tightly, don't let go."

"Now, roll forward and attach to another group," they said in unison and rolled forward.

"Now copy yourself again!" one of the groupings said.

"We duplicated three times," a fragment of Astars said.

This went on and on. Soon they were duplicating themselves in large groups of unequal ratios and connecting into different sizes and shapes. Repeatedly, more of them filled the mountaintop with seemingly no end.

"Keep joining together," the many forms said in unison. "But stay in your groups."

As the fractal patterns continued to form and link together, they created a larger illusion. Slowly it began to take shape and started to form into something bigger than themselves. Lifting slowly from the ground, all the sections started to rise as a larger version of himself, a piecemealed Astar giant.

As the fractals kept coming together, a giant-sized Astar rose from the mountain. First his head, then his shoulders formed. Then his arms, chest, and waist. He stretched up and lifted upon two feet that materialized under him. He raised himself in this pixelated form and stood some sixty feet high. As he rose unsteadily, remnants of smaller bodies fell away. But the smaller copies never hit the ground—instead they were absorbed back into the whole before struck the ground. The giant Astar became coordinated in his movements, turning them into fluid motions. He practiced his coordination, lifting his arms and legs, with full control of his hands and feet. Overall, the fractals of Astar could function as a single entity. A giant fractal Astar was complete. Holding out his hands, he looked to see smaller sets of multiplied Astars hanging on to form them.

Now the giant spoke.

"Impressive," he said. But these words did not come from the fractal Astar's mouth. A thousand voices comprising the whole unit thundered out in unison, synchronized as one voice.

"Very impressive indeed." The voices were deep and loud and echoed through the canyon.

"Now, let's rearrange the pattern!" the voices cried out. The fractals rearranged their positions, crawling on top, and underneath, and through the existing complex, which rearranged their shape. The shifting and sliding into different proportions caused a momentary whirl of chaotic movements on the surface. Soon they settled down into just the right places to form an ugly, one-eyed behemoth, the form of a giant ogre. Steadily, with the addition of even more fractal copies duplicating rapidly on the scene, a war club took shape in the ogre's hand. Once the club was complete, the ogre swung it. As he did, the ogre let out a frightening growl.

"Arrgh!" The fearsome creature lifted its arms, shouting in a menacing cry, while swinging its club through the air.

Then, all the Astars laughed at their angry visual display.

"This is working!" the excited voices said. "Now, let's change to something else. Let's make a dragon."

"Yes, let's rearrange again," more of them said. As before, the outside fractals rotated, the insides shifted. For a moment, all the movements created a blur of general chaos, a shifting mass inside and out of the massive being. When all the pieces were settled into place, the fractal ogre had changed in form to a fractal dragon. Astar's dragon stomped around the mountaintop, spreading its wings and hissing violently. Occasionally, with quick movements, several random Astars fell off here and there. But this did not harm the whole.

"Overall, a fearsome creature!" the Astars agreed.

He wondered what else he could do. But before he could experiment further with his fractals, his other forms, back at the Temple of Valor, spied something coming that needed his immediate attention. For now, his experiment would have to wait.

"Eh? What is this? Someone is approaching the Temple of Valor." But no one was approaching the fractal dragon in the mountains. These visions were coming from the other eyes of Astar left at the Temple of Valor. It was them that called the rest back. Astar's dragon dissolved with a multitude of sounds. The fractals absorbed, the many into one, merging into just a single Astar.

He found himself outside the Temple of Valor. There, all of the thousands of copies from the mountain had come back to merge into a single version of himself, the one keeping watch on the distant ridge.

The wagons of the Nomads of Spiron were approaching.

Be no more time spent

Crying over spilled milk

Be no more nights spent

Sleeping under red silk

Excerpt from *The Witch's Songbook*

What he did not count on was that before he
crossed that dark threshold of death,
he would be haunted by the ghosts of his dead sons.
— Excerpt from *Kilmer's Ghost* (Chapter 28)

BEYOND PRYING EYES

ORACLE MOUNT

"My Lady Valen," an acolyte reported. "A train of wagons is coming down from the ridge. The soldiers have opened their siege lines to allow a caravan of wagons to pass through. They drive right through the Red and Blue, right past the military lines upon the upper ridge."

Their wagons bore the resemblance of rolling houses. They were not cheaply made canvas wagons. These wagons were finely constructed homes on large rolling wheels, built from solid hardwoods. They had framed windows and elaborate doors. Orange-and-black flags flapped overhead, as they came wobbling down the hill. These were the Nomads of Spiron, and they snaked single file into the valley rolling toward the Temple of Valor.

Reaching level ground, the caravan of wagons proceeded to roll through the flat, long valley separating the high ridge from the Oracle Mount. As they got nearer to the Temple of Valor, the wagons slowed; the drivers had to navigate carefully to avoid running over the sick people camped in the grasslands. Eventually, the first of the wagons pulled up close to the Oracle Mount, below the Temple of

Valor. When the wagon train stopped, it marked the end of a long two-day journey.

Once halted, the door to the first wagon swung open. A curious-looking man leaped out without using any of the steps. He landed on the ground in a cloud of dust wearing hard black boots. The man was oddly dressed in a fashion they had never seen before. His garb was of the traditional orange shirt and black vest of the Nomads of Spiron. He had darkened hair that protruded from underneath a headscarf of burnt umber. Gold bracelets jangled on his wrists. He wore many chains of silver and gold around his neck and a handful of jewelry on his fingers.

Amtor and Aberfell approached the man to greet him. But before they could say a word, the Nomad shouted to all and extended his arms open.

"Friendly greetings to the Temple of Valors! The Nomads of Spiron have come to you now! I am Boldo, prince of our tribe and brother to the queen. Please allow me to introduce, Nadya, the Queen of Spiron." Boldo waved his hand with a flourish and backed away from the door with the lowest of bows.

Nadya emerged from her royal wagon. She gracefully stepped down the stairs and out of the lead wagon. Her boots were shorter than her princely brother's but no less dazzling; they were embedded with jewels of rubies and opals. She wore black pants under her short orange skirt. A thick leather belt, a large ruby in its center, kept her garments held fast together against her petite body. Her bracelets jingled in golden brilliance, as did her hanging diamond earrings. Other precious metals and stones adorned her slender fingers. A jeweled dagger tucked into her belt signified a certain danger, the price of her beauty, wealth, and power.

Nadya stood straight and dignified before them. She spoke to the onlookers. "The Nomads of Spiron extend warm greetings to the

Temple of Valor and all who come here. We bring you gifts, a bounty of supplies for your sick and wounded. We are happy, so glad, to offer all we have to you, to all of you."

"Queen Nadya." Aberfell approached and bowed low. "You and the Nomads of Spiron are quite welcome here. This is Amtor, King Leopold's first Minister of War. And I, of course, as I am sure you recognize me, am Aberfell, the Supreme Historian—"

"That will do just fine, Aberfell," Amtor interrupted before he got carried away. "Welcome, Nadya. We have been expecting you. Astar told us you would be coming."

"Oh, Astar…" Nadya gave a bow as Astar approached.

Astar approached Nadya. "I am glad you found safe passage from the clutches of the Demonic."

"Our liberation has begun," Nadya said. "We have broken trust with the Demonic. The penalty for that breach of our agreement is they will hunt us down and kill us all. On that, they gave their word. Though at present, I don't think they can. Or they simply don't care as much. I think they are more preoccupied with you, Astar. At any rate, we Nomads of Spiron consider ourselves to be free. Even though it meant we had to leave our ancestral homelands."

"Only for a while," Astar said.

Amtor looked up at the soldiers on the distant ridge. "How did you get through their siege?"

"It was Lord Whitney who gave us his blessing to pass," Nadya told Amtor. "He convinced the others we are noncombatants bringing food and supplies for the sick and wounded. And so it was that Lord Whitney gave the order. Some of the others up there though did not appreciate our presence."

"Make no mistake, we Nomads of Spiron are fierce fighter," Boldo told them. "On that point, they were in great disagreement on the upper ridge about that. A lot of disorder. No one seems to be in charge up there."

"Always a good man, that Lord Whitney," Amtor said. "Solid as they come."

Lady Valen approached Nadya with a beaming smile. "Oh, generous Spiron! You are most welcomed here!"

Queen Nadya greeted Lady Valen with a kiss. "My lady, we left our ancestral home seeking sanctuary from the Demonic. But we were told to come here, not because of our needs, but we come in your hour of need. We offer to you abundant resources but had no idea there were so many."

"Such a gracious and timely gift. We have much to do, and these supplies will comfort many," Valen said. "Blessings to you, and all the Nomads of Spiron, Queen Nadya."

Behind Nadya and Boldo, the rest of the Nomads began climbing out of their wagons. They set up camp and off-loaded supplies quickly. In accordance with their custom, as they worked in unison, they played music, danced, and began to sing the most delightful songs.

Oh, I have a river! Cut through the middle of my heart.
Oh, I have a river! Saved for the lover of my heart.
Oh, sometimes,
The river overflows, just like my aching heart.
And it makes me wonder, where does the water go?
Ever since we've been apart.
But I know that it flows, farther down the stream,
That's where I dream, about the lover of my heart.

The queen approached Amtor speaking very softly, "Amtor, will you please come with me? Some travelers came with us. They would very much like to see you in private, if you don't mind?"

Amtor and Nadya, along with Aberfell, walked through the Nomads as they sang on:

Oh, I have a river! Cut through the middle of my heart.
Oh, I have a river! Saved for the lover of my heart.

Amtor followed Nadya. They made their way through the caravan. At last, they came to a long black wagon without any windows. It had been painted all black with golden trim. The door was emblazoned with the orange-and-black insignia and coat of arms of the Nomads of Spiron.

"This wagon is a private transport for visitors and guests who wish to remain anonymous," Nadya told Amtor.

Boldo opened the door and motioned for Amtor to go inside. "No windows for prying eyes."

Once up the steps, Amtor had to duck to get through the low door. Behind him, Aberfell followed. But Boldo barred his entrance with a cool extension of his arm, an outward palm, and a toothy smile.

"The request was just for Amtor," Boldo said kindly but firmly. He smiled and a gold tooth flashed at Aberfell. The door closed behind Amtor.

"You mean they didn't ask for me too? The Supreme Historian?" Aberfell said, patting himself on the chest. "Who in the world is in there?"

"Guests of our queen," Boldo said, walking away, almost daring Aberfell to try to open the door on his own.

"Hmph!" Aberfell said, deflated, knowing it was trouble to attempt to barge in. He wanted no bad blood with the Nomads of Spiron. Instead, he walked away.

Entering the cabin, Amtor immediately recognized the man who had saved his life so long ago.

"By the Gods! Kilmer? Is that you, my friend?"

"Amtor! Well, just look at you," Kilmer shook the large man's hands. "It has been twenty years! You look healthier than ever. I see you recovered from your wounds."

"Ah, the Mauveguard Pass. Yes, the place you saved my life and pulled me out of that deep pit of death."

Amtor took Kilmer in his arms and held him in a warm embrace.

"Glad to see you," Kilmer laughed. "So much time has passed that we were never sure to see."

Amtor noticed who else was there.

"Gensen, Micah!" Amtor said. Then while examining Micah, the boy's skin was chalky white and pale, and dark circles rounded his eyes, deeply sunken in their sockets. His lips were tinted in an unnatural bluish-purple. "Micah? Are you—?"

"Amtor." Gensen stood and approached, interrupting his statement. "You look so healthy and refreshed, but...Amtor..." Gensen turned him away by the elbow. "Micah is not well. He has been turned to something...well, something not Micah."

"Aye, then it is as Astar told us," Amtor said. "What condition is he in?"

"He has become...a flesh-eater," Gensen whispered watching for Amtor's reaction. "After he was carried away by the Devourers, he was bitten by the demoness Langula, who infected him with a deadly venom. We have come here to seek out Lady Valen. Surely, her healing powers can find a cure for him."

"Of course, Gensen, of course," Amtor reassured him. "I'm sure she can help him too. Look, Gensen, I have nightmares of watching those vile creatures, the Devourers, carry our boys away. I am just so glad you have found Micah."

"Amtor," Gensen lowered his tone again. "Astar came to me in the underground He appeared out of nowhere. Thinking he was a demon appearing to me in a familiar disguise, I tried to strike him down. I'm sorry, Amtor. But I could not strike him. He convinced me of his miraculous power. He showed me the way out. Saved my life when I was on the brink of death. I am only alive thanks to the actions of your son, Astar."

"Gensen, Astar is the recycled spirit of Ehlona. The one foretold by the Star of Ehlona."

"All these years of knowing Astar, I had no idea my son's playmate was the reason for the Star of Ehlona. I always thought of it as a coincidence that on the day Astar was born, the Star of Ehlona started to shine. I never even thought to make the connection. Such an ordinary boy. I think I, along with the rest of the world, expected Ehlona's child to be someone's daughter, not someone's son, Amtor. Even if you would have told me, I would not have believed you. Until I experienced it for myself."

"Amtor." Kilmer approached, and speaking softly, placed his hand on Amtor's back. "In the Sanguine Forest, we watched Astar destroy Castle Orlo with his blade."

"Aye, Kilmer! We thought that explosion might be Astar in Orlo. He is in full possession of Soothsayer now. Astar and Ehlona, along with the power of the ancient Gods, have been joined," Amtor spoke loudly now, for all the others to hear. "Why, just look at me! My wounds are gone! I was cured with the magic of the new Gods. Astar and Lady Valen did this. Their power will be able to help you too, Micah. Yes, yes, I am sure of it."

Micah looked at Amtor with tired eyes, unimpressed. "Can she raise the dead?"

There was a long pause.

Hearing such a pause, Kilmer introduced his wife, Darla, and their young son, Kory, along with Oaks and Melvin.

"It is a pleasure to meet you, Amtor," Darla told him. "We have heard so many stories about you."

"Oh, yes, yes. There are many stories!" Amtor laughed with a nod to Kilmer. "You have come a long way from that day in the Mauveguard Pass. And you all have done well to come here."

"*You never would have believed, all the things that I've been through,*" Kilmer sang, reciting the words of a popular song from *The Witch's Songbook.*

Amtor laughed. "Well said, old friend. Well said. So nice to meet all of you, all my new friends."

"Is Gilglad with you?" Kilmer asked.

The humor suddenly left Amtor. They all noticed the quick change.

"No, no, she's not. A fire a long time ago."

"Oh, I am sorry to hear that," Kilmer said. "I didn't know."

"But there is more about her I think I must tell you."

"What other dark secrets and dangers have you been keeping to yourself?" Gensen asked. "After you told us that demons had fed on you, how much can you expect us to bear?"

The mention of demons made Kilmer take notice.

"A ray of hope for you, Gensen…and Micah. You see, Gilglad did not die in the fire that night as you were led to believe."

"She is alive?" Gensen asked. "After all these years? I don't understand."

"Gilglad did perish in that fire, but she did not die in it. She was changed, Gensen. Changed into someone else. She was changed into Lady Valen. Valen and Gilglad—they are one and the same."

"Are you saying…" The concept was too confusing for Gensen to understand. "What are you saying, Amtor? How is this possible?"

"We cannot understand it completely, Gensen," Amtor told him. "This is the Gods at work."

"I find all this hard to comprehend," Gensen said. "I'm just a blacksmith. These concepts are beyond me and my understanding. Give me hot iron, *that* is something I can understand."

"Just know this—when you speak to Lady Valen, you are speaking to the memory of Gilglad. Be careful here at the Temple of Valor, the magic of the Gods is on display here. We should all be mindful of that. We will either be saved by what happens here or be swept up by darker events. All I know is that powerful forces are at work here."

Kilmer overheard and turned to look at Amtor. "Amtor? Did I hear Gensen say that a demon fed on you?"

Amtor turned to look at Kilmer. "Aye, you heard it right, Kilmer. A serpent came to me in the middle of the night. What I thought were dreams, but she was there in real life. She fed on me and collected my blood. She collected more than blood at times."

"A serpent?" Kilmer asked, "Langula?"

"It is true," Amtor admitted. "She mesmerized me. I was with her against my will."

Kilmer asked, "Do you know what she did with what she took from you?"

Amtor went silent and avoided his gaze.

"I know what she did," Kilmer said. "For she made me do these things too."

At this point, Darla stood and wisely took Kory out of the wagon. Melvin went out with her. But Oaks remained, transfixed to the story. Kilmer hesitated for a moment, watching his wife and son leave. When Darla and Kory were clear of the door, he continued, but still in a quiet voice.

"She used us, Amtor, to breed a new generation of vampiric demons. They call themselves flesh-eaters. She used my blood to birth a red-skinned demon. The demon named Grim."

"Oh, he is the most ferocious one of them all," Micah whispered.

"I met this demon," Gensen spoke now. "Once out from the underground, I was offered as the Nomads' sacrifice for the feast of the Demonic. The red demon Grim came with Micah to accept me as that sacrifice. But discovering that I was Micah's father, he rejected me as the offering. The Nomads would incur the Demonic wrath for it."

Amtor asked Kilmer, "How can I know if my blood was used for a demon? I only ever saw the blue demon, Langula herself. I have never seen this red demon, Grim, you say."

"There are three demons I know of. Frost the blue-skinned, created in Langula's image. My blood was used for Grim," Kilmer told Amtor. "That would leave Monticello, the firstborn. The demon with the spots."

"Oh! On several occasions, I caught a glimpse of them, Kilmer. Demons, spying on me and my family. Langula came with the same spotted-skinned escort."

"The demon Monticello," Kilmer said. "They have blood connections with whomever incubated their Demonic egg. I don't think Monticello was spying on your family as much as he was spying on you, Amtor. With his blood connection he wanted to make contact."

"Blood connection?" Amtor asked.

Kilmer told him, "Call it a father connection. Grim had it with me. Monticello must have it with you."

"Your blood was used for this demon?" Amtor asked.

"I was captured and tortured by Langula and the Zorn. My stomach was torn open. I was forced to watch my blood incubate the Demonic egg," Kilmer said. "And the other things she made me do."

"But Grim is gone now," Oaks interjected. "We watched him leave on the Endless Sea, after a very strange meeting with Kilmer on the southern shore, close to the ancestral home of the Nomads of Spiron."

"I don't think you would have anything to fear from Monticello," Kilmer told Amtor. "He just wants to connect with you, like a son wanting to know his father. He may even be trying to protect you."

Micah spoke as he stood up with Gensen's help. "I can tell you this is true. Ever since Langula bit me, I have had a connection with her. I can *feel* her. As if she is standing in the middle of my bones. It gets worse the closer we are. That's how I know she's coming, and when she is near."

"Amtor," Kilmer spoke again. "If Monticello has your blood, he will want to find you, connect with you. Maybe that is something we can use."

"And all this time," Amtor replied, "I thought Langula and her spotted demon were after Soothsayer. When maybe Monticello was just trying to connect with me all along."

"All this time, all of this was happening in our little village of Homestead?" Gensen looked at the drawn-in face of Micah. "Amtor, why did you never tell us?"

"Gensen, these were not things I could share with you. These were things I did not understand myself. Only now can I make sense of them, of what happened then."

Then Kilmer spoke. "We must be careful here. As Amtor said, the Temple of Valor is a playground for the Gods. We are mortals among immortals. Stay alert, all of you. This place is dangerous."

Kilmer turned to Micah. "Micah, since you and Langula share a bond, maybe you should stay here and stay inside. You can be protected better if you stay in one spot where we know where you are. Plus, if you do not know what we are doing, you will not give Langula any indication of our actions."

"I am so hungry," Micah said. He climbed into a bunk inside the wagon and covered himself with a blanket.

Gensen followed him with sad, helpless eyes. "Should I get you... something to feed upon, Micah?" Gensen asked.

"No," Micah interrupted him. "I need nothing but Valen's healing. I do not wish to give in and satisfy these Demonic cravings. I only need a cure for this hunger. But I'm not sure how long I can hold out. It is easier if I sleep."

Gensen left the wagon. The rest of them followed, and slowly filed out.

Aberfell had patiently waited outside the wagon. As the door opened, he stepped up and introduced himself. "You must be Lord Plum-Kilmer. I am Aberfell. You've probably heard of me, no doubt."

"Aberfell?" Kilmer said as he joined Darla and Kory. Together, they looked at the hooded man. Kilmer smiled thoughtfully at Aberfell, then shrugged. "I'm sorry, I don't think we have heard of you."

"The Supreme Historian?" Aberfell raised his eyebrows. "Born on the blue comet?"

Kilmer and Darla looked at each other, then back to Aberfell. They shook their heads.

Aberfell's eyebrows burrowed down, as he huffed. "The boy who cannot forget?"

"Oh!" Kilmer said, snapping his fingers. "The boy who cannot forget. Yes, of course!"

"Must be nice. To forget, that is," Aberfell mumbled, slightly annoyed. "I remember you, for I cannot forget anything. I was just a baby then, when I was brought to your wedding. It was held on the Green at Castle Odessa. I remember everything that day, of course. It was the first time you were ever referred to as Lord Plum-Kilmer. The day King Leopold announced your real blood lineage of the Plum family to the entire kingdom. A rather dramatic day for you, I would say. The king gave you his dagger and offered his own neck to satisfy your vengeance. But instead of stabbing the king in the throat with it, you threw it over all the assembly, tossing it over the side of the Green, where it fell down the thousand-foot summit of the Blue Mountain. 'I choose life,' you shouted. Very nice, very touching."

Kilmer's face lit up. "I'm sorry I forgot you were there, but I do remember the day very well. Chen-Li was there with his First Wives too."

Aberfell lowered his head. "May they rest in peace."

"What do you mean, rest in peace?" Kilmer asked. "Something happened?"

"Tyla and Myra." Amtor nodded. "Cut down by the demon Langula."

Darla turned pale with a gasp.

Kilmer became sad. "They are dead? Tyla and Myra? They are the only reason I am alive today. Hard to believe."

"I don't want to believe it." Darla started to cry. "Oh, poor Tyla and Myra."

"Damn that demon," Amtor added. "I have my own reasons."

"Very sad, troubling," Kilmer repeated. He comforted Darla.

"Langula must be stopped," Darla suddenly said to Kilmer with uncharacteristic aggression. "Send her back to the hell she came from."

Oaks had walked out of the wagon and made his way among the Nomads of Spiron, fascinated by their music.

Oh, I have a river! Cut through the middle of my heart.
Oh, I have a river! Saved for the lover of my heart.

To Oaks they looked like the happiest bunch of people he had ever seen. A very pretty Nomad girl came to him and asked him to dance. He could not help but accept her invitation, even though he had no experience in dancing or merriment like this. But Oaks soon found it came naturally to him. The pretty Nomad girl patiently showed him the steps, and laughed when he got it wrong. Afterward, she took him to the banquet table, where they ate rich foods and laughed even more.

"I have never celebrated like this before," Oaks shouted over the music.

"Well, why not?" the girl asked. "We celebrate every day of our lives."

"Nothing much to celebrate, I guess. We were just lucky to be alive."

"Being alive is the best cause of all to celebrate," she told him. "You do not have to stay the way life found you. Don't you know that? Celebrate what is within you. That is our custom. We Nomads of Spiron celebrate life."

"What's your name?"

"Tamara," she leaned close to his ear. When she withdrew, the smell of her sweet, perfumed hair lingered.

"Oaks." He smiled and she smiled back.

The music played on.

Hollow Face appeared to Kilmer. The ghost wasted no time showing him a vision. The vision was screaming and destruction. Images of death permeated Kilmer's brain. This was a warning. A mighty battle was coming. Hollow Face did not, or could not, show Kilmer the outcome of the struggle. It was either unclear or unknown.

"Darla," Kilmer whispered as he came out of his vision. "Take Kory and get to cover."

"What? Why, Kilmer?" Darla asked with her hands full of medical supplies.

"Hollow Face," Kilmer told her with a serious expression. That was all she needed to hear. Darla dropped everything in her hands, and quickly took Kory by the hand. They ran.

The Nomads filled the air with singing, laughing, and talk of the past. Melvin smiled at them, then turned his attention to the Red and Blue upon the ridge. As he wandered up the Oracle Mount, he kept watch on the ridgeline observing their activity.

I used to be one of them, he thought.

Melvin became curious at the activity he saw. Their movements became increasingly more active than before.

Now what are they up to? Melvin watched with more focus.

Seemed to Melvin like they were hustling, busy at work. He gave a chuckle. He could sense the stress, the barking orders, and the scrambling compliance. Privately Melvin was glad to not be subject to it any longer. As he watched, he saw the arm of a catapult quietly flex forward, and a large, jagged rock silently lift into the air. Melvin froze, the tumbling rock was growing larger in complete silence as it started hurtling down directly toward him.

Melvin's eyes widened. He could hardly make a sound. He stumbled as he turned to run. Finally, he found his voice.

"Artillery! Take cover! We are under attack!"

There's a storm cloud coming

Coming over me

A storm cloud coming

Won't you please cover me?

Excerpt from *The Witch's Songbook*

He was free to get up, and he walked to the door.
But upon looking back, he saw his body still in bed fast asleep.
— Excerpt from *Kilmer's Ghost* (Chapter 29)

INTO THE MOUTH OF THE DEVOURER

ORACLE MOUNT

The first impact smashed into the Temple of Valor with a loud explosion, collapsing the outer wall into dust. The heavy debris crushed those near the impact, killing them instantly. Then, another projectile struck the ceiling, sending chunks of rock and broken plaster down upon the people inside. The temple rocked on its foundations with each new strike upon it.

With Frost dead, Brother Barker's malaise over King Leopold was broken. The king came out of the fog slowly. It took him a moment to collect his bearings. He scanned the situation on the ridge, seeing it clearly for the first time. He stood abruptly to learn the Red and Blue were on the ridge overlooking the Oracle Mount. Looking down the lines, Leopold saw the catapults launching projectiles on the Temple of Valor.

King Leopold's eyes widened. He sprang into action, running across the ridge, shouting as loud as he could, "Cease-fire! Cease-fire!"

One last launch and then the catapults grew silent.

"On whose authority do you attack the Temple of Valor?" King Leopold asked.

"On the orders of Brother Barker distributed yesterday."

"Ignore that order," the king breathlessly told them.

Just then, Lord Whitney and Lord Rhodes came running to the king's side.

"All orders from Brother Barker are hereby rescinded," King Leopold declared. "Lord Rhodes will be the commander of the Red and Blue. He will be in sole command of all Red and Blue forces in the field on my authority. Lord Rhodes only and no one else. Am I clear?"

"Yes, sir," all the men responded.

"Lord Whitney?" the king turned to the tall Lord Whitney.

"Yes, Your Majesty?"

"Take your command and return immediately to Castle Odessa," the king ordered him. "Defend the castle and begin preparations to repair the Green. Do you understand?"

Lord Whitney smiled a broad smile. "Yes, Your Majesty, I understand! I will depart immediately."

"What are your orders, Your Majesty?" Lord Rhodes asked.

"Defend the temple," the king said.

Lord Rhodes asked, "Defend it from what, Your Majesty?"

"Them," King Leopold pointed to the sky.

Lord Rhodes searched where King Leopold was pointing. Three distant shapes, still far away, were coming closer. Their darkness seemed to suck the light from the sky.

Lord Rhodes immediately turned from the king. He shouted at the top of his lungs, "Form into lines! Form into lines! Prepare to march! Quickly! Quickly!"

"Follow me to the Temple of Valor when they are ready, Lord Rhodes," the king said, pulling out his sword. "I am going on ahead."

TEMPLE OF VALOR

Astar and Valen huddled over a family of sick children. They help-lessly watched as the arched bridge collapsed inside the Temple of Valor. Pieces of stone debris splashed into the blue pond.

"Why would they attack the Temple of Valor?" Valen asked. "This is a place of healing not of war."

A large projectile rolled down the slope of the Oracle Mount. It collided with a crunch and came to a stop on one of the black wagons. When the stone came to rest near Amtor, he could see it had a smooth surface of polished green limestone.

"They are attacking the Temple of Valor with pieces of the broken Green!" Amtor shouted. "They are blind in their vengeance."

No one other than Aberfell heard him over the noise of the attack and the screams of entire families who lay dying. Kilmer shielded Darla and Kory. Oaks and Melvin huddled close by.

In the Temple of Valor, Astar multiplied himself to shield Lady Valen. Soon, she was shielded by a group of Astars. Oher copies of Astar started popping up everywhere, shielding groups of wounded people.

Then, just as suddenly as it started, there were no more projec-tiles. The Temple of Valor settled in dust, debris, and cries of the wounded. The sound of explosions was replaced by falling rocks coming to settle all around them. Now the moans of the sick and the dying began to grow in intensity.

Oaks spoke, "The shelling has stopped."

"It has, but for how long? And why?" Melvin rushed through the clouds of dust to see if he could help anyone.

"They stopped the artillery barrage to march in infantry," Amtor said, glancing quickly back up the ridge.

Kilmer told them, "See what is coming next."

Kilmer, Oaks, and Melvin joined Amtor and Aberfell. They could see King Leopold's forces assembling, coming down the hill now.

"Half of them are leaving," Melvin shouted. "The other half is coming through, marching down the ridge in columns toward us."

"They attack the Temple of Valor?" Oaks said.

"They are not in an attack formation," Kilmer observed.

"They are in single file," Amtor finished Kilmer's thought. "Not a skirmish line."

"Maybe they think they don't have to," Aberfell said, looking out over the damage.

The Nomads of Spiron suffered only minimal damage to one of their wagons. The Temple of Valor had taken the brunt of the attack. It now sat cracked and crumbling on top of the Oracle Mount.

A sudden scream sounded. Nadya and Boldo pointed up. "Look, there, in the sky!"

"The Devourers." Gensen immediately recognized the threat. "Coming down and fast!"

"King Leopold's troops are coming too," Melvin said, pointing. As Leopold's army came running across the valley now, Melvin pulled out his sword. "Get ready! Here they come!"

Oaks pulled Kilmer close. "Kilmer, if we are captured, they'll hang us!"

"Then fight like never before! Take them all with us!" Kilmer looked back at Darla and Kory. Darla heard but continued attending a fallen acolyte with a wounded child. Kory helped his mother comfort the child.

"Retreat to the Temple of Valor!" Kilmer shouted and all of them started to run. "Go back to the temple!"

A tremendous wind blasted by them, followed by a loud heavy boom, the first Devourer landed. It surprised a camp of sick people and, upon swinging its razor-sharp wings, disemboweled them in one rapid motion. They fell away in sprays of trailing blood. Then, the Devourer turned its large mouth to face the Temple of Valor and let out a roaring growl.

The second Devourer perched on top of the temple, shaking it on its foundations as it landed there. The creature's mouth opened wide and let out a vicious scream of rage.

Amtor was the first to act. He swung his battle-ax and rushed to meet the Devourer that landed in the field. Kilmer closely followed, his sword pulled back to strike. Oaks and Melvin came next, fully armed, and running toward the beast.

Aberfell, the self-professed watcher, was not accustomed to hand-to-hand combat. Still, he armed himself with a knife, the one Amtor had given him. He stayed well out of the fray, and inside the confines of the Temple of Valor. From there, he could see the third Devourer. It was flying overhead in a circle. Upon its back, the green Skeletal King rode the last Devourer. Aberfell could tell it had only one foot.

As Amtor neared, the beast turned to face him and the oncoming rush. With a sudden thrash of its razor-sharp wings, the Devourer sliced the air in front of Amtor, nearly slicing him. But Amtor was fast and avoided the creature's sweeping wings by the slightest of margins. Then, Amtor stared into the dark abyss of the Devourer's wide gaping mouth.

Kilmer arrived and flanked the monster on the left. Now both men circled it on opposite sides. Working together, the two men succeeded in confusing the beast on which way to turn.

More help arrived. Oaks and Melvin joined in. Gensen ran up with his sword named Vengeance. Nadya and Boldo rushed in with long spears soon after. Seven armed defenders surrounded the first beast.

"That's it, circle it." Amtor motioned with his hand. "Surround the creature."

The Devourer did not know in which direction to defend itself. In frustration, the beast screamed as it continued turning in circles. Kilmer and Oaks moved to the right. Gensen and Melvin moved to its left. Nadya and Boldo poked at the creature from behind. In the front, Amtor kept its large mouth at bay with his sharply honed battle-ax.

Darla kept watch on her husband. She saw how they had surrounded the oily black creature. She quickly finished patching up the woman she was working on as best she could.

"I've got to go," Darla said to her. "I'm sorry, but I must go."

"No, please don't leave me," the injured woman begged. "Don't leave."

"I'll be back for you," Darla said. "Kory, you stay here, hold this bandage in place, and don't move."

"I'll stay with you," said an aspect of Astar who suddenly appeared. "Go to Kilmer. I'll watch out for Kory. You go."

"Thank you, Astar," Darla said and quickly pulled her sword. She saw Aberfell standing in the archway watching the battle. Darla ran to stand beside him.

Lady Valen, at just that moment, had her fingers inside an old man's stomach, when another copy of Astar appeared to her. "Lady Valen, we are under attack by the Zorn's Devourers! We need to do something. Take my hand."

"My lady?" the old man asked as she pulled her fingers out of him. "Where are you going?"

"I must go now, my love," Valen said, wiping her hands. "You sleep now." She put her hand on the old man's forehead. He gently fell into a deep sleep. "That will keep him safe for now," Valen said and took Astar's hand.

When they clasped hands, the energies and power of the Goddess were joined. Astar's Blade started to glow in a green light. A flash pulsed from them sending a circular wave of emerald energy rippling out. Inside the Temple of Valor, the wave of energy pulsated out. Magic sparkled on the recipients' skin as they received a blast of healing from the ancient power. Lady Valen embraced Astar. When she did, more energy was released between them. Their wave grew in both power and frequency. Emerald waves pulsed from them like ripples on the surface of a lake. The waves pulsated outside the temple, fortifying those on and around the Oracle Mount. For those engaged in battle with the Devourers, the green wave refreshed and provided them with additional power and strength.

The beast circled and turned its back to Amtor. Taking advantage of the opportunity, Amtor rushed forward and attacked the Devourer. The battle-ax rang true. A vicious blow right between the wings stuck the beast hard, lodging deep in the creature's back. It let out an agonized scream.

The second Devourer now swung into action. Tucking its wings and darting like an angry missile, the behemoth dived toward the fray from high on the Temple of Valor. It plowed into Amtor, pinning him in between the two Devourers. The newly joined beast opened its mouth to consume the mighty warrior. But Amtor was fast and moved quickly. He gave the battle-ax a pull and it came sweeping out of the first beast. In one smooth motion, Amtor spun the handle and thrust the battle-ax vertically into the creature's mouth. The battle-ax created a wedge that prevented its jaws from closing. As the Devourer applied its lethal bite, the axe handle bent but held the monster's jaws apart.

"I will not be food for your supper today!" Amtor shouted at the beast. But as he spoke, sharp claws ripped across the warrior's chest. Amtor grimaced but his newly gained black armor took the brunt of the damage.

Pinned in the middle of the Devourers, Amtor's bravery inspired the others. They rushed into battle, stabbing and slashing both of the beasts with the tips of their spears and with their swords. Every strike made the great beasts groan in agony.

Surrounded by fierce attackers, the Devourers lashed out on their own. Flailing their claws and wings, they shook their heads wildly in every direction. Yet the more they struggled, the more they continued taking damage at every turn.

King Leopold and the Red and Blue army were getting closer. They were running now toward the temple grounds, swords drawn, spears at the ready.

Without a warning, Astar's fractal dragon appeared overhead, diving at the advance of the soldiers, catching them midway in the valley. The fractal dragon, made of hundreds, if not thousands, of duplicated versions of Astar, kept the Red and Blue at bay. The army's advance stopped in fear of dragon. The front lines stopped, and the rear guards slammed into them. The distraction created a chaotic congestion of fearful troops. They shouted in panic, refused to go on, and pointed at the dragon. Many retreated, refusing to go a step farther. Yet some overcame their fears and found sufficient courage to run past the dragon. The brave ones pressed on, despite the fractal dragon, toward the Oracle Mount.

"*Stop!*" the dragon called out in a loud voice of many Astars. "I don't know why you've come here! But I can't let you go any farther!"

"We've come to fight the Devourers!" Some of the troops up front shouted.

But Astar only heard that they came to fight. As Astar struggled with the army, the Zorn, riding on the maimed Devourer, turned sharply to avoid Astar's fractal dragon.

"Zorn!" the dragon exclaimed after him.

• ⋅ ⊷●ᗪ●C●⊶ ⋅ •

"Darla, look up there," Aberfell said.

Darla looked up to where he was pointing. He was pointing to the Temple of Chen-Li.

Aberfell continued, "The spirits of the White Eminence are launching their spiritual Lis."

Darla could see the trails of vapor, thousands of them. The coming of the White Eminence. The Li spirits of the warrior-priests coming up in trailing streams high on the Fangs. Darla ran through the archway to watch them come. They were arcing like missiles launched from the Temple of Chen-Li, arcing down to strike the Oracle Mount and the Temple of Valor.

"Here they come!" Darla and Aberfell screamed and dived out of the way.

In a series of flashing smoke, the White Eminence slammed into the ranks of the advancing Red and Blue soldiers along their front. Like ghosts when the Li spirits hit the soldiers they disappeared deep into their bodies. The first soldiers fell, absorbing the Lis. Each one hit now wrestled in an individual battle, an unseen struggle, for spiritual control of their own bodies.

Lord Rhodes was hit. He fell to the ground. His eyes rolled backward as the invading spirit sent him into convulsions. It did not take long. His battle of possession was over. Lord Rhodes, unpracticed in the ways of spiritual warfare, was no match for the Li. As it went with so many of the other soldiers around him, several of his men now stood in the field under someone else's control. They faced away from the advance on the Temple of Valor and turned on their comrades. Lord Rhodes was not in command any longer. Now, the army began attacking itself. Possessed soldiers attacked unpossessed soldiers. Even Lord Rhodes, a prisoner in his own body, was powerless to stop himself as he struck down and killed his own men.

Among the chaos, men burst out screaming, as one single fiery streak moved about them. From one soldier to the next, they ignited in blazing fire. Chen-Li was attacking, roasting the soldiers alive from the inside out.

Lord Rhodes could only struggle for control of his own body, watching all these awful things with a tear in his eye.

The spirit of Chen-Li was heard shouting, "You will regret the day you attempted war with the White Eminence!"

As the Red and Blue were killing each other, the White Eminence advanced from the dead and dying soldiers to new ones. Even more soldiers began to retreat back up the ridge.

Amtor snatched the long-handled battle-ax out of the Devourer's mouth. He swung it and buried it deep between the Devourer's oily black eyes. A stream of purple mist sprayed from its head. Amtor withdrew the battle-ax and spun it back into its mouth, preventing another attempted bite. As the creature crunched down, the battle-ax bent but held.

"We've got you now!" Amtor shouted.

The Devourer, still spraying purple blood from its head, turned to face Amtor. Making it pay for turning its back on him, Kilmer thrust his sword deep inside its back. The creature cried out. Kilmer dodged a razor-sharp wing, as the beast turned to attack him again. Just then, Oaks delivered a wide slicing sword swipe that cut through a section of the creature's wing. Melvin thrust straight and deep into the beast, driving his sword into the chest of the creature. Gensen sliced a great gash into the creature's side with his sword. Nadya and Boldo drove their spears deep under its thick hide, stabbing at the heart of the Devourer. The beast was taking damage from all directions.

"It is working!" Oaks shouted.

"We are going to kill it!" Gensen exclaimed.

Amid the struggle, the inevitable happened.

Snap!

Everyone heard it. The Devourer had snapped the long handle of Amtor's battle-ax in its mouth!

Amtor's eyes widened. He reached down and pulled out a long dagger he kept in his boot. As he did, the beast spit out pieces of his ax. The Devourer spread its enormous mouth over half of Amtor. This time, he could not prevent it. The upper half of his body was suddenly covered by its enormous mouth. The Devourer lifted the large warrior up off the ground.

Inside the Devourer's mouth, the air was rancid with hot breath. In utter darkness, somehow Amtor managed to roll over onto his back.

"I bite back, you nasty bastard!" Amtor shouted for all to hear. He thrust his dagger up and through its lip from the inside. Out of the great beast's mouth the sharp blade of Amtor's dagger thrust out of the Devourer's face. The blade wiggled as Amtor strained against it to cut himself free. Seeing Amtor struggle inside the creature's mouth, the fighters raised shouts of roused fury. Their attacks on the

Devourer became desperate in an energetic rush. Kilmer stabbed the beast. Gensen swung his blade. Nadya and Boldo leaped forward. Melvin and Oaks undercut the belly of the beast.

Inside the hot darkness, Amtor clenched his jaw in pain as row upon row of the Devourer's sharp teeth constricted around his waist. The rows of teeth began to pierce him, compressing around and stabbing him, pushing into his waist. Helpless to stop it, his body started to quiver. Blood poured out from his waist, ran down his legs, and sprayed out from inside the Devourer's mouth. Then, with a sickening crunch, the lower half of Amtor's body fell away from the mouth of the Devourer.

Aberfell stared from the Temple of Valor in disbelief. Astar, in his fractal dragon form, turned to look. Amtor, his father, had been severed in half.

All time stopped. A single version of Astar appeared on the battlefield.

"Oh, Father! What have I done? Why did I not stay with you?"

Unexpectedly, like a rushing wind, the voice of the Goddess Ehlona came to Astar. *You cannot save everyone, Astar. For each man must fulfill his own destiny, as you must fulfill yours. Amtor lived most of his life as only half a man. In death, he died a whole man again.*

Astar started to cry. "Can't we go back in time? Yes, yes, that's it! Show me how reverse time, not just stop it! We can go back—I can save him. I can be by his side. Then I can start time again, and we will be able to reverse it."

But the voice of Ehlona did not speak.

"He was the greatest man that ever walked upon this world. Help me!"

My powers are not unlimited, Astar. I can't go back in time. A thousand times I wished I could. But what is done cannot be undone. The spirit of your father has already passed. He spirit has traveled on to the Cosmic

Creation. Now he joins all the others, an equal to the great mystery. I am sorry, Astar, you must let him go.

"No! I don't want to let him go!" Astar burst into tears. All around him, scenes of battle froze.

He continued to cry for hours in stopped time. While time was stopped, every movement he made created an echo of his body. While he rose to stand, at the same time, he remained kneeling beside his father. And as he backed away, he created a tunnel of previous versions of himself. He could see through a tunnel of Astars, on to the remains of his father's body. He finally turned away.

Duplicating himself a hundred, then a thousand times, the fractal dragon began to take shape again. The dragon returned to the place in the sky where he was before he stopped time. Once he was back, a great light flashed. Time started again.

The battle resumed.

I see the rain

It's coming tonight

Stab me in the back with all your might.

Excerpt from *The Witch's Songbook*

Five deaths in total.
Those who went into the Sanguine Forest never came out.
— Excerpt from *Kilmer's Ghost* (Chapter 30)

WHEN I TAKE MY LAST BREATH

TEMPLE OF VALOR

A hush fell over the Oracle Mount. A slow realization crept over them. Amtor had been killed, bitten in half. Amtor was dead.

"No, not Amtor!" Aberfell shouted, turning inside the Temple of Valor.

Lady Valen wanted to run to Amtor, but Aberfell intercepted her.

"No, my lady, don't go out there," he said.

"Why? What are you protecting me from?" she asked.

"It's Amtor." Aberfell dropped his head. "He has fallen."

"Amtor? My champion? No, it is not possible." Valen searched outside. "Maybe I can heal him."

"He is beyond your help." Aberfell would not let her go. "And it is far too dangerous for you to go out there."

Looking over Aberfell's shoulder, Valen could see the bottom half of Amtor's body lying on the ground. "Oh, Amtor."

The Devourer snarled, and with a swing of its razor-sharp wings, the beast repulsed Melvin and Boldo, propelling them backward. Spinning, it then struck the legs of Kilmer and Oaks, causing them both to tumble over. Nadya and Gensen ducked, narrowly avoiding the deadly spikes of the Devourer's wing.

When Kilmer fell, one of the Devourers leaped upon his chest and landed heavily. Knocking the wind out of Kilmer, the creature's sheer weight was crushing him. Kilmer's face turned red as his chest was caving under the massive weight.

Darla saw what happened to her husband and rushed to Kilmer's aid. Only a few steps outside of the temple, Darla was waylaid by the demon Langula. Tightly constricted in Langula's coils, Darla fell in a cloud of dust and rolled together with the demoness upon the ground.

Aberfell rushed to help Darla but was met with a swift backhand. Langula's blow sent him reeling backward. As Aberfell lay on the ground, groggy, with red claw marks on his face, Lady Valen rushed to his side invoking her magic. Energy sparked from her fingertips and provided healing to Aberfell's wounds.

Under the weight of the Devourer, Kilmer tried to call out. But he could find no air. His face turning redder as he was being crushed. Through bloodshot eyes, Kilmer could see Darla struggle with Langula just a short distance from him.

The Devourer held him fast, tightly piercing him with its claws. Then, the Devourer spread its mouth open to consume him, the same way it just had with Amtor. Kilmer could see deep down into the Devourer's purple throat. From out of that tooth-filled hole a hot and rancid breath blew on his face. The beast was preparing to swallow him.

Outside the temple, Langula used one hand to put Darla in a choke hold. She squeezed Darla's throat with sharp, hardened nails.

With her other hand, Langula held any other rescuers at bay. Darla let out a scream and Langula's serpent coils constricted her, ever tightening, squeezing the very air out of her. The demoness dragged Darla around the side of the temple, disappearing from Kilmer's view.

At the very moment the Devourer opened its mouth to cover Kilmer, purple blood splashed warm and thick across his face. The tip of a sword had burst powerfully out of the Devourer's open mouth. The sword withdrew, quickly disappearing. Its absence left the monster gargling in its own purple blood. Then, the sword reappeared; this time it came out of one of its oily black eyes. The sword was there for a moment, then withdrew and was gone. When the sword appeared again, it was hacking through the head of the great beast. As a steady current of blood splashed on Kilmer, the Devourer's body faltered.

As the beast rolled off Kilmer, he saw who was responsible for his rescue. King Leopold stood there, sword in hand, and dripping of purple blood! The king was the only one of the Red and Blue that made it up to the Oracle Mount. He had run through the gauntlet. The fractal dragon had not dissuaded him. The White Eminence could not possess him. Even though they tried but failed. Unlike the others, his blood had the Zorn's immunity. His willpower was far too strong to yield to the force of these spirits.

The king gave a brief smile to Kilmer but then acted swiftly. He took a position over the creature and held his sword with both hands. With another great swing, the Devourer's head was now only held together by the finest strand of stringy hide. The king gave the beast one more thrust in the opposite direction, cutting through the last remaining thread, to make the action complete. As its head came off, the beast fell heavily, leaving Kilmer to squeeze out from underneath its dead weight and sharp teeth.

King Leopold withdrew his sword and moved off to the next foul creature.

Now free from the beast, Kilmer rushed to the side of the temple. Turning the corner, he received a whip from the demon's tail that drove him to the ground.

"The girl is mine!" Langula hissed. "She belongs to me!"

There was a wisp of black smoke, and Langula and Darla disappeared into a misty vapor. Kilmer reached into the scattering vapors but grasped only air. They were gone.

Up above another conflict was unfolding. "Astar! Astar! I am not here to fight you! I came here to help you!" The Zorn, flying high over the Temple of Valor, called out for a parlay from the back of the maimed beast. The Devourer flapped its wings to stay aloft and stationary. Astar's fractal dragon, many times larger than the Devourer, approached the Zorn and examined him closely.

"You! You have caused this destruction," the dragon spoke in the angry voice of a thousand Astars.

"I tried to get them to stop. I-I cannot stop them," the Zorn pleaded with Astar. "Langula, Monticello, Chen-Li—they all have gone mad! Langula has struck out on her own! She does not serve me anymore! Not since Chen-Li killed Frost... You've got to help me, Astar. Everything is getting out of control."

"What do you want?" the fractal dragon asked.

"Astar, I want my flesh back. I want to be restored! I want to be free from the Skeletal King. I knew neither you nor Valen would help me if I carried out an attack on the Temple of Valor. But Langula has attacked here because she wants to keep me the Skeletal King."

"If you are deceiving me, you will pay with your life, Hazor," Astar said.

"I just want to be whole again!" the Zorn shouted. Despite his hideous condition, his vanity was still absolute.

The dragon thought. "I need to help you, Zorn, to make my plan complete. But heed my warning: if you are deceiving me, in any way, I'll blast you back to the Cosmic Creation myself."

"I know you can do it. I am not deceiving you. You can trust me," the Zorn said with a nod. Then the Zorn veered away on the maimed Devourer. Astar's fractal dragon watched him for a moment. Just the words, hearing the Zorn say *trust me*, were unsettling.

The fractal dragon then turned and swooped beyond the land behind the mountains. Once on the ground the Astars dispersed, and the fractal dragon came apart. As the Astars disconnected, they absorbed back into the remaining Astars on the temple grounds.

Astar looked toward the mountains. The Zorn was riding out of sight.

Hmph! Astar thought. *Trust me. That will be the day.*

Meanwhile the battle with the remaining Devourer continued. In a shower of sparks, Chen-Li came screaming out of the sky to strike the remaining Devourer. Following his lead, the Li spirits of the White Eminence likewise swept down from the skies. They repeatedly struck the remaining Devourer, knocking it off balance.

Remember the First Wives! they cried as they struck the beast. *For the First Wives!*

After his possession, Lord Rhodes came to his senses and looked over the carnage. His men had been decimated, many lying dead in the field. A rush of anger seethed out of him. He realized the king's words had come true.

We can't fight against them. We can't and we won't. These are spiritual forms. Our men will have little hope of defending against their skills at possession. You will have to wait, Lord Rhodes, until they inhabit the bodies of our troops. Then, as they turn our own men against us, you will be able to kill them. We have provided all the materials they need. Fifty thousand bodies that they can possess.

The surviving soldiers began to regroup and were picking themselves up off the ground. They joined together with those who had fled in retreat. Now they came together and continued their dogged advance to the Oracle Mount.

"Come on, boys!" Lord Rhodes encouraged them on. "Forward!"

They rushed through the field, through the remaining spirts of the White Eminence. Shortly, the first soldiers finally arrived at King Leopold's side. They helped surround the Devourer, stabbing at it with their spears.

The Red and Blue raised their call. "Remember the Green! Remember our dead!"

Yet the beast rallied. It stood upright and tall, growling in a fit of rage. Planting its feet firmly in the ground, it stomped and swung its mighty wings. The powerful blast propelled its attackers away.

But King Leopold stood firm, still facing the Devourer. He leaped forward, lunging through the air with a warrior's shout. His sword buried itself through the lips of the great beast, fastening them together and holding them tight.

The Devourer stumbled backward, away from the king. The sword had penetrated its lips diagonally. While the Devourer pawed clumsily at its face, trying to remove the sword that held its mouth together, the king reached down and pulled out a long dagger from his belt.

"Now we finish it!" Leopold approached the loathsome creature.

Leopold took only one step closer to the beast, when he was struck in the neck. It was Amtor's broken battle-ax that had cleaved full and heavy into him. The attack came from behind, striking deep and hard in between his neck and shoulder. The king never saw it coming.

Chen-Li's burning spirit halted. Aberfell and Valen were assisting Kilmer, when they all looked up. Melvin, Gensen, and Oaks stared in shock. Nadya and Boldo lowered their spears. Those of the Red and Blue hesitated. Everything seemed to stop as they saw their king fall.

King Leopold's eyes widened. He grasped his throat and dropped to his knees. Behind the king, Monticello held the short end of Amtor's broken battle-ax. The spotted demon, incubated from the blood of Amtor, had picked up his patriarch's weapon and struck down the king with it.

The White Eminence were the first to act. A flurry of spirits descended upon Monticello. They pelted him in a rapid succession of off-balancing strikes. Monticello recoiled, falling backward. He released the broken handle of the battle-ax embedded it into Leopold's neck. As the spotty demon fell backward, even more of the spirits slammed into him.

King Leopold struggled against the battle-ax to remove it. Painfully, he pulled it out, sticky and wet with his warm blood. He threw the thing to the side. Blood cascaded thick out of his neck, fast now. He tried to stop the bleeding, but he couldn't—it was too much. Turning pale, he collapsed on his back in a cloud of dust.

After the spirits knocked Monticello on his back, the demon tried to scramble to his feet. Suddenly, Monticello's eyes widened as a spear punctured his chest. Micah stood over him holding it. The pale boy, white as chalk, stared with darkened dead eyes down at him. Clenching his lips, he gave a second downward thrust that drove the point of the spear deeper through Monticello's heart. Staring down at Monticello's face, Micah watched death form in the demon's eyes.

"Die, you bastard demon!" Micah gave the spear another thrust, until it stuck in the ground under Monticello's back. Then, he added a turn for good measure. Holding the spear, Micah watched the life run out of his former captor.

The remaining Devourer, mouth still pinned by Leopold's sword, was unable to use his most devastating attack. Yet it continued to defend itself by swinging its wings and claws. Knowing it was cornered and overwhelmed, it tried to get away. Attempting a retreat, it spread its wings and tried to fly away. The creature lifted slightly in flight. But several brave men of the Red and Blue dived upon it, attaching themselves to the beast and weighing it down. The Devourer flapped its wings harder and began to rise higher. Yet it was in vain as still more men came to hold on. The Devourer's left wing faltered, collapsing under the weight of the men. With the left wing failing, the creature listed that way. The beast continued to flap furiously with its remaining unburdened right one. But it was greatly encumbered, and flight was no good. The Devourer fell back down to the ground flat on its back.

Once down, the Devourer was immediately overwhelmed by a rush of soldiers with swords and spears. They repeatedly and wildly pierced and stabbed the creature, until it was motionless on the ground. Even after the great beast was dead, they kept stabbing it, long after it had stopped moving.

"Cease-fire! Cease-fire!" Lord Rhodes shouted above the din. "The Devourer is dead."

One by one, the spears and swords stopped stabbing the dead thing.

"It can no longer hurt us," Lord Rhodes told them.

Kilmer pushed his way through to King Leopold. Leopold held his hands over his wound. He had lost a lot of blood. The battle-ax had severed the main arteries in his neck. Despite the seriousness of his wound, the king tried to talk.

He whispered so softly Kilmer could not understand him and had to move closer. Kilmer leaned to him, turned to the side, and put his ear against Leopold's lips.

The king whispered, "Who...was...it?" Leopold coughed out some of the blood. He whispered again, a little louder this time. "Who... killed me?"

Lord Rhodes joined Kilmer. Aberfell, Oaks, and Melvin as well as a host of others, including soldiers from the Red and Blue, formed a wide circle around the fallen king. Even the spirits paused in mid-flight to witness the last moments of King Leopold.

Kilmer attempted to stop Leopold's bleeding with linens handed to him by the acolytes. But it was to no avail. It was hopeless. The king was dying. He would be dead soon.

"Was it...*you*...Kilmer?" Leopold made short gasps for air. Whispering softer, he said, "Darius Plum."

Kilmer looked over and saw the body of Monticello nearby. The spotted demon was dead, a spear sticking out of his chest. The broken-handled battle-ax of Amtor lay nearby in the dirt, stained with the blood of the king.

"I am sorry," Kilmer cried.

"No...no, don't...be." King Leopold shook his head, his face pale. "If anyone...deserved it...better you...than..."

Leopold let out a long exhale.

Lord Rhodes quickly checked him for a pulse. Finding none where he checked, he moved to check in several other places on the king's body. Still finding none, Rhodes reluctantly withdrew his hand from the body. He slowly looked up at Kilmer and shook his head.

Kilmer laid King Leopold's head gently back on the grass. He took one last look at the king's pale face, then covered it with linen. Kilmer now stood and looked at his hands. The blood upon them was bright red and thick. An acolyte handed him a linen, but for some reason, he did not take it or wipe away the blood.

Lord Rhodes rose too now. Feeling a multitude of eyes upon him, Kilmer spoke.

"Am I under arrest?" Kilmer asked without looking at Rhodes. They both continued staring down at King Leopold's body.

"I cannot bear to do that. Such a despicable thing to do, especially to you of all people," Lord Rhodes said.

"What about Melvin? He fought hard today," Kilmer asked. "Without a pardon, he will hang. Helping a condemned man escape is death. He broke the law helping you escape. He'll have to answer for that."

Kilmer asked Rhodes, "After all you two have been through? You would be able to send him to the gallows?"

"I can't," Rhodes said. "I will defer his sentence to my superior officer."

"Lord Whitney?" Kilmer asked.

"I will not pardon Melvin, but as my superior, you can do with him what you will." Rhodes stopped staring at King Leopold's body. He now looked up at Lord Plum-Kilmer. "Brother Barker is dead. Before all this happened, the king granted me all authority in the field. Maybe he knew something like this was going to happen. Do you think Leopold could have known what was going to happen?"

"He always seemed to know what others did not," Kilmer said. "It wasn't magic, you know. He just had a talent for observation. It just seemed like magic."

"I'm going to grant you a full pardon, Kilmer. Full restoration of your title and position." Rhodes patted Kilmer on the shoulder. "Welcome back, Lord Plum-Kilmer."

"Thank you, Lord Rhodes. But there is no rest for me, until I get Darla back."

Just then, Kory Plum-Kilmer walked out of the temple's archway holding a bloodstained linen. A worried look darkened his face.

"Papa," the five-year old's voice pierced the silence. "Where's Mama?"

Kilmer was covered in blood—purple blood from the Devourer, bright red blood of King Leopold, some of his own, all mingled together. The crowd parted, allowing Kilmer to make his way through the circle. He walked away from Leopold and toward his son.

Kilmer knelt to Kory. Their eyes met, and Kilmer's swelled with watery tears. No words came immediately. Instead, emotions welled up and Kilmer did not know what to say. Finally, he told Kory, "I'm going to get her back. I promise."

One of the Astar's walked over to where Kilmer knelt embracing his son. They both were crying.

"Kilmer," Astar whispered. "I know where she is."

"You know where she is?" Kilmer sniffed. "Darla? Where?"

"She is safe and unharmed," Astar said. "Langula has taken her to the Temple of Chen-Li. I can see you're worried but don't. For I am up there with them right now. While I am here with you, I am also up there with her at the same time."

Kilmer gave Astar look of astonishment. "Astar, bring her back to us. Let no harm befall her." He gripped Astar by the shoulders.

"Please, I beg of you. Use all your powers. She means more to us than anything. You must bring her back to us."

"I know, I know," Astar said, reassuring him. Astar removed Kilmer's hands. "Events are unfolding as we speak. It won't be long now."

Inside the Temple of Valor, despite the tragedy outside, Valen continued to work. She knelt by an injured child. Her arm was inserted deep inside the little girl's stomach, applying her healing touch. Valen had tears running from her eyes. She was mourning the loss of Amtor, remembering the life she had with him. She mourned for all who died today. She sang a song she knew from *The Witch's Songbook*. Her voice broke the shocked silence.

> *You remind me of a warm summer breeze,*
> *That blows there beside me, but I'm too afraid to breathe.*
> *Once I saw her struggle against the waves*
> *A love, lost, and dying, but too afraid to breathe.*
> *Once I looked into eyes so green*
> *They dreamed of a child, but I was too afraid to dream*
> *And the days of tomorrow are blowing in the trees.*
> *They fall like the mourning, and too afraid to leave.*
> *A love, lost, and dying, and too afraid to breathe.*

The sound of her voice faded away. Hearing Lady Valen's song affected each person differently. But none who heard her was left unmoved. Each person reflected in their private way on the events of this day. Now the sky was dulling, and the clouds were turning to reddish-orange.

The little girl, waking from her long nightmare, spoke to Lady Valen now. "My stomach feels much better now."

"Love has healed you," Valen said, wiping her tears, wiping her hands.

Just then, the wind picked up and blew through the chimes. Lady Valen reacted when she heard them. She gave the chimes an upward glance, noticeably acknowledging them. Then, she looked the girl in the eyes. Lady Valen smiled softly to her. "Listen to the chimes, my dear little one. The spirits of those we loved and lost are moving through the wind."

The little girl nodded.

"They are saying goodbye before they fly away."

ACT V

Every Part

of the Whole

The fire's dying slow, the embers glow
And is all nearly gone.
So why do we hurry?
We've got time.

Excerpt from *The Witch's Songbook*

The king reached under his red fur cloak and
pulled out an eight-inch dagger.
— Excerpt from *Kilmer's Ghost* (Chapter 31)

SUNSET AT THE TEMPLE OF CHEN-LI

The Temple Of Chen-Li

Langula appeared on the high walkways that lined the top of the walls at the Temple of Chen-Li. She held Darla tightly in her serpent's coils.

"Let go of me!" Darla twisted and struggled against her captor.

Langula looked down over the high railing. Below, in the courtyard, the priests of the White Eminence sat motionless in illuminated meditation, their bodies separated from their spirits. Their Lis had gone below, currently attacking the Devourers at the Temple of Valor. The Devourers had proved to be a perfect distraction. No one noticed Langula had arrived. There was no movement anywhere. The courtyard was calm and still.

No one, except for one. Amid the silence and stillness of the courtyard, a single voice called out.

"Hello! Hello, up there!" It was Astar. He was there, moving through priests in the courtyard. He waved to Langula from below. "She will not be able to resist you. Her name is Darla. You can release her now."

"I said, she is mine!"

"She will not move, won't even struggle. None of these others can either." He smiled at Langula. "I've stopped time. You and I are not affected. See for yourself."

"You lie!" Langula sneered. She turned back to look at Darla. Somehow Astar was right. The woman was completely still, her expression frozen on her face. Everyone in the temple was the same. Everyone seemed to be stuck in time, except Astar and Langula.

"Just let her go," Astar said. "There's no reason to..."

Langula uncoiled. Darla fell hard on the walkway like a sack of potatoes.

"That's not what I meant..." Astar started to say. "But never mind."

Langula peered over the railing again, giving Astar her full attention. She hissed at him. "You have done this?"

"The ancient power has," Astar told her. "I thought you knew what I was capable of?"

In a blur, Astar was up on the high walkway with the demoness. He stood adjacent to her on the western walkway, but not too close.

Astar asked, "Why have you come here to the Temple of Valor amidst all this chaos? Didn't you know how outnumbered you would be? Frost is dead. There is nothing you can do for him anymore. Just like there is nothing I can do nothing for my father. Or Chen-Li for his First Wives."

"Outnumbered? By these priests? They are nothing but empty husks," Langula told him, looking at them over the railing. "They make war below."

Astar walked along the western parapet on the high walkway. "Did you instruct Monticello to kill Leopold?"

"Leopold ruined everything!" Langula said with a spit. She slithered over Darla's body, lying prone on the walkway. "He outlived his usefulness the day Frost was murdered. Five years! Ruined!" She slithered closer now to where Astar was in the parapet, though she kept anxiously looking over the railing to the courtyard below, half expecting the White Eminence to snap to life at any moment. "You have the magic to stop time, then? You are a powerful wizard, Astar. More powerful than the Zorn. In another life, I may have enjoyed serving you, but that does not matter anymore."

"Time is for mortals, Langula, not us," Astar said strolling through the parapet coming closer to her. "The place you came from has always been this way. Do you not remember? Can you not remember your past?"

Astar considered Langula for a moment. Her eyes darted in all directions. Her hands were shaking. She was breathing very rapidly.

"What do you want, Langula?" Astar asked. "Why did you come here? Do you want to die?"

"Do not threaten me with oblivion, warlock! I have been there—I remember what it is," Langula said.

"Astar," she then whispered, "I have been betrayed. The Zorn is betraying the Demonic. His kindred flesh, betrayed. He doesn't care for any of us. He only cares about saving his own skin. Only cares about the restoration of his rotted flesh."

"Come now," Astar said. "I'm sure he didn't mean to—"

"Frost is dead!" Langula interrupted him with a shout. Astar noticed her eyes were watery and wondered if a demon was capable of crying. "Frost, my beautiful creation! The prince of demons, *my* proud blue demon. Frost was the best part of me. The best of all the Demonic. Now, just a pile of ash! Rotting in Haverhill. Lost in annihilation. Obliterated by fire. That Chen-Li! That is why I am here! I will have my revenge! And the Zorn? He cares nothing for avenging Frost's death or any of the others. Monticello is dead. Grim is missing. This is the end of the Demonic. My Demonic! He is killing us off like he did the Zornastic Order. Now he comes for my beautiful essence. We are nothing to him. He has sold us all to repair his desiccated body."

"He needs redemption, Langula, things have gotten out of control," Astar said. "He needs to be restored."

"He doesn't deserve to be restored! He will stay the Skeletal King forever!" Langula shouted. "But first, Frost, Monticello, and Grim need to be avenged!"

"I see." Astar turned his back and walked farther away from her now. "Death and revenge are the only things you are capable of."

"There is nothing else," Langula said, a hard conviction in her voice. "Why do you care?"

"I care about all living things," Astar said. "I am the God of Beauty, and beauty can be found in all things—even you, Langula. But only if you are willing to change."

At that moment, Chen-Li sailed over the north wall in spirit form. He stopped to hover over the wall across from Langula.

She seethed upon seeing him. "You!" She pointed a sharp claw at him. "You killed him! Killed my Frost!" She slithered back through the parapet and returned to Darla. She coiled around Darla, using her as a human shield.

"Tyla and Myra!" Chen-Li shouted. "The First Wives will have vengeance!"

"If you come any closer to me, Chen-Li, the girl dies," Langula said from behind Darla's shoulder.

Chen-Li's eyes blazed with fire. He clenched his fists. They ignited in flame as concentrated energy materialized in his hands. His eyes locked on Langula in a burning fury. "If the girl dies, you die with her," Chen-Li told her. As he spoke, the flames spread up his arms, through his shoulders, then down his hips. They finally crept down into his legs. His whole spirit flared in rolling, licking flames.

"Careful, Chen-Li," Astar called out to him, holding his palms out. "Do not cause harm to Darla."

Fully consumed in material flames, Chen-Li erupted in pulsating rings of fire.

"Stand back, both of you. Any closer and I disembowel this tender morsel." Langula traced a single claw, sharp as a razor, down the front of Darla's torso. "Bring me your body, Chen-Li. Bring it to me now. We'll trade her life for yours."

"Here is my counteroffer," Chen-Li told her. "Your life for the lives of my First Wives!"

Just then, a screech could be heard overhead—the last Devourer. The Zorn was coming, riding atop the monster. He came in from the west. Riding directly over Astar, he crossed the open courtyard of frozen priests and landed on the eastern walkway.

The four immortals now stood opposite one another, each on one of the four walkways, high above the courtyard. Below the empty priests of the White Eminence kneeled frozen in time.

"Langula!" the Zorn said. "You have gone too far this time. Come now, let us leave this place before something happens that will be irreversible. Leave Chen-Li to his temple."

"Something irreversible? Like Frost and Monticello? Dead! You mean that kind of irreversible?" Langula shouted. "It is too late for that!"

"Come now, please," the Zorn pleaded with her. "We have all of eternity to make more demons."

"That is not true, Hazor. I'm afraid I cannot allow it. That is not my purpose in this world," Astar said. "After this day, our era will be at an end. All of us, me included, will become unwelcomed Gods in this new era."

"You! Your treachery is legendary!" The Zorn pointed at Astar. "Your treatment of me has been nothing short of horrific! You speak to me about dignity...while you destroy my Castle Orlo, my birthright? Your duplicity goes beyond belief. Your lies are astonishing."

"Treachery, Zorn? You would know all about treachery," Chen-Li said in his fiery form. "You corrupt the mind of the king with Barker's orders to attack the Temple of Valor?"

"Do not ever speak the name of Brother Barker again," Langula warned Chen-Li.

"Don't you understand, Chen-Li? I tried to stop them," the Zorn said to his brother. "Instead of attacking the Temple of Valor, the army had to fend off attacks from the madness of the people I infected. I spread the disease of madness to weaken their forces, and it did weaken them. I was trying to protect the Temple of Valor. I needed to protect Lady Valen."

"So, you admit it!" Langula screamed and the Devourer growled. "In your own words, you have just confessed it. You intentionally betrayed the Demonic!"

"There was no other choice with Astars here, Astars there. Astars popping up everywhere! His confounded multiplicity got in the way of all our plans." The Zorn pointed at himself. "The Lady Valen is my only hope. I could not let anyone kill her."

"I can't serve you any longer," Langula told the Zorn. "I relinquish you, Hazor the Scorned! I do not need you anymore! I will make more Demonic eggs for new Demonic creations. I will steal what they need to fertilize and incubate them into Demonic life. They will be loyal to *me*! Not you! You never cared about them because no part of them were any part of you!"

As Langula spoke, she thrashed Darla from side to side. Her grip on Darla was twisting and tightening.

"Langula," Astar said. "Put Darla down."

"No, I will never let go!"

"Then you die this day, you dirty demon bitch!" Chen-Li screamed, then pointed at the Zorn. "And *he* will do nothing to stop it. Because he knows that if he does, we will be forced for all eternity into a great negation."

"You want this woman?" Langula turned quickly to shout at Astar. "Then give me your blade! Give me Soothsayer and I will give her over to you to do as you will."

"That's preposterous!" Astar said. "I'm not giving you the most powerful weapon in the world."

"Give me the blade!" Langula repeated louder. "Or I kill Kilmer's wife and you will have her blood on your hands. You alone will have to answer for why you did not save her life when you had the chance. Will you barter with me for her life? Did you not hear Chen-Li's words? He aims to kill me. I need the protection of Soothsayer. Now, give it to me!"

"I'm afraid that is out of the question—I can't do that," Astar told her.

"I will kill her, then." Langula pressed her claw into Darla's neck causing a thin trickle of blood to run down her throat. "You will watch her die."

"Let her do it." Chen-Li's flames turned hotter. "Then I will boil her alive."

"Wait! Stop, don't hurt her," Astar told Langula. "I'll give you Soothsayer."

"No! Astar, you can't," Chen-Li said. "No, do not give her Soothsayer."

"Langula, you can't," the Zorn pleaded. "Soothsayer is too powerful for you. Look what it has done to my face, to my flesh. Even I can't wield it. Look at what it did to me."

"I saw how it twisted you, Zorn. That's because you were not Demonic enough. But I am! I am a complete demon, unlike you."

Langula laughed. "Valen needs Soothsayer to heal your flesh. You will never have it! I shall keep it forever. Without it, no spell will ever be powerful enough to cure your flesh! You will remain the Skeletal King forever! Now, give it to me, Astar! Or I kill the girl!"

"Astar?" The Zorn trembled. "You're not really going to give it to her, are you?"

"Fools! There can be no other way!" Langula pressed her claw deeper into Darla's neck. "With just a bit more pressure, my claw will make her bleed to death in front of your eyes. Is that what you want?"

Astar looked at Chen-Li who burned with vengeance. Next, he looked at the Zorn, whose bony green face had transformed with worry and concern for his restoration.

"If you give her that accursed blade," the Zorn informed him, "there will be no controlling her."

Astar could see Langula pressing her nail deeper in Darla's throat.

"Don't do it, Astar," the Zorn said. "Don't take away the only hope."

Astar pulled the massive blade from his back, as light as air itself. Its smooth gold surface reflected up in his face. In its reflection, he could see his own eyes looking back at him. Soothsayer rippled in energy up the length of its blade.

"All right, Langula," Astar finally said. "I see I have no choice."

"No, no, no, don't do it," the Zorn continued to plead. "The power of Soothsayer is too immense. She will kill us all!"

"Chen-Li," Astar said. "Do not make a move or she will kill Darla. So, be careful."

"Let her do it," Chen-Li said. "It will be the last thing she does."

"Calm now, be steady, Langula." Astar held Soothsayer out in front of him. "I'm coming over to you to give you Soothsayer."

"No tricks!" Langula pulled Darla closer as Astar approached.

"Astar, you don't know what you are doing!" the Zorn said.

"Don't hurt her," Astar said. "And I'll give you Soothsayer."

Astar continued walking slowly toward Langula, until he came to within an arm's length of her. Delicately, he offered Soothsayer to her.

"No tricks!" Langula shouted again.

"No tricks. Here, take it and give me Darla."

Langula gave a final look at Chen-Li and the Zorn. She turned to face Astar. Keeping her claw pressed into Darla's neck, she reached out and took Astar's Blade.

Immediately after taking Soothsayer, she darted back from Astar laughing loudly. She did not give up Darla. Instead, she pulled her back with her. Langula pointed the blade toward Astar. When she leveled Soothsayer, blue energy crawled up her hand, pulsating through her arm.

"I feel so much power!" Langula laughed. "I have never felt anything like this before!"

The Zorn shook his head, turned, and mounted the Devourer.

Chen-Li anxiously waited for Darla's release, coiled to strike, waiting to attack and kill the demon. But Langula did not let her go. With newfound power, she swung the engorged sword first at Chen-Li, then at the Zorn. She laughed maniacally.

"Give her to me," Astar told her, holding out his hands. Astar reminded her, "A deal's a deal! You promised."

Langula laughed at Astar. "You made a deal with a demon. What did you expect? I planned on killing her anyway. Now I can kill all three of you with this!"

"No, Langula, don't do it!" the Zorn shouted. "It won't work the way you—"

Langula's laughter became uncontrollable. When Astar stepped closer, she swung Darla to the rear and pointed the blade directly at him. Her willpower was now melded as one with Soothsayer. Her thoughts became the actions of the blade. Her energy became one with it.

Langula stopped laughing. Rising on her serpent's tail, she tilted her head and looked down at Astar. "With this power, I strike down the ancient spirit of Ehlona inside you. I am Langula the Serpent Queen, and I will rule over a new era. I am the new Goddess of a new Demonic generation!" She let out a loud scream, then willed the full release of the blade's power directly upon Astar.

Astar shielded his face defensively. He could not watch as the blade swelled. Bulging and growing bigger, all of the souls inside it were waking to release their fury.

The Zorn wheeled the mighty Devourer around, and quickly pushed off the walkway. He took to the air on the back of the Devourer, trying to get away. He disappeared over the temple walls.

Astar turned to face Langula again. He dropped his hands from his face. Somehow his face had changed—the look of concern was gone, replaced with a sneer. "They can harm no part of the whole."

Langula thought those would be Astar's last words. Over the hum of the building energy in the blade, it continued to swell in her hand. The blade swelled from the center dramatically, appearing as an overfilled waterskin about to burst.

"The Timmutes," Astar said. "They can harm no part of the whole."

Since no explosive force came from Soothsayer, Langula changed her mind. She tried to drop the blade, but Soothsayer had already melded to her hand. She no longer grasped the blade, the blade grasped on to her. Unable to release the power of Astar's Blade, fueled by the energy of thousands of Timmutes, Langula aimed the power of the discharge at Astar.

Astar. The reincarnation of Ehlona, who created the Timmutes with her blood. Through blood the Timmutes and Astar were one and the same. Joined by the same blood and governed by a solemn blood oath.

"They can harm no part of the whole." Astar laughed again at her.

Langula watched the energy building with wide eyes. She was so frightened; she did not even notice the shadow looming large above her. A giant hand reached over the wall of the Temple of Chen-Li. The giant fractal ogre was made from hundreds of Astars. At the last minute, Langula turned to see the hand coming at her. She screamed in terror and lifted her hands to protect herself. Soothsayer was stuck firmly onto her hand, and she could not let go of it. Astar's fractal ogre reached toward her but did not touch her. Instead, it snatched Darla away. Then the ogre's hand withdrew.

Once Darla was free of Langula, Chen-Li flashed toward Langula. It was vengeance for the First Wives. But he also wanted to protect the thousands of physical bodies frozen in time below. Chen-Li had to kill her before she could kill them. But it was too late for all of them.

As Astar's fractal ogre withdrew with Darla in his hand, the Astar that had given Soothsayer to Langula also absorbed into the retreating fractal ogre. Just like that, Astar was gone, and time started again.

As soon as time started, Soothsayer exploded. A blinding white-hot light flashed in a massive explosion. The temple rumbled under the tremendous blast. The explosive force cracked apart the marble foundation, rocking the Temple of Chen-Li. The walls of the temple collapsed and crumbled down the mountain. Its pillars toppled over and came crashing down.

In the center of the blast, Langula's screams could not be heard. She burned apart in layers, disintegrating down to her skeletal black frame, before the walkway collapsed. She disappeared below, merging into the falling debris.

When the blast occurred, Chen-Li was caught halfway to Langula. He was struck with such force that it extinguished his flames. His spirit rolled away on a powerful gust of pure force, he blew away from the Temple of Chen-Li, like dust in the wind.

The Zorn's Devourer was hit by a wave of force and tumbled awkwardly. Unable to stay aloft, the Zorn was dislodged and fell off the beast. Once on the ground, he and the Devourer were caught in the crumbling of the eastern wall. They fell down the side of the temple and were buried under the debris.

The physical bodies of the priests of the White Eminence were immediately destroyed. The blast hit them with a torrent of hot wind that disintegrated their bodies into nothing but ash.

Astar's fractal ogre shielded Darla from the force of the blast and protected her from plummeting down the mountain. The many fractal Astars absorbed the damage.

When the fractal ogre landed in the valley below, Darla was shaken but otherwise unharmed. A fiery cloud rose over their heads, looking like a demon lifting to reach the heavens.

As Darla watched, the giant ogre began to dissolve. Bit by bit, the fractals were absorbed, until finally, only a single Astar remained with her.

"Astar? What happened? Where am I? Where did everyone go?" Darla asked him. But before Astar could answer, debris from the explosion above started coming down all around them. Darla shielded herself with her arms from the falling debris. "What happens to us now?"

"Now, we pick up the pieces and start over," Astar told her.

"Where is Langula?" Darla asked.

"Back to the oblivion that sent her," was Astar's reply.

Another day is ended
A new one's just begun
And she's back where she started
With the rising of the sun
She's waiting for the one.

Excerpt from *The Witch's Songbook*

"The darkness is oppressive," he said.
"I don't remember it being so black."
— Excerpt from *Kilmer's Ghost* (Chapter 32)

THE RETURN OF MYLEX

Demon Realm

Moments ago, Langula's eyes widened as the sword vibrated, and she could not let go of it. She could only watch helplessly as Soothsayer engorged in her hand. Unable to release it, she clung on to it in desperation.

In the seconds before the explosion, Langula had a strange thought, a memory that came to her from long ago. Strange because the memory was not hers. It belonged to Astar—a conversation Chen-Li once had with the Witch of the Great Mapes Forest.

"What about the Timmutes? I know they are a very formative power you have created. Will they help me?"

"No, that's impossible. They made a blood pledge with me. That explains why they allowed you to approach through the Great Mapes Forest unharmed. Because you are of my blood, and they believe that any one part is equal to the whole. So, as they see you, they see me, and they will not harm you. Unfortunately, they will see Hazor the same way. Because of their pledge, we are all related, and they cannot kill any part of the whole."

Where the memory came from, Langula did not know, but the meaning was clear.

She barely had enough time to realize that Astar had tricked her!

The Timmutes made a blood pledge!

They can harm no part of the whole, Astar had sneered at her as the fractions of seconds rolled.

Astar's Blade stuck to her hand. Soothsayer enlarged, engorged by power that had nowhere to go. The sword bulged dramatically, growing out from the middle, wildly vibrating and humming, getting bigger and bigger. Soothsayer was being stretched to its absolute limit.

Then, it burst! With a brilliant white flash, the sword finally broke. It erupted with a massive release, a monster of energy. Langula's mouth stretched wide in a dreadful scream of pain. Instantaneously, layers of her flesh began disintegrating in the heat of the blast until her bones were exposed and burning. Her frame changed in color from ivory to black. The force collapsed the upper walkway where she stood. She fell into the falling marble dust.

Her fall did not stop at the courtyard. Langula continued to fall, well past the floor of the temple. Then, she descended farther down into darkness, falling into a void of utter blackness. As she continued to fall, sounds filled her ears and senses. First, she heard Soothsayer exploding, and the sound of the falling temple still echoing in the void. Falling farther away from them, those sounds faded. Next, she smashed through another collapsing floor, then another. She fell farther and farther down, penetrating through more barriers. The repeated crashes produced sparks, and the barriers were becoming increasingly hot and fiery.

She screamed again as she dropped through the darkness that was giving way to a radiant and red molten glow. The fires from the underground started to swell all around her. Yet she continued falling, deeper down into the pit.

As she descended, small parasites came and bit her. They chewed upon her neck and face with sharp teeth and round clamping mouths. They locked on to her, causing her pain, and would not let her go. Langula shook violently, trying to rid herself of the demon leeches that fed upon her. But she could not make them go and they stayed fixed to her. She crashed again through levels of increasing heat and fire.

Without warning, she hit solid ground, a violent impact that jarred her senseless. She lay there for what seemed like hours. She had come to a stop flattened on a stone. She was all alone. Around her, molten rock gurgled in tumbling, rolling clumps. She watched the liquid crawl along, superheated, spraying out into spurting geysers. Around her fires sparked and lava splattered red like blood. Beyond the horizon, the wavy mirage of heat rose in bright colors of orange and crimson.

Langula struggled against the parasites that latched on to her face. She pulled at them, and her skin pulled unnaturally long. Yet, the demonic leeches remained fixed to her. Releasing them, her skin snapped back.

She let out a scream of pain and frustration. That's when, as if in reply, she heard distant, wretched screaming. The screams were getting louder, coming closer. Without warning, the parasites let go. They quickly scampered away, as if they knew what was coming.

Through the distant waves of heat and ash, a large horned demon, black as the darkest night, rose out of the fire. The demon appeared as a shadow, featureless, except for its eyes, which were the finest slits of superheated magma.

More demons appeared under the large shadow demon. Five smaller demons appeared. These demons were human-sized, and they rushed out to meet Langula.

"Oh, I can smell the stench of the upper world on this one!" a dark green demon with a scorpion tail and sharp claws said. The demon held a chain and gave it a violent pull. Out from the coals below, the naked figure of a man with blond hair and sharply angled yellow sideburns emerged.

Langula recognized this man. This was the sadistic leader of the now defunct Red Guard, a man by the name of LaNew, the vilest, most hated man in the world.

"Come, my brothers!" The dark green demon gave the chain another pull. The other end of the chain was connected to LaNew's neck by thick meat hooks. When the demon pulled the chain, LaNew stumbled forward. Langula got a better look at LaNew's condition.

The front of LaNew had been expertly carved to exact pain upon him. A flap of skin protruded from his chest. He had been cut from nipple to nipple, and then down from each nipple to almost his waist. The cut created a three-sided rectangular flap, which had been peeled down and hung out in front of him. Sticky flesh was exposed underneath from where the skin should have been. But the top of the flap had cleverly been connected to his feet by way of a series of small fishhooks and chains. So, every time LaNew took a step, his feet pulled against the fishhooks, peeling the skin further off his chest. With every step he took, he kicked against the chains, and the chains pulled against the flap. LaNew screamed as the green demon pulled him forward.

"Please, please, no more, no more," LaNew pleaded. His pleas amused his demon.

"Look upon your worldly mistress, LaNew. She has come to us to whet our appetites."

Langula had been summoned to the surface world and had lived there among the mortals comfortably for many decades. She had escaped the demon world for a time. But now returning, she reeked of humanity. The stink of man covered her.

The largest of the demons, the black shadow one, extended a dark finger. He reached out with a never-ending arm and pressed his finger upon her forehead. He burned into her flesh a steamy brand, an ancient Demonic symbol, grotesque as it was intricate. Langula screamed as her flesh roasted.

"Ah, that sweet smell!" The black demon roared with laughter.

Another demon, this one pure white, had a long mane of fur around its face. The white demon ran its bright claws viciously down her chest. He tore three large gashes in her torso, and in so doing, slashed the corset she wore, exposing her breasts.

"Now, that is what we like!" The white demon laughed at the bloody wounds in her apparition.

Next came a yellow demon who carried a spiked staff. The yellow demon had large pointy ears and small puckered black lips. Grasping her cheeks between its thumb and first finger, squeezing her tight with a powerful hand, the yellow demon forced her mouth open. Then the yellow demon leaned over Langula's face and drooled acidic saliva down her throat. Langula tried to spit the acid out as the demon mocked her.

"Just a little kiss," the yellow demon giggled with a high-pitched laugh. "Oh, we are going to fill you with all kinds of things."

"It burns! It burns!" Langula cried.

But the demons only repeated her cries. "It burns! It burns!" they mocked her.

A flurry of smaller demons appeared next. These were hairy little demons in the shape of pigs with sharp bristles down the length of their backs. They rushed at her with handheld hooks that penetrated and pulled against her skin. They drove their hooks into her serpent tail and tugged at her, stretching her flesh in different directions.

As they tormented her, Langula could see that the little pig demons were crying. She stared into their faces, and saw they were human faces. Faces of mortals that had offended the Gods somehow, cursed to spend eternity with their small, bristled bodies and sharp hooks.

Following the little demons was the pig master. A gray-and-blue demon that growled as he rustled up his little pig demons. "It has been a long time, since we have tasted your suffering, Mylex."

"Mylex? My name is not Mylex!" Langula insisted.

"How quickly you have forgotten, Mylex. How quickly you have forgotten us!" the big black shadow demon said.

"We will make Mylex remember," the white demon snarled.

"Wait! You have the wrong demon! My name is Langula! I have performed well for the Demonic! Supplying you with a steady supply of souls!"

"What does that matter, Mylex?" the yellow demon shrilled. "You are here with us now! There is nothing but pain here."

Time seemed to stop for Langula as the demons pressed closer. But Langula was no more. She was now Mylex.

The dark green demon jumped back into the fire and the magma. As the demon sank deeper, the chain attached to LaNew dropped down with him. LaNew saw the slack unwind and was almost gone. He turned quickly to address her.

"I should have never trusted you. I should have been a better human being."

Just then, the slack in the chain tightened around the manacled neck of the filleted and flapped LaNew. The force of the chain yanked him off his feet. He lifted backward, staring at her the whole time. He and the chain disappeared below the hot coals. A second later, she could hear him screaming.

The black demon snickered in her voice, mocking her. "Magnificent! Perfectly demonic!"

"You think everything is magnificently demonic!" The yellow one imitated the Zorn's voice. He stopped laughing and pulled her hair. Then he paused to stroke her face with the spiked staff.

"Come now, Mylex, let us show you what you've been missing." The yellow demon picked her up and carried her away. Together they disappeared under a rushing wave of magma.

A second later, a gut-wrenching scream erupted from the fire.

Well, I just hit the bottom
Of this bottle of wine
Just hit rock bottom
My broken watch shows no time

Excerpt from *The Witch's Songbook*

It looks like a burning wagon wheel. Like glowing spiderwebs.
Like a bright glowing net cast over the mountains.
— Excerpt from *Kilmer's Ghost* (Chapter 33)

WHAT A STRANGE LIFE

ORACLE MOUNT

Astar stopped time just moments before the explosion. Micah's first indication of this was when Gensen stopped moving.

"Father?" Micah asked. "What's wrong?"

Then searching the immediate area, no one was moving. Why had everyone stopped in midmotion? Micah had no idea. The soldiers, the Nomads, the acolytes—all were paused. Even the spirits in the sky were frozen in place. Micah walked through the field. All the motionless people were like statues.

He stopped to investigate. He came to a scene where two young soldiers were tossing a dead body on a heap of others. The corpse was defying gravity, motionless in the middle of being thrown, suspended inches off the ground. Micah was examining the space under the man, when he heard a voice.

"I wanted to talk to you privately." Astar appeared to him. He extended his hand to help Micah off the ground. Then, they strolled the grounds of the Oracle Mount together.

"What's happened here, Astar? Why are we the only ones moving?" Micah said.

"What happened is that time has stopped," Astar said. "Micah, do you remember how I used to trick you? When you thought I was in one place only to appear somewhere else?"

"I always wondered about that," Micah said. "How did you do it?"

"Micah, I was born into a mysterious power. I inherited an ancient ability, one passed down from a long time ago, because I have been infused with the recycled soul of Ehlona. Since the days of the Star of Ehlona, I have been able to stop time. And when I do stop it, I tend to leave traces of myself in the present. This is how I am able to duplicate myself. It used to only work when I would sleep or get overly excited about something. But with some experience, I got better at it. The older I got, the better I could control it."

Micah looked at him with eyes of silver, face pale, and lips blue. "You did this? You can control time?"

"I cannot *control* it. I can't go back in time to the past. I can't jump ahead in time to the future. No one can do that. But if I could, I would go back to save my father."

"I'm sorry about him," Micah said. "He was a great man."

Astar's eyes watered.

Micah scanned the grounds around the temple observing the scenes of life suspended all around him.

"Why am I not frozen in time like the rest?" Micah asked.

"Because time only affects mortals," Astar said.

"So, why not me?" Micah asked, but then thought about the obvious. "Because I am not mortal anymore, am I? They told me my body would die this way."

Astar asked, "The demons, Grim and Monticello?"

"They said I would become like them, a flesh-eater," Micah said. "But I'd rather be dead."

"But you're not dead, you're still alive," Astar said.

"I'm neither alive nor dead anymore," Micah said. "Aberfell calls it 'being undead.' And that's what it feels like."

Astar watched him for a moment. "Langula's venom, meant for me, has turned you into an immortal."

"Can the Lady Valen cure me?"

"She could neutralize the poison. But without a functioning body, well, she cannot raise the dead."

"There is no hope for me, then?" Micah asked. "I have to stay this way. Eat flesh to survive?"

"It's hard to see any good options right now, Micah," Astar said.

"No, I will perish first, rather than turn into a ghoul."

"Just know this, Micah. Whatever happens, I'll be here with you." Astar let that settle for a moment. "Do you want me to start time again?"

"Sure, Astar, if you say you can, go ahead."

"Get ready, there's going to be a boom," Astar said. Then, he started time.

All the activity around them began again.

As soon as Astar started time, a deafening explosion rumbled under their feet. Vibrations from the Temple of Chen-Li. The boom unsettled the damage to the walls at the Temple of Valor. Kilmer and Aberfell knew what happened immediately. They saw the bright light above as the Temple of Chen-Li erupted.

"Oh no." Kilmer stood. "Darla!"

Everyone at the Temple of Valor stopped to look up. A great ball of flame enveloped the temple. After which, a large rolling cloud ascended higher and higher. Shortly, a rain of falling rocks and pieces of debris started to fall out of the sky. The people on the Oracle Mount ran for cover.

Aberfell held his hood over his head. Kilmer pulled Kory close to protect him. They hurried for cover inside the Temple of Valor.

"Astar destroyed the Temple of Chen-Li, just as he said he would!" Aberfell said.

"What if Darla was up there?" Kilmer could not watch. He covered his face with hands.

"Kilmer?" a soft voice asked. Kilmer thought he heard her voice. He peeked through his fingers and saw that Darla stood right in front of them.

"Darla?" Kilmer uncovered his face. "Darla, is it really you?"

"Something happened to me, Kilmer," Darla said. "But I'm afraid I don't know what it was." Darla rushed into Kilmer's arms in an embrace, as debris fell all around them, raining down in smoky trails.

Kilmer shielded her from the debris as best he could. He quickly moved her under an archway of the Temple of Valor.

"Oh, Kilmer." Darla embraced him. "Where is Kory?"

Kory saw his mother and ran to her. "Mama!" Kory rushed to embrace her. "You're back! Oh, Mama! I was so afraid. I'm so glad you're back."

Kilmer stared at her. "I thought I lost you."

Oaks came and gave Darla a warm embrace. "You had us scared to death. I nearly died when I saw Langula take you. We have lost so many this day. I thought we lost you too."

"Are you all right?" Kory hugged her.

"A little scratched," Darla said, rubbing her neck. Her big brown eyes welled up with tears. "I don't know. Everything happened so fast. I am not really sure how to explain it."

Just as they made it under cover, a heavy plate twisted and bent, landed just a few feet away. It captured Kilmer's attention, and he quickly ran out to retrieve it. Securing the heavy plate, he returned to under the archway. Kilmer wiped the carbon off with his sleeve and saw this was the golden plaque King Leopold dedicated to Chen-Li and the First Wives. The golden plaque had been given in a ceremony on the Green of Castle Odessa. Kilmer read the words inscribed upon it:

This Golden Plaque of King Leopold
Is hereby presented to:

Chen-Li and the First Wives

In Eternal Friendship
Castle Odessa Year 842 HRT

"That was twenty years ago," Kilmer said after reading the inscription. "So much has changed since then."

"Can I see?" Aberfell asked.

Kilmer handed the golden plaque to Aberfell.

"Seems like such a long time ago," Aberfell said.

Darla looked around. "Where is Astar?"

"I'm right here." Astar stood behind her.

"Astar, I recall seeing you up at the Temple of Chen-Li. But that was the last thing I remembered before the explosion," Darla said. "It all happened so fast, like only a blur. What happened up there?"

"Just a blur of time is all it seemed to you?" Astar said. "A lot happened up there. Let me tell you about it."

For the next few moments, Astar relayed the story to them. They took it all in, and once anything was told to Aberfell, the Supreme Historian would never forget it.

A determined Gensen had other things on his mind, like saving his son. He approached Valen and spoke to her, "You can help my boy, can't you, Lady Valen?"

"I can cure him of the poison. But he will need a living host to inhabit," Valen said. "Without one, if I cure him, I will just be killing him. The poison is the only thing keeping him alive right now."

"But we've come all this way—" Gensen was on the verge of tears. Then a shout interrupted his thoughts.

"Incredible!" Aberfell pointed to the sky. "Listen!"

My body, my body! They heard the spirits of the White Eminence launch into a cacophony of desperate screams. After the explosion, they had raced back up to the Temple of Chen-Li to enter their physical bodies. Once there, they found everything destroyed—the temple, their bodies, everything. One by one, their cries rang out.

Aberfell commented on their fate, "The spirits of the White Eminence have been abandoned outside their physical forms. They will be forced to roam this world forever like ghosts. The implications of this will not be fully realized for some time."

Melvin asked, "Will they die?"

"Like Micah, they are trapped between life and death," Aberfell said. "With so many needing living hosts they will be in short supply for some time! Unless, of course, they go rogue."

"Go rogue?" Oaks asked.

"Steal someone's body, inhabit it without the host's consent," Aberfell said. "The very idea would go against their beliefs—everything the White Eminence ever stood for."

Kilmer looked over and saw Hollow Face looking up, watching the spirits. After seeing Hollow Face and thinking about his dilemma, Kilmer replied, "Forever is a long time to hold on to a belief system without a body."

"Indeed, it is," Aberfell said. As the seventh son of Fortis Plum, Aberfell knew it well. Aberfell then walked over and recovered Kilmer's sword. He wiped off the dirt and grime. He took a moment to examine it. The sword was highly crafted, made by the best artisans of Haverhill.

"Pure Haverhill," Aberfell whispered to himself. "This sword was given to Kilmer his first day in enlistment with the Amalgamates. He lost this sword once, when it was confiscated by the Zorn himself. But he recently found it again when they took up residence in Castle Orlo. It would be a shame for him to lose it again."

Melvin and Oaks watched as Aberfell walked the sword up the hill to Kilmer.

"I found your sword, my friend," Aberfell said with a pat on Kilmer's back. "You are going to need this. There is still work to be done."

Once the debris stopped falling, Kilmer and Darla were arm in arm. Kory clung tightly to them. They cautiously stepped out of the archway. The ruins of the Temple of Chen-Li smoldered on the mountaintop.

Oaks said, "I wonder what happens now."

Kilmer took a deep breath. He was still covered in blood. He looked at the scene, and all the people around him. He had his wife and his son. He had his friends.

"What a strange life this is," Kilmer sighed. "Let's go home."

You got a reason to hate me
I'm not the kind to just forget
You're dealing with a feeling
Of fear and regret

Excerpt from *The Witch's Songbook*

Following the baby's cries, he discovered it was not a baby at all
but a demon mimicking one.
— Excerpt from *Kilmer's Ghost* (Chapter 34)

THE KING IS DEAD

TEMPLE OF VALOR

The entire field stood in stunned silence, reluctant to speak or make a sound. A thousand fighting men, the sick and the mad, stood in a circle. In the center, the fallen king lay in a puddle of darkened crimson.

Then, the hushed whispers began. They spread like wildfire through the crowd.

King Leopold is dead.

Acolytes covered King Leopold's body. They covered Amtor as well. This was a custom they did to show respect, to give them humility in death. They left Monticello out in the open.

"What should we do with them?" an acolyte asked Lord Rhodes. "Should we cover the bodies of the Devourers?"

"No, leave them," Lord Rhodes said. "I want the world to see what foul creatures killed our king."

With the heel of his boot, Lord Rhodes rolled one of the Devourers over. The beast settled upward, exposing its belly. Rhodes pulled his sword from the scabbard. It was still stained with blood. He lifted it over his head, then brought it down. He thrust it into the beast's belly. Rhodes commenced to cut the beast's midsection open, exposing the contents. Jets of putrefied, vaporous fumes vented out from the creature. Rhodes made a sour face, then continued. With a few more cuts, a rush of disgusting odorous bile spilled out.

Rhodes knelt beside the opening and inserted his arm all the way into the beast's stomach. The inside was lined in a thick soup of slimy mucus. He pressed still deeper into the creature, searching with his bare hand. Finally, with a gut-wrenching sound and a splash of gall, the upper half of Amtor's body slid out wet and bloody. His remains were immediately covered by the acolytes who stood nearby with linens.

After the grisly discovery, Lord Rhodes stood up covered in slime. He spoke to Amtor's remains. "You were never fit to be food for this beast. We will give you a good and decent burial in your village of Homestead."

Covered in smelly stink, Lord Rhodes backed away and saluted Amtor. Oaks and Melvin came and carried Amtor out of the filthy puddle of the beast's fluids to where his lower half waited. They rested the upper half of his body gently together with his lower half. They made the alignment of the two as best they could, reuniting his two severed halves. Now Amtor lay together under a single white sheet.

Gensen and Micah stood over the body of Monticello. The demon was on his back. His fangs were motionless inside his gaping mouth. His red eyes were open, staring blankly but seeing nothing. The spear still protruded out of his chest. A wide circle of dark blood stained his fancy white shirt.

Gensen looked at his pale son.

"Are you hurt?" Micah asked him.

"No, are you?"

"No more than I already was," Micah replied.

"He cannot hurt you anymore," Gensen said. "He cannot hurt anyone anymore."

"What will they do with him?" Micah asked.

"Burn him, I suppose," Gensen said. "Send him back to the fires where he came from."

Nadya and Boldo came and joined them.

"The alliance of the flesh-eaters is over," Nadya said. "No more sacrifices to supply their Demonic feasts."

"We are free," Boldo said, wrapping his arm around Nadya. "Yes, my sister. We are free to live once again."

But Nadya looked through dark eyes. She knew better. She could never be free. She could not help noticing the stares. Those that had sacrificed loved ones would never forgive her. It showed in their eyes. The hateful stares of the Gellers who chose the black stone three times this year alone. Then, the Adsons passed by. They refused to make eye contact with her and looked in the opposite direction. Children of the Ullis were told not to go near her. The Atrams and the Oparks were more open in their hatred, with rude gestures. They spit when they saw her. The Edmans and the Walloons were just as overt; they huddled together and called out, "Who are you going to kill now, Nadya? Who will it be this month?"

Overhead, the White Eminence began to question what they had just done.

"These soldiers were coming to help us kill the Devourers, not to attack the Temple of Valor," one of the spirits said.

Another one answered, "We are responsible for those innocent lives."

"Chen-Li was burning soldiers alive, for no reason at all."

"Can we ever make it right with these men? Will they ever forgive us?"

Likewise, the surviving soldiers of the Red and Blue cursed the spirits of the White Eminence.

"I thought the White Eminence were on our side."

"They killed our friends."

"These spirits are evil."

"The blood of our dead on their heads."

But the Red and Blue had more immediate concerns to attend to. They had to provide aid to the survivors, while others fanned out in the valley to collect the dead. Piles of bodies were stacked like firewood in the fields.

The Kingdom of Odessa was another chief concern. "Who will be our king now?" many asked. "Now that Leopold is dead, who will bring order to this chaos?"

Lord Rhodes heard the men and took charge. Climbing to the top of one of the damaged wagons of the Nomads, he rose to a high place where all could see him. Then, he shouted, "Listen to me! Listen, all of you! We have lost King Leopold, and though I do not claim kingship, I am the highest-ranking soldier in the field. By order of the king before he died, I have been placed in command. That is the way it will be until we get back to the castle. Until Odessa can select a new king."

"What are your orders?" a voice called out.

"We will return to Castle Odessa but let no cheer go up," Lord Rhodes commanded. "These have been the darkest of all days. Our king is dead. And we must go back in disgrace. To look our wives and mothers in the eye, without our king. So, not a single cheer shall rise, for now is a time of grief and great reflection. This is not a proud day for this army. The Red and Blue has a lot of healing to do. Now prepare the dead for the long march. Then let's go home.

"But first there is one thing I must do." Lord Rhodes jumped down off the wagon. The soldiers watched as he approached the body of the second Devourer. He lifted his heel and stamped his boot upon its face. He reached down and withdrew the sword that pinned its lips closed. Once removed, the creature's jaw opened, sloppily and slack, causing a disgusting stench to release. But Rhodes ignored the creature's breath. With a clean linen, he wiped King Leopold's sword clean. Once satisfied, he laid it gently on top of the body of the king.

On the battlefield, Aberfell reached down and picked up Amtor's broken battle-ax. The handle was broken into two. Aberfell took a moment to admire the craftsmanship. Melvin and Oaks stood nearby and watched him.

"Aberfell?" Melvin asked. "How will history remember what happened here today?"

"History will remember King Leopold as the orphaned boy who became king. He was aged forty-two years or thereabouts. His exact age is unknown. Died in the fields of the Oracle Mount, under the shadow of the Temple of Valor. Murdered in cold blood by a demon with spots, the demon Monticello."

"I heard rumors that he murdered his own mother," Oaks asked. "Is that true?"

"That would be rumor of the Massacre of Umbrick," Aberfell recalled. "It is mostly true. He burned down the orphanage he grew up in, killing everyone inside. The headmistress was his primary concern, a woman named Sister Luna, the object of his rage. Sister Luna was his mother, although he did not know it at the time. He was just settling an old score. So, I suppose the rumor is true, but for all the wrong reasons. He did not know the truth of it for some time. When he found out, he was greatly upset. Mostly because she was his mother, but I don't think he regretted it much. For she had been very harsh to him as a boy. Very abusive."

"What about Amtor?" Melvin asked. "How shall we remember him?"

Aberfell sighed. "Oh, Amtor. The first Minister of War of the Kingdom of Odessa. Died heroically saving the lives of others. Amtor lived fifty years and had recently regained his strength again. He lived out his last days as a full man, before he was bitten in half in the mouth of a Devourer. He was a fighter and only lost one fight in his life. That one loss was to Leopold. Ironic that it was Amtor's battle-ax that took Leopold's life. There might not have been any love lost between them, but even so, Amtor would not have wanted it to turn out this way."

Aberfell looked at the broken battle-ax in his hands.

"Amtor's battle-ax. The sharpest of any weapon in the kingdom. He made doubly sure of it. Always honing it on the grindstone. As many as four times a day. I know, because I watched him do it."

Aberfell lowered the battle-ax and placed the two broken pieces upon him. He aligned the two broken halves on the corresponding halves of his body.

"Seems fitting, doesn't it?" Melvin said, watching what Aberfell did. "Two pieces of the battle-ax, lying on separate halves of Amtor."

"Fitting indeed," Aberfell said, standing up. "Oh, the irony of it all.

You remind me of a warm summer breeze

That blows there beside me

But I'm too afraid to breathe

Excerpt from *The Witch's Songbook*

Leopold could sense he was getting closer now,
and nothing slowed his progress in the slightest.
— Excerpt from *Kilmer's Ghost* (Chapter 35)

THE WINDS OF CHANGE

CASTLE ODESSA

Lord Whitney marched his column out of the Oracle Mount the day before, riding with ten thousand men heading back to Castle Odessa. They marched in step, their cadences ringing out!

Here comes the Red and Blue!
Knocking over trees!
Here comes the Red and Blue!
Fall to your knees!
So, go ahead! Raise your mighty sword!
Lift it high! High against the Zorn!
You smile and grin and crown your head!
Well, we better not find you!
Or you'll be dead!

About two hours out, Lord Whitney guided his horse to the side of the road. His mount stepped up a rising mound—a bare and dusty rock that led up to a flat grassy top. Along with him was his aide-de-camp, Gregor. They stopped to watch the passing troops and, maybe more importantly, to have the troops see him. Lord Whitney knew it raised morale to see the leader enduring the same hardships as them. He ate an apple while he and Gregor watched them pass. As they did, many waved and shouted greetings to their commander.

Some soldiers spoke to him as they passed by.

"How's that apple, Lord Whitney?"

"Aren't you glad to be going home, Lord Whitney?"

"I know I am!"

"No more hardtack!"

"Stop by and see me after this," Lord Whitney replied with a laugh. "We'll eat some more delicious hardtack together!"

"We want to get some of that home cooking!"

"Yeah, can't wait to see my girl!"

"My mama will be glad to see me again!"

Lord Whitney waved at them. Then he stopped. He stared in the distance, deep in thought.

Gregor noticed. "Are you all right, sir?"

"Strange. I was just thinking about LaNew."

"That awful villain, sir?" Gregor asked.

"Funny. I had not thought about him in years." Lord Whitney continued to stare blankly. "I had a dream last night, Gregor. In my dream there was a strong wind that blew across the waters. I watched it from a tall tower and the gale blew across some beach below. In the distance, a little cottage stood. When the wind blew strong against the cottage, I thought it would surely break apart. Yet the cottage was built solid and broke the wind instead of being broken by it. From the tower I looked on. Searching the sky, I saw the wind blowing through the clouds. But the clouds, having no firm foundation, could not stand up against the wind, and twisted into wicked and menacing shapes. That was it, really. That was the whole dream."

Gregor asked, "Were you for the wind or against it?"

"Neither," Lord Whitney said. "I was just an observer, feeling safe in the tower, watching the changes."

"Sir," Gregor interrupted. "A messenger is approaching."

"No doubt from Lord Rhodes," Whitney said, watching the messenger's horse pass through the ranks.

In the meantime, the column continued marching and singing in cadence with ten thousand voices.

> *Our king is the mighty Leopold!*
> *Here comes the Red and Blue! Do what you're told!*
> *So, go ahead! Raise your mighty sword!*
> *Lift it high! Use it against the Zorn!*
> *You smile and grin and crown your head!*
> *Well, we better not find you!*
> *Or you'll be dead!*

The messenger rode through the troops in a cloud of dust to Lord Whitney and the aide.

"Sir, we are receiving reports from our scouts in Haverhill," the messenger said. "They said they have found a dead body, sir, badly burned. It is one of ours."

"Any idea who it was?" Lord Whitney asked.

"It was Brother Barker, sir," the soldier said.

"Brother Barker?" Lord Whitney asked. "Are you sure?"

"The scouts who checked his possessions were sure, sir," the scout reported. "Should we retrieve his body, sir?"

"Oh no, no, leave it where it lies," Lord Whitney said. "Brother Barker was a stranger to honor. Either in King Leopold's court or anywhere else in this life, I presume. I can't imagine he should find honor now that he's dead."

"As you command, sir!" The messenger saluted and started to leave. Before he could go, Lord Whitney reached out with his hand and stopped the messenger.

"Wait, no, disregard that," Lord Whitney said. "We can't leave a charred body for the villagers of Haverhill to stumble over, can we? That would be irresponsible. Do this: send two soldiers to go find the remains. Have them bury Brother Barker where they find him. Once done, I don't ever want to hear his name again. Ever! Understand?"

"Yes, sir!" The messenger saluted again and left the hill.

After the messenger left, Lord Whitney said to his aide. "It's the least we can do for the people in Haverhill."

"Yes, sir." Gregor smiled. "Here comes another messenger, sir!"

Lord Whitney saw the second messenger. This one passed through the line at a slower downtrodden pace.

"He doesn't look terribly cheerful, does he?" Lord Whitney commented.

The messenger rode up slowly to Lord Whitney and saluted. Lord Whitney found the messenger's behavior quite strange. For after the salute the messenger leaned forward to whisper his report quietly into Lord Whitney's ear. After receiving the message, Lord Whitney bowed his head. He said something under his breath that his aide could not hear.

Lord Whitney quietly told Gregor, "Have the commanders form into their lines."

Immediately, orders rang out from every mouth. "Form up! Form up!" The commanders shouted.

Troops ran in chaotic patterns to come together in orderly units in front of their leader. Soon the units were counting down the lines and throughout the column.

"All present and accounted for, sir!" the aide told Lord Whitney, then backed away.

Lord Whitney looked out over ten thousand soldiers in smartly dressed lines stretching before him. The flags of the Red and Blue flapped in a light breeze. Lord Whitney watched them silently for a moment and an intense silence followed.

A darkness fell upon Lord Whitney as he briefly remembered the dream again. He was in his high perch again. His words were to be the wind to break those who lacked a solid foundation. Now he understood what his dream meant.

"Lord Rhodes has sent word of a tragic development at the Oracle Mount," Lord Whitney said. "There has been another attack of the Devourers!"

A great gasp could be heard, and murmurs followed.

"Attention!" The commanders quieted them. "Attention!"

"The Devourers were killed by the Red and Blue. One of them dispatched by King Leopold himself."

The Red and Blue gave an impromptu cheer for their king.

"Attention! Attention!" Again, the commanders had to quiet the troops.

"However, in the battle with the Devourer, King Leopold has fallen in the field."

A gasp of disbelief segued to the inevitable announcement.

"The king is dead," Lord Whitney announced. "King Leopold is dead!"

A gasp rippled through the ranks. This time the commanders, in shock for themselves, could not quiet the ten thousand. They did not even try.

Lord Whitney shouted in a loud voice, "Remember this day, for the rest of your lives, Odessa! Remember it until you are old men, the day you heard that King Leopold is dead!"

The ten thousand soldiers murmured.

Someone shouted, "Lord Whitney is king! Lord Whitney is the new king."

The soldiers began the chant. "King Whitney! King Whitney!"

Lord Whitney heard their cries. He could not think about that or allow his men to.

"Attention!" Lord Whitney himself cried out loudly. He shouted it again, "Attention! Do not lose your bearing!"

"Attention! Attention!" The commanders eventually got them under control.

The soldiers quieted.

Lord Whitney addressed the men again. "Do not concern your-self with who will be next on the throne. That matter is for later. For now, the time is to mourn for our fallen king. To make preparations for when he comes back home. Back where he belongs. We will con-tinue our march! To Castle Odessa! Prepare the way for the king!"

The troops murmured, some cried, unsure of what to do.

"Red and Blue!" Lord Whitney commanded. "Left face! Forward, march!"

The army was marching to Odessa once again. Along the way, Lord Whitney let them relax and talk while they walked. Almost all the conversations were about the death of the king.

Two more hours they had marched, when a loud explosion and a bright flash of light erupted behind them. Everyone, including Lord Whitney, turned back to see a rising pillar of fire and smoke on the eastern horizon. The soldiers gasped, pointing to the rising cloud. The large gray plume lifted in a rolling cloud behind him.

The questions started pouring in.

"Where was that blast?"

"What could cause an explosion like that?"

"It came from the Temple of Valor!"

"No, that's the Temple of Chen-Li!"

Lord Whitney let the soldiers watch and talk about it for a long time. At length, the towering pillar started to dissipate into the wind shear. Lord Whitney urged the column back together, encouraging them westward. The men turned away and started to march orderly again, as the cloud continued to rise behind them. Occasionally some of the soldiers glanced back to watch.

The column continued marching to the Mauveguard Pass. Lord Whitney took the lead. He marched the ten thousand to the west. As they marched, the soldiers talked in the ranks. Lord Whitney heard them and let them talk freely. Between news of King Leopold's death and that massive explosion on the horizon, they had a lot to talk about.

Hours later, they reached the turn to the pass. Immediately, they came across debris from the Green that had rolled all the way to the opening of the Mauveguard Pass. As they marched higher they encountered larger pieces.

Eventually, Castle Odessa came into view. But it was not the welcome, familiar sight they had all grown accustomed to seeing. Upon the upper reaches of the castle, a large white blemish scarred its once glorious outer skin from where the Devourers had broken the Green.

Lord Whitney stopped directly under where the Green had collapsed. Here, the pieces of the Green lay in the largest chunks—those that had fallen straight down and were buried deep in the ground. Under the weight of many tons of the debris were the smashed and destroyed memorials put there commemorating war sacrifices of thirty years ago.

Lord Whitney wasted no time. He got the ten thousand safely back inside Castle Odessa. Just as quickly, he tirelessly organized the cleanup of the Green. He put men to work with pickaxes and wheelbarrows. They started stacking rocks in wagons and hauling them away around the clock. Stonecutters were deployed to the quarry pits to chisel out more of the famous green limestone for the rebuilding of the Green.

More terrible news arrived from Lord Rhodes. He was still at the Oracle Mount. Rhodes reported that Amtor had also been killed, savagely bitten in half by one of the Devourers. Lord Rhodes communicated to Whitney that Amtor's remains would be taken by an honor guard back to his beloved little cottage in the village of Homestead.

"It is fitting and proper," Lord Whitney wrote back to Lord Rhodes. "Homestead is where Amtor belongs. The place he would want to be."

Lord Whitney rubbed his face. Amtor had been a good leader and friend to him. Whitney passed the somber news along to the Red and Blue.

"Sometimes it feels like this is the end of the world," Lord Whitney said to himself.

Lord Whitney remembered his dream of two nights ago. He now applied it to Amtor's little cottage in the woods of Homestead. *The little cottage that could withstand the wind. That sounds like Amtor.*

More messengers started to arrive from the east.

Lord Rhodes reported that the Temple of Chen-Li had been destroyed, which explained the explosion he and the ten thousand had seen. In addition, the White Eminence had been wiped out, destroyed. Their physical bodies obliterated inside the Temple of Chen-Li when it exploded, leaving thousands of spirits wandering throughout the land. Lord Rhodes added, *be on the lookout for unwelcomed inhabitations.* It was clear that Lord Rhodes did not trust them.

Additionally, Lord Rhodes wrote that Lord Plum-Kilmer had been discovered fighting in defense of the Temple of Valor. For Lord Plum-Kilmer's courage in the field, Lord Rhodes was granting him a full pardon, restoration of all titles in the Kingdom of Odessa, and restoration of military rank in the Red and Blue. Melvin, the renegade, had also been seen fighting alongside the Red and Blue and had been subsequently confined and released on the authority of Lord Plum-Kilmer.

Finally, Lord Rhodes reported the demoness Langula was dead. The Zorn was last seen in the collapse of the Temple of Chen-Li and presumed dead until proven otherwise. "Back to that damnation that sent you," Lord Whitney whispered.

I don't want to go
But I don't want to live here anymore.
What are fighting for?
The hurt heals so slow.

Excerpt from *The Witch's Songbook*

He was as large as a bear, tall and thick around the chest, his biceps like
bands of thick muscle. Amtor had a thick mane of dark hair and a long
lavish beard.
— Excerpt from *Kilmer's Ghost* (Chapter 36)

A TIME FOR IMMORTALS

ORACLE MOUNT

Chen-Li survived the explosion but only in spirit. His Li came back to the Temple of Valor dulled, his held head low. An army of other spirits numbering in the thousands followed. These were the sad-faced spirits of the White Eminence.

Valen saw them approaching. "Chen-Li, you survived."

"But I have not, Lady Valen," Chen-Li said. "My physical body has been destroyed along with the Temple of Chen-Li. The White Eminence have no bodies to return to. Look what I have done to them."

No longer having a temple or physical bodies to return to, the spirits of the White Eminence loudly wailed, "All is lost."

"I am forced to listen to them. What have I done to these faithful souls? Their cries, these torments. I can't stand it."

Lady Valen approached the spirit. "I am so sorry, Chen-Li."

"Do not feel sorrow for me, Lady Valen," Chen-Li said. "Feel sorry for them. The spirits. The priests of the White Eminence. Feel sad for them."

The condemned spirits of the White Eminence circled Chen-Li with their agonized cries. "We have failed."

Chen-Li lifted his head from crying. "The First Wives have been avenged, but revenge comes at a heavy price. There can be no solace, no peace of mind. We cannot rejoice. A great tragedy has beset us. How blind I was. Tyla and Myra are still dead. Langula's death did not bring them back."

The sprits called out. "The sons of the Gods have destroyed this generation."

"Listen to what the spirits are saying," Chen-Li lamented. "Oh yes, it is so true. We have failed this generation. I fear the times now are even worse than before. The Zorn and I have wasted so much precious time fighting each other, rather than living in this world together, making it a better place. I see now what Astar meant when he said another era must begin. This message is clear to me now. With the destruction of the Temple of Chen-Li, the balance has finally been achieved."

"No, Chen-Li, there has been no balance achieved, only defeat," a voice came from among the rubble. It was the Zorn, the Skeletal King, limping to Chen-Li and Lady Valen in clothes torn and dirty. "We have all been beaten down in equal measures. There are no winners."

He held his hand over a large rip in his jacket that exposed the greenish and tarnished rib cage underneath. He met Chen-Li's gaze and held it steady. "My brother and I have each failed in many ways."

Just then, a shout came. "There! There they are! Get those dirty bastards!" It was the Red and Blue. The soldiers saw them standing together. "Come on, rush them with your spears! To glory this day! Kill them! Kill Chen-Li! Kill the Zorn! Kill them all!"

Lord Rhodes commanded them to stand down. But their impulsive reactions of vengeance had taken hold. He stood in front of his men and tried to stop them. "Cease-fire! Stop this madness! Get back to your units!"

But the soldiers turned into a mob that Lord Rhodes could not control. The soldiers drew arms and charged up the Oracle Mount.

Nearby, Astar heard the commotion of the crazed soldiers. Suddenly, the coming onslaught of soldiers froze in their actions like sculptures. Astar had stopped time before events got out of control and ruined everything. Astar, Micah, Valen, Zorn, and Chen-Li were left to move about freely, but every other mortal was frozen in time. This was a time for the immortals.

Astar came and spoke to Chen-Li. "I'm afraid you have made many enemies in the Red and Blue. There has been a lot of death in their ranks. They want revenge. You are no longer the hero you once were. They fear you now as much as they do the Skeletal King."

"How could I have allowed myself to become that which I myself despised?" Chen-Li shook his head. "How could I have let that happen?"

"And you." Astar turned to the Zorn. "Their longtime enemy. They sing songs to your demise. For everybody involved, I had to stop time, or else the full fury of the Red and Blue would come down on us all. If these men kill you, it would only make matters worse. Killing us now, before we do what needs to be done, would alter the balance and all the hard work already completed. With time stopped, the five of us can talk. So, let's talk."

"Micah, you need to be a part of this, too," Astar told him.

Micah approached with his face white as ivory, his body thin and frail, his eyes silver and sunken in dark hollows. "I fear there is no hope for me, I—"

"I want my flesh restored," the Zorn interrupted Micah. Astar could tell the Zorn's mind was churning rapidly. "I want to be made whole again. You said you could do it. Well, can you? And if you can, will you? What is the price? Or just another one of your lies?"

"And what of them?" The Lady Valen pointed to the White Eminence hanging in the sky above. "We need to do something about them, these pitiful souls."

Astar turned from the circle. He walked a couple of steps, looking out over the sea of sick people surrounding the Oracle Mount. At last he spoke, "Hazor, you made these people this way, first in sickness, then in madness. Can you make them whole again?"

"I suppose I could if I wanted to," the Zorn replied. "But why would I?"

"All this bitterness and scorn you have against the mortals must stop. It is the price you shall pay for saving your own skin." Astar turned to the group. "Why would any of us help the others? Why would I want to help any of you, if you are not willing to help each other?"

"This is going nowhere," the Zorn spoke. "You talk about helping each other? There is too much resentment in this circle. Just release the Red and Blue. Let them do their worst. Can't hold them back forever."

"Maybe I will release them, Zorn. Do you think I am not tempted to do so? It would be entertaining to watch them hack you to pieces," Astar told the Zorn. "But I, at least, am willing to give one last effort to try to resolve what needs to be resolved. But I cannot do it alone.

I must have the help of all of you for this to work. This is the only way. That is what this new era has in store for all of us. We must either learn to live together or we will die separately."

"Now, each of you," Astar spoke to each of them in turn. "Hazor, you want your flesh restored?"

Astar turned to Chen-Li. "A body for your spirit and the souls of the White Eminence?"

To Micah he said, "A cure for the venom and a living host?"

Then finally to Lady Valen he said, "You want an end to the sickness and madness, and healing for all these people?"

"But, Astar, how much can you do without Soothsayer?" Chen-Li asked. "Your blade has broken. I watched it explode in Langula's hands."

"You mean this?" Astar pulled the golden dagger out from under his cloak. Soothsayer in its minor form.

"How can that be?" Chen-Li asked. "I was the closest to it when it exploded. I saw it explode in Langula's hand."

"You saw *that* blade explode," Astar told Chen-Li. "Don't you know? I can reproduce a million of them if I so desired!"

"I see, but the blade has discharged its energy," Lady Valen observed. "How will you charge it? Will you call upon the Timmutes again?"

"No, the Timmutes have served me once already, and once is enough," Astar said. He now walked toward the spirits streaming behind Chen-Li. "What about them?"

"Of course, the souls of the White Eminence," Chen-Li said. "They could recharge Astar's Blade."

"But *will* they?" Astar asked. "Will they make the sacrifice, or will they be content to wander about this world without form, without hope, stealing bodies as they come by them? That will make them hated and despised by humanity. What will they choose?"

"Why would they make a sacrifice to satisfy the wants of the Zorn?" Chen-Li asked.

"It would be an unselfish sacrifice to rid the world of a monster?" Astar asked. "They could also take heart in knowing that they would be ushering in a new era."

"And curing the multitudes of the sick and the mad," Lady Valen added.

"All noble-enough causes to redeem themselves," Astar continued. "That is the trade-off. They can either exist as body thieves, or be gratefully remembered for a selfless sacrifice. They could heroically atone for their spiritual possessions and murders of the Red and Blue. They can wipe their slates clean and achieve forgiveness for the lives they took. Making this sacrifice, they would be serving the greater good. Relieve their souls of the eternal burdens of their guilt."

"What about me?" Micah asserted himself. "You told me before, I cannot be cured of this venom without dying. My body has stopped functioning. I keep moving the levers, in this flesh prison, but it will not sustain my restoration. I need a living host. Are you suggesting that I too sacrifice myself to charge the blade?"

"No, that is not what I had in mind for you, Micah," Astar told him.

"What about us?" the Zorn said, pointing at himself and his brother. "Chen-Li and I cannot even touch without invoking the Great Negation. That would send us back to the Cosmic Creation. Trapping us together eternally."

"No, that has never been true," Astar said. "Only violent *intent* between the both of you enacts the Great Negation. But nonviolent contact between you poses no threat at all. You have been at war with each other for so long, you have never given peace a chance. Think about this, Hazor. At one time, before you both were born, you shared Ehlona's womb. Did you forget that? It can be that way again."

The Zorn shouted, "Are you trying to trick us, the sons of the Gods, into negating ourselves?"

"I am the Goddess incarnate!" an angry Astar said. "I do not need to mislead you to eliminate you. You have done quite well to accomplish that on your own!"

Astar softened before continuing, "If there is no malice in your hearts, no violence in your intentions, you need not ever worry about a Great Negation."

After he said that, Chen-Li and the Zorn looked at each other.

"Now, I want you to touch hands," Astar told them. "Go ahead."

"How can I?" Chen-Li asked. "I am only but spirit."

"Reach out with your spirit hand," Astar said to Chen-Li.

As Chen-Li extended his translucent hand, the Zorn looked skeptical. "But he has no body."

"Spirit to spirit," Lady Valen whispered.

The Zorn's yellow eyes studied the warrior-priest. Then the Zorn allowed Chen-Li to reach through his skeletal green hand.

Like Astar had promised, nothing happened. No Great Negation. No explosions. Nothing happened to them externally. But what the Zorn said next indicated something may have changed.

"Remember when we were children?" the Zorn reminisced. "All the others hated me. It was because I made them hate me. I wanted them to hate me, so I could hate them back. But you, Marus, I did not hate you, for you did not hate me first. Your only sin against me was that she, the Goddess Ehlona, loved you and not me. I wanted to blame you for that."

"Ehlona was the Goddess of Love," Chen-Li said. "But really, she loved no one. That was true with you, Hazor, and true with me too. But I never hated you. You were always my brother."

Astar said softly, "Marus needs your body."

The Zorn pulled his hand back from Chen-Li. "I knew this was a trick! You want me to give him my body?" The Zorn laughed. "What's the point of restoration of my flesh if I cannot be around to enjoy it?"

"It is not that way," Astar said. "Chen-Li will not take control of your body—he will become a part of it. He will be merged into you. Together, the both of you will form someone new."

"The way Gilglad's and Ehlona's power merged into Valen," Lady Valen said.

"Something new?" Chen-Li asked. "A new person? I'm not too sure about this. I need a body but share one? With him?"

"What kind of new person will we be? What will we be changed too?" the Zorn asked.

"You share common blood," Astar said. "You already share what is common among every mortal. For every man has the two distinct voices of Chen-Li and the Zorn already inside them. In this way, you will be more like them. One side will temper the other."

"Why would we do that?" Chen-Li was skeptical. "How is that any better than the Great Negation?"

"Because if you don't," Astar told them both, "the disease that took Hazor's flesh will continue to get worse and soon kill him. He knows that, don't you, Hazor? You feel that what I say is true. As for you, Chen-Li, you can wander in your spiritual form but only for a limited time. In a matter of weeks, your energy will weaken and dissipate. Finally, you will just blow away on the wind. You either become a new creation with your brother, or very soon, you will both die separately. But more than that, if you don't do this, you will miss the one and only opportunity to make amends for what you both have done. This merger is for the greater good, to restore your dignity. But I leave it for you to decide."

"And what will become of me?" Lady Valen asked. "Am I to become the receptacle for Micah?"

"No, my lady, you will not. But you can no longer remain immortal in this era. The healing, the blessing, the extension of long life. All of these have been viewed, in the Cosmic Creation, as deviancy. They violate assigned destiny. In short, they alter the predetermined timetables, schedules, and resources set aside for each person, as they go through life and death. They must go on as intended, and they are not being allowed to. So, my lady, a time is coming when Valen will no longer be needed. Being needed is in the essence of you. It is in your heart. With no one to heal and no one to love, you will find only sadness and depression. You will turn from godliness to pettiness. This lack of love will torment your mind and eventually break you. Your days will be filled with misery and madness. But these burdens I can lift from you and return you back to the delicate flower you once were. There, you will find duty and purpose, and happiness, and love, for all your days."

"What will happen to the Temple of Valor?" Valen asked, crying.

Astar explained, "The Temple of Valor will remain a place for the sick to come to find healing. But please understand, the new era will be an era for the people, not for Gods or their magic. People will still be born and people will still die but in their own time. In between birth and death, they will live out their lives naturally. They will get sick and will be healed but through the medicine of the mortals, without intervention from us. This will be an era of nature and science. Free from our magic, free from us Gods. There will be no more extensions of life through blessings. There will be no more curses. We must be the first to set the example. But, like it or not, the era starts today."

"What am I to become?" Valen asked.

"Your powers of Ehlona will be removed," Astar said.

"I wish Amtor could be here now," Valen said. "I so would have liked to be reunited with him."

What Astar said next stunned them all. "*I* will become the vessel for Micah's new body."

"What? Astar, you can't do that," Micah insisted. "What would happen to you?"

"In the coming era of the mortals, none of us can remain. Not you, Zorn. Not Chen-Li. Not you, Lady Valen, or Micah. Not even me," Astar said. "I am leaving this world too. After I give Micah my body as a host, then I will go my own way."

"Go away how?" the Zorn asked. "Without a body, where will you go, and how will you get there?"

"That is my business," Astar told him. "And none of your concern. Plus, you will find out soon enough anyway."

"Everyone feeds on something, Langula once told me," Micah said. "I guess that was true then, and applies to all of us, and our needs now."

"Stupid," said the Zorn. "Utter nonsense."

"What will be left when we are gone, Astar?" Chen-Li asked.

"The kingdom of mortals," Astar said. "A new era, the kingdom of men."

All of them looked at each other. At last, the Zorn spoke. "I, for one, take no pleasure in this."

"Everyone stands to gain something," Lady Valen said. "And everyone loses something."

"I have lost enough already," the Zorn said. "I am all that remains now."

"As have I," Chen-Li agreed. "I am now despised by the mortals."

"I have been despised my entire life," the Zorn recollected. "You'll be all right."

"Maybe a new creation is better than what we are now, Hazor," Chen-Li said. "But once done, there is no turning back."

None of them could find any reason to disagree.

"It is settled, then," Astar said. "I am going to start time again."

"What about them?" Micah asked, pointing with his thumb to Lord Rhodes and the Red and Blue rushing toward them.

"Don't worry," Astar said. "I'll handle them."

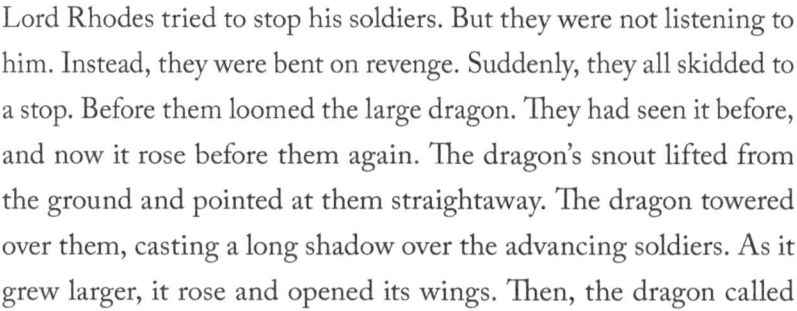

Lord Rhodes tried to stop his soldiers. But they were not listening to him. Instead, they were bent on revenge. Suddenly, they all skidded to a stop. Before them loomed the large dragon. They had seen it before, and now it rose before them again. The dragon's snout lifted from the ground and pointed at them straightaway. The dragon towered over them, casting a long shadow over the advancing soldiers. As it grew larger, it rose and opened its wings. Then, the dragon called out in a thousand voices.

"Stop right there! Go no farther! Do not interfere with the immortals! Collect your dead and leave us to our own business!"

Astar's fractal dragon stood in the way between them and the immortals. Lord Rhodes and the others quaked at the sight of the giant dragon. Quivering in shock, they dropped their swords and ran in the opposite direction, realizing they could not fight against it.

But not Lord Rhodes. He stood firm for a moment, looking past the dragon at the spirits that once inhabited his body and made him kill his own men while he helplessly watched. He called out to them. "You are murderers of men!" Lord Rhodes shouted.

The great fractal dragon that loomed ahead now stepped toward them, invoking the cries of the men. After the great dragon dispersed the soldiers, he pursued them down the Oracle Mount. The soldiers scattered before the giant dragon, allowing time for the immortal parlay to continue.

Chen-Li turned to face the priests of the White Eminence. He stopped to listen to their cries of anguish.

"Are we to roam the world, stealing bodies from the living?"

"That would make us no better than those we fought against."

Chen-Li explained to them that by sacrificing their spirits to the blade, they could serve a higher purpose. After his explanation, the priests responded.

"Should we seek to sacrifice our priesthood in the fulfillment of a righteous purpose?"

"If so, then let us be as one."

"May it be a dignified and noble offering, in memory of Tyla and Myra, the First Wives, and those that were lost!"

"In the end," Chen-Li told Astar. "There seems only one decision worthwhile."

"So be it," Astar responded.

Astar held the small blade over his head.

The spirits of the White Eminence circled the blade for a moment. The first few spirits absorbed into the blade, invoking small crackles of blue sparks. Then, other spirits followed, then more came. Each absorbed into the blade, causing it to crackle. Astar's Blade hummed with electric life, vibrating in his hand as it grew larger. The spirits swirled down quickly now in force, in long descending clusters, swirling around the ever-growing blade. Soothsayer enlarged, gorging upon the souls entering its golden surface. Until, at last, all the spirits of the White Eminence had been absorbed. Astar lowered the massive sword as effortlessly as he would the weight of the little dagger.

Lord Rhodes and the soldiers observed what happened in wonder.

The great dragon spoke to them again. "The spirits of the White Eminence have sacrificed their lives for you, to usher in this new era of man. They did this to atone for their wrongs against you, for your Red and Blue," the giant dragon said. "It is true, you have suffered and have been wronged by them. But behold! Tens of thousands of sacrifices were just made for you, for the era of all men. Now take your vengeance, take your dead, and begone from this place of the immortals! Never return to the Temple of Valor, lest I come back and slaughter you. Now begone!"

Lord Rhodes and the soldiers all stood looking at each other, hesitant to leave. Then the dragon shouted again in a loud voice.

"*Go!*" the giant dragon commanded. The shout echoed across the Mid-Run Valley.

Lord Kilmer came and took Lord Rhodes by the arm. "Come on now, Rhodes. This is none of our business here. Things are happening we cannot control."

Lord Rhodes backed away with Kilmer's help. He and the other soldiers sheathed their swords. They left the dragon guarding the Oracle Mount. Together they walked away from the Temple of Valor without further incident.

Once a safe distance from the dragon, Kilmer talked to Rhodes.

"Darla and I will accompany you back to Castle Odessa," Kilmer said. "We would like to go home. Oaks and Melvin can help get the king safely back home too. It will be nice to finally find a home for our son, Kory."

"It would be an honor to ride with you again, Lord Plum-Kilmer," Rhodes said.

"Kilmer?" Oaks approached. "I'm not going back to Castle Odessa."

"What do you mean, Oaks?" Kilmer asked.

Behind Oaks, Tamara stood waiting. Oaks looked back at her. He smiled and she nodded. Oaks continued, "I'm done being a soldier, Kilmer. There's no future in it. I've been asked to go south with the Nomads of Spiron."

"With Tamara?" Kilmer asked.

Oaks returned Kilmer's smile with a smile his own.

"You're leaving us?" Darla asked. "I am going to miss you."

Astar spoke. "Me too, Oaks, more than anyone else. It was you who found me in the woods, freezing to death from the Plum River."

"How could I forget?" Oaks said with watery eyes.

"We've been together all this time," Darla said, holding back tears. "Especially when Kilmer and Kory left to fight in the war…" Darla's voice trailed off as she looked at the younger Kory.

"The first Kory," Oaks tussled the younger Kory's hair. "Your namesake, squirt."

Kory smiled. "Are you really leaving?"

"Just for a little while, squirt," Oaks said. "But the next time I see you, we will have a big fire. One the likes the Mid-Run Valley has never seen."

"But us—you and me—we've never been apart, ever." Darla gave Oaks a big hug. "I'll miss you so much. Take good care of him, Tamara."

"I will. You'll have to come see us on the south shore," Tamara said. "You are always welcome with the Nomads of Spiron."

"We'll come back to Castle Odessa to see you too," Oaks started to say, but then his voice cracked choking back emotion. "I miss you guys already."

"Don't miss us too much. You have your own life to live. You deserve a fresh start," Kilmer said. "It's time you start living."

The wagon was readied with King Leopold's body. The elite guard rode on horseback in front and back. Banners of red and of blue were slowly furled, to represent the death of the king's colors. They would not be unfurled until the selection of a new monarch.

Kilmer, Darla, and Melvin sat mounted on their horses ready to escort the funeral procession. They turned and waved at Oaks and Tamara, standing arm in arm with the Temple of Valor in the background. They both waved back. Lord Rhodes gave the order to march and, with an abrupt rap of the drum, the column started to move. The funeral procession began a slow arduous march away from the Temple of Valor. Keeping in time with the beat, Kilmer was afraid of turning around to look at them again. But Darla and Kory did and cried as they waved. The long line of mourners rode up the ridge and out of view. They were heading home, toward Castle Odessa.

The giant dragon watched all these developments, until the Red and Blue were gone from sight. A soldier or two stayed behind to prepare Amtor's body for transport to Homestead. But they were no cause for any concern. They worked dutifully about their business. So, the dragon spread its wings and flew away.

That left only the Nomads of Spiron and the Immortals.

"We should begin," Astar told the immortals.

ACT VI

What Has Happened Before

Will Happen Again

Candy apple treat
I place my face inside the beast
Stumble from the feast
Headless and bleeding.

———✦◦◦◦✦———

Excerpt from *The Witch's Songbook*

When the spirit moved in front of the fireplace, rather than cast a shadow, the ghost refracted the light like a kaleidoscope in bright prismatic colors upon the opposite walls.
— Excerpt from *Kilmer's Ghost* (Chapter 37)

FUNERAL FOR A KING

CASTLE ODESSA

The funeral procession moved in time to a single lonely beat on the half step. First came the drummers. Next, the solemn cavalry rode upon jittery mounts. They all marched up the Mauveguard Pass in a double line. Their colors, their bright banners and flags, were all furled and dipped into a mournful salute. Everyone stepped in time with the drum.

The dour escorts preceded a single funeral wagon, painted in black. Inside the black wagon, a single casket adorned with bundles of white flowers had been covered with the king's colors of red and blue.

Lord Rhodes and Lord Plum-Kilmer rode on horseback. Kilmer looked back to make sure Darla and Melvin still rode behind them. They all rode together with a host of King Leopold's aides and personal elite guards. Each person in the procession wore a black armband.

Behind the king there were more wagons carrying more caskets, also draped with flags and flowers. These caskets held the soldiers killed in the action against the Temple of Valor. Most of the dead were killed in the field by the survivors who rode with them now. Their friends and fellow soldiers came bearing the guilt of having succumbed to the possessions of the spirits of the White Eminence. These were the bitter dead and the guilt-stricken living.

The Mauveguard Pass was lined with people who had come from the villages to watch the funeral procession pass by. Word had reached them that the king was dead. They came to pay their respects. They started crying as the dead passed and removed their hats to honor them. Some took a knee as the caskets passed by.

"Murderer!" An abrupt shout burst the silence. Amid the mourners, a woman loudly insulted the king as his casket passed. "You finally got what you deserved! Murderer!"

The woman was quickly subdued by the other mourners, until guards came and took the hysterical woman away. But as they hauled her off, she continued to shout louder indignations.

"Remember Bowling! The massacre! Remember the flames!"

Then, just as suddenly, across the way more abrupt voices joined in. This time, a group of men started shouting.

One man shouted. "He burned my son to death! Butcher!! Leopold was no king!"

"Do not mourn this man!" Another man tried to walk into the funeral procession but was held back. "Remember Umbrick! Killer of children! Killer of women and orphans!"

More disrespect sounded. "Die Leopold! Death to the king!"

One person ran toward the casket carrying a bucket of pig's blood but was intercepted before reaching the king's casket. The blood spilled all over himself and the soldiers who held him back. The man was taken away shouting, *"Die! You Murderer! Die"*

Just then, another man from the other side rushed the casket and tried tipping it over. He too was quickly caught and removed.

The mourners and onlookers started wailing in a great commotion. Soon, people were pushing and shoving each other. The funeral procession got out of step. The soldiers were heightening their aware-ness, looking around, waiting, and watching for more trouble.

Worried that it might get out of hand, Lord Rhodes shouted an order, *"Red and Blue! At the ready!"*

All the swords and spears went from carrying their weapons to holding them out in front. They snapped to a more aggressive stance. They were ready to use lethal force if necessary. The crowd noticed and immediately suppressed their collective agitation.

Lord Rhodes shouted to everyone, "No one approaches the casket!"

Kilmer turned to Darla and gave her a concerned look.

Melvin learned toward Darla. "Looks like a lot has changed since we left."

ORACLE MOUNT

Ironically, at the same time, at the Oracle Mount, a growing mob of angry Nomads surrounded Nadya and Boldo.

"You betrayed us. Betrayed your own kind," a woman shouted at Nadya. "You will never be forgiven!"

"My grandfather was food for the demons!" a young man cried out. "Damn you, Nadya! Damn you!"

All of those families who had selected the black sacrificial stones over the course of the past year shouted at Nadya. Those who had not selected any black stones tried to calm the other families. But the riotous families would not be calmed. Having made no sacrifices, the others were quickly ignored and chastised for even attempting to keep the peace. The anger they expressed to Nadya was escalat-ing and quickly spiraling out of control. They spit upon Nadya and pelted her with rocks and garbage.

"Stop it! Please, I submit!" Nadya put her hands in the air. "I submit to you!"

The crowd expressed more outrage.

Nadya continued, "So much death! So much pain and suffering! It is all around me. I mourn your families. I mourn them all. I remember them all! I see their faces! I hear their sobs. Their ghosts haunt me! I see them at night! I see them during the day! I see them all the time!" Nadya covered her eyes as she spoke. "My soul has been corrupted! Month after month, I brought them your loved ones. Had I not, the Demonic would have destroyed us all. I cannot live with what I have become. I am no longer Queen of Spiron."

"Let's kill her!" somebody shouted.

CASTLE ODESSA

At Castle Odessa, the funeral procession arrived at the top of the Mauveguard Pass without any more incidents or any more protests. While the drum continued the lonely beat, they turned the corner and entered Castle Odessa.

Lord Whitney had been waiting there, expecting to receive them. A host of soldiers stood at attention at the ready. As the wagon bearing the king's casket rolled into the courtyard, it came to a stop as the drum stopped. After becoming accustomed to the steady beat for so long, the silence seemed to ring in the ears. An eerie silence followed. An intense stillness fell across the courtyard. The quiet had the effect of shrinking the courtyard into a very small space.

At length, Lord Rhodes alone dismounted. The sound of his boots was the only sound. He approached Lord Whitney and stood quietly in front of him. They waited for the mournful stillness to take hold again. In the silence they found a long reflective, respectful moment to their fallen king. Thousands of onlookers watched in silent reverence, afraid to breathe.

"Report!" Lord Whitney broke the calm with a commanding voice, while executing a quick, sharp salute.

Lord Rhodes returned the salute. "King Leopold has returned!"

"Well done!" Lord Whitney looked straight ahead at nobody. "A grateful Kingdom of Odessa commends you."

The men dropped their salutes. Lord Whitney turned and faced the front. He gave a nod. Then, a multitude of voices, both young boys and girls, permeated the silence, and the king's choir started to sing:

> *Sing me a song! One final song!*
> *Sing me a song for the departed!*
> *I'm almost gone, I'm almost gone.*
> *The things that I wanted are slipping through my hands*
> *And I'm all, almost gone. Oh, I'm all, almost gone!*
> *Let me look at you, the way I used to look at you!*
> *I want to look at you once more!*
> *Let me feel your lips, pressing down upon my lips*
> *The way we used to kiss before.*
> *I've been giving away everything that means anything to me!*
> *I've been crawling on my hands and knees.*
> *I hear the whispering. But can't you hear my plea?*
> *I just want to say these words, that you never heard*
> *Before I get what I deserve,*
> *I'm sorry!*
> *I'll give you all the reasons,*
> *Why my heart feels like it's sinking*
> *Round the drain inside my soul,*
> *And I'm all, almost gone. Oh, I'm all, almost gone!*
> *Sing me a song! One final song.*
> *Sing me a song for the departed.*

After they were finished, a single bell in the tower rang slowly. The rabble-rousers encountered along the road had been eliminated from the public. For whatever reasons they had, now it made no difference whether Leopold was a good king or a bad man. Either way, he was just as dead now.

ORACLE MOUNT

Boldo came to defend Nadya. He shouted back at the crowd, "Wait! Did you not hear? Nadya has abdicated as Queen of Spiron."

"She must die for her crimes against us!" someone shouted back.

Another angry voice shouted, "A life for a life!

"The Demonic would have killed you all!!" Boldo shouted. "If not for Nadya, you would all be dead now!"

The mob looked at Boldo. His face was deadly serious. It gave them some pause. They knew him to be a man of reason, who often spoke out against Nadya.

He continued, "Killing Nadya will not bring back your dead. Can't you see what is happening up at the Temple of Valor? Everything is changing. A new era is hinging on the future, not on the past. Things will go more favorably for you if you do right by it now. A new leader must be chosen. Do that if you must! Yet let Nadya live."

CASTLE ODESSA

Lying in state, the king's casket was transported to rest under the large overarching chapel constructed above the catacombs. Colorfully adorned honor guards, smartly dressed in red and blue, were posted with long pikes at the four corners of the king's casket. For the next week, the king's body would lie in repose. Thousands of tearful people walked by to pay their respects. Many of them desired to touch the flag-draped coffin and look upon the body of their king.

Many of the mourners spoke of his courage to kill a Devourer. They talked about how he faced death, so gallantly, and finally met his fate. They cursed the cowardly battle-ax-wielding Monticello, who struck him from behind.

"What do you expect from a dirty demon?" they said to each other.

Meanwhile, in the upper reaches of the castle, a committee formed to determine the next king. On the committee were Lords Whitney, Rhodes, and Kilmer as well as other village dignitaries who were also given a voice at these proceedings. The committee was heavily sequestered. Throughout the week, the committee members appeared at certain times and eulogized the king. But still, no announcement of a new king, or regent, came.

Then, on the seventh day, a messenger came running to a balcony overlooking the chapel. He shouted down at the mourners, "Ring the bell! A new king has been selected!"

ORACLE MOUNT

"Come one! Come all! All you Nomads of Spiron!" the barker cried. "Cast your vote for the next monarch of the Nomads of Spiron."

Several men and women passed out ballots on slips of paper. The process was simple. Whoever had the most votes, as selected by the people, would be their next ruler. No one advocated for the post directly. There were no campaigns. The Nomads registered to cast one vote each. They were encouraged to keep their vote a secret. But in darkened places, one could not help whispering about rumors and innuendo throughout the process.

Nadya sat dejected outside one of the more common wagons. This one, a sparsely decorated one, was in the back of the caravan. She had to stay away from the royal first wagon. She did not cast a vote to select her successor. Instead, she only watched, as the people filed through the line to get their votes counted.

Finally, a man shouted, "Is that all of them?" He held several strips of paper in his hands. "Has anyone *not* cast a vote?"

The ballots were all collected and the counting began. It took several hours to count them all. Finally, the last strip of paper went through the last set of hands.

"Was that the last one?" the counter asked.

All the counters looked through their piles, checking twice. "That is the last of them."

"Then let's compare notes."

A crowd gathered around the counters, anxious to hear the results.

"Is that it? Are we sure?" The counters coordinated.

"Yeah, that's right." They nodded in agreement. The counters then handed a single folded slip of paper to the barker who would make the announcement. The barker unfolded the paper, read and understood it, then climbed to the top of a high wagon. There, he stood alone high above the crowd.

"Can you see me?" the barker asked.

The crowd impatiently said they could.

"Can you hear me?" the barker then asked.

"Get on with it, you old dog fart," the crowd laughed.

"All right, then. Can I have your attention, please! Attention, all you Nomads of Spiron," the barker shouted. "The votes have been cast and counted. I have the results here in my hand!"

A general hush fell over the crowd.

"By an overwhelming majority of five hundred and thirty-eight votes, the new ruler and king of the Nomads of Spiron is Boldo, the Prince of Spiron!"

"King Boldo!" A general cheer went up. But the celebration was subdued. Some others were not so happy.

"No!" someone protested. "Boldo is Nadya's brother! Why did you vote for him?"

"He has courage," another Nomad said. "He speaks of safety with honor. He will be a good king!"

"Three cheers for King Boldo!" someone shouted and others joined in.

As Boldo approached the crowd, girls threw flowers at him, and men hoisted him upon their shoulders. Dancing and singing burst forth as they passed around Boldo, the new king.

He addressed the crowd, "The dark days of the feasts are over. A new and better day is coming for our generation. So, dance and celebrate, for a new day is dawning for the Nomads of Spiron!"

They danced, drank, sang, and laughed. The celebration continued throughout the day.

Nadya watched them celebrate from the shadows. Her thoughts turned to leaving. But then, where would she go? She knew nothing but the Nomadic ways she had grown up with. No, she would stay and live out her days in the familiar world she had grown accustomed to. To start her new life, she turned and faded into the plain wagon to take a long deep sleep.

CASTLE ODESSA

After the bells, the horns announced the arrival of the Lords Whitney, Kilmer, and Rhodes. They gathered in front of the chapel for all to see. They stood behind the flag-draped coffin of King Leopold, which was made to resemble a sacred offering. The horns finished announcing their arrival. Then quiet filled the chamber.

Lord Whitney was the first to speak. "Following the tragic and untimely death of King Leopold, and over the course of the past three days, a committee to determine the next king and the proper transition of authority from His Majesty to the next ruler of our kingdom has convened. To this purpose, the committee has reached a conclusion. It is now our solemn duty to announce to the world who will be the next sovereign over the Kingdom of Odessa."

Here, Lord Whitney stopped speaking from his notes and looked out over the crowd.

"But first I want to address the protesters." Lord Whitney paused for a moment, letting his words hang in the air. Then he continued, "Let us not forget that before he was king, Leopold was a man—an imperfect, fallible man. Before he was king, he had a vision bigger than himself. A vision of a unified Mid-Run Valley. My thoughts often wonder, what kind of tyrant could he have become? Who could have prevented it? Yet, on his own, he promoted a common good. I cannot justify all his actions. I am not asking you to forget those who were lost. But at least grant yourself peace. Make this a time for healing. The Kingdom of Odessa will live on, although the man does not."

A silence filled the hall.

"Now," Lord Whitney cleared his throat. "For the business at hand. The committee has adopted a citation, a unanimous decision. I ask that Lord Plum-Kilmer comes forward to read the citation."

Lord Plum-Kilmer came forward with a long scroll. He unrolled it to reveal large flowing calligraphy eloquently written in black, red, and gold. With a little nod to Darla, Kilmer addressed the crowd, "To all subjects in the Kingdom of Odessa, to all who can hear these words, let it be known and signed into law from this day forth, the solemn duty and sole responsibility to govern, rule, and protect, to preserve these lands and realms of Odessa, from the Gray Mountains in the east, to the Blue Mountains in the west, to the Great Mapes Forest in the north, to the shores of the Endless Sea to the south, and to all of the amalgamated lands of the Mid-Run Valley, one man who shall rule, be given that grace to rule as sovereign King of Odessa. That man's name is Lord Oskar Whitney."

The crowd let out a resounding cheer. Lord Whitney stepped up beside Lord Plum-Kilmer. Lord Rhodes came and lifted a golden crown high in the air.

"Your Highness, what name do I crown you?" Lord Rhodes asked, holding the crown over Lord Whitney's head. The crowd hushed to hear him say the name of the new king for the first time.

"King Leopold II," he said, and another loud cheer erupted.

Lord Rhodes gently placed the golden crown on his head, thereby coronating the next king, King Leopold II, of Odessa. Immediately after placing the crown, Lord Rhodes took a knee. Seeing this, Kilmer, Darla, Melvin, and the entire crowd of thousands repeated the action.

Members of the elite guard came and honored the new king by draping the traditional red bearskin upon his shoulders. Then they started a long procession line. People came from all over to present him with gifts, including a decorated golden rod and an ornamental staff.

The king turned to Lord Rhodes and laid his golden rod gently upon his shoulder.

"Rise now, Lord Rhodes, make the official announcement," the king said.

Lord Rhodes stood and turned to the onlookers. "People of the world, rise and behold your new king, King Leopold II."

A loud cheer rose up. Flowers erupted in the air. The trumpets blared. The bells rang out. Music cut through the gloom. A new feeling of euphoria swept through the people.

Across the Mid-Run Valley, the news spread very quickly. In the villages, bells soon rang out. People cheered and celebrations were held to honor their new king.

In the first days of his reign, King Leopold II quickly got to work. The first order of business was to continue organizing the repairs to Castle Odessa. Scaffolding was constructed along the front of the castle. The work began to reconstruct the Green. In the days and weeks that followed, Castle Odessa became a flurry of activity. Repairing the castle's former glory was a welcome and positive distraction for a kingdom that had just lost its founding monarch.

The people loved King Leopold II. He had not murdered his way to power. He had earned it through building lasting relationships. With Lord Rhodes ratifying, the king signed into law that no further prosecution should ever be lodged against Lord Plum-Kilmer, his family or his loyal friends. He was given a full pardon of the past trumped-up charges and full restoration of his titles.

Lord Plum-Kilmer and his family settled into their old residence in Castle Odessa. But they did not stay long. Just a couple of years later, the family made plans and left for a fresh new start in Haverhill.

Before Lord Plum-Kilmer retired from public service, Leopold II fashioned a golden ring for him. It symbolized the wealth of the Plum-Kilmer family for all time. King Leopold II presented the ring to Kilmer in a small ceremony attended by Lord Rhodes and Melvin, as well as Oaks and Tamara who came up from the south. The ring represented a physical manifestation of the law, that no one shall ever question the loyalties of Lord Plum-Kilmer, his family or friends again. The ring would give Kilmer and his descendants access to vast Plum-Kilmer financial fortune.

On the morning Kilmer was to leave for Haverhill, Hollow Face appeared to him. This time, there were no visions of death. Kilmer could only speculate that the ghost's presence was a sign of good things to come. The ghost faded away as it usually did. But the benign appearance of Hollow Face got him thinking. And Kilmer reflected on all he had been through.

"I have lived such a blessed life," Kilmer told Darla. "There were times it was hard to see. I think these blessings come to us like ghosts. Hard to see and even harder to believe. But I see them clearly now. They have always been there, not as ghosts, but right there in plain sight, right in front of me."

"Right in front of me," Darla smiled. "Like the king's poem on our wedding day."

Kilmer nodded; he remembered every word.

For all the times we have devoted looking
Over all the years we went searching.
In our desire to grow wings, we flew high to find hidden things.
Like the secrets in our minds, and in the center of the skies.
But as we searched our questions still cry.
Then we find, to our surprise,
That everything we were looking for was here the entire time.
Always right in front of us.
This is the meaning of love

Kilmer gently laid his forehead upon hers.

Shortly after, they rode out of Castle Odessa, never to return again.

One day, when King Leopold II was alone and looking over some reports, something very peculiar happened. A voice interrupted his thoughts and startled him. Thinking he was alone, the king looked up from his reports.

"Your Majesty? Hello, I don't believe we have ever met."

A man in a green cloak stood there in front of his desk. When the man pulled his hood back long blond curls spilled out. His eyes were of the brightest blue.

"My name is Astar, I am the only son of Amtor."

The king was surprised to see him here. "Astar? I have heard much about you."

"As I have heard about you, King Leopold II." Astar bowed politely.

The king gave a nod back to him. "I did not hear you come in. Were you announced?"

"My apologies, Your Majesty, I was not announced."

"I see. One of the things I have heard about you is that you are very mysterious in your nature, Astar. Kilmer has told me about how you destroyed Castle Orlo with your blade, Soothsayer. Later your blade destroyed the Temple of Chen-Li, destroying the demoness, whose name I care not to mention. Since you have done all these miraculous things, I don't suppose it would be any great feat for you to get by my guards undetected."

"No, it was no trouble at all, noble king. And I apologize for this disruption, I know you must be busy. You needn't worry about me—I present no danger. I only bypassed your staff so as not to be seen by others. I needed to talk to you privately."

"Of course, of course. What may I do for you, Astar?"

"I want you to know that I will be leaving soon."

"Leaving?" The king tilted his head. "Where are you going?"

Astar said, "To the northern lands, beyond the Great Mapes Forest. Into parts unknown."

Leopold II puckered his lips. "I have heard unconfirmed reports—just vague speculation really—of what may lie beyond that impenetrable forest. Are you in need of any assistance? Is there anything that I can do for you? Anything that may be in my power to provide?"

"Very kind of you, my king. Such a joy to hear good, kind words again." Astar brought the dagger out from behind his cloak. He held the blade in front of the king. The golden dagger sparkled in a most extraordinary way.

King Leopold II's eyebrows rose and his eyes widened. Holding his palms out in front of him, he startled when Astar produced the dagger. "Astar, what are you meaning to do with that?"

"Oh, sorry to shock you." Astar realized he had scared the king. "This is the blade you spoke about. This is Soothsayer, the most powerful weapon in the world. And I would like to give it to you. A priceless gift for safekeeping."

The king lowered his eyebrows in wonder. He looked first at the blade, then back to Astar, then back again to the golden dagger. "You are giving me Soothsayer?"

And it burns me up inside

When the tears swell up my eyes.

You said you loved me

But you left me

Here to die.

Excerpt from *The Witch's Songbook*

The three beacons illuminated the sign to the whole world
that a new God had entered their world and
had come to heal them—with love.
— Excerpt from *Kilmer's Ghost* (Chapter 38)

THE ERA OF THE UNWELCOMED GODS

ORACLE MOUNT

"It is time to begin." Astar rolled up his sleeves and reached to hold Lady Valen's hand.

She let out a sigh as she took Astar's hand. Then Valen and Micah clasped hands.

"Now you, Chen-Li," Astar said. "Grasp Micah's."

Chen-Li reached through Micah's hand and found his spirit.

"Good, now finally, the Zorn," Astar said.

After much consideration, the Zorn slowly extended his hand. "I have nothing to lose."

"Nor do I," Chen-Li said. He first looked at his brother's bony hand, then his own ghostly one. He reached his hand into the Zorn's bones.

"Now, Hazor, touch the blade. Carefully, use the palm of your hand." Astar dipped Soothsayer forward.

The Zorn nervously watched the blade's shadow cover his face. His eyes widened in fear, as it lowered closer to him.

The Zorn could not look at it. "Look what it did to me last time I touched it."

"This time it will be different," Astar said. "This time it will restore your flesh."

"I have a hard time trusting you," the Zorn told him. "Not just you—I can't trust anyone."

"Your choice," Astar said. "Touch the blade and live or die as the Skeletal King."

"Go on, touch it," Chen-Li encouraged him. "What more can it take away from us?"

"Ah, maybe you're right." The Zorn's dry purplish tongue darted out of his mouth to moisten his lips or something equivalent to that. Still, he stopped just shy of it. He rubbed his fingers.

"The circle must be complete," Lady Valen said. "All of us are in this together."

The Zorn laid his palm on Astar's Blade.

Throom! The blade suddenly roared to life.

Soothsayer rippled in waves of energy that encompassed all five of them with fantastic color. They watched as the energy ascended and descended over them. Rising from the tops of their heads, the wave fell to their knees, only to go back up again. Each of their muscles tensed as the energy waves increased in intensity. The waves grew brighter, glowing and spinning around them.

Phoom! Another burst of energy pulsed from the blade.

The Zorn rocked forward, doubling over as in pain. He grimaced and let out a scream. Meanwhile, Chen-Li also looked in pain. He screamed as his spirit started blinking in and out of existence in strobing light. Micah began convulsing, his eyes rolling back in their sockets as his spirit began shedding its body. Valen's hair was blowing wildly upward as if caught in a hurricane wind. Astar's skin crept with living veins of lightning.

Energy funneled through Soothsayer, through the Temple of Valor, and around the Oracle Mount. With power siphoned from the Zorn, Soothsayer was reversing the sickness and the madness, undoing the spells he first cast upon them. With the healing power of Ehlona from Valen, their wounds grew new tissue, injuries spontaneously mended, and where there had been disease and broken bones, the people started to rise and stand to walk on their own. But as the sickness healed, Lady Valen's auburn hair started turning a darker brown.

The Zorn was changing too. His sickly green bones changed to ivory, pink, and then bloodred. Skin started to crawl in a living tangle over his bones. Blue veins and red arteries burrowed, like worms, forming muscle and sinew. New flesh connected onto the Zorn's bones. It twisted up his neck, then crawled under his chin. Throughout, a spiderweb of fleshy gore crept over him, entwining, and began to pump blood.

Chen-Li was being pulled inside the forming flesh of his brother. As the Zorn's skin formed, Chen-Li was absorbing into it as a drain attracts water. The shape of Chen-Li's body stretched into a screaming deformity as his spirit was dragged deeper inside the Zorn.

"This … is the end… of Chen-Li!" He gave one last cry before being completely absorbed.

Micah's body was ripping apart into long painful lacerations of his skin. Through these ruptures, like steam hissing, his spirit was leaking out of his body and streaming into Astar's.

"It is happening!" Astar shouted over the rumbling and crackling. "The change is coming!"

The Lady Valen shouted now as the structures of her face painfully rearranged. "All shall be healed!" Valen closed her eyes.

The Zorn screamed too, his face was becoming whole again but still pale like a cadaver. Skin continued to grow. Muscular structures convulsed into wet and sticky sinews that connected and sealed into place. His eyes grew larger, filling the hollows of his once-empty sockets. Inside and outside the transformation was completing.

Astar received Micah's streaming spirit into his own illuminated body. Micah's lifeless body fell to the ground. When this happened, the circle came apart.

Thack! Thack! Thack! The golden sword kicked wildly and repeatedly in Astar's hand. The power funneling through Astar's Blade began to sputter.

Boom! The blade released a final thunderous sound and a blinding flash of light.

For a moment there was only pure white light. All around the Temple of Valor, people saw the light. They heard the boom. Those in the circle were kicked to the ground. Slowly the Temple of Valor returned to view sitting on the Oracle Mount. First, it seemed to have no color. Then gradually its tones returned, the hues of greens and blues started to blend in and take shape.

Never had anyone seen such power before. Witnessing all this, King Boldo knelt to the power of Astar's Blade. The tribes of the Nomads of Spiron followed his lead and knelt too.

The Lady Valen had been blasted out of the circle. She could tell she had been changed. The magical healing power of Ehlona was gone. Lady Valen was gone. She could tell that she was Gilglad once again. She looked up to see what happened.

Astar had fallen beside her. His body was covered in a steam. No sign of Soothsayer was anywhere on him. She tried to bring him back to consciousness with a shake.

"Astar?" Gilglad asked.

He started to stir. "Where am I?"

"You are still at the Temple of Valor," Gilglad said. "Do you remember anything?"

"Astar? I am Micah. Who are you? Where is Lady Valen?"

"Micah, it worked! You are alive and in Astar's body! No more will you suffer from Langula's venom. But where is Astar?" Gilglad asked. "Where did he go? Or is he in there with you? Do you feel him inside, anywhere?"

"Yes, yes! I am in Astar's body. I'm not undead anymore," Micah replied. "But I don't know where he is." Then, Micah saw his former body lying facedown. "Over there, is that my body? Is it dead?"

"Astar? Micah, you had no knowledge of his plan afterward?" Gilglad shouted out. Receiving no answer, she shouted louder. "Where is he? Astar! Where are you!"

"This is his body, but I can't feel any trace of him," Micah asked. "Where could he have gone?"

"Oh, Micah." Gilglad hugged him. She had a tear in her eye. "I am mortal once again."

Micah looked past his former body. "Who is that over there?"

The unfamiliar man started to sit.

"Astar?" Micah asked.

Gilglad scrambled over to the new man and helped him sit.

"What happened to me?" The man shook his head. "What has Astar done to us?"

Kneeling beside him, Gilglad saw his eyes were no longer tiny yellow orbs. They were big and bright blue, the eyes of Chen-Li.

"Your flesh has been restored, just like Astar said it would. Do you have any memory? Are you Hazor or are you Marus?"

"Hazor? You called me Hazor?" the man asked. "That is not who I am."

Gilglad whispered, "Maybe Marus, then?"

"Marus. No, I am neither, yet I am both," the man said. "We have become one, fused together, as one being, together in one body. Now, like all men, we are comprised from light and the darkness.

Our memories are still there. They remain intact. This is good. We cannot allow a repeat of the wrongs committed in the past. We have been given a new start. The choice is ours to make. To live or to die. To maintain the balance inside ourselves."

"What is your name? Do you have one? What will you call yourself?" Gilglad asked. "Hazor or Marus?"

"Lazarus—I am Lazarus."

"Lazarus," she repeated.

Gilglad looked out beyond the Temple of Valor. She ran into the fields and valleys of the Oracle Mount. All around her, as far as she could see, the sick and injured had been healed! They were free to live their lives again.

"It worked. It worked. The people are healed!" Gilglad said, laughing and crying at the same time. "Look at them! They are standing on their own! They laugh! By the Gods, I will laugh with them!"

The Nomads of Spiron made celebratory, joyous yelps. They pounded on the drums and started singing, realizing a celebration of life was in order. Dancing burst out all around the Oracle Mount.

Gilglad's laughter and tears mingled with dancing, and with cymbals, drums, and flutes. Those who had been sick or stricken with madness joined in the celebration. Gilglad extended her arms and turned in circles, liberated from the endless labors and emotion of Lady Valen. She was free!

The remaining soldiers joined in too. The Nomads welcomed all. Laughter and shouts of joy burst out all around the Temple of Valor, down the Oracle Mount, and across the Mid-Run Valley. Even the Temple of Valor's acolytes, exhausted from months of unceasing labor, joined in the celebration.

Gensen ran to his son but stopped in shock. He looked down and saw the dead body of his son. A look of horror darkened his face.

But then Micah, now inhabiting Astar's body, came over and hugged Gensen. "Father, look at me. I am in Astar's body. I have been cured."

Gensen looked at him, confused. "Astar? Micah, is that you?"

He told Gensen. "I am Micah still. There is no Astar anymore."

Gensen walked to his son's dead body lying facedown in the grass.

Micah asked him, "Can we ever be the same? Will you be able to accept me as your son in this body?"

"I have always loved you and I always will," Gensen said. "And I loved Astar as my own. I get to love you both of you now."

Aberfell watched Oaks dance with Tamara along with all the others. Among the celebration, Oaks held Tamara close. Then, in the middle of the celebration, they kissed. When they kissed, they seemed to make the rest of the world disappear.

"This is not Astar's magic—this is the first blossoms of new love." Aberfell chuckled, watching from them from the archway. "Well, it has finally happened. The new era has begun."

Just then, someone screamed. "The Devourer returns!" Around the grounds the cry went up. One gray shape was coming toward them. It was the injured, maimed Devourer pumping then soaring on its wings.

As it circled overhead, Lazarus said, "It could not have chosen a better time to strike us, than while the camps are celebrating. Our guard was down."

There were screams around the Nomads' celebration. Abruptly the people scattered, running for their lives. The Devourer glided around and finally down to make a heavy landing on the roof of the

Temple of Valor. Archers from the Nomads of Spiron stepped up with nocked arrows preparing to launch a deadly volley. Out came the long spears and swords to attack the beast.

But the Devourer did not growl. It did not threaten them in any way. Instead, it leaned over the wall. It sniffed and searched the area. Then, a most unexpected thing happened. The enormous Devourer began to speak in the common tongue.

"Don't shoot! Do not fear me," the Devourer spoke clearly. "It is me, Astar." The Devourer spoke in Astar's voice for all to hear.

"Astar?" Cautiously, people peeked out from the archways of the Temple of Valor. They slowly came out of hiding behind cover and looked up at the creature on the roof. This mighty Devourer showed no signs of aggression. The Devourer merely watched them and looked at them with oily eyes that now seemed to somehow possess a more sympathetic sparkle.

"Come, come! Don't worry, I am really Astar. I will not harm you," the Devourer said. "When I discharged the blade, I sent my spirit into this poor creature. It is the last of its kind. This Devourer was as much a victim of the Demonic as Micah was. They are simple beasts. The creature only did what it was told it do. They have no natural animosity or hatred of men. Being controlled by Monticello, they were in pain. That's why they looked so fierce. Poor mindless beast. They did not know what they were doing. This hearty creature survived the explosion and would have wandered aimlessly with no master, until humans would have hunted the creature down and killed him. That didn't seem fair. So, I came to its rescue. I needed a body, and it needed a master. It wouldn't be right to leave such a noble creature to die out here all alone. Especially one that survived all these hundreds of years."

"Astar?' Aberfell asked. "Are you sure you are not hurt?"

The beast said, "I've never felt better! I told you, beauty can be found in all things. Plus, I have dreamed of having a magnificent form such as this. I will make this creature my own, and in it, make my exit from this land."

Astar spotted Micah. "How's the new host working out, Micah?"

"It's wonderful! I have been cured of the venom. Thank you for your sacrifice," Micah said.

"What are friends for, Micah?" Astar said. "Lazarus, the longer we remain here the more we must leave. With your flesh restored, you are a new creation. But you remain immortal. Unlike Gilglad and Micah here, who are now mortal. But you and I, Lazarus, we can no longer stay. We cannot be a part of this world anymore."

"But I have something for you." Astar held up the flabby arm of the Devourer. A golden chain dangled around one of its claws. Connected to the chain was the magic feather given to Chen-Li by the Witch of the Great Mapes Forest. "I thought you could use this."

Lazarus extended his palm, and Astar dropped the chain with the magic feather to him. Lazarus smiled. He opened the chain with both hands and studied the feather. Then he put it around his neck.

"You must be careful now, Lazarus," Astar said. "Immortality is not what it used to be."

"Look! The birds, the crows." Lazarus searched skyward. The sky was filled with the scavengers. The birds circled Lazarus overhead. "Seems I can still summon them, the lowliest of creatures. That is a start." Lazarus touched the feather around his neck. He looked at Astar. "Thank you, Astar. This means a lot to me."

With the power of the magic feather, Lazarus lifted from the ground. He rose even to the roof and came face-to-face with Astar. "Is there any hope for us, Astar?"

"Of course there is, Lazarus. Wherever there is life there is hope. Remember that and be well. I wish you the best."

Lazarus rose and met the crows in sky, in the center of their circle. He welcomed them with outstretched arms. Then, Lazarus and the crows flew off together to the east.

"There he goes," Aberfell said as Lazarus flew away.

"Somehow, he looks right at home," Gilglad said.

"I wonder what waits for him out there," Aberfell mused.

"I don't know," Astar said. "No one has been that way before." Astar turned to look at Gilglad. "You look like my mother again. Did you ever think you would be capable of giving birth to a Devourer?"

Gilglad laughed. "I'll take you however I can get you, Astar."

"Will you go back to Homestead now?" Astar asked.

"No, I can't go back there," Gilglad said. "No, I think I will stay here, at the Temple of Valor. Here, I can continue to comfort and cure people. Helping people is not prohibited, is it?"

"Not at all, and I would expect no less from you." Astar laughed. "No, the mortals will always continue to invent ways to help and hurt each other. It is in their nature. Through the course of ordinary time, they will get better at both. But for the time, it will be without magic or immortal Gods to help them along. Eventually their accomplishments will seem like magic unto itself."

"Are you going back home to Homestead, Gensen?" Astar asked him.

"That was always my plan," Gensen said. "Be good to finally see it through. Now that I have Micah back and he's cured."

Micah said, "I can't wait to get back home and eat regular food. I'm starving."

Gensen put his arm around Micah. Then they turned once more to the Devourer on the roof.

"Good luck, Astar, and thank you," Gensen said. "None of this would have been possible without you. If you ever need us…"

"I know where to find you." Astar nodded with the wide toothy smile of a Devourer.

Astar looked at the Oracle Mount. "I see the remaining soldiers have prepared my father's wagon for transport back to Homestead. I believe I'll fly on ahead and make sure the way is clear."

"Amtor will get a Devourer's escort home," Aberfell said. "Fitting and proper for the extraordinary life he lived."

"What will you do after that, Astar?" Gilglad asked the Devourer again.

"You never know," Astar told her. "But I assure you, prophecy will not be in it. We are beyond prophecy now. We are heading into uncharted waters."

"I'll miss you, Astar," Gilglad said. "I'll think of you always."

Astar looked upon her with a sad Devourer's face. "I'll always remember you just as fondly. I'd better be off now." Astar turned into the wind. They waved at the Devourer as it spread his massive wings and took to the air. The Devourer was headed west, and it took no time at all before it flew completely out of sight.

"There he goes," Aberfell mused. "Into those unchartered waters."

Then you leave me,

Here alone, alone, alone.

When I saw you,

I should have known

Love only comes once upon a time.

Excerpt from *The Witch's Songbook*

Memories of that night haunted him.
— Excerpt from *Kilmer's Ghost* (Chapter 39)

INTO UNCHARTERED WATERS

THE ENDLESS SEA

Grim's little lifeboat had been tossed on the waves for months. He was an insignificant speck in a vast expanse on the watery horizon. When caught in storms, gale force winds, and raging swells, the boat had capsized multiple times. Each time, he managed to stay with it. He spent those days adrift, floating along where the currents would take him. He did not try to paddle in any direction, for every direction looked the same to him now. The blazing sun beat down on him. He had torn off his shirt and tied it around his head. His lips were parched, his skin cracked. When the rains came, he collected rainwater in his shoes. At other times, the sea became flat and dead calm without any wind.

Being a flesh-eater, Grim needed little food to survive; and so, he was the perfect creature to attempt a crossing of the Endless Sea. He hunted using his unique Demonic vision. With it, he could see the warmth of life-forms under the surface. In his eyes, living things glowed in reddish-orange shapes. Then using tremendous speed, he would catch his supper. He ate sea turtles, fish, eels, whatever happened to float by. Sometimes he had to hunt farther away from the boat. Sometimes he had to dive deeper than he wanted or thought possible.

Grim was demon-born, which meant he possessed inhuman abilities. He could swim as fast as he could run, which was very fast. He could hold his breath very deep and for a long time; and whether he caught something to eat or not, he had no trouble rising to the surface. Finding the boat was another matter entirely though, of which he had several close calls, locating then swimming back. On a couple of occasions, he almost did not make it. But all this effort required energy, and that was getting short in supply.

After many months, his strength had faded. He could no longer take excursions out of the boat. He simply caught what would swim up close, or he went hungry. After days of no food, and a lack of fresh water to drink, the sun baked away his endurance. The demon could cheat the immediate hunger, as he could go many days without eating but finally starvation took its toll. His frame had evaporated into skin and bones.

Most days he lay on his back. His shirt covered his face, protecting him from the brutal sun. During these long and lonely moments, he had plenty of time to think. He often thought about what he had left behind. He thought about the ancient ancestral curse of the Plum family's blood coursing through his veins.

When Grim reached up and removed the shirt from his face, he saw Hollow Face sitting in the boat with him. The ghost appeared with the sun blasting hard behind him.

Grim sat up. "You've returned to finish what you started haven't you? To watch me die out here?"

Hollow Face raised an arm to Grim. He reached out and touched bony fingers upon his head. He induced a vision in Grim's mind.

In the vision, Frost was propelled backward. When he landed on the ground, his body started to shake. Frost reached out and his hands were on fire.

"Help me!" Frost pleaded. "Mother, please!"

There came a *whooshing* sound, and Frost erupted in fire. The flames engulfed his entire body. He was left burning in a field as his flesh roasted.

Grim's vision returned to the merciless sun out on the rocking Endless Sea. "Frost is dead? What an end to burn like that."

Hollow Face touched his head again. He showed him another vision.

The king reached for his throat, as he was struck from behind. An ax protruded out of his neck. Monticello held the ax and watched as Leopold died. Then suddenly a spear thrust through Monticello's heart. "Die, you dirty demon bastard!" Micah held the spear! Monticello's eyes closed in death.

"Both Leopold and Monticello too?"

Then a third vision was given to Grim. In this vision, Grim saw himself standing in front of a great pyramid. The vision ended with the giant pyramid swallowing him.

As the vision faded, Grim's vision returned to him. Hollow Face remained in the rocking lifeboat.

"What the hell was that?" Grim asked Hollow Face. "As usual, no reply."

"That boy, Micah. He ended the life of Monticello? Maybe I gave that boy too much of a chance. Frost, Monticello, King Leopold, all dead. Kilmer was right, all your visions have death in them. Even so, I appreciate you showing them to me, Hollow Face."

No. The ghost shook his head.

"No? What do you mean no?" Grim asked.

No. Hollow Face shook his head slowly.

"Is there something else you want to show me?" Grim asked.

Yes. Hollow Face nodded.

"Go ahead, then, ghost."

Hollow Face lifted a bony hand again. Another vision penetrated Grim's mind.

Langula tried to drop the sword but couldn't. There was an explosion. In the center of the blast, Langula gave a raucous scream as the particles of her flesh stripped away to the bare dark bones of her burning skeletal frame. The walls of the temple collapsed. The resulting explosion destroyed the Temple of Chen-Li.

Grim sat up abruptly, rocking the lifeboat. "Langula is dead? I thought that was impossible! Am I the only one who survived? Is the Zorn still alive?"

Hollow Face did not answer.

"Well, Hollow Face? Does the Zorn still live?"

Hollow Face sat there for a moment. Then, he disappeared.

"Hollow Face!" Grim reached out for the ghost, causing the boat to shake in the water. "Hollow Face! Oh great. Sure, just leave me in suspense."

Hollow Face did not return.

Several days passed. Grim was very weak now. He had had nothing to eat or drink in days. His ribs protruded through a thin layer of skin and flesh. His face had become drawn and gaunt. He was too weak to lift his arms anymore.

Near the end, he thought. *Going to die soon.*

Grim was too physically drained to keep himself alive anymore. He shut his eyes not expecting to ever open them again. Still, he floated for another full day. He was thankful when a cloud occasionally obscured the sun.

Fickle things, he thought about the clouds as he drifted along. *Too few. Too far between.*

He thought, *I wish I would just sail off the end of the world.* He relished the thought of coming to the end.

A cool wind blew over him. A short reprieve from the heat. Opening one eye, he found only hot glare in his vision. A shadow passed between him and the sun for the briefest of moments. Then another shadow. It happened again. His ears registered high-pitched squeaking sounds. It took him a while to notice that the fleeting dark shapes circling the sun were birds. Focusing his eyes better, yes, he saw birds. Seagulls flew overhead.

He felt a hard rumble under the boat. His forward movement had come to an abrupt stop. He watched the birds until he found the strength to pull himself up. He pleasantly discovered he was in the shade of a large palm tree. The boat had drifted ashore. The question was, a shore of a distant land, or did he drift back to the Mid-Run Valley?

Grim turned to look at the shoreline and saw Hollow Face floating on dry land. Behind Hollow Face, a great green landscape stretched out consisting of rocky cliffs, trees, rocks, and sand. He saw cascading waterfalls, lakes, and streams. Colorful birds sprinted along with the tide to pick through snails on the shoreline. Above, the seagulls called out.

Grim crawled over the side of the boat. His body fell with a splash. He pulled himself onto the beach, right up to the feet of Hollow Face. He reached for the ghost, but his hand passed through him.

Then he must have passed out. When Grim opened his eyes, time had passed. Hollow Face was no longer there with him. Several of the gulls had taken a liking to him and were pecking at his flesh. They backed away when the demon started to move. With alarming speed, Grim picked off one of the gulls in a flurry of white feathers. He gnawed at the bloody raw flesh. The first time he had anything to eat in over a week.

The gull restored a little of Grim's energy. He wandered his way to a waterfall by a rocky cliff. The waterfall tumbled down into and fed a small pond. He let his entire body fall into the water. Greedily he drank the cool fresh water. Now having eaten some seagull guts and hydrating some, he felt some strength return.

Grim walked into the hills of this land. Under a starry sky, he followed the water upstream, trying to determine if he was back in the Mid-Run Valley or somewhere else. He came to the base of the waterfall and looked up the rocky cliff. Finding a good purchase on a vertical draw, he began to climb. It took him minutes, but he reached the top. A long flat plateau now stretched out before him. But there was more…much, much more. His eyes widened at what he saw.

A long straight avenue of marbled stones had been embedded in the ground before him. On either side of the avenue, torches were placed, illuminating the way ahead. In the distance, a full moon rose perfectly over the apex of a great pyramid-shaped monument. Even from a distance he could tell the pyramid was constructed of heavy, large, earthen blocks of stone.

Grim wandered ahead while he dusted himself off. He made his way down the path perfectly aligned with where he was and the pyramid structure. He could also see the torches were not in sconces but held in the hands of tall people who stood silently on the sides of the avenue. These people did not make a sound or any movement. They did not acknowledge Grim's presence. These people were decorated in paint, nearly naked, except for adornments of brightly colored feathers and exotic scarves. They all held their torches perfectly aligned straight and remained quiet and motionless as Grim walked by.

As he neared the pyramid, a host of more elaborately dressed people waited for him. They stood on the bottom steps of the pyramid. They wore open robes and golden jewelry. The tallest of the bunch wore a multi-pointed crown of gold.

Grim stopped before them. The crowned one stepped forward and considered him for a moment. He slowly extended his hands, palms up. Then he spoke. But the words were in a language Grim had never heard before. Grim patiently listened, but he did not understand what the man was trying to say.

He kept using the word, *Chimera. Chimera.*

The leader said his words and looked to another member of the group. A small man came to him and held up a little effigy. Looking closer at the doll-like image, the effigy had red skin and curly red hair. Grim determined it looked exactly like him. Then two women came. They carried a red robe and carefully draped it over Grim's shoulders. Grim had no idea what to make of this.

The leader with the crown approached Grim again. He reached up and removed his crown. He stepped forward and placed the crown on Grim's head.

"Chimera," the tall noble one repeated. "Chimera."

Grim turned to look at one of the women who draped the robe over him. She returned to her spot with the others. The tall royal remained, pointing all around him, repeating the word. *Chimera, Chimera.*

"Grimera," the red demon said.

The man corrected him, "Chimera."

"No," Grim corrected him back. "If you are the Chimera, I am the Grimera!"

The man gave a wide smile, and laughed, delighted they were communicating.

"Grimera," the noble one addressed Grim. Then he turned to the others and said, laughing, "Grimera."

"Yeah, now you've got it." Grim laughed with them. "Grimera!"

Still with a laugh the man repeated, "Grimera!" He motioned with his hand, shouting for all to hear. *"Grimera! Grimera!"*

Now all the people holding the torches beside the avenue erupted with laughter. They left their positions like a mob and came running to surround Grim. They were all chanting, *"Grimera! Grimera!"*

A bell rang out. Celebrations ensued. The people of the pyramid honored Grim as their new guest and king. The Grimera was the red god from the sea they had long waited for.

Somewhere in the crowd, unseen by Grim, Hollow Face was there. But now satisfied, the ghost turned to leave.

The people brought the Grimera all he could eat and drink. After a while, Grim was feeling much better, like his old self. Afterward, the nobles walked up the steps of the pyramid. They asked the Grimera to follow. Which he did.

At the very top of the pyramid there was a twenty-foot-tall rectangular chamber with its doors open. On the very roof of the rectangular chamber was the pyramid's squared capstone. Grim followed the nobles up the steep steps. They ascended to a great height. Grim turned and looked behind him. The view was magnificent. From here he could see all the lands bathed in moonlight. At the bottom of the pyramid, the torchbearers crowded at the base of the steps. They did not or were not allowed to climb the stairs with them.

They reached the top of the pyramid. The nobles all entered the rectangular chamber. They beckoned Grim to come inside with them. He entered the crowded chamber along with the nobles, then turned to face out.

Somewhere below, Grim could hear an apparatus spin on unseen cogs and gears. The chamber started to lower, smoothly and uniformly with all aboard. As the chamber descended it went into a column within the pyramid. Grim watched as the view changed to finely polished stone rising in front of him. As the masonry work rose, it revealed impressive carvings of skillful artwork and symbols indicating stars and kings. When the chamber descended twenty feet down, an airtight seal stopped the column. Unseen above them, the pyramid capstone sealed in place, aligning perfectly flush against the linear angles of the pyramid's sides. The finished seal made the lines of the pyramid perfectly straight from top to bottom. The pyramid had swallowed Grim into the depths. Just like Hollow Face had showed him.

While back inside, the chamber had stopped to allow access to a platform that led to a winding staircase. The staircase went farther down into the pyramid. Grim started to exit, but the nobles did not let him. Instead, another apparatus reeled below, and a platform shifted below their feet. A sub floor of the chamber telescopically released and extended downward. The nobles' descent continued, this time through a round column cut in the stone below.

Finally, at the same place where the stairs ended, they reached the bottom of the chamber's shaft. In front of Grim, a long hallway was lit with the warm orange glow of torches. The light reflected on golden walls. They exited the chamber and walked through a corridor stretching out before them. Along the way, columns supported the massive weight of the ceiling. Upon the columns, two-dimensional depictions of people were chiseled in artwork to show common objects, animals, and events in these people's history.

"Chimera." The tall noble pointed to the carvings. "Chimera."

In some of the depictions, there appeared a snakelike entity, a woman, along with a spotted demon and a blue demon with white hair.

"Langula! The Demonic!" Grim touched the column. "Chiseled here in ancient stone. How is this possible?"

The tall noble touched the serpent woman with a gentle palm. "Mylex," the noble said.

Soon, they passed a bas-relief carving showing a Skeletal King.

"Could this be the Zorn?" Grim asked. "And here is one of Astar and Soothsayer." There were carvings representing a bright star and a boy with a golden dagger.

There were others. There was Castle Orlo, the seven-spired stronghold, the place he was born. There was Castle Odessa, drawn with its dramatic overlook. Farther along the way, there were artist renderings of the original Gods—Hexor, Heironomus, and Ehlona. Hexor and Heironomus battled each other inside a fixed sun. The Goddess Ehlona came out of the mountains in colorful rainbows.

"Hollow Face," Grim said, looking at carvings of a ghost in a long, hooded robe.

These carvings had been chiseled in the stones centuries earlier. How could these people have known?

Then, he saw pictures of himself, interacting with the Chimera, chiseled in stone, probably a hundred years old.

"Is this a foreshadowing of what is to be, or has all of it happened before?" Grim asked them. He did not receive an answer because the Chimera did not understand his language.

A single dark hallway continued, lit by only a single torch. The Chimera would not go there. Grim took a few steps into the dark hallway. When he turned back to look at the others, they would not follow him. Not into this chamber. They were scared. However, they did encourage him to keep going on his own. Grim frowned at them and continued anyway.

The torchlight revealed a stone throne. Seated on this throne sat an old corpse. Grim looked behind him. Even though the nobles were scared—they peeked in to watch at a distance. But they would go no farther.

"Eh? What's got them so jumpy?"

Grim walked closer to the body sitting on the throne. The corpse had been skillfully mummified. Its skin dried to a gray color. The body was dusty, placed here a long time ago and had not been moved. Whoever this was had been dead a long time. The more he examined the corpse, the more he realized he was looking at himself. The body was an aged, bearded, and older version of himself. There was no doubt in Grim's mind. This man on the throne was him.

"Who is this?" Grim asked, looking back at the nobles.

The tall one extended a palm. "Grimera."

"Grimera?" Grim repeated. "That's me, I'm Grimera. What is going on here?"

Making his way through the nobles came an old man with a bald head and gray beard. He came to Grim carrying a large book in his hands. He approached Grim and extended the book. He encouraged Grim to take it.

After giving the old man an inquisitive look, Grim ultimately took the book.

"*The Provenance?*" Grim read the title.

The book had a date written on the first page Grim could understand. The date indicated it had been written in 1042 HRT.

"But that date is still in the future?" Grim asked aloud. "This is 862. Either you have a different time standard or..." Grim stopped and searched the faces inside the room of the pyramid. "…or this old dusty book is from the future?" Grim mumbled. He turned to look at the leathered body sitting on the throne.

"Could it be?" he wondered. "You Chimera…a time-traveling race? Too preposterous to believe. But what if it were true?"

The Chimera stood with their heads bowed.

"You could teach me," Grim said to them, although they did not understand his words. "Teach me, yes. But I wonder? It begs the question. Did any of this happen, or is it still to be? And if so, could any part of it be changed? Could all of it be changed? What if I had the power of Astar's Blade? What other cataclysmic events could occur we would have no knowledge about? Maybe more important, what good is the present if the past suddenly falls into question?"

His arrival to these lands had been foretold and chiseled into stone for hundreds of years. The Chimera built a pyramid in anticipation of his coming. The stone avenue had been constructed aligned to the exact spot he would appear above the cliffs. On the exact night of his arrival, all the torchbearers were in their places. Waiting with their torches lit. They knew the exact night, the precise time, he would wash up on their shores.

These mysterious Chimera knew that Grim was a flesh-eater before he came. They knew he was born from the blood of Plum ancestry, and haunted by an ancient ghost.

They coronated Grim the Red as King of Chimera. They worshipped him as king. They did all they could to make him comfortable. For the Chimera it came as a high honor in Chimerian society to sacrifice their flesh to eat.

Grim stayed with the Chimera. He came to understand these people better, learning their language, perfecting their magic, and living in their customs. Their powers became his powers.

And so, Grim the red demon did not die lost in the Endless Sea but washed away in a sea of time.

I could fall to pieces tomorrow
Would you still be around?
Or I could decide
To climb that mountain tonight
And if I do
I'm never planning on ever coming down

Excerpt from *The Witch's Songbook*

After several minutes, Amtor painfully rose.
His old war injuries newly reaggravated.
He helped Astar off the ground.
Together they walked inside the cottage.
— Excerpt from *Kilmer's Ghost* (Chapter 40)

ON TOP OF THE WORLD

Temple Of Valor

The two halves of Amtor's body were carefully prepared with delicate surgical stitching. A tight wrapping of fine linen helped keep him together as one. His face was left unwrapped so that, on his sojourn back to Homestead, all could see his magnificent face. Although he would have considered it much too fancy, his long beard was washed and combed to an exquisite luster, upon which fragrant oils were applied, something he never would have approved of had he still been alive. After all the diligent preparations, Amtor looked peaceful. As if he was merely at rest, relieved of all his worldly burdens. His body was carefully placed in a red-and-blue casket, then lifted and placed onto a flat wagon, pulled by a team of four horses and attended to by an honor guard of two soldiers.

Gensen and Micah prepared to go with them, back to Homestead, and to accompany Amtor on his last journey. They said heartfelt goodbyes to the Nomads of Spiron, thanking them for all the kindness they had received. Then the wagon bearing Amtor started to roll on its solemn journey to take his body home.

As the procession passed through the villages, some had heard he was coming. They stood on the side of the road with their hats in hand to pay their respects as the funeral procession passed. There were no protestors along the way.

As the casket passed, people started to speak rumors of seeing the maimed Devourer flying overhead. Still others witnessed something unidentified they said was a dragon. When called out on it, people said they saw the thing with their own eyes.

"It was not a dragon, I tell you," some of them refuted. "Why, I don't think you saw anything at all."

"It was a dragon, I tell you," another villager said.

"Aye, maybe you saw something, but what you saw was no dragon. There is no such thing."

"The beast I saw had only one foot," one of them said.

"The beast I saw was one of them Devourers," another said. "And it certainly was not missing a foot. It had all four."

"What I saw had a long dragon's neck, and a long dragon's snout."

"That's not how I remember it," another would say. "Didn't much look like a dragon to me. Didn't have a long neck either. Why, I thought it had no discernable neck at all. And it was not missing a foot either. Actually, it had no feet. And it flew through the air like a flying snake."

"How many beasts are there that inhabit this land?"

Whether real or imaginary, these rumors fueled a general fear for the villagers. These rumors and retellings of embellished eyewitness testimony are how the legends of dragons live on still to this very day.

VILLAGE OF HOMESTEAD

Amtor's funeral procession arrived at the little cottage in Homestead. The house remained exactly the way Amtor had left it. Gensen and Micah exited the wagon and approached the cottage.

"Sure is a welcome sight," Micah said.

"I never thought I would see this place again," Gensen said.

Gensen turned to look at Micah—with the blond curls of Astar under the green cloak. His new but familiar appearance would take them both some time to get used to.

"Yes, it is good to be back home," Gensen said.

The wagon carrying Amtor's body was guarded by the soldiers. A contingent of villagers, well-wishers, and curiosity seekers came to earnestly pay their respects.

Gensen and Micah opened the door to Amtor's house. Upon closing the door behind them, Gensen immediately noticed the foot of the dreadful beast was gone.

"Someone stole it?" Gensen muttered.

"Stole what?" Micah asked.

"A giant foot was right there," Gensen said, pointing into the kitchen. "Amtor left it here on the table. Some thieves or villagers must have slipped in here and taken it as a trophy."

"Why would someone steal a foot?" Micah asked. "Weird thing to steal. Aren't there more valuable things?"

"Timmutes sawed it off a Devourer," Gensen said.

"Oh, those adventures," Micah said. "I think I've had my fill of those."

There came a cry from outside. "Dragon! Dragon!" A crowd was forming around the house.

But like all the other times, there was nothing there.

"Do you think Astar is really gone?" Micah whispered to his father. "All these rumors?"

"Anything's possible," Gensen said, scanning the roofs. "But I don't think so. He would not go back on his word. He won't be back."

"I miss him," Micah said. "He was my best friend."

The next morning, the soldiers interred the remains of Amtor with a small ceremony. His body was laid to rest under the stone he'd used to conceal Soothsayer so long ago. After they finished burying him, they chiseled his epitaph upon the stone. The inscription simply read: *Amtor.*

No words were spoken. It was exactly the way Amtor would have wanted it. For he was a strong man of very few words.

ORACLE MOUNT

The Nomads of Spiron were packing up to leave the Oracle Mount. They quickly finished loading their pots, tables, and the rest of their field gear into the wagons. Some men of the tribe, skilled in carpentry, repaired the wagons damaged in the artillery assault.

Boldo sat on a wagon talking with Nadya. His sister felt disgraced and lucky to be alive. The Nomads of Spiron would forgive her eventually. She would someday take her place as an ordinary, but discreet, member of the tribe. But that day was still many days ahead. For now, none of the Nomads would even look at her. For there was too much bitterness, bitter memories of the sacrifices, and the Demonic feasts. They hated everything she represented.

"I would have been better off dead," Nadya told Boldo. "You should have just let them kill me. Staying alive keeps me in greater pain."

"Don't say that, Nadya. You heard what Astar told Lazarus. 'As long as there is life there is hope.' These people of ours are fickle and headstrong. It is both their strength and their weakness. But they are good at heart—they will come around in time. They will see that what you did protected us. Give them time. You have some allies. Let them help convince the others to see the truth. They will talk it out and understand better in time."

She stared off in the distance. "I have not slept in a very long time. Every time I close my eyes, I am haunted by dreams of the Demonic and the sacrifices of the tribe."

"Well, you can rest now, Nadya," Boldo told her. "Things are going to get better."

Nadya looked out and saw Tamara and Oaks carrying boxes to the supply wagons. Once completed, Oaks held Tamara in his arms. They kissed longingly and lovingly. Just seeing their young love, fresh from two different worlds, made Nadya smile. *Maybe there was still some hope left after all.*

"Thank you, brother." She slipped her arm around his and rested her head on his shoulder. "You tried to warn me. I didn't listen."

"You did what you thought best," Boldo said. "You held on to hope when there was none."

Gilglad and the acolytes approached. With a kiss to Nadya, Boldo jumped down to speak with them.

"Gilglad, I'm glad you'll be staying at the Temple of Valors," he said, grabbing a garment trunk and handing it to one of his Nomads. "It is here you can help people the most."

"Dear Boldo, thank you for all your help and support. And all the Nomads of Spiron. We are very excited for you and Nadya, that you are to return to your homeland. It was quite an adventure."

Gilglad gave Boldo an embrace. Then he climbed back up on the wagon and took the reins.

Aberfell approached them now. "Goodbye, Spiron, may the Gods be with you."

"Aberfell, we are heading south, back to the southern shore. Remember this and take it as a standing invitation. Come visit us in our ancestral lands down by the sea," King Boldo told them. "You and yours are always welcome in Spiron."

"We will always remember your celebration of life with gladness in our hearts," Gilglad said.

King Boldo laughed. With a nod, he snapped the reins and the long line of wagons started to roll. Aberfell and Gilglad backed away and watched as the caravan rolled along from the Temple of Valor. Their wheels kicked up dust through the valley, then up and over the top of the high ridge, then out of sight. Before the last of the wagons disappeared from view, Aberfell turned to Gilglad.

"Gilglad, I am going to sorely miss your loveliness," Aberfell told her.

"Aberfell, you flatter me," Gilglad said. "What will the Supreme Historian do now?"

"What I do best," he told her. "Remember everything. Someday I'm sure I'll be asked to recall it for someone. Who knows? Maybe I'll write it all down someday and write a book."

Gilglad said, "Will you write a book?"

"Well, I think it will be more like a few tomes, I suppose." Aberfell nodded. "Maybe so."

Just then, voices cried out from a distance away. They turned to look.

"Gilglad! Gilglad!" the voice called again. A woman was running over the ridge, calling her from far away. She was coming from the direction of the village of Estes. The woman was not alone—she was accompanied by children. There must have been forty-five of them, boys and girls, between the ages of three to seventeen.

"Do you remember?" The woman who looked to be very youthful herself, in long blond curls and blue eyes, was familiar to Gilglad. She and the children came closer, running through the valley.

"Sister Jule?" Gilglad called out. It was one of the original Sisters of the Orphans. By now, despite her youthful appearance, Sister Jule would have been in her advanced years. "But how did you know?"

"Word spread quickly that you, Lady Gilglad, were Lady Valen, the recycled spirit of Ehlona," Sister Jule said. "We came here to thank you and show you all you have done. What you put in motion."

"Why, Sister Jule," Gilglad said. "You look young and beautiful. It's as if you haven't aged a day."

"How I wish that was true," Sister Jule laughed. "I am eighty-two years old."

"It can't be," Aberfell said. "You look twenty."

"But I am," Sister Jule continued. "The other sisters, Chavise and Catosa, passed a few years ago. But Sister Dunhi still lives—she is ninety-five. Lives in the village of Rynholt. We are the last two Sisters of the Orphans. We remain youthful thanks to the Goddess

Ehlona's beautiful blessings. We wanted to come and show you the vision she had for the St. Ehlona's Orphanages. The children, Mother Goddess, look at all the smiles and goodness you have done in this world."

"Oh, Sister Jule!" Gilglad cried. As she knelt, children surrounded her. They touched, hugged, and kissed her. All thanking her.

Jule and the children stayed for a while and played games. After the dreadful events of the past few weeks at the Temple of Valor, it was good to see children at play and hear them laugh.

"Such a blessing," Gilglad kept repeating with tears in her eyes. "Such a wonderful blessing."

"Aberfell," Gilglad called the Supreme Historian. He had been preparing to go. "Where are you going?"

"In search of Timmutes and mountains," Aberfell chuckled, and at just that precise moment children burst through loudly laughing and screaming. One of them bumped into him. "Far from...distractions."

"I so hate to see you go. You know are always welcome here. But if you must, I will miss you the most, Aberfell, more than anyone else. Won't you come back, so we can see each other again someday?"

"I would like that, my lady," Aberfell said. "More than anything."

"I gladly look forward to that day," Gilglad said. "My heart beats fondly for you, Aberfell. Be well, my friend. May you always be blessed."

"Goodbye, Lady Gilglad," Aberfell said and the two smiled. "May Ehlona's light always shine upon you."

Then Aberfell set out for the east on foot, while Gilglad returned to the children.

It took Aberfell forty minutes of walking to get to the top of the first hill. The sprawling mountains and the Dragonbreath loomed large and lay spread out before him.

Yet, as Aberfell stood overlooking the sprawling and spectacular view, he turned to look back one last time. From this height he could still see the wagons of the Nomads of Spiron rolling snake-like, heading south toward the shores of the Endless Sea. Around the Oracle Mount, where there had once been thousands of people, now only a few remained, hammering and making repairs. He watched for a moment longer and privately bid farewell to the Temple of Valor.

Then he turned to the steep hills, and with a deep breath, continued his long arduous walk east. As he began, a few golden orbs joined him. Seeing they posed no harm, he gave them little attention. Soon, more came and danced all around him in little golden lights as he walked.

Below at the Temple of Valor, the crowds and the children had all left. Some acolytes stayed on, but some had left for adventures of their own. But whether they stayed or left, it did not matter much. There was nobody left to treat. Those who remained, a handful of acolytes and some soldiers left by Lord Rhodes, repaired the damage to the Temple of Valor.

As proof that the new era of scientific discovery was underway, some scholars arrived, scientific people, who had come with an interest in biology and anatomy. They had come to examine and catalog the remains of the dead Devourers. After some initial measurements, they packed the big flabby bodies on flat wagons and took them away for further examination and study. Good riddance.

The ruins of the Temple of Chen-Li smoldered above. Its once beautiful, fluted columns were gone, collapsed under the weight of the falling roof. Inside, the scorched and ashen remains had scattered away in the winds. It would be months before it would cool sufficiently to enter. But even then, no one dared, for the Temple of Chen-Li was now a tomb for the dead.

GREAT MAPES FOREST

Gensen and Micah stood looking into the deep pit. The massive hole to the underworld had produced all three Devourers. Even now, it still smoldered in yellow steam lifting up from the world's molten depths.

"This thing is a hazard," Gensen said. "We have to cover it. Someone could fall into it and never be seen again."

That being said, over the course of the next few weeks, Gensen and Micah collected stones in and around the Great Mapes Forest. Stacking them in a wheelbarrow, they transported the stones to the pit site. Very methodically, they worked together and started placing the stones around the pit.

As they stacked the stones, Micah asked Gensen a question while they worked. "Do you think he is really gone?"

"Who, Astar?" Gensen stirred a thick mixture and applied it to adhere the stones together. "Last week, a farmer from the south of Conner came north, all the way up here. He said a person matching Astar's description was seen in those parts."

"That's funny," Micah said, unloading heavy stones from the wheelbarrow and placing them near the pit. "I heard that a sailor from Rynholt saw Astar. That he had been spotted down there.

Surely, you don't think... Astar did not leave me with the last copy of himself. Do you think?"

"Don't rightly know." Gensen shrugged and continue to smear the stones. "Astar was something special all right. A real one of a kind. I guess in the end, he could do whatever he wanted."

Gensen paused from adhering the rocks to look at Micah. His son's face and features no longer resembled the dark-haired, brown-eyed boy that Gensen knew as a child. Micah had become the fair-haired, blue-eyed Astar. Amtor's son. The more Gensen thought about it the less he could remember what the old Micah looked like. It was no matter. He continued the stonework.

"Makes no difference anyway," Gensen told him, returning to his labor with the stones. "There is only one of you. There is only one Micah, no matter what you look like, and that is all that's important."

After working this way for several hours, a small wall was forming. As the adhesive dried, the wall held firm in its construction of stone and mortar. It rose oval-like in a ring around the outside of the pit. But the two of them did not stop there. They continued working to build up the wall. Soon, they not only constructed a wall, but an entire stone dome that encased the pit.

They did however, leave a small opening, a pumpkin-sized hole, in the top of the dome. That allowed the steam, yellow and putrid in sulfur dioxide, to continue to vent. If not, the pressure of the steam would build and blow the dome apart, thus exposing the pit again.

On the day they finished the dome, they were surprised to see Timmutes. The orbs appeared to them once again as they had so long ago. Micah never liked them. Gensen was equally startled. But they came anyway. Soon the two men were surrounded by the golden orbs for the second time in their lives. The Timmutes did not harm them, only swirled around them for a few moments.

"I take this as a good sign," Gensen told Micah. "A good omen. I think they are blessing our little dome out here, letting us know that they have our backs. Maybe they will stay around to protect us." As they walked away from the pit site, they left the golden orbs swirling around.

On the way back home, they passed a single marker they had also erected. A flat stone to signify the place where they had laid Micah's body to rest. The stone simply read: *Astar.*

In memory of the friend that was no longer with them.

THE GRAY MOUNTAINS

Even in his youthful and spry condition, Aberfell was no match for the treacherous Fangs. He tried to scale the mountain heights, but he was no climber. The Timmutes helped him. They carried him, lifting him up on the steep side of the mountain. On the descent, they lowered him. Aberfell found he could trust the little things, and need merely jump in the air, and the Timmutes would carry him to the top of the next summit. Without their help he never could have ascended any of them.

The Timmutes supplied Aberfell with as much food and water as he needed. There were other things too. The simple comforts of life, like teakettles and cups, plates, paper, inks, towels, and a wide assortment of other things.

With the Timmutes' help, he continued up the mountains…that is, until he reached the base of the tallest of them all. The Dragon-breath Mountain. That was when the Timmutes took full control. Aberfell leaned back and the Timmutes caught him. They would not allow him to fall. Gradually he began to rise and seemed to float up. He rode upon a swell of tiny golden orbs. He continued rising through the extreme heights of the Dragonbreath, until he came to a height where there was not enough oxygen to breathe and he passed out from lack of air.

When he awoke, he was lying on the summit of the cloudy Dragonbreath Mountain. He had been lifted through insufficient air until they reached the ever-present cloud. Inside the cloud, the air was thick and rich. The Timmutes had seen to it.

The first thing he witnessed was a beautiful tree. The tree was a white oak that had grown in the shape of a woman. The branches were posed like outstretched arms, lifting to the heavens. The trunk looked like here legs, one crossed over the other. A small protrusion between the two main branches resembled the head and shoulders, uplifted, and praying to the Gods.

As Aberfell admired the tree, the Timmutes were coming and going all around him.

He walked a short distance through the fog, up the gentle slope of the summit. There, he saw the dim image of a little cottage. This was the house of the witch so long ago.

"Well, if it was good enough for her," Aberfell said out loud, "It's good enough for me."

The Timmutes opened the door as if to invite him in. Entering the little house, Aberfell saw there were only three pieces of furniture—a table to the right, a sleeping bench to the left, and a rocking chair by a large bay window.

"Perfect. Sparse but cozy," Aberfell said. "What more would a man who cannot forget anything need? The less to remember, the better."

He approached the window and looked out. There was nothing to see but the never-changing white fog of shapeless clouds. "Perfect. I didn't come here for the view anyway. At least I'll be able to tell night from day."

He sat down in the rocking chair with a squeak. A glass came floating to him, full of cold spring water, carried by the unified microscopic hands of the Timmutes. He accepted it and drank it down. When he finished, the glass floated away on its own.

Over time there were other things, vegetables, fruit, cheeses, wine, beer, bacon. Anything he wanted and never had to ask for. The Timmutes seemed to know what to bring, and they always came to him in a steady supply. He ate what he wanted. When he could not eat another bite, the food kept coming anyway.

"Oh, stop! Are you to fatten me to death?" Aberfell finally had to scold them.

Finally came the paper and ink, along with a quill. Aberfell licked the quill. Then he began writing down his extensive memories.

The first thing he wrote:

> *I have successfully divorced myself from the masses, those who have hounded me for a chance of immortality. The fools! Thinking immortality comes by whispering inconsequential blather in my ear! They have all been eliminated, as I sit here at the top of the world. I remain in the company of the Timmutes, until such time as someone worthy finds me here. Once the feat of attaining the summit of the highest mountain has been accomplished by some future adventurer, then I will gladly pass on my knowledge of recent events. That will grant me the necessary time to write the provenance of my information. So the world can be assured what I say is true. Unless I miss my guess, I should not be here very long. Until then I'll stay here on top of the world and wait.*
>
> *Signed — Aberfell, the Supreme Historian,*
> *862 Human Recorded Time.*

"Until such time when somebody worthy finds me," he chuckled. "That's a good one."

Aberfell pulled a long bandage he took from the Temple of Valor out of his pocket. He blinded himself by wrapping and tying the linen around his eyes. Then, he stuffed the ends of the bandage into his ears to eliminate all sound. "There," he said getting settled into the rocking chair for a little snooze. "If I can't see or hear anything, I won't have to remember anything."

He laughed at how clever the whole idea seemed. After a moment, he sighed and spoke with confidence in his voice. "Shouldn't be too long."

ONE HUNDRED SEVENTY-NINE YEARS LATER
YEAR 1041 HRT
DRAGONBREATH SUMMIT

One night, Aberfell did not stuff the cotton in his ears, and he heard a noise outside. He ignored it. Just something flung by the wind, like all the other times. The noise continued.

"Impossible," he snorted out loud and settled back in his chair. "I've heard sounds like that before. It ended up being nothing. Just more of the same."

But after a while it sounded like more than that. Aberfell listened more intently now. He thought he heard the door open and the floorboards creak. It sounded as if someone had entered his house. *Could it be that someone is really here?*

The noise of footfalls was getting closer. Somebody really was there. *At last!* Aberfell could hardly believe it. Finally!

"Oh, there you are." Aberfell dropped his arm to the wooden chair, resulting in a cloud of dust. "I've been waiting for you."

Unwrapping the linens around his head, they fell into his lap. Free of the bandages, Aberfell turned his head. There was an audible crack of long stiff bones in his neck. A young man with curly red hair stood in front of him.

"You!" the young man spoke. "I thought you were dead. But you're not dead. You're not dead, are you?"

"No, I am not dead. I never have been," Aberfell said. "And any rumors of my demise were ill-founded."

"Who are you?" the young man asked.

"Well, I'll be… You mean you've come all this way, I've waited all this time, and you don't even know who I am? I'm Aberfell!"

"Aberfell? You mean the *real* Aberfell?"

"One and the same. Who were you looking for?"

"I-I wasn't looking for anyone," the young man stuttered. "Ghosts, dragons, maybe?"

"Dragons?" Aberfell rolled his eyes. "Yes, of course. No dragons here, sorry."

Aberfell slowly stood up with a series of snaps from his old bones. "I suppose congratulations are in order on your reaching the summit of the Dragonbreath Mountain. Quite an accomplishment. You are now the second person to get to the top of this mountain, second of course to me, and about ten million Timmutes. But don't worry, I won't tell anyone. No, you can claim the title of being first. I am famous enough already, and the Timmutes don't care about such things."

The young man looked confused. "The Timmutes?"

"Yes, yes, the Timmutes," Aberfell said, holding out his hands, motioning to the tiny golden orbs. "They have been taking care of me for a long time now. But be careful around them; they are a dangerous sort. They can be rather possessive. So, if you are here to end me, they might have something to say about that."

"I'm not here to end anyone," the young man said. "I mean you no harm."

"They never would have let you get this far if you did not have the right intentions. Somehow, they know; they always know."

The young climber looked around. "I did not expect to find anybody living on top of the tallest mountain in the world."

"I have been on top of this mountain for, well, one hundred seventy nine years, by now. I should be the oldest man in the world. I am 237 years old. Have you ever heard of anyone older?"

"No, not even close."

"Well, I have." Aberfell laughed. "There are much older. But I am, perhaps, the oldest *person* in the world. Some are older, but they are not persons; they are Gods. I think they are still around somewhere."

Aberfell considered the climber for a moment. "Who did you say you were?"

"Almon. Almon Plum-Kilmer."

"Almon Plum-Kilmer. A Kilmer, eh? Remarkable." Aberfell stared at Almon for a long time. "Yes, I can see the resemblance."

Chariots are coming, coming from below

Horses are dawn, onward they will go

Excerpt from *The Witch's Songbook*

Every night I lay down, I looked at that little door,
and just prayed that it would not open to expose some deformed
slobbering face staring down at me.
— Excerpt from *Kilmer's Ghost* (Afterword)

ALL THE TIME IN THE WORLD

TEN YEARS LATER
YEAR 1051 HRT
VILLAGE OF HAMMERVILLE

For three nights in a row, they met in a shadowy empty house. A place where no one would disturb them. There was a need for this type of privacy. On that all would agree. What the men discussed demanded a certain level of security and discretion. The last person that had openly discussed this information had disappeared without a trace just four years ago. Their friend, Almon Plum-Kilmer.

Two men entered the house in the morning. They found that, just like the day before, the same mysterious man was already there and waiting for them, even though it was early in the morning. They wondered if he had ever left the place the night before. The man always sat in the same spot, in the corner, away from the curtain-drawn windows. A partial shadow darkened his upper half. He always sat the same way too. Both hands resting on the table. Except for the chairs, this was the only furniture in the room. He wore the same dark red cloak. He kept the hood pulled over his head to obfuscate his identity. Only the man's hands rested on the table. He wore tight leather gloves, old and worn, the ends of which were ripped, seemingly intentionally, to allow his long black fingernails to protrude through. Now, the man ruffled his hardened nails rhythmically on the table, as he watched the man across from him drink his morning beer.

As the big man lifted the underside of his beer stein, it covered the front of his face. In the chair beside him, another man, smaller, thinner, and frailer, sat next to him. As the big man finished, he drained the last remnants of beer without a care. The hooded man watched him greedily gulp it down.

The smaller man watched nervously the way their shadowy customer continued rapping his fingers on the wooden table. The atmosphere was awkward and unnerving. The finger rapping. The beer slurping. The clock ticking. It all made his leg jitter under the table. But these were the only sounds in the house. The small man turned his gaze from the man behind the table, and gave his friend a look of anxious concern.

The big man lowered his stein to the table.

"More beer?" the hooded man asked in a deep but clear voice.

"Nope, good now," the burly man said. He shook his head, gave a silent burp, then wiped the excess off his bushy mustache.

"Mose?" the frail man said. "Maybe you should just continue with the story."

The hooded man stopped rapping his fingers. He shifted his head slightly, noticeably, even in the shadows.

"No need to rush. I have all the time in the world," the deep voice said from under the hood. "No hurry at all, Mr. Jacko. Please forgive me, it is just that impatience is in my nature. I am working on that. However, if you are comfortable and had enough to drink, maybe you are ready to continue. If so, please go on, Mr. Mose."

"Like I was saying, Mr.…Mr., you know, we've been meeting for three nights in a row and I haven't gotten your name."

The shadow man leaned forward. The diffused light exposed his face to them for the first time. His face and eyes were redder than the cloak he wore. Between his lips protruded ivory fangs that he did not try to conceal.

"Call me Mr. Grimera." He leaned back into the shadows with grin.

"All right…uh, Mr. Grimera," Mose said to him.

"Grimera? Like from the story?" Jacko whispered to Mose. Jacko's leg was pounding furiously under the table now. Mose gave his friend a sly nod, then pushed himself back from the table a bit. Jacko leaned back from the table as well. Both wanted some distance from the man in the hood. They both gave each other a worried look.

"Come now, Mr. Mose." Grim also sat back while asking politely. "Won't you continue?"

"W-where was I?" Mose stuttered.

Grim reminded them. "You were telling me about King Leopold II. How repairs to the Green were underway. How Castle Odessa had been transformed back to its former glory. I believe *that* is where you left it for the night."

"Precisely that it is. Yes, yes, that is where I left off, thank you, Mr. Grimera."

Jacko looked nervously at Mr. Grimera from the side, as Mose began, "Yes, as the history will show, the Kingdom of Odessa thrived under King Leopold II and settled into a peaceful reign. With the threats of Castle Orlo, the Sanguine Forest, the Zorn, Langula, and all the Demonic…"

Here, Mose looked up quickly at Grim. But he did not take offense. He only motioned with a finger for Mose to continue.

"Keep on going, Mose," Jacko told him keeping one eye on Grim. "You're doing great."

Mose continued, "Yes, well…like I said, with all the other 'threats' gone… an era of prosperity was enjoyed by most in the kingdom. Once repaired, the castle hosted many a celebration and ceremony. Leopold II repaired most of the monuments in the Mauveguard Pass. But he left the biggest pieces of the original Green, those big pieces that fell from thousands of feet above. He just left them. They remained half-buried in the ground where they fell. Even to this day. They serve as a sad reminder and warning of what could happen when men are influenced by greed and hate. King Leopold II dedicated many more memorials for those who perished fighting off the Devourers and those who died at the Temple of Valor. That was when the obelisk was erected. It stands sixty feet at its base in the Mauveguard Pass. The names of those who died, in what came to be called the Siege of the Temple of Valor, inscribed upon it."

Mose wiped the perspiration off his face. "Old King Leopold II lived to be seventy-two. Then in the year 875 the man once known as Lord Oskar Whitney took his last breath of peaceful, natural causes. The kingdom grieved that year. A new king was crowned the following year.

"Lord Rhodes was king after that. Many wanted Lord Plum-Kilmer to be king next. But Kilmer would not return. He had no interest in returning to public life. So it was that Lord Rhodes, the hero of the Sanguine Forest and the Temple of Valor, ascended to be the next king.

"Rhodes would not be King Leopold III. He made a break from that so-called name of power. And King Rhodes I was coronated as the third king of Odessa."

"Tell me more about what happened to Kilmer." Grim leaned closer.

"Lord Plum-Kilmer lived out his days in a fine home in Haver-hill. Hollow Face remained with him up until the very end. He passed away at the age of eighty-two. When Kilmer died, the spirit of Hollow Face passed to his son, Kory Plum-Kilmer, who grew to manhood with Kilmer's ghost."

At this, Grim dropped his head. His countenance changed and he seemed to grow darker. "And what happened to Kory?"

"Well, after Kory, a succession of Plum-Kilmers followed."

"I understand that the ancestral line has recently ended," Grim said. "This happened recently, in your lifetimes."

"Yes, eventually Erland Plum-Kilmer, a very wealthy hunter, was passed the ghost, Hollow Face, on the death of his father. When Erland got sick and died in the Mid-Run Valley, the curse of the ghost passed to our friend, Almon Plum-Kilmer. But after an adven-ture to the top of Dragonbreath Mountain, he suddenly disappeared, only some four years ago. Almon Plum-Kilmer ain't been seen since. He was the last descendant from the original Plums."

"Are you sure there is not anyone else out there with the blood of the Plums?" Grim asked.

"We really wouldn't know," Jacko spoke up.

"We have no way of knowing. But after Almon disappeared, we found this in his house." Mose held up the ring. "The Plum-Kilmer family ring and insignia. This represents the Plums' inheritance, a sizable fortune. But no one has come forward to claim it. Can only assume that Almon was the last of them Plums."

There was a pause from Grim. Then he asked Mose a question. "What of Lazarus? Whatever became of the new creation between Hazor and Marus?"

Mose read from the document before him. "Using the magic feather that Astar saved for him, Lazarus flew deep into the Gray Mountains, where no living person would find him."

Here, Mose looked at Grim. "The manuscript says that Lazarus wrestled with insanity for years, repeatedly trying to end his life. But unable do it, eventually, he quit trying and came to peace with what he had become."

"Is he still alive after all these two hundred or so years?"

"Aberfell, the Supreme Historian wrote as recent as four years ago that the Timmutes reported seeing Lazarus alive. He lives alone, as a hermit, deep in isolation of the Gray Mountains. They say he lives like an animal."

"What a miserable existence that must be." Grim turned to look out the window.

Mose stopped there for a moment, staring at the man in the hood.

"Why did you stop, Mr. Mose?" Grim turned to ask. "Do you want more beer?"

"When you say you are Mr. Grimera, are you really…" Mose hesitated "You know? *The* Grim? The one from the stories? Maybe a descendant?"

"I was the third demon born of the demoness Langula. Bred from the blood of Lord Plum-Kilmer," the man in the hood said. "Yes, I am *that* Grim."

There was a long pause.

"Are you going to hurt us?" Jacko asked. "Because I really don't want to die."

The man in the hood did not answer. It was as if he was still thinking about it, and not really sure himself. Finally, he asked them a question.

"You have these manuscripts of *The Provenance*?" he asked. "And you wish to sell them?"

"Y-yes, we have all that. *The Provence* and the other two," Mose stuttered. "The *Temple of Valor* and *Kilmer's Ghost*. Three manuscripts in total. All written by Aberfell, the Supreme Historian."

"The boy that never forgets." Grim gave a little laugh.

Mose and Jacko gave forced chuckles.

Grim looked at them. "I will pay you for them, of course. I can double your original asking price, triple it if you throw in the ring. That will make you both very rich men. But I must have all of them. And I will be taking them with me when I go." Grim leaned forward, bearing his face once again into the light. "But first, tell me, Mr. Mose. What ever became of Astar's Blade? Legends say Soothsayer is gone. But I happen not to believe it. Did Astar hide it somewhere before he left? What do the manuscripts say about it?"

"I must tell you, Mr. Grim, I have no knowledge regarding the whereabouts of Astar's location. If he is alive or dead. To your point concerning the blade, the manuscripts say he gave a copy of Soothsayer to King Leopold II."

"But Whitney could not wield Soothsayer," Grim said. "No one could, except for Astar himself. What did King Leopold II do with it?"

Mose and Jacko told him where Soothsayer had been hidden.

The conversations lasted well into the night. Yet when Mose and Jacko left the empty house, they had finalized a deal with Grim. They came to an agreement to make their way to the south coast in the morning. There, they would meet again at Port Harbor. Grim had arranged that a ship would be waiting for them. The ship's name was *The Celestial II*. Grim had filled the stores under *The Celestial II* with a great treasure of gold, supplies, and other valuables. In exchange for *The Celestial II*, Mose and Jacko would trade Grim the works of Almon Plum-Kilmer and Aberfell, and the Plum family ring.

Mose and Jacko could not wait to get the manuscripts off their hands. They considered them cursed anyway and could not wait to be relieved of them for a good price. For they knew in these manuscripts lay the forbidden information of the history of the world, of three eras, and of the history of the Gods. But in the end, information worthy to them of a ship full of gold.

In the meantime, as they waited for morning, Grim needed no rest. He used his speed and ran fast, faster than the speed of the wind. He hurtled past landscapes that blurred by him as he ran across the Mid-Run Valley. He ran until he saw the sixty-foot pinnacle, the monument at the base of the Mauveguard Pass, dedicated to the Siege of the Temple of Valor. He turned and sped up through the pass, twisting his way around all the monuments and half-buried boulders of green limestone before finally screeching to a halt.

He looked up through a blue night deep with stars. The high towers and arched roofs of Castle Odessa appeared grayish white and pale as a ghost. Drifting behind the castle, the clouds gave it just the briefest illusion of movement. Grim searched the castle for the Green, the spectacular overhang that made Castle Odessa famous. He studied it at length. Grim knew that Leopold II had put a round medallion in the center of that green limestone. Under that medallion was a carefully crafted secret compartment. There, buried under tons of stone, lay the most powerful weapon in the world—Soothsayer, the golden dagger. Astar's Blade.

This is what Mose and Jacko told him Aberfell's manuscripts said. That Astar presented Soothsayer to King Leopold II for safekeeping. The Kingdom of Odessa and all the future monarchs would ensure the safety of Soothsayer, as long as the Green remained intact. And after the Devourers broke it once, the chances of that ever happening again were beyond astronomical.

Grim knew he couldn't use it. Mose and Jacko couldn't either. No one could wield the blade, not kings, not heroes nor anybody else that would come after them. Only one could wield it. This was Astar's Blade.

Grim only wanted to see where it was. Now he knew.

PORT HARBOR

The next day, they met in Port Harbor as planned at *The Celestial II*. Mose and Jacko came with thick documents wrapped in linens and carried in backpacks. They came nervously suspecting a trick. After all, they were making a deal with a demon. They had to be extra careful because this was the same Grim written about in the tales. The Grim of the Demonic. The Grim of the Chimera. But coming to them now indicated he had waited many lifetimes to make this deal. Why jeopardize it now with petty treachery and deceit, being this close to the goal?

As promised, Grim stood on the dock alone. Mose and Jacko approached him. As they narrowed the gap between them, the sound of ropes tightening in the rigging mingled with the waves lapping against the side of sailing ship.

"Did you bring the manuscripts?" Grim watched them intently. "And the ring?"

"All right here," Mose said, and he and Jacko dropped the backpacks.

"Very good," Grim said. "The treasure is yours. You may board her and inspect it all you want."

"What about our payment?" Jacko asked. "The one we agreed to back in Hammerville?"

"I don't understand." Grim looked a little befuddled. "Why, the whole ship is yours, *The Celestial II*, and everything in her. Do with her as you will."

"The whole ship?" Jacko asked. "Um, Mr. Grim, please excuse me and my partner while we have a brief conversation."

"Of course, I have all the time in the world," Grim said.

Mose whispered, "The whole ship? I didn't know we were getting the ship too."

Jacko took Mose by the arm and turned him away. "If we go on that ship," Jacko told Mose. "We will never leave it alive. Look, it's a ship, and a good ship at that, as far as I can tell. But we'll die in there. It's a trick, can't you see that?"

"But a ship just the same," Mose said. "What should we do? Can't go back to Hammerville empty-handed, can we?"

"Don't have to get on that boat either," Jacko said. "At least not right now."

The two came back to Grim.

"We'll take it," Mose said.

"No need to board her just yet, um, I'm a little prone to seasickness. Guess I should have mentioned that before. My apologies, Mr. Grimera." Jacko folded his arms. "We...we trust you. But we'll wait until you leave before we board her. Here are the manuscripts, Mr. Grimera, and the ring."

"Of course," Grim smiled. "Have it your way." Grim approached the backpacks. When he came closer. Mose and Jacko moved backward in step with him. They gave him plenty of room to inspect the contents of the bags.

"Everything seems in order here," Grim told them after a rudimentary search. "We will take the manuscripts; you can have *The Celestial II.*" Grim motioned with his hand. A mist formed on the docks, and several Chimera appeared, seemingly out of the clouds. They came forward brightly adorned in animal hides, bone jewelry, and long elegant feathers. They stepped through the mist and collected the backpacks. Having them under their control, they backed away, and turned. The cloud of fog followed and covered them completely. When the fog lifted, the Chimera were gone. It was as if they were never there to begin with.

Grim smiled. "This concludes our business, gentleman." He turned to walk away.

"Mr. Grimera," Mose asked. "If you don't mind me asking, what are you going to do with them?"

"What? The manuscripts?" Grim asked. "Do you care?"

"I-I was just wondering if, I don't know, if we did the right thing?"

"What do you mean?" Grim took a step closer to them.

"I mean, you wanted them really bad for a reason. We just can't see it. We couldn't think of what to do with them. But up until you contacted us looking for them, we couldn't decide what to do with them. Just wanted to know what we were missing. Now that our deal is done, didn't think it would hurt to tell us, you know?"

"You really want to know?" Grim asked.

Mose and Jacko remained silent, afraid to state it either way.

"We are the Chimera. The prophecy-makers. From a different place and time. The ancient Gods once looked to us for divine guidance. It can be that way again. We wanted the manuscripts to take back with us. With this information, we control destiny."

"Are...you going to change history?" Jacko asked with an awkward laugh.

Grim answered, "We are going to *tell* history. How it *really* happened. How it *will* happen. This concludes our business deal, gentlemen. Mr. Mose, Mr. Jacko. Farewell."

With that, Grim walked down the dock. As he went, he became surrounded by a cloud similar to that which took the Chimera. Soon both he and the cloud were gone. Returned to wherever they had come from.

"Did you see that?" Jacko asked.

"I'm not sure what I just saw," Mose responded.

Much later, Mose and Jacko crawled down into the ship's keep. They had to watch out for the limited clearance for their heads. The entire interior of the vessel sparkled with the thrill of gold and riches. *The Celestial II* had been stuffed full of all manner of gold. Items such as plates, cups, armor, swords, doubloons, and overflowing chests of even more, just pouring out.

The two men were overjoyed with exuberance. They laughed and played with the treasures, hardly believing their good fortune.

Then, Jacko started thinking. "Mose," he said.

Mose was busy wearing an ill-fitted golden helmet and strands of gold necklaces. "Yeah, Jacko."

"Does any of this feel right to you?"

"Oh yes," Mose laughed, plunging a pile of gold into his pockets. "This feels so right."

"I mean, what about what Grim said? The future, of how it will happen? Do you think that—"

"Now see here, Jacko!" Mose sat up abruptly, the golden helmet crooked upon his head. "You mean if we are going to disappear like Almon or Aberfell?"

"Like Grim or the Chimera did?" Jacko added. "I mean think about it, Mose, they took those manuscripts back with them, to what time did they say?"

"They didn't. Probably sometime before the great cooling," Mose said. "Long time ago."

"Yeah, that would be like, almost six hundred years ago at least. Ever since they took them bags from us, they will have over six hundred years to be looking at them, studying every word. I got a bad feeling about this, Mose."

"Look, Jacko, we're alive. We're still here—nothing has happened. And we're rich!"

"Yeah, I guess so," Jacko said with a chuckle and a shrug. "Come on, let's find ourselves something to eat, I'm hungry."

"Sure, Jacko, me too," Mose said. "I tell you what, my friend. Lunch is on me; I'll just grab a few gold coins to use for our dinner."

With their pockets full of gold, Mose and Jacko climbed out of the hold and back topside. They turned and headed down the gang-plank. That was when they noticed *The Celestial II* was no longer docked in Port Harbor.

In front of Mose and Jacko stood a pyramid. A lengthy column of Chimera lined a long stone avenue straight to the pyramid. The avenue came right up to where they exited *The Celestial II*.

In the distance they could see Grim, wearing a crown, no longer adorned in the dark red cloak. He now wore the luxurious fabrics of royalty. He stood in front of the pyramid in the middle of the avenue. Behind him a large contingent of a thousand Chimera stood with long spears.

"Mr. Mose, Mr. Jacko, it has been a very, very, long time. At least for me!" Grim said. "We've been waiting for you! Thank you for returning *The Celestial II* to us, and all the treasure inside her."

Mose and Jacko froze in shock. They now stood at the same time, but in a completely different place, then when they walked onto *The Celestial II*.

"Gentlemen, gentlemen. Take your time." Grim opened his arms. Behind him the Chimera marched toward Mose and Jacko with long spears.

"I have all the time in the world."

The End

GLOSSARY

CHARACTER NAMES

Aberfell	*The boy who remembers everything, the Supreme Historian*
Amtor	*Wounded Minister of War of the Kingdom of Odessa*
Blaize Plum	*Head Council of Haverhill, General of Amalgamates*
Boldo	*Prince of Spiron / King of Spiron*
Brother Barker	*Spiritual Advisor to King Leopold*
Chavise, Sister	*One of the three sisters who left the Temple of Valor to find Ehlona in Husband. She was blessed with the Orphanage of the South*
Chen-Li / Marus	*Warrior, name of Marus, son of Heironomus and Ehlona, meaning Body and Spirit*
Darla	*Orphaned friend of Kilmer / wife of Kilmer*
Darius Plum	*Son of Justus and Rosa Plum*
Fortis Plum	*Trader, tracker, hunter, and adventurer of Clan Plum*
Frost	*Blue Vampiric Demon of Langula*
Gensen	*Blacksmith in Homestead*
Gilglad	*Healer and Amtor's wife, Astar's mother*
Gregor	*Whitney's aide-de-camp*
Grim	*Red Vampiric Demon of Langula*

TEMPLE OF VALOR

Hazor / the Zorn	Son of Gods: Ehlona and Hexor. The Skeletal King of Orlo, the Master of Evil
Heironomus	God of Light
Hexor	God of Darkness
Jacko	Bartender
Jule	Youngest Sister of the Orphans
Kilmer	Saves Amtor's life during the Battle of Mauveguard Pass
Kory	Orphaned friend of Kilmer / And the name of Kilmer's firstborn son.
LaNew	Sadistic captain of the Red Guard
Langula	The half-woman, half-serpent demon
Lazarus	A new being formed from the souls of two others.
Leopold	An orphan of St. Ehlona's Orphanage, he becomes the first king of the Kingdom of Odessa.
Marus / Chen-Li	Son of Ehlona and Heironomus
Melvin	Member of search party, youngest, low-ranking, inexperienced
Micah	Son of Gensen
Monticello	Spotted Vampiric Demon of Langula
Mose	Bartender
Myra	One of the First Wives
Nadya	Queen of Spiron
Oaks	Orphaned friend of Kilmer
Oskar Whitney / Lord Whitney	Cousin of Jakob Whitney, an engineer in Bowling
Rhodes	Commander, Red and Blue
Talbot	Lawyer
Tullis	Lumberjack
Tyla	One of the First Wives
Valen / Lady Valen	Healer at Temple of Valor
Zorn / Hazor	The Skeletal King of Orlo, the son of Ehlona and Hexor

JOE LYON

COUNTRIES

Chimera   *South Endless Sea*
Kingdom of Odessa   *Leopold's growing kingdom*

CITIES, TOWNS AND VILLAGES

Blaize   *Village*
Bowling   *Village*
Chase   *Village*
Darby   *Village*
Estes   *Village*
Hammerville   *Village*
Haverhill   *Seat of the House of Erland, village.*
Homestead   *Village where Amtor and Gilglad make their home*
Jorleston   *Port and Lighthouse*
Olzen   *Village*
Plum   *Village*
Port Harbor   *Largest Port*
Umbrick   *Destroyed village*

PLACES OF NOTE

Blue Mountains   *Mountain range of the west*
Castle Odessa   *Leopold's castle in the Mauveguard Pass*
Castle Orlo   *Hazor's castle*
Dragonbreath Mountain   *The highest point on the map*
Gray Mountains   *Mountain range of the east*
Mid-Run Valley   *The central lowlands*
Oracle Mount   *The hill of the Temple of Valor*

Sanguine Forest *Haunted forest*
Spiron *Nomadic tribes*
Temple of Chen-Li *Marus's / Chen-Li's temple and home*
Temple of Valor *Ehlona's Temple of Healing*
Wilds, the *Untamed lands where the ground dips dramatically to create enormous cliffs*

CREATURES

Rock Larvae – ancient wormlike underground creatures
The Timmutes – a society of microscopic humanoids
The Demonic – flesh-eating demons
The Devourers – three wide-mouthed winged monsters

ORGANIZATIONS AND GROUPS

Acolytes of the Temple of Valor
Amalgamates (Army of the Mid-Run Villages)
Chimera (ancient race of people)
Nomadic Tribes of Spiron
Red Guard (defunct)
Red and Blue (Leopold's army)
Star Prophets
White Eminence
Zornastic Order (defunct)

Joe Lyon is no stranger to storytelling. He grew up in Springfield, Ohio, creating monsters and characters for homemade comic books. In his first fictional epic fantasy series, *Astar's Blade*, Joe creates a world some have called "wonderfully epic with great texturing and grand scope worldbuilding." Joe currently lives in Aiken, SC, with his family, two dogs, and a horse. Joe has a master's degree in business administration, a former Military Intelligence School graduate, a US Army veteran, a musician and prolific songwriter.

CHECK OUT MORE STUFF BY JOE LYON:

WWW.ASTARSBLADE.COM

EMAIL ME AT:

JOE.LYON@ASTARSBLADE.COM

OTHER BOOKS BY JOE LYON

The Provenance (Book One of Astar's Blade)

ALL HIS LIFE, ALMON KNEW THE PLUM-KILMER FAMILY
HAD BEEN HAUNTED BY SPIRITS OF THE DEAD.

*For over two hundred and fifty years, the ghost had cursed his family,
but not Almon. He thought the curse had finally run its course and may
have skipped him. When the ghost finally does come, it strains his sanity.
Unprepared, in growing madness, he is driven to the mountains. There,
the ghost waits for him, either trying to save him or lead him to his doom.*

Kilmer's Ghost (Book Two of Astar's Blade)

THE LEGENDS SAY THE SANGUINE FOREST
IS HAUNTED BY EVIL MAGIC.

*Those that dare go in never come out alive. But those are just tall tales,
aren't they? Ever since he was a young boy, a ghost had been appearing
to Kilmer in an unlikely other-worldly friendship. Making Kilmer the
perfect choice to go into the Sanguine searching for the King's missing archer.
Guided by his ghost and bent on revenge, he is doomed to bear witness to
the cataclysm around him. Helpless to prevent the birth of a brand-new
evil, his life comes down to if Kilmer's Ghost can save him.*

Temple of Valor (Book Three of Astar's Blade)

ASTAR HAS POWERS.

It had been a year since the Star of Ehlona, leaving the world to wonder if the soul of the Goddess of Beauty had returned. But while a weary world looked to the heavens for answers, a new terror was being unleashed from below. Deep in the steamy darkness hatches a plot bent on vengeance. When powerful forces collide, there is no safe place. Will any survive in the final battle over Astar's Blade?

CHECK OUT MORE STUFF AT THE WEBSITE:
www.astarsblade.com

MUSIC BY PURPLE TOAD:
available on iTunes and streaming services.

Music to Swim By (1984)
Legacy (2013)
Self-Inflicted Wounds (2016)
Anything You Want (2017)

Thank You

"I hope you have enjoyed reading this epic adventure, as much as I have enjoyed writing it."

Joe

www.ingramcontent.com/pod-product-compliance
Lightning Source LLC
Chambersburg PA
CBHW052348020726
47503CB00001B/156

Patrice Sinave

CHRONIQUE D'UNE EXTINCTION MASSIVE

Livre I

-

OULAN BATOR

ISBN 978-2-9814470-0-5

Dépôt légal - Bibliothèque et Archives nationales du Québec, 2014

ISBN 978-2-9814470-0-5

Page :2